A BULLET IN TIME SAVES NINE

When he looked back, the Hunsackers were clearly within range. He moved his rifle sights around ever so gently, so that he was focused on the broad chest of Jim Stock. Now he could see the man clearly. He was wearing the brocade vest that he was known to wear. His rifle was still in the boot, but Longarm had no doubt that this was a man who would cause him trouble. He leaned down over his sights, calculating the wind, calculating the distance, calculating the drop of the bullet. Then, very gently, he pulled the trigger, and the sharp crack of the shot rang harshly off the rocks . . .

DON'T MISS THESE
ALL-ACTION WESTERN SERIES
FROM THE BERKLEY PUBLISHING GROUP

THE GUNSMITH by J. R. Roberts
Clint Adams was a legend among lawmen, outlaws, and ladies. They called him . . . the Gunsmith.

LONGARM by Tabor Evans
The popular long-running series about U.S. Deputy Marshal Long—his life, his loves, his fight for justice.

SLOCUM by Jake Logan
Today's longest-running action Western. John Slocum rides a deadly trail of hot blood and cold steel.

BUSHWHACKERS by B. J. Lanagan
An action-packed series by the creators of Longarm! The rousing adventures of the most brutal gang of cutthroats ever assembled—Quantrill's Raiders.

TABOR EVANS

LONGARM

AND THE NEVADA NYMPHS

JOVE BOOKS, NEW YORK

LONGARM AND THE NEVADA NYMPHS

A Jove Book / published by arrangement with
the author

PRINTING HISTORY
Jove edition / December 1998

The Penguin Putnam Inc. World Wide Web site address is
http://www.penguinputnam.com

ISBN: 0-515-12411-7

A JOVE BOOK®
Jove Books are published by The Berkley Publishing Group,
a member of Penguin Putnam Inc.,
375 Hudson Street, New York, New York 10014.
JOVE and the "J" design are trademarks
belonging to Jove Publications, Inc.

PRINTED IN THE UNITED STATES OF AMERICA

10 9 8 7 6 5 4 3 2 1

Chapter 1

Longarm peeked out the door of the empty storefront, and looked toward the big stone house that stood at the end of the dusty street like some sort of monument to the dead ghost town. There was nothing to be seen except a couple of rifles protruding from second-story windows. Other than that, there was no activity anywhere.

Longarm knew the stone house well. He had reconnoitered it from every direction, and it was as solid as a fortress. He didn't reckon there was any way that one man was going to get past the rifle fire, somehow breach the stone walls of the house, and get at the Hunsacker clan that was holed up inside. He understood that they had plenty of food, plenty of ammunition, and plenty of time. He was at his own discretion to either wait them out, go for help, or just go.

He moved across the street and closer to the house, hurrying through the dust and tumbleweeds of the main street, stepping up on the rotting boardwalk and ducking into what

1

had formerly been the sheriff's office. The town, at one time, had been named Lodestar, after the main silver mine that had given it life. But when the silver had run out, so had the miners and so had the storekeepers and so had everyone else. Now, it was just so many framed buildings rotting in the dry, high air of Nevada.

All except for the stone house, which had belonged to the mine's owner. The man had gotten out with a considerable fortune, enough that he could walk away from such a sight as the eight- or-nine-room house he'd built to celebrate his success.

Longarm hunkered down by a window in the sheriff's office, where he could see the best part of the stone mansion, as he got out a cigarillo and lit it, wishing he had a drink. His whiskey was back in his saddlebags at the livery at the opposite end of the street from the stone house. He reckoned he could do without it. He had a gallon canteen of water with him, and he eased it off his shoulder and took a long drink. He was armed with his .44-caliber revolver in his cross-draw holster. Besides that, he had his carbine, which also fired .44-caliber to eliminate the need for different types of ammunition. He also had a .44-caliber double-barreled derringer attached to one end of his watch chain. It had saved his life more than once.

Longarm wanted to cuss his boss, United States Marshal Billy Vail, for the trouble that he now found himself in, but he had to admit that it was nobody's fault but his own. Billy had had no part in pulling him away from the job that he had been sent out on and putting him on the path of the Hunsackers. But now he had run them to earth, and was determined to have them. He had been chasing the clan for years, and he vowed that before the month was many nights

2

older, he would have the bunch of them in jail. Those that weren't buried, that is.

He was United States Deputy Marshal Custis Long, called Longarm by both friend and enemy alike. The name came partly from his last name, and partly from the fact that he had made it a religion to chase his quarry to the ends of the earth if need be. He never quit on a trail, hot or cold, and he never failed to get his man. He was the long arm of the law in person, or more simply, Longarm.

He sat there, smoking, trying to think of some way to get at the Hunsackers. No immediate solution came to mind. He could see his face in the dirty window. Already he had a few days' growth on his face, and he looked tired and felt like he could use a bath. But there would be no bath in this part of the country, unless it was dust for water and tumbleweed for a towel.

His face said forty years of age, but his big arms and hands and shoulders and his quick and lithe way of moving said closer to thirty. Longarm was one of those men whose age was a mystery to everyone but themselves, and they weren't telling. He had been a U.S. deputy marshal a good deal longer than he cared to think about. He could have been a chief marshal, and Billy Vail had offered to put him up for the promotion many times, but somehow it didn't go with Longarm's idea of being a lawman. Billy Vail's job now was to sit in an office in Denver, Colorado, and send other men out to do the work. Longarm had seen Billy shrink every day he sat there. Longarm didn't want a job like that.

There had been very little conversation between himself and the Hunsackers. He had been on assignment in Virginia City, Nevada—sent there by Billy Vail to investigate the

3

murder of a state senator. It had proved to be an easy piece of work. Even though the sheriff had been corrupt, Longarm had managed to roust out the killer and get him dispatched. After that, he had, by chance, jumped seven members of the Hunsacker clan in Reno.

The Hunsackers were four brothers, the old man, and two cousins. They had fled at the sight of him, and had had a good start by the time he could get himself organized, but he had trailed them mercilessly, riding almost night and day. He had two horses, which was fortunate, and their trail had gone along a way where there was plenty of water. He had managed to kill one of the so-called cousins with a long rifle shot. After that, they had loaded up their belongings like jackrabbits and taken off.

It had surprised him when they had gone to ground in the stone mansion in the town of Lodestar, but considering the surroundings, it really wasn't a bad place to hole up. If Longarm went for help, he'd be gone for so long that they could scatter to the ends of the earth. If he simply tried to wait them out, they would win, because he didn't have the provisions or the patience to last. The one fortunate thing was the pump in the livery station that kept a big wooden tub full of water so that he was able to water his horses and himself. Otherwise, he would have to make do with what provisions he had in his saddlebags.

There was no question of attacking the place frontally. They could riddle him at least a half-dozen times before he even got thirty yards in front of the building. He sat there by the window, watching the evening get low, bringing with the lowering sun a little relief from the intense heat. The air was high and cool at night, but when the sun was cutting through it, it was like sitting on the edge of a hot skillet.

After watching for a while, Longarm ducked out of the door and skittered down to the livery stable to see about his horses. He noticed that the Hunsackers seldom fired at him, even when he was within a hundred yards, which wasn't a particularly long rifle shot. Maybe they were enjoying playing with him. He couldn't be sure. All he knew was that there were a lot of jobs that he would much rather have than the one he was presently employed in. It was taking too long, and he couldn't see any way to bring it to a satisfactory conclusion.

The Hunsackers were one of the numerous outlaw clans that populated Longarm's territory, which was generally Arizona, New Mexico, Colorado, Texas, and Nevada. It seemed as if most of these families had come West hoping to discover an El Dorado, a wealth of riches, either in the gold mines, in ranching, or in farming. When they'd realized what a hard-bitten country they were in, they'd turned to crime as a way to make their fortune. The Hunsackers were not much worse, and no better, than half-a-dozen other such outfits that Longarm had run across in the last ten years. Several he had wiped out, and several were still running at large, just like the Hunsackers.

The Hunsackers were murderers. They were thieves. They were burglars. They were train robbers. They were stagecoach robbers. They were whatever it took to get your money in their pockets. Of the Hunsacker bunch, Longarm calculated that the oldest son, LeeRoy, mostly called Lee, was the most dangerous. For pure cunning, the old man, J.J. Hunsacker, was no slouch himself. The rest were somewhere in the middle between bad and awful.

Longarm figured this band now had about ten members in all. He didn't know where the rest of them were hiding, but he had the uneasy feeling that they might be somewhere close. That would be all that he needed, to have three or five or six others come riding in to catch him unawares. He had all he could handle with the six hemmed up in the stone house. He didn't need to be caught in the cross-fire between two well-armed and well-provisioned parties of men who could shoot. As a general rule, he could deal with odds of four or five to one, but he had never cared for much higher.

Longarm settled himself in the stables, looked his two horses over with a critical eye, and saw that they were in good shape. He dug in his saddlebags and got out some cheese, dried beef, and biscuits that were rapidly becoming one day too old, and made himself the best meal he could.

In that high elevation, the sun stayed up a long time, but when it went down, it went down in a hurry. Fortunately, it seemed like the moon and the sun were balanced against each other. Once the sun was down, the moon popped up to take its place. In the clear air of that altitude, the moon put out nearly as much light as the sun, a fact that made it all that much harder to slip up on the stone house.

Longarm wondered why the mine owner who had built the house had made it so much like a fort with small windows and a heavy door. Maybe he had figured that the day would come when the miners who were making five dollars per day while he was making five thousand dollars per day would decide that it was time to turn the tables.

Longarm had not the slightest idea of how he was going to get the Hunsackers shaken loose from their hiding place. There seemed to be no way. He had only provisions for a couple more days. After that, it would mean going back to Reno or Virginia City or to Mono Lake. There was still some moldy hay in the livery stable, and his horses were making our fairly well on that, along with a couple of sacks of oats that had been left behind. But Longarm wasn't going to make out very well on the cheese that was getting harder than his teeth.

After he had eaten, he sat, smoked, and had a nip of the Maryland whiskey he tried always to carry with him. He didn't have many luxuries in his life—the odd woman here and there, and the silken taste of the whiskey. His job was such that it ought to have paid about ten thousand dollars a month, but Billy Vail couldn't seem to see it that way. Longarm drew what pay he could, and shipped what horses he could back home and tried to make a little profit on the side.

Lodestar was like a hundred other deserted towns in Nevada. Longarm had seen a good many of them. He had seen them in their flush days when storefront running footage cost forty dollars a foot, when there were ten saloons, when there was even talk about building a school, when there was even a fire department and police—all that while the mines were paying off.

Then one day, just like a water tap being cut off, it would change. Overnight, people slipped away. Overnight, the buildings were vacated. You might even walk into some of those towns and find a beer still sitting on the counter of the saloon, not a soul in sight. Lodestar was not anything extraordinary. Longarm wondered, however, if it was the headquarters of the Hunsacker clan, or if was just one of a half-dozen or so places where they knew they could hole up and give anybody a good fight.

Longarm waited until about nine o'clock, and then went out the back door of the livery stable and slipped down the backs of the line of buildings on the main street until he got to the corner. He was within twenty-five yards of the stone house now, and he could see it clearly. The rifles were still on guard.

He called out, at first softly and then with increasing volume, "LeeRoy. LeeRoy Hunsacker. Lee, it's Longarm. I want to talk."

There was a pause before a voice came back from one of the upstairs windows. "What the hell do you want, Longarm? Why don't you get on your damned horse and get out of here?"

"Listen, Lee. If you boys will surrender to me, I can guarantee to get you to jail without nobody else being killed. But I've got a party of deputy marshals on the way, and I can't guarantee you what will happen then."

Hunsacker laughed softly. "You say you've got a party of deputy marshals heading here to back you up? Is that right, Longarm?"

Longarm said, "You heard me, Lee. Now, they'll be here tomorrow or the next day, and I can't account for what an active interest they might take in this affair. There could be some thinning out of the ranks."

Hunsacker laughed again, this time out loud. He said, "Longarm, you get more full of it every day. Just exactly when did you send for this passel of deputy marshals? It would appear to me that you just barely took time to tighten the cinch on the saddle before you jumped on it and took out after us."

Longarm said, "Well, Lee, that's where you are wrong. I had plenty of time to give you all a look to see which

8

way you were heading before I ducked back into town and got off a telegram. I am telling you, Lee. You're going to get a surprise."

"And where are they supposed to find us? I take it you gave them directions to this place here? We're forty miles from Reno, Mr. Deputy Marshal Custis Long."

"Lee," Longarm said, "you're taking chances with your own life and the lives of your brothers and your daddy. Let me talk to the old man. Maybe he's got some sense."

Hunsacker said, "No, I don't reckon, Longarm. The old man is sleeping. He don't need to be roused up by you. Now, let me give you some advice. You can't get at us. You can't even get near us. I doubt seriously that you have enough provisions, especially for your horses, to hold out very long. If you'd like to rush this place, you're more than welcome."

Longarm said, "No, listen. You boys have done some tolerably bad business in your time, but you ain't ever shot a United States marshal. If you get into that bracket, you're liable to be plumb sorry."

LeeRoy Hunsacker said, "Listen, Longarm. It's my turn to come off watch, and I don't feel like sitting here jawing with you. It's plain that you ain't got a card in your hand to play, so why don't you just get on out of here and leave us to be?"

"Lee, go and wake your daddy up. I know he's got more sense than you do. I'd like to talk to him."

"I done told you, he's sleeping and he don't want to be woken up."

"Well, it's the law saying that he ought to be woke up, so you go on in there and get him. I want to talk to him."

There suddenly came the sound of another voice, an

9

older, fuller one. "Is that you, Longarm?" It was J.J. Hunsacker. "What the hell do you want? Don't you have no better sense than to come around here at this time of the night and wake people up, bothering the good at heart?"

Longarm laughed. "Well, J.J., I'd reckon that I'd have to yell mighty loud if I was going to bother anybody that was going to be described as good at heart. I don't know anybody in the immediate vicinity that could be described like that."

J.J. Hunsacker said, "Well, I reckon that you know yourself as it is." His voice faded as he turned his head. Longarm could hear the old man say, "Go on to bed, Lee. I'll take the watch for a while."

Hunsacker turned back to the window and said, "Now, here you are, Longarm, in the big middle of the Nevada desert. You ain't got no idea of where you are really, 'cause this ain't your natural stomping grounds. You're by yourself. Just what in the hell do you plan to do against the six of us? And by the way, I don't appreciate you shooting that boy yesterday."

"That boy, as you called him, one of your cousins, I think, was wanted in about ten states for everything from road agentry to bank robbery. Besides that, he was doing a pretty brisk job of shooting at *me*. You shouldn't have left him as your rear guard if he was so valuable to you."

J.J. said, sounding careless, "Well, to tell you the truth, he wasn't that much of a hand. He wasn't actually kin, you know. We just kind of took him in. Naturally, he'd be the one that we'd leave as rear guard. I was curious to see if you still had your wits about you. I thought he might catch you off center and plug you one."

"Sorry to disappoint you, J.J., but it just didn't work out

10

that way. Now listen here. Now that I am talking to the head of this outfit, what do you say to you and the balance that's left coming on out and surrendering and let's go back to Reno and get this foolishness over with real quick. You know that you can't stay in that rock house forever. Sooner or later, you've got to run out of groceries and water and whiskey and smokes.''

The old man chuckled. "Oh, Longarm, I think it will be a long time before we run out of what you ain't got now.''

Longarm said, "J.J., you don't know how I'm fixed. You talk mighty well for a man who ain't completely in the know about all matters. How old are you anyway, J.J.? You fifty?''

Chapter 2

Hunsacker said, "Well, I don't reckon that that'd be a damned bit of your business, Longarm. But since it's you asking, I'll tell you that I'm eight years over forty and still able to do my day's work when the time comes."

Longarm said, "J.J.,we don't call robbing banks and holding up people on the road work. Work is something you do with cattle or with goats or with a plow or a shovel. You've got it kind of confused. Taking other people's money when they ain't willing to give it to you ain't work."

J.J. Hunsacker cackled slightly. "Longarm, why don't you step out in that patch of moonlight so I can get a good look at you?"

Longarm said, "I'd be glad to, J.J., but I am afraid that with your eyesight, as old as you are getting, that you might hit me in the foot or someplace where it might hurt. The light ain't quite good enough for me to be taking any chances on your aim."

Longarm could hear Hunsacker cough and spit. Then he heard the gurgle of a bottle. "Listen, Longarm," the old man said. "Why don't you take on off and do us both a favor? I tell you what I'll do. I'll pitch five thousand dollars in gold out the front door, and you can pick it up and take it with you."

"Well, I'll be damned," Longarm said. "You mean that you're going to offer me a bribe? I've never had a bribe offered to me before, J.J. That's damned interesting of you."

Hunsacker said, "Can't you see that we've got a Mexican standoff here? You can't get at us, and we ain't going to get at you, and there's not a damned thing either of us can do about it. You ain't got no help coming. You might as well turn around and ride back to Reno and wire for some help. In the three or four days that'll take you, we can be out of here and be gone to ground someplace else, and you won't be getting your bunch into a gunfight, and nobody will be hurt, and everybody will be happy. How about that?"

Longarm said, "Well, if you don't mind, J.J., I think I'll just stick around here for a little while."

Hunsacker snorted, "Well, at least go to bed. Hell, I can't stand these all-night talks much longer. If you ain't planning on shooting us, don't talk us to death."

Without a word, Longarm stepped back along the line of empty buildings, disappearing while J.J. Hunsacker was still talking. He slipped quietly into the livery stable, checked on his two horses, and then spread out his bedroll on a mound of straw and hay he had raked up. He lay down, not bothering to take his boots off or loosen his belt. He left his revolver in the holster. Using his saddle for a

14

pillow, he put his hat over his face and settled down to sleep.

He didn't plan to sleep very much. He had taught himself over the years to take short fifteen-minute naps, and then come awake long enough to sense what was happening around him before drifting back into a light sleep. But tonight, he couldn't get quite settled. He got out his watch and looked at the time, and saw that it was nearing ten o'clock. He had a bottle of his Maryland whiskey out and near to hand. He took time to pull down a snort, cork the bottle, and then settle back again on his saddle and makeshift bed.

Longarm's mind was busy. It was a puzzle what he would do. By the time he was able to get together enough of a party to attack the stone house, it would be four or five days before they could make it back to the ghost town of Lodestar. By then, the Hunsackers would have scattered to the winds, going to any one of a dozen hideouts. Longarm didn't see any other choice but to stay here as long as he could. Maybe they weren't as well provisioned as they had bragged to him they were. Maybe they didn't have as big a supply of water. Maybe there wasn't water aplenty for their horses. He didn't know.

The best he could do would be to hang on until the very last moment. He and the horses could make it back to Reno without any fodder, and there was water along the way. When the food ran out for the horses, he would have to make a decision as to what to do, but until then, he would just keep the Hunsackers bottled up and uncomfortable. He planned to fire a few shots through the windows from time to time, just to interrupt their sleep. Truth be told, he wasn't that long on ammunition and he didn't think the game was

15

worth a candle. It might cause them a little inconvenience, but it would cause him a little more than inconvenience to run out of ammunition.

As he lay there ruminating on his latest problem, waiting for sleep to come, Longarm thought back to his last encounter with the Hunsackers, one that had come to a fight. He had not fared as well in the situation as he might have wished.

Longarm had gotten information that the Hunsackers, after several robberies in the panhandle of Texas, had fled to New Mexico and were in the Las Cruces area. He had taken the train from Denver to the area around the mining town just south of Sante Fe. The Hunsackers had been much easier to find than he had expected. There had been fourteen, more or less, holed up at the ranch house about five miles outside Las Cruces.

He had recruited several sheriff's deputies, and they had surrounded the place as much as four men could surround any place. He had called on J.J. Hunsacker to come out. When the old man had called back that he would see him in Hell first, a brisk gunfight had come about. Unfortunately, Longarm had lost one deputy who had been a little too daring—he had taken a bullet in the thigh. It had taken Longarm most of the first part of the gun battle to bind up the deputy's wounds.

After that, Longarm had been able to work his way to the back of the ranch house, and firing through a back window, he had hit several members of the gang. But then, they had rushed out to the back corral, firing as they came, and Longarm had been forced to seek cover. He had been able to kill two more as they had fled, but another deputy had gone down, and Longarm was faced with the choice of chasing after J.J. Hunsacker and his family and friends or getting medical attention for the two young deputies. He had chosen to see after the deputies.

Never, at any point, had he been able to get J.J. in his gunsight. It just never seemed to happen. In the several forays he had had with the robber band, Longarm had never been able to cut the old man out and gun him down, and the same went for his favorite sons, LeeRoy and Shank and either Joe or Jack—he could never be sure of the boy's name. They were all of a similar cast, mean and rough and able to fend for themselves without much regard for other men.

It had been a close thing, getting both of the deputies back into the town to a doctor. But in the end, neither one had died. It had made Longarm even angrier toward Hunsacker and his gang. Three times he had had them under gunfire, and three times the old man had gotten away with just the loss of a few distant relatives or friends or hangers-on or whatever they were. Lying there now in the stable, Longarm gritted his teeth. Once again he had the old man dead to rights, but he still had to put him in jail or in a shallow grave in the sandy soil of Nevada.

Longarm thought on about the gunfight in New Mexico. The Hunsackers had left a young Mexican woman at the ranch when they'd fled. It had turned out that she belonged there, and had only served as a maid for the gang, who'd little time to get settled before Longarm jumped them out.

He remembered the night he spent in the ranch house after he had gotten the deputies into town. He could still see the lovely form of the Mexican woman silhouetted in the moonlight gleaming through a large window of the bedroom in the house. He guessed her to be in her early twenties. Her name was Juanita, and she burned with a fine hatred against all of the Hunsackers, LeeRoy, Shank, and the old man in particular. The Hunsackers had come into the ranch, killed the owners, and run off everyone except her. They had kept her on only to serve them. Her hatred had transferred itself into gratitude toward Longarm when he'd routed the gang.

That night, she undressed him, stood him in a tub of warm water, and slowly and carefully washed his body. After that, she took him to her bed and its clean sheets, and dried him with her kisses, working her way all up and down for as long as he would allow it. Finally, shivering and shaking with excitement, he pulled her up to him, loving the feel of her silken skin against his fingertips and his lips. He explored her soft belly with his mouth, and then moved down to the inside of her thighs.

Then, when she groaned impatiently, he thrust himself into her, and they rode and tumbled across the bed as they humped away toward the goal of a climax, their excitement building. Finally, he was no longer able to contain himself. He almost crushed her with his strong arms as the feeling that had swept through them exploded on top of the mountain. He tumbled downward, little by little, until he finally fell off and lay flat on his back, his arms outstretched, gasping for air.

That had been a good memory of the fight at the ranch. The only bad part had come when Longarm set out to try to pick up the trail of the Hunsackers and find the direction they had taken. Two men jumped up before him about a quarter of a mile from the ranch, firing as they came. He killed both, spinning one around with a bullet through the side of his chest. He killed the other a little slower with a slug through the gut. They both died, but it amazed Longarm that J.J. Hunsacker could demand such loyalty that two men would stay behind, practically giving up their lives. Longarm had no doubt that the two men had expected they could kill him, the odds being what they were. He thought probably that Hunsacker had given the men to understand that Longarm was a slouch and could be easily taken. J.J. Hunsacker was no friend, not even to his friends. Now it made Longarm shake his head as he worked toward sleep. This, he decided, was one old man who wasn't going to get away.

Longarm awoke for the last time just before dawn. It had been cold all night, and he had slept uncomfortably and chilled. His light bedroll was not up to the job of handling the desert night air. With creaking joints, he got up, looked carefully around, and then saw to his horses, doling out some grain in a feed trough for both of them. He patted the nearest animal on the rump. He was a roan gelding, sixteen and a half hands high, that Longarm had bought in Virginia City. The second horse had been an afterthought, a little bay that had surprised him with her staying power. She was gentle to a fault, but she did tend to shy and spook at the least thing.

The Hunsackers had been on his mind almost from the instant he had opened his eyes. Now, he got some of the dried beef and some of the bread, and made breakfast as best as he could. Having no coffee, he made do with some water sweetened with a little whiskey.

The taste made Longarm grimace. He turned and looked out the livery's back door toward the brilliant sunrise as it cleared the last mist of night away and heated everything it touched with its rays. It was going to be a hot day, all right.

Longarm sighed, got up, and busied himself, getting ready for the day. He needed a shave, but he was damned if he was going to go through the trouble. The Hunsackers were going to have to surrender soon, or Longarm would have to surrender to the hunger.

Longarm walked out the front door of the livery stable, casually smoking a cigarillo. The livery was at the north end of the town, with the stone house being some four hundred yards distant to the south. He turned right and walked toward it, puffing on his cigarillo and admiring the day, which had not quite reached the acme of its temperature. It was still just pleasant enough to where a man could stand it.

The first store was fifty yards toward the stone house. He walked through the dust and sand, then stepped up on the boardwalk, walking carefully so as to avoid the rotting places and the broken boards. There was a roof over the sidewalk all the way down the street, and it gave enough shade so that it was deliciously cool as he walked along. He wasn't going anywhere in particular, certainly not too near the stone house. He hadn't even brought his rifle, and he certainly didn't plan to get within pistol shot of the house.

As he walked, he looked at the stores and thought about the inhabitants when the town had been a going concern. He passed the general mercantile, and wondered how many saddles and sacks of beans and feet of rope and cans of nails the place had sold when the mines were working and people were convinced the town had a future. They had been convinced in spite of the fact that there had been thirty

20

other towns that had gone to seed ahead of them. He took a puff and blew out the blue smoke, watching it through the occasional hole in the boardwalk roof that allowed little shafts of brilliant sunlight through.

He had gone another half a block when there suddenly appeared small holes in the porch roof. He heard the high-pitched whine of bullets as they ricocheted, and then the crack of rifles being fired from somewhere up ahead. He never paused, just whirled and went through the first door he could find. The firing stopped. He squatted in the corner of a deserted cafe and cursed softly under his breath.

They had seen him come out of the livery stable, and they had seen him walk under the awning in front of the stores, and had been able to catch sight of him through the big holes in the roof. They had made a guess of where he was, and then put up a furious fusillade of rifle fire. Hell, the damned fools could have killed him. It made him furious.

Longarm found the back door out of the cafe, and then ran down the buildings toward the stone house. When he came to a corner where he couldn't be fired upon, but where he could be heard from, he let out a yell. "J.J.! J.J. Hunsacker! Come out of your hole. I want to talk to you, you sonofabitch."

After a moment, the man's mild voice came back. "That you, Longarm? What's the matter? You got a burr under your saddle blanket?"

Longarm said, "Listen, you sonofabitches. I was just walking along. I wasn't messing with you all and the next thing I know, you let out a volley of rifle fire on me. You damned idiotic sonofabitches, you could have killed me."

J.J. Hunsacker said easily, "Is that a fact, Longarm? Do

tell. Well, that would have been a most horrid shame.''

"Listen, Hunsacker," Longarm said, "this ain't no more fun for me than it is for you. This shooting at me is going to get your ass in trouble. The best thing you can do is to come on out of that joint and go with me. The less trouble you give me, the less trouble on you. You ain't got no wanted poster notices on you for murder yet. But the day is coming, if you keep on like this, when there will be. You take my meaning?''

"Oh, I take your meaning, all right, Longarm. Did you take our meaning a while ago?''

"I took your meaning that you were trying to hit me.''

"That's generally why we pop the cap on a cartridge, to hit something. Don't see no damned point in shooting to miss. But if you took our meaning, then it looks like you'll haul your freight and get the hell out of here. We ain't coming out and you ain't getting at us, so you might as well get on out.''

Longarm said, "Am I bothering you all? I never recollect being so unwanted in any one place in all my life. You all don't seem to want me around. How come is that? You got someplace you need to be?''

Hunsacker said, "Hell, Longarm, you can't watch us all the time. If we wanted to slip out, we could do it when you're asleep without any trouble.''

Longarm said, "I wouldn't be so damned sure of that, but I am sure you are damned anxious for me to be out of this part of the country. Makes me wonder.''

"Well, you just keep on wondering. Meanwhile, I am going to have to get you to excuse me. I've got some breakfast to tend to. I've got some ham and eggs that need eating. You have any ham and eggs this morning, Longarm?''

22

Longarm was silent, thinking about the dried beef that he had eaten.

J.J. said again, "Why don't you come on up here and have breakfast with me, Longarm? It would be a treat to have your company."

Longarm turned away. "Go to Hell, Hunsacker. Just go to Hell."

He walked slowly back to the livery stable, his mind busy and his head full of thought. He couldn't see any clear-cut plan. He could slip around and make a try for their horses, but he reckoned that would be pretty risky. The horses were in a small corral at the back of the house, and he imagined that they were guarded by more than one rifle, night and day. No, getting at their horses was not the way. Getting at *them* was what was going to be necessary.

He stepped into the livery stable and spent an idle moment rubbing down the roan gelding with an old empty feed sack. Nothing could come to his mind about getting at the Hunsackers. The alternative was to go for help, but he knew that when he left, so would they. All he could do was to hold out as long as he could. He didn't know how long that was going to be, maybe one more day.

Because of his reputation of always running down and bringing back his man, he hated giving up on them, but he was beginning to believe that this was one of those situations where he was going to have to. Oh, sure, he could go back to Reno and wire and have a half-dozen deputy marshals or local law available in a few days, but by then there would be no catching the Hunsackers. It made him want to mash his teeth in frustration.

Finally, he got up, had a drink of whiskey, and then walked out the back of the livery stable until he had the stone house in view. He settled down on a rock and commenced to watch the house to see what kind of a routine, if any, he could figure out and make use of.

Watching the stone house made for a very slow morning, but then he really didn't have much else to do. In the afternoon, for the sake of variety, he went around the livery stable and watched from the other side. It had nothing to do with shade or being cooler, because there was no shade to be found, not anywhere, not where he could see the stone house. He reckoned a man could dig down seven or eight hundred feet and it might get a little cooler, but he didn't feel much up to the effort.

His surveillance of the Hunsacker hideout yielded very sparse results. Occasionally, he would see a flicker of a body passing one of the windows, mainly upstairs, and occasionally he would hear a dim sound, but other than that, the harvest was pretty slim.

He ate as little as he could, not so much to preserve his provisions, but to make sure he didn't completely poison himself on the beef and cheese, both of which were starting to get a kind of funny taste. The biscuits had expired. He thought of burying them and holding services, but decided that was too much trouble. He had about one day's grub left, and it was not fit to be eaten. Something was going to have to happen.

It gradually grew dim and then dark. He went into the stable, put out more grain for the horses, and made sure they had water. They seemed perfectly content with the arrangement. What was time to a horse? They certainly didn't mind the wait. He reckoned, given a choice of being in a cool livery stable or carrying his 190 pounds over the hot desert sand, he'd probably choose the livery stable too.

Longarm determined to do very little sleeping that night. He had a feeling that the Hunsackers just might try to make a break sometime before daylight. It was his belief that he had caught a tone of desperation in J.J.'s voice that morning. He thought it might mean that they were thinking about running out. If that was the case, Longarm wanted to be watching.

He determined that he would take an early nap and then be on the watch from about midnight on. He calculated that if they took off, they would do it sometime in the early morning hours when it was the coolest and they could make the most tracks. The moon would go down about two or three and it would be pretty dark, but they could still be moving along and putting distance between them and him if they were able to get clear.

Longarm determined to get to bed just as early as he could. He wanted to get about an hour or two of sleep, and then be ready to stay up the balance of the night. He made what supper he could, washing it down with the whiskey and water, and settled down to sleep, if sleep would come. He set his mind to wake himself up about midnight.

He didn't know how a man could do that, but he knew that it had always been an easy trick for him. He guessed that a man got so used to telling time by a watch that he could just feel it inside of him. Longarm had never been a man to overcomplicate his mind, or any other situation, with thinking that had nothing to do with the job at hand.

It was difficult to get to sleep so early, but finally he slept. Then shortly, or so it seemed to him, he was awake again. He had his watch lying beside him, and by a shaft of moonlight that shone through a back window, he could see that it was about ten minutes until midnight.

25

Longarm made no attempt to get up. It was best to rest a bit, let his body get attuned to the job at hand. What he planned to do was make a great circle in the desert and come up on the stone house from the back. He would be carrying his rifle, and he would have to take advantage of the lay of the land. It was going to be hard going through the cactus and the sand and the rocks and the greasewood. He would just have to snake along through the low places, and duck down behind the humps and the mounds, until he could get to where he would have a good vantage point to see if they were going to try to make a run.

He sat up yawning, thinking about getting up and starting the two-hour walk. He figured he would need at least that much time to make the big wide circle. As he yawned, he heard a sound. It wasn't a sound his horses would make. It wasn't the sound a stray cat would make. He distinctly heard the sound of a booted foot in the front of the stable.

He sat up, slowly drawing his revolver as he did. It seemed that he had visitors. He was just about to lean forward and look around, when some sense told him that there was a presence behind him. Longarm whirled, flinging himself to the dirt as the shotgun roared and the pellets clattered into the stable wall above his head. He whipped his revolver up, sighting toward the empty back door, but the person who had fired the shotgun was off and running by the sound of the boots striking the ground. There was still the other fellow, so Longarm didn't think he could get up and run to the back door of the stable without exposing himself to whoever was out front. He eased around the partition and tried to see through the gloom.

Somewhere near the front entrance, he saw the slightest motion, and he fired, aiming low. The only reaction was a sudden scuffling run, and Longarm saw a dark figure slip around the edge of the door and take off. After that, Longarm got to his feet, walked to the back door, and looked down along the line of the back of the buildings of the ghost town. Three or four hundred yards away, a dark form was clearing the last of the buildings and running diagonally to the stone house.

The whole scene left Longarm puzzled. They had come down to get him. Instead of simply taking off into the night, they had come down with the intention of killing him. He couldn't understand that. J.J. Hunsacker and his son, LeeRoy, were outlaws, and they were low-down and they were varmints, but they weren't stupid. You didn't kill a United States deputy marshal unless you had no other choice, and they had another choice—the choice of running. They had chosen instead to come and ambush him.

Longarm walked back into the stable, found his whiskey bottle, took a drink, and then stood by his road horse, thinking the matter over, running all the details around and around in his mind.

He couldn't for the life of him figure out what they must have been thinking. To him, it had been a damned fool play. What did they have to gain from killing a United States deputy marshal other than biting off a hell of a chaw of trouble?

Surely, they could have figured out to make a getaway. If they had to, as a last resort, they could have lain in wait for him on the trail and crippled him or his horse. There was a lot of things they could have done instead of attempting to assassinate a member of the Federal Marshals Service.

Something else was up. They wanted him gone, and it

wasn't to make a getaway. He wondered if the attack had been a bluff, if its main intention had been to scare him off. One thing for certain, they weren't going to tell him, and he doubted that he could figure it out, not even using their way of thinking. Finally, Longarm shook his head and gave it up as one problem too many, took another drink of whiskey, and then with his carbine in his hand, went out into the street to see what was transpiring down at the other end of the street where the stone house stood.

He walked about halfway down until he was about two hundred yards from the house, then casually threw six shots through the upstairs windows. Even before the echo of the shots had died, he could hear a considerable amount of yelling and excitement. It made him smile. If they weren't going to allow him to sleep, he didn't see any reason to let them have their peace either. When some of the commotion had died down, he yelled out, "J.J., that's just a little of what you're going to get in the next few days! I've got six deputies on their way!"

He waited a few moments for a reply, but when none was forthcoming, he turned and trudged back to the livery stable and into the gloom of the back. He was well and truly puzzled. It was unlike anything he knew about their past history. They were sneaks rather than folks who would confront you and take you on in a fight. Longarm took a moment to light a cigarillo, and then he sat down on a couple of sacks of aging feed, smoking, thinking, and trying to figure this situation out.

One thing was certain. The attack didn't change his plans. As bad as he dreaded the idea of footing it in a long circle around the stone house, he didn't really see any way of getting out of it. If anything, their midnight visit made it all that much more important that he take a scout and see just exactly how they were situated. It wasn't pleasant now, and it wasn't going to be pleasant. But then, as Billy Vail would say, if it was so damned much fun being a deputy marshal, they wouldn't bother to pay you. Well, he could always reply to Billy Vail that he, Longarm, made more money playing poker and trading horses than he ever did getting paid by the United States Government for wearing a little tin badge around.

Longarm faced the fact that he would have to leave and make the trek. He checked his rifle, and then put a dozen extra .44-caliber cartridges in the pockets of his jeans and his shirt. After that, he went out the back entrance to the stable, leaving his horses to get along as best as they could. It was about 1:15 by his watch when he left.

Chapter 3

The going was rougher than he had imagined. The sand was loose, and there were thousands of little rocks and stones and cactus plants every ten feet or so that pronged him as he stepped. He hadn't gone a hundred yards away from the livery stable before he had stuck a cactus thorn through his jeans and into his calf. It hurt so bad, he nearly cursed out loud. As it was, it was tough going to keep himself concealed from the stone house. If anyone had been on careful guard, he imagined they would have already seen him. But he had gotten a break. It was a dark night, clouds shadowing what moonlight there was in the desert.

He headed almost due west for five or six hundred yards, before he turned back toward the south to go past the house and come up from behind it. The loose sand was the biggest irritant. After a half mile, his legs were so tired from the work required to walk through the nasty stuff, he wasn't sure he could make it. If he hit a soft spot, his boot would sink halfway into what was supposed to be firm ground.

He cursed under his breath most of the first part of the trip. The second part, he didn't have the breath to curse.

He ran across a small gallery of scrub brush, mostly greasewood with some mesquite mixed in. With that as a cover, he was able to stoop down and make some time.

There was only one window on the west side of the house. It was dark, but he still kept his eye on it looking for any signs of movement. Finally, he was beyond the house and could start curving back to the east so that he could see what was happening at the back. If they were going to leave and try to lose him, they had to get their horses from the back.

From a position about a mile south of the stone house, Longarm worked his way forward, moving from one clump of mesquite to a high place in the ground to a gully, and then to any other kind of cover he could find to keep himself well hidden. He was approximately six hundred yards short of the house when he went to ground in a little gully, stretching his rifle out before him. He got out his watch and by the moon's dim glow, he was able to see that it was 2:30. It had taken him about an hour and fifteen minutes to come not much more than two miles—a long two miles. For a man who didn't make a habit out of walking, it was a damned long two miles. While he waited, he took his time, pulling both boots off and pouring out the sand. He couldn't figure how sand could get by his jeans, which covered the tops of his boots, and then get down inside his boots, but he reckoned there was a coffee cup full of sand in each one.

He watched the house, and nothing happened. He was close enough that he could see the Hunsacker horses distinctly. There were ten of them. He reckoned that four of them had been used as packhorses or maybe just extra mounts. Several of the horses were sleeping, standing up, one hind foot cocked and lifted off the ground and then let back down just on the toe of the hoof. You could always tell when a horse was sleeping because his tail was still. Never mind that his head was down. Most horses did that a lot of the time, but their tails were seldom still unless they were asleep.

Longarm grew restless. It was 3:30, starting toward four. There still hadn't been a sign of movement from the house. If they were going to be leaving, they were taking their own good time about it. Perhaps, he thought, they might have spotted him.

Yet there had been no disturbance, no sign of movement from the house. It had been as still as a graveyard. At four, he stirred and raised up slightly. There didn't seem to be much point in waiting much longer. He crawled out of the gully and then began working his way backwards a few hundred yards before he found the kind of cover he wanted. Once he headed west, he took it slow, watching the house and the horses, listening for any movement. Finally, he came even with the west side of the house again, and paused to look the situation over. He was in a clump of mesquite and greasewood, and it was a good a place to take a rest. His watch said it was near five o'clock, and there was still no movement from the house.

After a short break, Longarm pushed on north, hurrying a little because it was coming dawn and he didn't want to be caught out in the desert on foot just in case the Hunsackers were watching for him.

The growth of greasewood and mesquite ran almost a thousand yards, and he made good use of it. His legs were tired from lumbering through the loose sand, and he paused to rest every so often. It didn't really matter because by now, he was out of rifle range and there would damned little they could do about it even if they did catch sight of him. He was nearly even with the livery stable, but he was still some six or seven hundred yards to the west of it. He paused at the last of the mesquite and sagebrush to kneel down on one knee and take a rest. He was damned if his job involved walking four miles in one night in high-heeled boots in loose sand that was full of rocks and cactus and probably a whole lot of crawling things he didn't want to run into.

Toward the east, he could see a faint glow in the sky that told him the sun was rising. It hadn't nudged its way over the horizon yet, but it was fast coming. He yawned, got out a cigarillo, and lit it. While he smoked, he looked toward the northwest, toward the open country that led to the foothills of the mountains. He was surprised that the Hunsackers hadn't held up in there. That was their natural habitat. It was full of all kinds of hidey-holes and gullies and blind canyons where a man could get lost for a thousand years. As he was looking, he thought he saw movement in that direction. He strained his eyes, but whatever it was had gone to ground.

He was about to turn his attention to the stone house for the last time when, out of the corner of his eye, he caught the movement again. He whipped his head around and stared long and hard. Yes, it was definitely something moving across the desert. It was a good ways off, maybe four or five miles, maybe more. It was difficult to tell in the clear, still mountain air, but he could tell that it wasn't a mounted rider. It was too big. As it came on, he was finally

34

able to distinguish that it was a mule-drawn buggy. At least, that was what the brief glances he got of it made him think. It disappeared from time to time as it hit low spots in the desert or ran behind a rise.

Now he turned and watched it intently. It seemed to be moving at a pretty good pace. Whoever was in the buggy, if it was indeed a buggy, was interested in getting to where they were going before the sun got up and too hot. As near as he could figure, and he knew it was still too early to be making such calculations, the contraption seemed to be heading toward the town of Lodestar. He wondered if the sheriff at Reno or some deputy had become curious about him and had come to see after his welfare. But no, he thought. That couldn't be. The buggy was coming from a direction well to the west of Reno. In fact, it was coming out of the mountains.

It came on, and now he could tell that it was a buggy being pulled by something that didn't look exactly like a horse, so he assumed it was a mule. Mules were used to the desert country. A mule could go longer without water or feed. They were tougher than horses. Also, their hooves were softer and splayed out to where they could get a better grip in the sand and soft going.

Knowing it was a mule didn't answer any of the several questions that were in his mind, the main one being who was in the buggy and what they were doing headed for such a spot as Lodestar. The only people in Lodestar were him and the Hunsackers, and he doubted very seriously that whoever was driving the buggy was looking for him. That meant that whoever was coming had to be an ally of his quarry in the stone house. It behooved him to keep them from joining up with the old man and LeeRoy and the rest of the clan.

Longarm started moving westward in a line to intercept the route of the mule and the buggy. For several hundred yards, there was the cover of the bramble of the mesquite and greasewood, and he moved from clump to clump, moving as slow as he could, yet at the same time making certain that he'd be in a position to intercept the path of the buggy. He could not quite make out the passengers, but he could see that the mule wanted to get to wherever they were going before it got hotter. Mules were smart that way.

He had moved some 150 yards west when he knelt to watch the buggy. Now, it was no more than a mile away. He studied the passengers, and had a difficult time coming to a conclusion. They looked too colorful for members of the Hunsacker gang, and they weren't exactly wearing the kind of hats that most gunmen and cowboys and road agents wore in this part of the country.

He moved as quickly as he could through the bramble of bushes for another hundred yards. The buggy was now less than three quarters of a mile away. This time, as Longarm studied it, a startling thought occurred to him. There were three people in the buggy, and it appeared that they were women. He couldn't for the life of him figure out what three women would be doing flying across the desert floor at five-thirty in the morning, unless they were three of the Hunsacker men who'd decided to wear dresses for disguise.

Longarm moved west rapidly. For certain, he intended to stop the buggy. With it less than a half mile away, he could see that there were women on the seat of the buggy. He couldn't make out their features, but he could tell that two of them had long blond hair and the one in the middle, who was driving, had short, raven-black hair. It made him lick his lips unconsciously. He was hungry for a woman.

He had just gotten to know a female faro dealer in Reno when he'd run across the Hunsackers. In fact, he had been planning on inviting her for some very pleasant lovemaking the night he had taken out chasing the Hunsackers. He'd regretted more than just the loss of the woman's soft body. As far as he was concerned, faro was the worst odds a gambler could get, and yet he had sat there for several nights in a row, losing at a sucker's game while he smoothly let the good-looking woman dealer get to know him. He reckoned that she had gotten to know his money a good deal better than she had gotten to know *him*.

He crouched behind the mesquite bush and watched the buggy as it neared, steering straight as an arrow for the stone house. He itched mightily for the pair of binoculars that were, right then, back in his saddlebags. He hadn't taken them with him when he had gone to trek around the stone house because they weren't much good at night. Now it was daylight, and he wished he could see what type of ladies were occupying the buggy. He wondered if they were kin to each other, or if they were kin to the Hunsackers, or just what their relationship was to the whole matter. He doubted that they were new cooks hired to come out.

The buggy was less than a half mile away. He was going to have to do something. What, he was not certain, but the one sure thing he could do to stop them was to kill the mule. He hated to do that. It seemed like a good animal, and he had never been one to shoot horses, mules, donkeys, or any animals that you couldn't rightly eat, although he had eaten horseflesh a time or two when there wasn't anything else.

Longarm began moving, trying his best to intersect the line the buggy was making as it headed south and toward the stone house. He would be out of cover before he reached that line. Whatever he did, he was going to have to do it at comparatively long range. After fifty yards more, he was at the end of the mesquite and greasewood clump, and the only other thing that was in front of him was a broad expanse of clear sand. Clear, that is, except for small rocks and cactus.

The buggy was coming on at a fast pace. It was less than two hundred yards away. Longarm had no time to debate any longer. He put his rifle to his shoulder, pulling back the hammer with his thumb as he did. He aimed a little above and in front of the mule and fired.

Longarm saw the mule shy slightly and the women jump. The mule had spooked at the sound of the bullet as it whistled right over his head, and the women were surprised by the noise of the rifle when it reached them. But for all the good it did, he might as well have saved the bullet. The mule once again picked up his rapid trotting pace, and other than looking around, the women paid no more attention. As quickly as he could, Longarm jacked another shell into the chamber. This time, he fired the bullet right across the mule's face. The mule stopped and reared up. The women, he could see, were frightened and nervous.

He heard the black-haired one cry out shrilly, "J.J.! J.J. Hunsacker! Is that you, dammit?"

The women were no more than fifty yards away. Longarm stepped out of the clump of mesquite and started toward them, his rifle at the ready. The black-haired woman picked up the reins she had dropped when the mule had reared up. She made as if to slap the still-nervous animal on the back.

Longarm yelled out, "Hold it, lady!" He put the rifle to his shoulder. "You hit that animal and get him going, he'll be a dead animal!"

All three of the women were looking at Longarm. He was within forty yards. Already he could see that the black-haired one was older, and the two blond women were in their mid-twenties, he guessed. He walked steadfastly forward. He said, "Don't move a muscle. Drop those reins. Do it, lady! I am a United States deputy marshal, and I will use this gun if I have to."

The black-haired woman glared at him. The other two just looked interested and sort of innocent. From somewhere behind him, he heard a dim clamor and clatter and shouting and the sound of rifle fire. He turned and looked back toward the stone house. In the windows of the upper story, he could make out the dim figures of several people who appeared to be waving their arms and yelling. Now and again, one fired a rifle. He wasn't too much worried about the rifle fire, for unless they had a Sharps buffalo gun or something similar, they were well out of range of the Winchester carbines that they most likely had in their possession.

Longarm walked up to the buggy and reached out, taking the reins out of the woman's hand. He could see now that she was forty or so. The girls—he began to think of them as that—next to the hard-faced, old battle-ax that had been doing the driving, were even younger than he had thought at first.

It was a two-seater buggy, a carriage really, and he bade the two young women to get in the backseat. He said,

"Now, if anybody's got a weapon on them, a pistol, a derringer, a knife, or even a long hat pin, this is the time to declare it. If you try to use it on me, you're going to get yourself dead."

The dark-haired woman said sullenly, "You say that you are a United States marshal? Well, anybody could say that. For all me and the girls know, you're some crazy man out here in the desert."

Longarm reached in his shirt pocket, took out his badge, and held it in his palm long enough for them all to see it.

He said, "I am a United States deputy marshal and I am hunting the Hunsackers. I have them run to ground in that stone house over yonder. I have a feeling that you were going to see them."

The dark-haired woman stared resolutely out across the desert. She said, "You can go to Hell. I don't like any law, and I sure as hell don't like the kind of law you represent."

Longarm said, "Well, slide over in that seat, lady. I'll be doing the driving now."

Longarm had to half-shove her over as he stepped up into the buggy and took the reins. Turning back so he could see the two blondes, he said, "You just stay back in your seats. Don't lean forward. Don't talk. Don't yell. Don't do nothing."

They didn't answer, and he wheeled the mule to the left and started directly toward the livery stables, which were some six or seven hundred yards across the desert. As he drove, he glanced over at the stone house. He could see that the outlaws were jumping around, waving their arms, and apparently not enjoying the sight of him in charge of the buggy and its passengers. His one worry was that they might suddenly get all braved up and mount their horses and charge him before he could get inside and fort up in the livery stable. But if they did, they couldn't fire at him without endangering the women, and from the way they were acting, he didn't think they wanted to do that. In fact, the more his mind toyed with it, the more he was convinced that the women might have been the best thing that had happened to him in the whole scheme of things.

He headed more to the north, intending to circle around and come up the street and into the livery stable through the front, since there was no room to come in the back way by buggy.

Longarm watched carefully to see what was transpiring with the Hunsackers, half expecting at any moment to see four or five horsemen come bursting around the big house with rifles in their hands. By then, he was sweeping around the north line of vacant buildings. The Hunsackers had made no move. He checked the mule, who was stepping along briskly, slowed him down to a walk, and then turned into the livery stable. He knew quite well that the Hunsackers were watching his every move.

He went through the big double doors of the stable, and pulled the mule up smartly before he could get into the back of the building. Longarm jumped down and tied the reins to a post. He turned around and looked at the three women. The two blondes looked back at him solemnly, but the black-haired woman had a furious look on her face.

She said, "By damn you, sir. What right do you have to stop us on our right and lawful and peaceful business? Just who the hell do you think you are?"

Longarm stood there, looking at them, his hands on his hips for a long moment. Finally, he spat, "I've already told you who I am and what my business is. Now, you all get down from that buggy. We're going to go into that office and everybody is going to take a chair and we are going to talk. Only this time, I'll be asking the questions, finding out about your business.''

For a moment, nothing happened. Longarm decided he better set the tone of the business so there would be no misunderstandings. He took a long stride to the buggy, reached in with his right arm, and got the black-haired, hatchet-faced woman by the arm, dragging her out of the buggy. He would have dragged her to the ground if she hadn't jerked back just enough to slip his grip. He was about to reach for her again when she waved him away.

''Hold on,'' she said. ''There ain't no use throwing me on the ground. I'll get down by myself.''

After that, the two yellow-haired girls followed suit, coming out immediately, stepping on the running board and then to the ground. He herded them toward the office, keeping an eye toward the street in case company came calling. The office was a fair size, and had glass on three sides, which gave him a good view to keep watch. He took a chair, and put his back to the stable part of the livery. He appointed the black-haired woman to sit behind the desk, and then let the two young women find chairs for themselves.

Longarm turned to the black-haired woman. ''What's your name?''

She was dressed in a high-necked gown made from some paisley print, with a brooch at her throat collar that gathered the material up into a becoming choker. He thought to himself that she wasn't all that bad-looking, except when she was furious, which was the only view he had really had of her.

42

Longarm said, "What is your name, ma'am? I'm not likely to ask you many more times."

She said, "I'm Mrs. Minnie Sewell, if it's any of your business."

Longarm glanced at the woman. "Is that Mrs. or Madam?"

The woman gave Longarm an outraged look. She said, "How dare you, sir! The late Mr. Sewell would rise to mark right promptly and you would not be bully-ragging a poor helpless woman like me!"

Longarm smiled. He nodded his head at the two young women. "And who are these? Your daughters?"

Mrs. Sewell said, "Well, now, Marshal. I'm certain they can tell you if they are of a mind to give you their names."

Longarm turned toward the two young women. They were sitting quite calmly, composed. The first one had a green ribbon in her hair that went very well with her coloring. He could see that she had used a little rouge on her cheeks and on her lips. He said, "What's your name, miss?"

She cocked her head, gave him a slight smile, and said, "My name? What do you want with my name? Men don't usually want my name. That's not what they're after. They want something other than my name."

Longarm looked at her for a long moment, thinking how right she was. He could feel the swelling rising in his groin just looking at her. She was right. It would be a damned fool of a man who would only want her name. He said, "Well, that's true, but for the time being, let's just pretend that's all I want."

"My name is Marianne Parsons, if it's any of your business," she said.

43

Longarm nodded. "All right, Miss Parsons. Thank you."

He looked over at the other young lady. She was not as flirtatious. She looked calm, but she also looked serious. Her yellow dress went very well with her wheat-colored hair. He could see now that they were different-colored blondes. Marianne Parsons had the lighter hair. This one's hair had a touch of brunette in it. He said, "I need to know your name, miss."

The woman looked over at Marianne Parsons, and then at Minnie Sewell, and then back at Longarm. She said in a cool, haughty voice, "I'm not certain that I care what you want, Marshal, if that's really what you are. But if you must know my name, it's Verlene Thomas."

Longarm nodded again. "That's fine. Actually, I didn't need to know any of your names. I don't really care what they are, but what I do care about and what I intend to find out is what brought you to this ghost town of Lodestar."

Longarm looked around swiftly at Minnie Sewell. He said, "I think that's the one you can answer, Mrs. Sewell. You were the one driving that mule. You knew what you were doing, where you were going. Let's have an answer."

Minnie Sewell folded her arms across her ample breast. Her face was set and her eyes piercing. "Listen here, Marshal," she said. "There are things that you ain't got the right to make me do. We ain't done nothing wrong. We ain't committed no crime and you can't say that we did. This is a free country. Where we were going and what we were going for is none of your damned business. So you just get that straight in your mind and me and you will get along just fine."

Longarm looked steadily at the woman. "Mrs. Sewell, I

have it in my mind that you are engaged in the business of prostitution.''

She opened her mouth to speak, but he put his hand up to stop her. ''Save your breath until I am done talking,'' he said. ''Maybe then you'll understand what I am trying to say. I have it in my mind that you have brought these two young ladies out here for the purpose of prostitution. That is illegal in every state and territory under the federal flag, and Nevada happens to fill that bill. So you might think that you haven't committed a crime or done any harm, but you'd be up the wrong tree, Mrs. Sewell.''

Her dark eyes had gotten even harder. ''You can just go to Hell, Marshal.''

''Deputy Marshal. You can address me as Deputy Long. The name is Deputy Custis Long. You didn't ask, but I am offering it to you in case you want to get my attention. That's the way you would do it.''

Mrs. Sewell said, ''I'd just be happy if I never heard your name again. In fact, I wish I had never set eyes on you. I said we were going about our business in a free and American way and you ain't got no right to interfere. As for this business about prostitution, you can't prove nothing. And secondly, prostitution is just as freely practiced in the territory of Nevada as it is everywhere else. Where you get off saying it is against the law is more than I can figure.''

Longarm nodded. ''I will agree with you that it is a law that is not often enforced. It's not a popular law, and it is probably only enforced in one or two states in the Northeast, but that doesn't keep it from being a law, and that doesn't keep me from enforcing it as an officer of the law any time I feel like it. And it just so happens that I feel

45

like it right now. Do you want to tell me what you were doing, where you were coming from, and who you are heading towards? I think I already know all the answers, but I would just like to hear you say them."

Minnie Sewell said, "Did I remember to tell you to go to Hell? If not, go to Hell."

Longarm swung his eyes to the two very pretty young women sitting in the room. He said, "I have the feeling that you two are the prize that goes with the ribbon. Now, Mrs. Sewell is not going to have anybody laying awake nights waiting on her. But I do believe that you, Marianne, and you, Verlene, could set the heart racing fast in some young men that I happen to know. Now, is it true that you were coming to this town for the purpose of prostitution?"

He was looking at Verlene when he said that. She turned and looked at Marianne and gave her head the slightest shake. Longarm caught the motion. He said, "Marianne, one of you is going to tell the whole story about why you decided to drive out from Reno on a forty-mile jaunt. Someone is going to tell me the truth of this matter before it's all over. Now, it could be you, Marianne. Or it could be you, Mrs. Sewell. Or it could even be you, Verlene. You can make it hard or you can make it easy, but it's going to happen."

Marianne suddenly blurted out, "We didn't come from Reno. We didn't come from more than ten miles away."

Longarm smiled. "All right, that's a good start. Now, where was this someplace not more than ten miles away?"

Minnie Sewell said suddenly, "Marianne, you shut your mouth. I'll come over there and slap some sense into you if you're not careful."

Longarm got up. He said, "You all stay still and I'll be

46

right back. You can't make it out that door into any place before I could run you down. Be assured of that."

He went out the office door, and then cut quickly back into the stable, going past the mule and the buggy. His saddlebags were hanging over a stall partition. He rummaged inside the left pouch, and came out with two sets of handcuffs. He put one set in his rear pocket, and then went back inside the office carrying the other one.

Before the woman could realize what was happening, he had snapped one of the cuffs over the wrist of Minnie Sewell and then dragged her to her feet and around the desk. She was out the door before she realized what was happening. As he took her toward the back, she tried to kick and slap at him with her free hand, all the while directing a torrent of abuse and cuss words at him. He paid her no mind. At the first post, he found where the jaw of the loose cuff would go around, snapped it closed, and left her anchored to part of the woodwork of the livery stable. He said, "Now, the only way you'll get loose is to pull that post down, and then if you do, the roof is going to fall down on your head."

She said furiously, "If I thought, by damned, that it would get you too, I'd be willing to take the chance."

Longarm nodded and walked back into office. The two young women had been whispering between themselves, but they fell silent as he entered. He said, "All right, now we are going to get down to some truth here." He reached into his back pocket, took out the other set of handcuffs, and then said, "Or else we're going to put these to use, and then there won't be but one of you loose. And that one is going to be worked on proper. So, you can do it however

47

you want to. Now, who wants to start telling me what you all are doing here and why and how all this stuff got made up? Who wants to go first? You, Marianne? Why don't you start?''

Chapter 4

Marianne gave Verlene a frightened look. It was clear to Longarm by now that Marianne was the more vulnerable of the two girls. Verlene was older and more experienced. It would be against Marianne that the best pressure could be applied. Longarm hated to come down hard on the pretty young woman, especially considering how long he had been out in the desert, but he felt that he had to do just that. He didn't know what purpose these women had for coming to Lodestar, whether they had been sent for by J.J. Hunsacker, or had come on their own, or just what the situation was. For all he knew they could be kinfolk to the Hunsackers. They might be engaged to some of the men. But to Longarm, they were bargaining chips to play off against the Hunsackers, and with the odds being what they were, he needed all the help he could get. He stood up, walked over, and stood near Marianne, forcing her to look up at him. Her lips were trembling, and she was blinking her eyes rapidly.

He said, "Now, listen to me, little lady. You've got your-self in over your head. You are fooling with the wrong folks. You've got yourself caught between some outlaws and the law. If you've got any sense, you'll cooperate with the law."

Marianne's lower lip started to tremble more, and Long-arm saw tears start in her eyes. She made a moaning sound, and looked toward Verlene again.

The older girl said harshly, "Oh, leave her alone. If you have to bully her so, why don't you come ask me?"

At that moment, the progress between them was inter-rupted by yelling and cursing from the interior of the stable. Minnie Sewell was making sure she was not being forgot-ten. Longarm gave the two women a look and said, "Don't either of you make a move." With that, he turned on his heel and walked out into the stable, untying the handker-chief from around his neck as he walked.

Minnie Sewell was in fine voice. She stopped when she saw him, but just for an instant. In the next, she let out a long string of curses. Longarm caught her with her mouth wide open, and jammed the handkerchief in and tied it around behind her mouth so that she was gagged but not bound. She could reach up and free the gag with the hand that was not handcuffed, so Longarm was forced to get out his key, unlock the cuff that was around the post, then force Minnie Sewell over to where he could get both of her arms around the post, and then click the jaw of the free handcuff onto her other wrist. She was much more uncomfortable now, but at least she couldn't pull the handkerchief loose.

Longarm said, "I hope you are satisfied. You've man-aged to get yourself into a very handy position. Let's see what you can do now. You had better hope that the Hunsackers don't go to shooting through the roof again. There's a damned good chance they'll hit you. You're just about in the middle."

She gave Longarm a look with wide, frightened eyes. She struggled to push the gag out of her mouth with her tongue, but wasn't successful. Longarm turned and walked into the office.

Verlene said before he could even ask her, "Well, if you have to know, Marianne and I are suppose to marry two of the Hunsacker family."

Longarm stared at her in disbelief. "Marry? You mean with a preacher or a justice of the peace?"

Marianne started to speak, but Verlene stared straight back at Longarm. She said, "I know you think we are whores, and maybe we have been, but a deal was made through Mrs. Sewell and we are to marry two of the Hunsacker boys. It's going to be a marriage, proper and legal, and you can think what you want to about it. But you've got no right to hold us, no right to keep us from going to men we are engaged to marry."

Longarm smiled slowly. It was even better than he had hoped. He'd thought that he had intercepted some whores that J.J. Hunsacker had hired to keep his stud horses in line. He couldn't believe that he had intercepted a bridal party. He said, "What about Minnie Sewell? Who was she going to marry? Old J.J. himself?"

Verlene folded her arms and looked out the front window. She said, "Whatever Mrs. Sewell's business is, it's none of mine and I doubt that it's any of yours."

Longarm said, "Next you'll be telling me that she didn't own the whorehouse that you worked at."

Verlene gave him a look. "Next, I won't be telling you

anything. Next, we'll be getting up and walking out of this office and going down to where we are supposed to be right now."

Longarm slowly took the extra pair of handcuffs out of his pocket and said, "I don't think you'll be going anywhere to see anybody."

Marianne said, "I wish we had never come. I wish we were home and it was all over with."

Verlene gave her a hard look. "Be quiet, Marianne."

Longarm said, "And just where is home? Where did you all come from? You say you didn't come from Reno? Where did you come from?"

Marianne suddenly said, "There's a little town about ten miles northwest of here where a mine is still working. There's a saloon and a whorehouse there. We were working there because it's got less competition than Reno and the money was better. Even the men were more grateful, if you understand what I mean."

Longarm nodded. "Oh, I understand what you mean."

Verlene said, "What do you plan to do with us? Not that you have right to do anything."

Longarm scratched the back of his head. "Well, Verlene, I haven't exactly worked all that out in my mind yet. I've got to figure out some way to get some contact with the Hunsackers and see what they want to do about this business—see what they have to trade. I can assure you of one thing—I ain't allowing you to parade up the street and finish up getting married to a couple of them boys that I plan to see hung before the week is out. So you can put that thought right out of your mind.

"As to what I am going to do, that I cannot say. First, I know I am going to have to secure you two so that you can't get to bouncing around and get loose. I don't need to be watching you every second of the time."

Marianne said, "Oh, you're not going to lock us up? Or chain us? Or tie us up? I couldn't stand that."

Longarm said, "Whatever I do, I'll see to it that you can handle it. I know that, right about now, both of you think that I am about the meanest man in the country, but that ain't necessarily the case. I ain't interested in putting a hardship on you that I don't have to. My interest is in those six or seven fellows down at the end of the street. By the way . . ." He switched his eyes over to Verlene. "Which ones were you and Marianne suppose to marry?"

Verlene seemed somewhere between disinterested and angry. "What does it matter?" she said. "Is it really any of your business? I understand that you want to put those men in jail. We were simply going to marry them."

Longarm started to say, "Sounds about like the same to me," but he caught himself in time. Instead he said, "Well, I reckon you can pretty well figure that the marriage ain't going to come off. I hope that you got some money on the deal already so that you won't hold it against me for interrupting the upcoming nuptials."

Verlene said steadily, "Whatever we got is our business. It's not yours."

Longarm said, "I am a little curious about one thing. You were coming here to marry a couple of these Hunsacker boys. Who was going to do the marrying? As far as I know, outside of me, there ain't another soul alive in this town. Who was going to be the preacher?"

Verlene drew herself up. She said, "Mrs. Sewell, for your information, is a licensed minister."

Longarm looked at her, blinking for a second. Then he

53

smiled slowly. "Oh, yeah," he said. "I'll just bet she is. I'd hate to find out which church, though. I'm pretty sure Mrs. Sewell is not going to be mistaken very often for a minister."

Verlene said, "Well, Marshal Long, you may or may not know everything. It appears that you think you do, but in this case, you just happen to be wrong. I have seen her diploma on the wall of her house. So there."

Longarm was about to speak when he heard the sound of a voice shouting from somewhere up the street. He jumped to his feet and ran to the big double doors of the stables. He could distinctly hear someone shouting now. With a cautious left eye, he peered out the door, looking up the street toward the big house. He could see three figures walking down the middle of the street. At times, one of them called out his name, and at other times, all three of the men called out, "Longarm! Longarm! Show yourself! We've got business to talk!"

The only one of them that Longarm recognized was LeeRoy. He was the one carrying the white flag. It was nothing more than what appeared to be a torn-up sheet tied to a slim piece of wood. Longarm slid his carbine around the edge of the door and dropped to one knee. He steadied his sight on LeeRoy, who was in the middle. He called out, "That'll do you right there. That's far enough. You can stop right there."

The men came to a halt. LeeRoy Hunsacker said, "That you, Longarm?"

Longarm said, "Were you expecting someone else?"

"We need to talk."

"What do you want to talk about?"

One of the other men spoke. He appeared younger and

54

lighter-haired than LeeRoy, but Longarm didn't know his name. He said, "It's about those women you took. They were supposed to be our brides."

Longarm said, "What's your name?"

The young man said, "Joe. Joe Hunsacker, and you have my bride in there."

LeeRoy said, "And you have mine too, Longarm. They ain't got nothing to do with the law, and you ought to turn them loose. You ain't got no business holding them there, and you have that Mrs. Sewell. She's a nice lady."

Longarm said, "Well, LeeRoy, you ain't got much to trade. I can see now, though, why you wanted me out of this town. You wanted me out of here before these ladies showed up. Well, it's a little late for that now. I've got the ladies, and you can have my share of the stale cornbread. I am about to get impatient with you and this carbine. So, just start walking backwards. The next time I see you, there is not going to be any talk of truce. Do you understand?"

The other two started backing away, but LeeRoy held his ground. He said, his voice almost in a wail, "What am I supposed to tell Daddy? What kind of a deal will you come to on this matter?"

Longarm said, "I don't know, but we ain't reached it yet. Make sure that Daddy understands that nobody else better offer me any money. That's a very unhealthy occupation."

LeeRoy Hunsacker shrugged his shoulders, turned, and started walking back up the street toward the big house. After ten yards, he turned and said, "Longarm, are them girls all right?"

Longarm chuckled. "Well, they ain't got anything to eat."

LeeRoy Hunsacker said, "You mean *you* ain't got nothing to eat."

"Well," Longarm said, "if I ain't got nothing to eat, that sure as hell means those girls have nothing to eat, now don't it, LeeRoy? Why don't you get on back to J.J. and tell him that the next time he wants to talk to me, don't send three fools but get himself up and we'll make a deal."

LeeRoy said, "Are you telling me that you will deal, Marshal?"

"Yeah, I'll deal if the proposition is right. Now, get on back and tell him that. But I want it understood right now, right clear so that you don't make a mistake. There ain't going to be another flag of truce. Anybody that comes waltzing down the middle of the street, waving a bedsheet, is going to catch one right where it will do him the worst good. You had better have your hands over your head the next time you give me a sight of you. Otherwise, I'll be shooting to finish the party. Now, get on back to your daddy and tell him to work out what he wants and what he is willing to give up. And I ain't going to be satisfied with just a little helping."

Longarm watched as the three men backed off a few steps, and then turned and walked off down the street toward the big stone house. Longarm knew his own position was weak. He had to get out while his horses were still strong enough to make the forty-mile trip back to Reno.

Thinking that made him remember where the women had come from. Ten miles, one of them had said, from the northwest. He didn't know of any town there, but she'd said it was just a digging. Some miners probably prospecting on a cold strike, maybe potlucking it, digging holes in the hillside and hoping to strike a ledge or a vein or a glory hole. Certainly there was no water, so it wasn't a placer mine. It was Marianne who had told him that they had picked the place because there was no competition. Well, he supposed that was as good a reason as any. He certainly had no competition from any law officers in this wonderful town of Lodestar.

Longarm got up, turned, and walked back to the livery office. As he did, he looked at Minnie Sewell. She didn't look particularly happy with her hands handcuffed around the post and a handkerchief in her mouth. She gave him as vicious a look as he reckoned he had ever received in his life.

He said, "Mrs. Sewell, I hope you are comfortable. Lord knows I have done everything to make you so."

She kicked out at him with her foot, stirring dust up from the floor of the stable.

He went in the office. The two young women were still sitting exactly as they had been when he'd left. He could tell they hadn't come very far by the freshness of their clothes. Both of them were wearing gaily colored dresses with low-cut bodices that revealed a great deal of cream-colored skin. It caused a stirring inside him, and brought that swelling he knew so well but had no intention of doing anything about. The women were prisoners of his. For all intents and purposes, they were accomplices of the Hunsackers, and they were hostages to be bartered.

He nodded at the two young women as he came through the door, and then went directly and sat in the chair behind the desk. They stared at him openly, but neither spoke.

He stared back just as openly. "One thing has got me confused, ladies."

Verlene said, "And what would that be, Marshal?"

"I am a deputy, as you well know, so quit calling me Marshal. You're doing it on purpose."

"Yeah, Marshal," she said.

Longarm shook his head and gave her a look. "What's got me confused is that you said that you had gone to the mining camp to avoid the competition. As easy on the eye as you two are, I don't see how you would have given much of a damn abut the competition in Reno or wherever it was that you were running from."

Verlene said evenly, with nothing in her voice, "It wasn't the quality of the competition so much, Marshal, as it was the quantity. In a crowd, it's hard to pick out the prettiest face, just like it's difficult to pick out one cow in a herd. We went where the living was much easier."

Longarm nodded. "Yeah, I can understand that. Makes sense to me."

Just then, Marianne spoke up. "Dammit, Marshal or Deputy, whatever you are. I'm hungry. When are we going to have something to eat?"

Longarm looked around at her, enjoying the bright sun-shiny look of her face, and the body enclosed in the tight-waisted frock she was wearing. He could see how her breasts were straining against the thin material of the dress. He said, "Well, Miss Parsons, or Marianne, if I may—the sad news is that I don't have much here to eat, and on top of that, the horse feed is going bad. This town hasn't served a good meal in some time."

Verlene gave him a fierce look. "If you're the law, you have no right to hold us here, causing us to undergo hardships, when comfort is just down the street. We haven't broken any laws."

Longarm reached around and scratched the back of his

neck. "Well, ladies," he said. "I'm not all that sure about that. You are consorting with known outlaws. And for all I know, you're planning on robbing a bank with them or holding up a stage or a railroad train."

Verlene made a disgusted sound. "You know better than that. Now, we have the right to be given humane treatment. We have the right to food, to comfortable living accommodations. Now, can you furnish us with those or not? If not, then we're going to march straight out that door and go down the street to where we can get them."

Longarm looked at her, frowning slightly. "Ladies, I don't want to have to put that other pair of handcuffs to work, but if you force me to, I will. I don't think you'll like very much being chained up, and I won't like doing it, so for the time being, you might as well shut up that kind of talk. But you do have a point that you have a right to food and shelter, and as a representative of the United States Government, it's my job to see that you get it. Let me put my mind to this thing for a moment. As it is, I was out of food myself. You sure you didn't bring none of that in the buggy?"

Marianne said, "Mrs. Minnie gave us to understand that the gentlemen we were coming to see would have ample provisions as well as a good assortment of beverages. She said we wouldn't want for anything."

Longarm made a sound like laughing, although he wasn't feeling humorous. "Maybe they do. It seems like a very unlikely place to be treated like you were staying at the Palmer House in Chicago. Let me set my mind to thinking on this subject and let me see what I can come up with."

Verlene said, "Well, I wish you would hurry up, Marshal. Some of us haven't had anything to eat since breakfast."

"Yes, and some of us didn't even have breakfast," Longarm said.

"Nobody is forcing you to be out here. Why don't you get on your horse and go back to wherever it is that you came from?"

"Because I am here because of what's here and that's what I came for, understand? Now, be quiet."

Longarm thought a moment more, and then suddenly smiled. He said, "Hell, yes. Why not?"

Without another word, he got up from his chair and walked out into the stable. He reached into his pocket for the key to the handcuffs as he walked. Minnie saw him over her shoulder as he came near, and she began making agitated motions with her head. He said, "Just calm down, Minnie. I'm fixing to turn you loose. I've got a little job for you."

As quickly as he could, he took the handcuffs off her wrists and tucked them in his pocket. Then, before she could use her own hands, he untied the handkerchief. The moment her mouth was free, she started in cursing, swearing, yelling, and flailing her arms all about.

He grabbed her by the shoulders. He said in a flat hard voice, "Shut up, or I'll handcuff you again. Don't make another sound. Do you understand me?"

It took a few moments, but she finally settled down enough so that he could talk to her. He said, "I've got a chore for you. It's an easy one."

She gave him a suspicious look. "What kind of chore?"

"I want you to go to the big house at the end of the street where your boyfriend lives, J.J. Hunsacker. Tell him that these girls are starving down here and that you need to get some food for all of you.''

She stared at him, startled by the request.

He said, "Do you think you could do that?"

She continued to stare at him for another long moment. Finally, she said, "Yes, I can do that. The question is: *Am I going to do that?* I'll tell you one thing, Mr. Marshal, and you had better get it straight off. I ain't leaving you alone with those two girls without a damned good reason.''

Longarm said, "How about if they tell you to go up there? I reckon they're just about hungry enough to do it.''

She narrowed her eyes at him. He thought, looking at her, that she wasn't half as plain as she'd first appeared. She did have a little wear and tear, but some of it was becoming. She said, "I ain't got nothing but the greatest case of dislike for you that there is, Mr. Marshal. If I do you any favors, it won't be for the sake of doing you any but for all of our sakes. You want me to go up there and ask Mr. Hunsacker for some grub? What makes you think I won't just stay with him up there?''

Longarm said, "I am counting on you planning on staying close to your stock in trade. I don't reckon that you'd let those girls go without your vigilant eye any more than a butcher wouldn't watch his steaks. Am I right about that?''

Minnie Sewell said grimly, "Just don't get any ideas about those girls. You haven't got the price in your pocket, Mr. Marshal, for either one of them.''

Longarm gave her a mocking laugh. He said, "Oh, do you sell them as a pair?''

Mrs. Sewell straightened her clothes, which had become disarrayed in her struggle with the handcuffs. She said, "I

61

am going to go, but it's not for any good for you that will come from it. How am I supposed to know that Mr. Hunsacker will help us out on this?"

Longarm said, "Oh, I think he will. After all, those two girls are his cattle that he'll be feeding. I think he will be more than happy to cooperate while he figures out a way to come down here and shoot me full of holes."

Minnie Sewell looked at him with a hard eye. "The sooner the better. That's what I say."

"All right, the sooner the better that you go and get that food, and get enough for four while you are at it. I haven't been grazing too high on the hog lately myself."

She turned away and started toward the office. "I'll just tell the young ladies what I'm about."

Longarm was right behind her. "We'll tell them together so we'll both get the special thanks."

She flashed him a hard look over her shoulder and said, "I told you to get that kind of thinking out of your mind."

It did not take the three women long to reach an agreement that they all needed some food, and without further argument with Longarm, Minnie Sewell was very shortly out the door and hurrying up the street as if she were escaping from prison. Longarm walked back into the office and looked at the two young women. He said, "Well, Maw has gone to the store to fetch us some vittles. I ain't real sure, however, that she'll be coming back."

Marianne said, "Minnie Sewell is not the kind to run out on her friends. If she's going to Mr. Hunsacker's to fetch something to eat, you can be sure she'll be back."

Verlene said, "Yeah, and pretty quick too."

Longarm put his feet up on the desk and yawned. "We will see. I'm betting that we've seen the last of her. I'm betting that I'm going to have to take you two to Reno with me in order to draw them vultures out of that stone nest they've got built over there.''

Verlene and Marianne turned out to be right. Within two hours, Minnie Sewell was back with a tin pail filled with different kinds of foods. Longarm thought she looked a little mussed. It appear that the wind or somebody's hand had rearranged her hair, but he didn't say anything. He was too interested in what she was carrying in the pail to inquire into her personal affairs.

She had brought cheese, canned beans, canned tomatoes, canned peaches, some smoked beef, and some smoked ham. Longarm thought that, if nothing else, the Hunsackers were certainly eating a lot better than he and his little flock of prisoners. Minnie Sewell also brought something else: word from J.J. Hunsacker. She said, cocking her head, ''J.J. said that if you don't turn me and those two girls loose right quick, he's going to find a way to separate you from your sanity.''

Longarm laughed lightly. ''Well, Minnie, why don't you trot right on back up there and tell him that he is not going to separate me from my sanity until he comes out from that stone fort. Now, I'd like nothing more than a chance to see him try, him and his boys, but they are going to have to come outside to do it. I will not play inside. My momma told me not to be roughhousing inside the house.''

She gave him a look. ''You think you're so damned smart, don't you?''

''Not so that you'd notice. If I was smart, first of all, I wouldn't be here. Second, I wouldn't be a deputy marshal, and third, I'd be in a lot nicer part of the country. So, what

63

I'm doing right now proves that I don't think I'm very smart."

They found some pots and a skillet in Longarm's saddlebags. He built a fire, and the women heated some beans and tomatoes. Mrs. Sewell had brought along three tin plates, none for Longarm. He said, "It doesn't matter—I've got my own. I thank you very much for choosing to omit me."

As they ate what was a combination of breakfast and lunch, he watched the three women, deciding when and how much he was going to tell them. During Minnie Sewell's absence, he had reached a decision. The only way to get the Hunsackers out from that stone fort was to make them believe that something they wanted was shortly going to be out of reach. He was going to have to leave and take the women with him, and depend on J.J. and the rest of the boys to get their noses right down next to the ground and come a-yelping and running like a herd of hound dogs.

He didn't know exactly how he was going to do it. He didn't know if he could handle three females, all of them pulling in different directions. You couldn't just pull a gun on a woman—she knew you weren't going to shoot her. He didn't think he could manhandle all three of them at the same time. The question of how to get all three of them going in the right direction was an important one. He knew once he got them out in the desert, he wouldn't have any trouble. Nobody was going to jump out of the buggy in the big middle of nowhere without any water or food or any protection from the sun.

He put off thinking about it until he was finished eating. When he had mopped up his plate with a piece of bread, and had chewed it slowly and thoughtfully, he said, "Minnie, I want you and Verlene and Marianne to go on back in the office and take yourselves a chair and sit right still."

Mrs. Sewell was getting up to scrape the skillet out. She looked at him and said, "What are you up to, Mr. Marshal?"

"It doesn't matter what I'm up to," Longarm said, shaking his head. "Just do what I tell all three of you. When you get finished, all of you get in the office and stay there. Don't be looking out the window. Don't be looking out the door. Just stay in there and be quiet."

Verlene said, "Well, aren't we the high-handed one? I guess you think you can push us around any which way you choose."

Longarm nodded. "Just when it comes to government business. No more than that." He waited until they had gone into the office and closed the door behind them. He didn't want them seeing him making preparations for their departure.

He walked to the end of the livery stable, away from the street entrance, and pushed and shoved on the big door there and got it open far enough so that the buggy and the mule would pass through. After that, he untied the mule from the front part of the stable and took him to the back door and tied him there. He then saddled one of his horses and put the other on a halter lead. He tied both of them to the back of the buggy. Probably he was going to have to drive the buggy himself until he got a little ways away from the deserted town. He thought the women would be willing to ride along, figuring that sooner or later he would have to release them and they could return to Lodestar. They had another think coming. Until he got J.J. Hunsacker and his boys in hand, the women were his permanent bait.

With the buggy in place, he opened the door to the office and called for Minnie Sewell to come out. She got up reluctantly from her chair, grumbling, "Now, what do you want?"

"I want you to come along with me, Minnie, and take a look at something. It has to do with this buggy of yours." He closed the door to the office behind him, and then walked by her as they headed toward the buggy.

She said, "What the hell did you move back here for?"

He took her firmly by the left arm. "You've noticed that, have you?"

She tried to stop and jerk her arm loose from his. She said, "Let me go, you rascal. What's your plan here?"

With a grim face and a closed mouth, he manhandled her onto the buggy and on up into the backseat. Before she could move, he had handcuffed her wrist to one of the wrought-iron arms of the seat. She let out a squall, but it didn't matter—he had the madam in place now.

He walked back to the office just as Verlene was coming out, summoned by Minnie Sewell's squalls. She took in the scene with a quick glance and started to turn on Longarm. She was too late. He had anticipated her move, and already had her by the upper arms and was hustling her toward the buggy. For some reason, she made no outcry. She didn't go along docilely, but neither did she put up much of a fight. He propped her in the seat beside Minnie Sewell, and quickly handcuffed her right wrist to the arm of the back-seat just as he had the older woman. He turned and went back after Marianne.

Longarm had left her for last because he had expected her to be the most docile of the three women, causing the least amount of trouble. But he was totally wrong. She fought, from the first moment he had to pull her up to her feet, until he got her tied down in the front of the buggy. In the end, he had to gag her, fearing that her bloodcurdling cries would draw attention from the stone house even as far down the street as it was. She had scratched his face and his hands, but he could still remember feeling her firm young breasts as he was trying to subdue her. He had not sought the proud flesh barely concealed by the thin material of the dress and her underclothes, but it had seemed to find its way to the softest part of his hands.

Now, he stood beside the buggy, breathing heavily, mostly from the exertion of fighting the strong young woman, but also from the images and the feel of her body that had inflamed his brain.

Then he said, "Now, dammit, Marianne. You had better behave yourself from here on in. I am not going to stand for any more of that foolishness. I've got a job to do and if it comes to it, I'll bind you up like a market-bound hog and lay you on the floorboard."

For answer, she turned her head and gave him a murderous look with her eyes. His handkerchief, which had once gagged Minnie Sewell, was now across her lips.

He said, "All right. We're going to take a little ride. I want you all to sit steady. You ain't going nowhere as tied up as you are and handcuffed as you are, but I don't want you to scare that mule and get him to kicking the buggy to pieces. At the same time, that mule could break a bone amongst you three."

He looked around to make sure he had everything. His rifle was in the boot of the saddle. His derringer was in his pocket, and his spare revolver was in the saddlebags, along with his spare clothes and socks and what little money he had with him. There wasn't really anything else left to take. He had two full canteens of water, but that wasn't as important as it might have seemed since there would be no place to water the mules or the horses, and if they gave out in the desert, it wouldn't matter how much water you had in the canteen.

He took the time to walk to the front of the livery and offer a glance down at the big stone house at the end of the street. He saw no one, neither near the house nor anywhere near the street. After that, he walked back to the livery and looked out the rear. It was still clear. The horses were behind the buggy, the buggy was loaded, and his passengers were loaded. There was nothing left but to get up there himself and take the reins and start out.

As he untied the reins of the mule, he could not help but take note of the fact that they were going out in the middle part of the afternoon, into the heat of the day. It wouldn't take long for him or the women or the animals to wilt under the unrelenting sun. But he had chosen the time because he thought it most likely that Hunsacker and his sons would not be expecting him to be take off then for open spaces, not in that country, at that time of year. Most likely, they were having a nap themselves in the coolness of the big thick building.

The mule and the horses had had their chance at the water trough. He flipped the reins over the dashboard of the buggy, and then climbed up beside Marianne, who was bound hand and foot. With a deft move, he circled the mule around a stall post and headed him toward the big daylight gap in the back of the livery.

They went out into the heat and light at a faster pace than Longarm had meant to, but then the mule seemed to have a mind of his own. Longarm was willing to let him express it so long as he didn't work himself to death. He acted like a mule that was ready to head to the barn. Longarm had little doubt that he could loosen the reins on the animal and the mule would take them straight to wherever the mining camp was that the women had come from. Not that Longarm was going to do that, because a mule was a mule and he had the sense of a mule, and no mule was smart enough to know that he couldn't last at a running trot across the hot desert for ten miles. This mule was no exception. So with firm but steady pressure, Longarm pulled the animal back down into a trot and then a walk, and then slowed him down even more than that, heading him in the northwesterly direction that the mule had naturally taken as they'd left the livery stable.

Longarm forced himself not to look back until he had judged that they had traveled for half a mile. Then he glanced back toward the town of Lodestar. It looked very still, very deserted. There was no movement, no sign of anyone rushing to get on their trail. Longarm frowned slightly. He didn't want to get away clean. He wanted them coming after them. Dragging bait in front of a mountain lion wasn't much of a trick if the mountain lion wouldn't cooperate. He wasn't interested in seeing these women home. He was interested in luring J.J. Hunsacker and his gang out into open where one man would have a chance against the six or seven of them or however many there were.

But Longarm was not too worried about having gotten away cleanly. He had a pretty good idea that he had been watched at frequent intervals ever since the women had arrived. He had not necessarily seen anyone, but he had felt their presence from a distance. He didn't expect that J.J. Hunsacker was fool enough to let his prize sit so close and not keep an eye on it. Longarm had never yet ascertained which girl went with which Hunsacker, including Mrs. Sewell. Not that it made much difference.

For now, he settled down to the serious business of driving a mule across the desert. The women seemed to be riding all right. The buggy top provided some relief from the sun, though nothing could provide relief from the unrelenting dead air and heat that surrounded them and seemed to almost suffocate them. He wasn't afraid of the Hunsackers attacking him with rifles at long range. They weren't about to do that out of fear of hitting the women. He had protection as good as a man was likely to get.

After a while, he snapped the reins on the mule's back and let him speed his walk up, but now the mule wasn't as responsive, and Longarm could tell that the heat was already going to work on at least one animal. He glanced back and saw that Verlene and Minnie Sewell were riding along stoically, looking to be none the better for the afternoon outing.

Now that they were clear, he saw no reason to keep the gag on Marianne. With his right hand, he reached over, and with his strong fingers, undid the knot and pulled it away. He expected a barrage of cussing, but all she did was pant. The heat was getting to her too. He took the reins in his teeth, and reached over and untied her hands where they lay in her lap. She gave him a half-grateful look of appreciation when the knots fell free from her flesh. She rubbed the reddened skin with each hand alternately.

They rode on across the desolate desert. The mule was quite content now to stay in a medium walk. Longarm was surprised that he had not had more protest from his backseat passengers, but he'd congratulated himself too soon. Verlene's voice came suddenly to his ears. She said, "Listen, Marshal. Where the hell do you think that you are taking us? You could get us killed out here in this desert."

Longarm said, "I'm taking you to safety, if that be its name. I'm taking you away from danger—danger posed by the Hunsacker gang, who are outlaws. If you become joined up with them, that would make you an outlaw too and I'd have to put you in jail."

From the front seat, Marianne said, "Oh, don't try that old story on us. We know very well what you are doing."

Longarm watched the mule's ears to see if they'd heard anything that his inferior pair hadn't. He said, "What am I supposed to be up to?"

Marianne said, "You're taking us off for your own self. We understand men like you, but you won't get away with it."

Minnie Sewell said in a sullen voice, "I've got some news for you, mister. You get us out in the open out here, and J.J. Hunsacker is going to fill you full of holes. You're going to look like an old dress that somebody left whipping in the wind."

Longarm looked around into the rear seat of the buggy. He said thoughtfully, "You know, Minnie, you're saying that just to get at me, but you might turn out to be right. I am taking a hell of a chance here and there ain't no maybes about it."

She stared back at him, too startled by his agreement to comment any further.

Chapter 5

It seemed that with every moment the heat increased, until
Longarm didn't see how it could get much hotter without
everything bursting into flames. They plodded along on his
northwesterly course. The only thing that disturbed the flat,
featureless landscape was a big outcropping of rock amid
what appeared to be trees. The outcropping lay just to the
right of his line of march, and was, he guessed, about three
or four miles distant. In that heat, and in that country, that
was a pretty good ways.

The women had lapsed into silence, content only to
spend their energy in a futile attempt to fan a breeze into
their face with their hands. Longarm was soaked with
sweat. The mule was holding up fairly well, but Longarm
was considering hitching one of the horses to the side of
the harness and seeing if the horse couldn't take some strain
off the mule and help him along a little.

From time to time, Longarm looked back at the deserted
town of Lodestar. He guessed they had come some four or

five miles in the hour they had been traveling. The place remained quiet. The buildings had shrunk in the distance, but they were still as solitary and as silent and as lonely. He glanced out ahead at the outcropping, wondering about it. He was used to seeing rock buttes in the desert, but these looked big. The heat waves shimmered off the desert floor and distorted shapes and distances so that a man had no real idea of what he was looking at or how far off it was.

The desert had taken an upturn, and the mule had slowed as he dragged the buggy up the slight incline of sand, cactus, and rock. For the tenth time, Longarm asked the women if he was on the right course for the mining camp. None of them bothered to even open their mouth on this occasion. Before, they had favored him with some choice cuss words, which had sounded strange coming out of such angelic-looking mouths—at least two of them had angelic-looking mouths. But they seemed under no compulsion to give him the slightest hint or direction. He hadn't worried. He figured the heat and the sun and the discomfort would do his work for him, causing the women to suddenly get cooperative, if for no other reason than for their own sake.

The mule had nearly reached the top of a rise. Longarm could tell that the long pull up the elevation in the desert had taken a lot out of the mule. He was determined to rest the animal at the top. As they pulled up, he stopped the mule right on the small crest. Now that he was looking downhill, the outcropping of big rocks looked much different. Looking back, he could see that the town of Lodestar was indeed in a valley, if you could say that a desert had valleys.

The mule was standing with his head down, and Longarm could see his ribs heaving in and out as he breathed.

It was clear that they were going to lose the mule if Longarm didn't give the creature some help. He got out of the buggy, taking both canteens with him, and went up to the head of the harness, where the mule was standing quite still. Longarm took off his hat, poured one of the canteens into the crown, and then offered it to the mule. The animal accepted the water and drank greedily, spilling as much as he was drinking. Longarm finished pouring the canteen into his hat, and let the mule keep on drinking. There had been a full five gallons when they had started, but he reckoned now there were only three gallons, and the mule could handle that much and more. Longarm opened the second canteen and gave the mule more water. It was playing hell with his hat, but he needed another one anyway. Besides, it was very doubtful that he needed to cut much of a figure of fashion where they were headed.

When he was through with the mule, he put his hat back on. It felt wonderfully cool under the blazing sun. He walked back to the buggy with one empty canteen and the other only half full. It was a serious matter to have as little water as they did and to be where they were now. He was going to remark on it to the women when he happened to glance toward the south, toward the deserted town. To his surprise, he saw several little black specks swirling around what he took to be the livery stable. He also saw several in front of the stone house at the end of the street. It was apparent that the Hunsackers had come alive and realized that they, he and the women, had left. Longarm supposed the Hunsackers could see him and the women just as well.

He looked around, not quite certain what to do next. Apparently, he was going to get his wish. He thought they would be having company is less time than it had taken them to travel this far. He expected that the Hunsackers were riding desert-hardened horses and that they would be bringing plenty of water. He needed to get to cover. He glanced over his left shoulder. The rocky outcropping had not moved. It appeared to be no more than a couple of miles away. It was best, he thought, to get started. That is, unless the women wanted to tell him where the diggings were and if they were even close.

He climbed into the buggy and took up the reins. The mule seemed more alert and lively now that he had had some water, and stepped off as they started downhill. Longarm resisted the urge to lift him into a trot. Whatever energy the mule had, he was going to need when they were on the flat.

From the backseat, Minnie Sewell said, "I see that they are coming."

Longarm turned his head and looked back at her. "That's right, Minnie. At least they're outside. I don't know if they have figured out where we are or not, but you can bet if they can find a bed in the dark, they can pick up our trail leaving that town. Now, I know it's your hope that they are going to shoot me to pieces, but I want to remind you all of something. I don't plan to let them get close enough to just concentrate on me. So go to thinking about bullets whizzing around your ear and trimming your hair for you. See what you think of that."

Marianne said, "They wouldn't shoot at us."

Longarm said, "I didn't say they would, but I'm going to stick mighty close to you three, and if they are going to shoot at me, they're going to be shooting mighty close to you."

From the backseat, Verlene's voice snapped out, "That's

a coward. There's nothing of a gentleman about that.''

Longarm laughed wearily. "Verlene, I wish the bunch of you would get it straight in your mind that I'm a United States deputy marshal. I ain't a gentleman and I'm not brave, at least not any braver than I have to be. I don't see any point in being brave when it's six or seven against one. Now, do any of you want to tell me where that miners camp is? Are we anywhere close to it?''

Minnie Sewell said, "You'll not get anything from us, Mr. Smart Aleck.''

Longarm nodded. "All right. Have it the way you will.''

He put the reins under his knee and held them back with pressure against the seat while he picked up his lever-action carbine off the floor. He worked the lever and put a shell into the chamber. Then he reached into his pocket, took another .44-caliber cartridge, and shoved it into the magazine of the rifle so that it now held seven shells. He glanced over at Marianne. "You be sure and point out the one that is intended to be your fiancé and I'll shoot him clean.''

She gave him a sour look and said, "You're not making yourself real welcome with us.''

Longarm spat over the side. "Lady, I ain't trying try make myself at home with you. You'd better make yourselves at home with *me* because you are going to be with me a hell of a lot longer than you think.''

Minnie Sewell said, "I think they're going to be wrapping you up in your best shirt, if you take my meaning.''

Longarm chuckled. "Oh, I take your meaning, Minnie. I just think I'm going to thin that bunch out a good deal before that happens.''

He looked back over his shoulder, but the rise that he'd topped blocked his view. He could not know if the Hunsackers were pursuing him or not, but for the next half hour, he began to get edgy. The mule was showing signs of fatigue, and Longarm was wondering if the fortress of the rocks was actually coming any nearer. He had visions of being trapped out in the desert flat with nothing more for protection than a buggy and three women. It was not an inviting prospect. He had no doubt about his ability to hold the Hunsackers at bay with a little cover, but he wasn't swimming in ammunition. There were forty or fifty cartridges in his saddlebags—a half a box—and in a running gunfight, that many caps could be busted in no time at all.

After another hour, Longarm could tell that the mule was definitely flagging, slowing down more and more. Longarm was going to have to do something and do it fast. He pulled the mule to a stop and jumped down from the buggy, taking his rifle as he did. He went to the back, untied the horse that was already saddled, and stepped aboard, shoving the rifle into the boot. Then he reined his horse around the buggy and up to the head, where the mule was panting a little harder than it should have been.

Longarm ordinarily didn't carry a rope with him, but he had one on this occasion. He threw a noose in it and used it to take a grip a on the twin shafts, intending to give the mule a little help. He dallied the rope off around the horn of his saddle, and then set out to take up some of the strain off the mule. As they started forward and the buggy jolted into motion, he was surprised to see Marianne slide over in the seat and take up the reins. Longarm noted with more surprise that she had just enough pull on the reins to give the mule something to lean against as they worked their way across the desert floor.

As he was mounted on horseback, Longarm had a much

clearer view behind him. Not only that, but as they had
drifted to the right, the rise had flattened and he could see
parts of the deserted mining town of Lodestar and the black
dots that had been scurrying around it. Now, the dots had
formed into one pack and were moving in a definite direction, toward him. It was a guess, but he judged that they
were some five or six miles away, perhaps further, but they
were on good horses and he knew it wouldn't take them
long to catch up. He had very little time to spare.

Urging his horse, Longarm hurried the mule along as
best he could. The rock outcropping didn't seem to be coming any nearer, but he knew it was. The desert played tricks
on your eyes. Things could look awfully far off and yet be
reasonably close by, and by the same token, something you
thought was only a mile off, you'd spend the better part of
the day killing your horse to get to.

The two women in back were leaning around as much
as their handcuffs would allow them to look out the back
of the buggy to see where the Hunsackers were. Marianne
was holding the reins and helping the mule along. Or at
least that was the way it appeared to Longarm, but he
wasn't quite convinced. If he hadn't had a rope on the shaft
of the buggy, he wouldn't have put it past the young
woman to suddenly jerk the mule around and try to beat it
back toward the Hunsackers. The mule wouldn't have made
it, of course, but there would have been no end of trouble.
He wanted that mule to survive until it got to the shadow
and help of the rocks. If he knew anything about deserts,
there was a good chance the place, which was growing
bigger and bigger with every step they took in its direction,
would be full of cool, dark caves. Their most immediate
concern was water. Two gallons of water wasn't going to

split very well between one mule, two horses, and four people.

He hurried the whole contraption along, figuring he could get into the rocks before the Hunsacker party could draw near. Longarm guessed them to be no more than two and a half miles off, and he still had a half mile to the rocks. They were coming fast, but he wondered how much horse they would have left by the time they made that last drive. He also knew that if they got within a quarter of a mile, he could slow them down considerably with his rifle. He hated to shoot horses, but he knew the quickest way to kill a man in the desert was to shoot his horse down. Horses couldn't carry double in these kind of conditions.

He glanced again at the rocks, and then back at the Hunsackers. They were still just a shapeless mob, no figures visible, but he figured the old man would be in the very forefront. It almost made him smile to himself, but he reckoned J.J. Hunsacker was curious about the whole state of affairs, and he knew that sending Minnie Sewell down for some grub for the girls and himself must have irritated Hunsacker no little bit. But the old man hadn't had a choice. He could not feed the women without feeding Longarm.

Longarm glanced toward the inside of the buggy, and was startled to see that Marianne had slipped quietly over to the side and dropped to the sand. As fast as he could, he untied the rope from his saddlehorn, dropped it, then wheeled his horse around and caught up with the girl before she had taken a half-dozen steps back toward the pursuing outlaws.

Longarm leaned down out of the saddle, grabbed her around the waist with his left arm, and lifted her up in front of him. She was light, and felt almost like a feather, except that she was squirming and kicking like a wildcat. She yelled in his face, "Let me go, you sonofabitch! Let me go! Take your big hands off of me!"

He turned his horse back toward the buggy and caught up with it. The mule was still walking patiently ahead, although his pace had slowed since Marianne had dropped the reins. Longarm rode up to his head, stopped the animal, and carried a protesting Marianne back to the buggy and shoved her inside. With her fighting him all the while, he retied her hands and her feet. He said, "Now, there. See if you can jump out of the buggy now. If you keep on yelling, I'm going to gag you. Do you want me to stick this back in your mouth?"

He pulled the bandanna out of his pocket and showed it to her. "Do you care for some more of this?"

She gave him a spiteful look. "Oh, you just go to hell, Mr. Big Man. You just think you're so tough. Well, you just wait until yet get caught and those gentlemen behind you make you holler."

Longarm smiled. "Well, to begin with, there ain't no gentlemen behind us. If you're talking about that bunch of outlaws and renegades and bushwhackers, that's the Hunsackers. You really don't want any part of them, but you don't know that yet. They'll put twenty years on your life overnight.

"But I don't plan on them to catch up with us. See, they're doing what I wanted them to do, which was come out into the open. That was the only way I was going to be able to trap them and then catch them. I know that puts a sour look on your face, but it's the truth of the matter. I did want them to come out. They're chasing me just so I can catch them."

From the backseat, Minnie Sewell said, "Oh, pshaw. That's just so much big talk. You know as well as I do if they catch you, you're just one dead sonofagun. Them Hunsackers will teach you and your grandmother to suck eggs."

Longarm stepped away from the buggy, went to his horse, led him around to the other side of the mule, and picked up the rope.

He said, "We're going to move a little swifter now, so you all just take it easy."

Minnie Sewell said, "Can't you at least unhandcuff us? Keeping us in chains like this is downright unhuman. What would happen if this mule were to run away? We could all be killed, the way you've got us manacled in irons here to the buggy seats."

Longarm smiled as he stepped aboard his horse and took a dally around his saddlehorn with the rope that was tied to the buggy. He said, "Don't worry, Minnie. If this mule were to run away, it would be a miracle about like it raining this afternoon. It's all this mule can do to keep on walking. I may have to bring that other horse on up here to help him."

Longarm quickened the pace slightly, though there was little danger of the Hunsackers coming up on them before they could be safely into the rocks. His biggest concern was what he was going to find when they finally did get in amongst the outcropping. He assumed that there would be a place where they could fort up, where they would have protection on all four sides, but that might turn out to be wishful thinking. For all he knew, what he was looking at could be just a line of rocks running east and west across the desert floor with no way to protect your back, no matter which side of the rocks you were on.

But then the rocks were so close, he could see the work of the wind and the weather. The outcropping was fairly tall, some forty to fifty feet in height for the majority of the butte-like humps. One big butte in the center went up like a giant chimney, rising perhaps a hundred feet. It was accompanied on each side by humps no less jagged and no less craggy.

As they neared, he was able to see a sight he was looking for—the outcropping was circular. He was able to tell that as he turned and led his party to the west or the left side of the group of rocks. Then an opening appeared, and he turned his horse, followed by the mule and the buggy, into the center of the rock formation.

It was almost like a little room without a roof. It was not so little, being perhaps fifty to sixty yards in one direction and twenty to thirty in the other, but it was good protection. No one could slip up on him and take him unawares without giving themselves away. As near as he could tell, there were only two openings in the wall of rock. One to the north and the smaller one to the west. He had no intention of letting the Hunsackers ever learn that there was a northerly approach. He was going to keep them bottled up to the south.

He led his party to the edge of the rock toward the lower portion of the outcropping. To his surprise and delight, he could see the mouths of several caves set in the earth between some of the big boulders. Some of them were six and seven feet high, a good place to hide the women and the horses and keep them out of the way of flying lead.

He made his way through the scattered rock lying on the

ground to the main wall of stone that had thrust up through the soil. He found a cleft in the rocks, and he was able to see the Hunsacker party in pursuit. He watched them as they came on over the rising and falling desert floor.

They weren't coming particularly fast. He reckoned they were finding out in a hurry that it was best, in such country, not to just jump on the nearest horse and set out in hot pursuit. He reckoned they were already wishing they had taken some time to better organize themselves, and maybe take along an extra horse or two, before they went running around in the Nevada desert. But Longarm figured that the minute they had realized that he had absconded with the ladies, the alarm had gone off and they had jumped up and got high behind.

He reckoned they were still at least a mile and a half away. At the rate they were going, he figured he had an hour, and that was plenty of time. He stepped down from the rock he was standing on and walked down the wall of stone. He came to the first cave mouth and stepped inside. He was disappointed to see that it was only a few feet deep and would serve for nothing unless a body just wanted to get out of the sun.

But the next mouth, which was at least six feet high, led back and downward. He walked ten feet into the cave, and after hearing the squeaking of a few bats that he had disturbed, he figured it would be perfect. It might be a block long. It might be no more than twenty feet long. He couldn't see, as dark as it was, but it would serve. He walked back out into the sunshine and started toward the buggy. He could see the women sitting stiffly where they were.

He came up to the buggy without a face being turned

toward him. It almost made him want to smile. But these were three ladies who were not going to affect him with either their charms or their lack thereof. He leaned his rifle against one wheel of the buggy, then untied Marianne, and then released the other two from their handcuffs, stuffing the manacles into his back pocket, putting the key in his right pocket.

As the women stepped down stiffly from the buggy, he said, "Take a good look at your new home and get used to it. Now, if you want to run out there into that desert and try to meet the boyfriends and the old man, you are welcome to do it. There's going to be lead flying here in about a half hour, and I would say that the chances are that you are going to be hit. And if you don't get hit, you're probably going to die of thirst out here, because you're not going to get to your fiancés. I'm going to be keeping them busy with my own rifle fire. Now, I've got a place for you to stay and I want you to get out ahead of me. I'll show you where it is."

He tried to herd them toward the cave he had in mind, but a smaller one off to his left had taken his eye, and he thought it would be worthwhile to investigate. He pointed out to Minnie Sewell where they could get shelter from the sun, and then set out on his own toward the smaller-mouthed cave. He was carrying his carbine in his right hand.

He said, as he parted from the women, "If you try to run, I may take it into my head to shoot one of you in the ankle. And I damned sure wouldn't go near that mule or those horses. In the first place, that mule is probably going to die if you take him more than a quarter of a mile, and those horses belong to me and that would make you a horse thief.''

He watched as they made their way over the rock-strewn desert floor heading toward the shade of the second cave. He turned and made his way to the third cave he had seen. It was mostly hidden by a big rock that had fallen from above. It turned out to have a fairly big mouth. The angle he had seen it from, with the rock in the way, had caused it to look much smaller. He walked up to the rock and, leaning his head down slightly, entered the cave.

The first sound and the first smell he got made his ears and mouth prick up. With a few steps, the sunlight still lighting that part of the cave, he saw a small but steady stream bubbling out of the ground and then running downhill away from the mouth. It was an underground spring, and it couldn't have been better located. By the sign of campfires and tallow from candles, he could tell the place had been used before—either by Indians or outlaws, he didn't know which—but he did know that he now had water for the horses. He did know too that he had better hurry. He wanted to get them watered and put up before the Hunsackers arrived.

He hurried out of the cave and across the open ground to where the mule and the buggy and his horses were. As quickly as he could, he unharnessed the mule, and then untied his horse from the back. Then, leading all three animals, he took them around the rocks and into the cave. They had all smelled the water, and they were all anxious and in a hurry to get to the source.

Longarm had to keep a tight hold on them, but he was able to take all the animals into the cave at once and let them drink from the underground spring. He himself wanted a drink badly, but he knew he could wait until the horses and the mule were through. He let them drink for ten or fifteen minutes, just long enough to satisfy them for the time being, but not enough to cause them to founder or to bloat. When they had had enough, he pulled and tugged them reluctantly away from the spring, and then led them along a ledge to the cave where the women had gone. When he led the horses in, the women set up a squawk. Minnie Sewell said, "We don't want them damned animals in here! Get them out of there! We've already got bats!"

Longarm said, "These horses need shade as bad as you do, so just shut up, Minnie. Keep these horses up on this end. I don't know what's back there. It could be a drop-off, it could be a black hole back there that you could fall into and never stop falling until you hit China. So keep these horses and this mule up here toward the mouth of this cave. You don't know, you might need them in case the Hunsackers put a bullet in me."

Verlene said, "You're going to let us go, that's what is going to happen."

Longarm said, "Lady, was I you, I'd stay in this cave and keep my mouth shut. If you want to run to your boy-friend, now's the time. There's a chance that you might make it before you die."

Marianne said, "You think you're so smart. You just make me sick, Marshal. Did you know that?"

Longarm chuckled. "I'm liable to make you more than that before this is all over with, Marianne, but you go ahead and think what you want to."

He started out of the cave, and then turned back to say, "By the way, there's another cave about ten yards to the right that's got a running spring in it, in case you're thirsty.

One of you might want to go to the buggy and get that basket of grub that Mrs. Sewell so kindly got for us from J.J. Hunsacker. Might be that you're going to get a little hungry, staying here in this cave.''

Minnie Sewell said, ''Are you telling the truth when you say that if we want to make a run for it, now is the time? You'd let us go? You wouldn't stop us? You wouldn't shoot us?''

Longarm looked at Minnie Sewell as if he wasn't hearing right. He said, ''If you're stupid enough to run out into that desert with a long two miles between you and any kind of help, you just do that. I don't think you'd last two hours, not unless you spend a considerable amount of time taking on water like a camel. But no, I don't care if you make a break for it, as you call it. Now, I've got to get to looking as to how I'm going to defend this place against your fiancés, who are apparently going to come riding up here with bad intent on their mind. But I've got some news for them. And remember this, Minnie, just in case you do try to get at them. I don't plan to let them get much closer than a half a mile, and that's a hell of a long ways to run across the desert floor.''

She looked at him, glaring with her hands on her hips. She said, ''I just may take you up on that, Marshal.''

He shrugged and left the cave, winding his way between the scattered rocks over to the buggy. He reached into the back and retrieved the saddlebags from the floor where he had left them. There wasn't much in them, just his extra revolver and the last of his ammunition, a clean shirt, a clean pair of jeans, and a clean pair of socks. He didn't figure to need the clothes, but he was going to need the ammunition, and he didn't figure it was going to be enough.

Standing by the buggy, he gave a careful look to the rock wall, searching for the most likely place to take up a defense. Finally, he settled on a spot where the rocks were all jumbled and it would be difficult for the Hunsackers to see where the fire was coming from, but where it still appeared to give a 180-degree view toward the south. Holding his rifle, with his saddlebags over his shoulder, he picked his way over to the spot. It was necessary to clamber up on several smaller rocks so that he was standing about five feet in the air.

He found that with the protruberance of the bigger rocks, there was a notch in the wall that gave him an excellent field of fire while affording him the most protection from incoming shots. Not that he was worried too much about their ability to fire back. They were going to be on the bald, bald desert, and they would have to stay out of range, and if they were out of range of his rifle, he was also out of range of theirs.

He climbed up into position, and then worked his shoulders until he was set in the notch of the rock wall. One glance told Longarm that the Hunsackers were not far off. By now, they were close enough that they had evolved into individual riders and he could take a count. He had expected six or seven, and he was amazed to find that nine men were coming toward him. Either they had gotten reinforcements, or there had been men in the house awaiting them.

He narrowed his eyes, squinting them to better see into the glazing sun and through the rising heat waves. He could easily pick out the old man, who was riding back in the back. His billowing, thick graying hair was easy to spot.

Up front, Longarm could see LeeRoy leading the pack.

To his right was the second oldest son, Shank. Longarm had never had any dealings with the young man, who he understood to be in his early to mid-twenties, but he had been told that Shank was the meanest of the lot. He had murdered and he had done robbed. Of course, that was no different from any of the rest of the Hunsackers, but it was said that Shank was known to relish his crimes.

Longarm didn't recognize any of the other men, though one of them appeared to be a man named Jim Stock who was a cousin to the Hunsackers. Longarm had come across him once before in a running gunfight as he and several sheriff's deputies had chased the gang into northern Arizona. If it was Jim Stock, it was a new problem, because Stock was said to be an excellent marksman, and it was said that he carried a rifle of greater firing distance than the average Winchester carbine, which was only accurate up to about a quarter of a mile. It was said that Stock carried a Sharps buffalo gun. If he did and it was sighted in, that made him dangerous from three times as far as the Winchester carbine.

Longarm watched the men coming on toward him, and thoughtfully put his thumb on the hammer of his rifle and drew it back, taking satisfaction from the *clitch-clatch* sound it made. The Hunsacker party was still a little too far away for a shot, but they were getting to the place where it would be time to thin their bunch out as much as he could and as fast as he could.

Then something flickered in the corner of his eye—some movement, some animation. He turned his head swiftly just in time to see Minnie Sewell vanish through the western entrance of the rock fort. He started to yell, but held his tongue for fear of giving away his position. He could not imagine what the woman was doing rushing out into the desert. He supposed that the woman thought she could make it to the Hunsacker party and that they would give her protection, but he had news for her. She was going to discover just how hard it was in the desert sand with the sun beating down on you so hard that it was driving you several inches deeper into the loose sand.

He waited, looking out the front of the little palisade of boulders with his eyes cut around to the right, waiting for Minnie to come hurrying around from where she had exited and appear heading toward the Hunsackers. It took a few moments, but he wasn't disappointed. Out into the sunlight, she staggered from the south side of the rocks. She was already struggling in the sand and sun, and she had only come some fifty yards. He would have yelled at her to get back to the safety of the rock outcrops, but he knew she wouldn't listen.

He watched as Minnie kept struggling across the sand, now and again falling to her hands and knees, and then rising quickly and going on. He noted that she had taken the canteen out of the buggy. He wondered if she had taken the time to fill it in the spring that was in the cave. He didn't really care, because she had clearly declared which side she was on. She was as much an opponent of the law as the Hunsackers.

Longarm brought his attention back to the advancing party. They were, he guessed, not too far out of range, and closing rapidly, or as rapidly as a horse could slowly walk. Now he could see how done in the mounts were. They were clearly dead tired, and most of them were covered with the white salty remains of dried sweat. He reckoned they didn't have much life left in them.

He sighted down the barrel of his rifle at Jim Stock, if indeed it was the man. But if it was, he posed the biggest threat, and Longarm had every intention of disposing of him as soon as possible. He was at the point of risking a long shot when a noise to his left made him raise his cheek from the rifle and glance quickly around.

There stood Marianne, looking, in spite of the dirt and dust and sweat and fatigue, as pretty as most girls could aspire to, even though she had a grim expression on her face. She said, "You had no right to let her go. You know how dangerous it is out there in that desert."

Longarm opened his mouth and stared at her. He said, "Are you crazy, girl? What in the hell are you talking about? I didn't let her go."

Marianne's eyes bored into him. Her bosom rose and fell, distracting his mind as he could see the nipples hard through the thin material of her dress. She said, "You could have stopped her. You would have stopped her if she had been one of us."

Longarm said, "If you'll recollect, I told you at the buggy that you were free to do what you wanted to do but that I wouldn't recommend you go racing off across the desert. You do remember me saying that?"

She shook her head angrily, making her hair swirl about her face. "Yes, but we're just women. You know what the desert is like, we don't. And now, Minnie has gone out there and anything could happen to her. You should have stopped her."

Longarm turned his face back to his rifle where he had it propped up between two small rocks. He said, "Well, I didn't. In the first place, I didn't see her until she was already outside. If you want to take a look at her, you can find a low place in these rocks and you will see that she is floundering along doing the best she can. It may not be good enough, but at least she is trying. If you look, I'd be damned careful because there's a man out there that's got the kind of a rifle that can reach from them to us, and he is going to shoot at any movement.''

She said, ''Oh, the hell with you.'' But there was not much conviction in her voice. She suddenly turned on her heels and walked back, heading toward the cave,where he supposed Verlene was with the horses and the mule. He watched her walk, admiring the sway of her hips and the dainty motion of her feet. He wondered what she would be like in bed, but he doubted that he was ever going to find out. As a general rule, working girls like her weren't much good when it was just for fun.

When he looked back, the Hunsackers were clearly within range. He moved his rifle sights around ever so gently so that he was focused on the broad chest of Jim Stock. Now he could see the man clearly. He was wearing the brocade vest that he was known to wear. His rifle was still in the boot, but Longarm had no doubt that this was a man who would cause him trouble. He leaned down over his sights, calculating the wind, calculating the distance, calculating the drop of the bullet. Then, very gently, he pulled the trigger, and the sharp crack of the shot rang harshly off the rocks.

Chapter 6

For an instant, it was if nothing had happened. Then Longarm saw Jim Stock duck his head as the bullet whistled
past him, and then he saw the party of men split in two,
the left going to the left of the shot and the right riding off
in *that* direction. Furious at missing, even though he knew
he had fired at too great a distance, Longarm quickly levered another shell into the chamber and sighted in on a man
riding behind and to the left of Stock.

This time, he held his sight on the man a little longer,
not allowing the shimmering heat waves to cause him to
aim too high. It was not a particularly hard shot because
the men were only walking their horses slowly. He
squeezed the trigger gently, felt the thump of the stock
against his shoulder, and then almost through the echo of
the explosion bounding off the encircling rocks, the man
that he had hit went backwards and sideways out of his
saddle. His horse stopped immediately as if someone had

jerked back on the reins. The man lay on the sand of the desert floor, not moving.

The man nearest him dismounted and came over and knelt down next to the body. It was clear that the prone rider wasn't going further. The rider that had dismounted caught up the dead man's horse, and then remounted, and they all started onward again, only now they were scattering to the left and the right, making Longarm's shots harder.

He wanted a shot at Shank. He figured that maybe Shank was the most dangerous of the bunch outside of Stock, but he could never quite get the man fully in his sights with the lines of sight offered him by his firing position. Instead, he settled on one of the other Hunsacker boys, one that looked like Joe. He fired, and saw the man clutch his thigh, and then suddenly jump down from his horse as it started to fall. The bullet had apparently just creased the man's flesh and then gone on into the horse. The horse was almost to the ground by the time the man was able to land on his feet and limp on around behind the animal before throwing himself to the sand, taking cover behind the dying animal.

Longarm cursed. He hated shooting horses. He levered in another shell and tried another shot at Joe, if that was who he had wounded. The bullet kicked up sand harmlessly a foot to the left.

But now J.J. Hunsacker was directing his men to fall back. He knew as well as Longarm did the range of Longarm's rifle, and he was directing his people to move a hundred yards to the rear. That was all right with Longarm. They could sit out there in the desert and fry for all he cared.

Suddenly, he became aware of Minnie Sewell, still struggling toward the party. She had made only some two hundred yards away from the rock face, and he wondered if she would make another two hundred, for by now she was staggering and floundering badly. He wondered if the old man would make a try to retrieve her. If he did, Longarm determined he would let him get away with it. Any man who was fool enough to ride into the covering fire just to save an old battle-ax deserved anything she could give him.

No horseman rode to Minnie's rescue. The old man didn't even seem to notice her as he wheeled his own horse around while shouting and gesturing for his men to get out of Longarm's rifle range. Longarm snapped off a shot at one trailing member of the gang, and was satisfied to see him pitch out of the saddle. It had been a long shot with long odds against him, but he had gotten lucky, at least this time. However, the shot had not done for the man. He had landed on his stomach, and almost immediately got to his feet, reached over for his horse's reins, and hurriedly limped toward the rear where Mr. Hunsacker was headed.

They had fired a few shots back, but they had done so out of frustration, knowing they were firing into a rock wall. The slugs had glanced and whined harmlessly away. Longarm doubted that any of the riflemen knew where he was holed up in his firing position.

His interest was once more drawn to Minnie Sewell. She had somehow gathered her strength, and was now marching resolutely across the hot sand. She had managed, however, to lose her canteen somewhere along the line. Longarm reckoned it had gotten too heavy for her. She was now out of range of his own rifle shot, so Hunsacker could easily send someone to fetch her into their midst.

They had all rounded up and dismounted some six hundred yards away from his position. They were standing around staring his way. He wondered just how they were going to like it when they realized that they didn't have any water. They didn't look like they had brought along any provisions either. He also wondered if they knew that he had water.

With a sudden stab of irritation, he realized he had let Minnie Sewell get away. She knew that he had a spring of water just inside his fort. That was a bad break. Now, they would attack him in a different fashion, knowing that he could hold out much longer than they would have previously expected. He had rather hoped for a long drawn-out battle of attrition during which he could take them down one by one, until there was some semblance of evenness between them and himself. Then he would have gone on the offensive and run them in the ground. Now he thought they would become bolder in their attack.

Of course, that depended on how bad the two oldest boys wanted Verlene and Marianne. They would be the ones pressing on the attack.

Longarm noticed that J.J. had spotted Minnie Sewell. He gestured to one of his men. It appeared to Longarm to be Joe, the next-oldest boy. Joe jumped on his horse, took the reins of another, and then carefully walked both animals across the desert until he came up to Minnie. He dismounted and helped her up into the saddle, her skirts billowing up around her waist, then remounted himself before they made their way to where J.J. Hunsacker and the others were waiting.

Longarm became aware of Marianne and Verlene standing beside him. They were peering out between the same gap where his rifle rested. They could see the scene as clearly as he could. He said, ''Well, looks like she made it.'' He shrugged. "You could have gone with her.''

Marianne said, "You'd no more let us go than you would jump from here to Reno.''

Longarm got an amused look on his face. He said, "Well, Marianne. Whatever makes you think that?''

The blond-haired girl said, "Because you think of us as bait. You don't fool me, Deputy Marshal Long. You're trolling them along with Verlene and me, ain't you?''

"Yeah, that could be,'' Longarm said.

"So, you'd no more let us get away then you'd fly. You'd have shot us if we'd try to make it, wouldn't you?''

Longarm shrugged. "I ain't shot many women this year. I don't know how I'd have felt about it.''

"You didn't shoot Minnie because you didn't think she was worth it.''

"You have a point there, Marianne. I have to admit it. Now, I hope that you're wearing some perfume and the wind is blowing in the right direction, because I'd like to see it fetch Joe and LeeRoy in here on the run.''

Marianne stamped her foot. She said, "You are a horrible man.''

Longarm nodded his head and spat on the floor of the rocks beneath his feet. He said, "Yeah, that may be so, but I'm the only one wearing a badge.''

Marianne shook her head, making her golden hair fly. She said, "You may not be as smart as you think you are. You think you are trying to trap Mr. Hunsacker and his boys, but it looks to me like you're the one who's trapped.''

Longarm gave her a small smile. "Well, we'll see. Now, you two had better get back in that cave and get out of this sun. It'll fry your brains.''

"Well, then, I reckon that's something you don't have to worry about."

When they were gone, he got out his watch. It was just after five o'clock, but the sun was still high in the sky. He reckoned there would be no sunset for another three hours, and the heat would burn just as intensely during that time as it was at the moment.

He settled down to keep an eye on the Hunsackers. It didn't seem like they were very much concerned. All they did was squat around in a semicircle with the reins of their horses in their hands and stare his way. The horses looked none too good for the experience, but at least they were able to stand still in each other's shade. The body of the man Longarm had shot lay on the light-colored desert floor. Longarm reckoned he'd swell pretty quick. Longarm looked up in the sky. Already he could see a few buzzards circling well up in the air.

Six o'clock came and went, and then seven. Longarm was beginning to think about having the two women do something about supper when his eye was suddenly caught by a strange sight. It began as a sort of oblong black object outlined against the desert still some two or three miles away. But as he watched, it grew larger and larger and larger. He could tell that it was a wagon being pulled by four mules. It made him give a slight snort of surprise. From what he could tell, Old Man Hunsacker had not jumped off in hot pursuit with no thought of the future as Longarm had originally hoped.

The wagon came on and on, and he saw two of the horsemen mount up and go to meet it. As it neared, Longarm could see that the wagon carried two big barrels, and he was willing to bet his last dollar that they were full of water for horses and the men. In case they didn't have enough, the wagon would make another trip and bring some more. He would also bet that they had plenty of grub and plenty of cartridges. Well, Hunsacker had said, "Let's go in a hurry," but he had also given the order to bring the supplies on out there. No wonder he had fallen back to a better position. Now, he really was in a position to outwait Longarm.

When the wagon arrived, all hands turned out to unload the supplies that it carried. Longarm had been right about the water. It was mostly for the animals. They had brought a big tub, and since the barrels of water were too heavy for the men to handle, they simply set a tub on the prairie next to the wagon, knocked out the bung hole, and let the water spout into the big tub. They brought the horses over two at a time and let them drink. Longarm watched enviously as they unloaded boxes of provisions and enough canvas for a tent to keep off the burning rays of the sun. Hunsacker knew the desert well.

Since Longarm could see that they were occupied with the business of fixing up a camp, he made his way to the buggy and brought out the grub that had been stored there. He went to the cave where the horses were, and told the girls to fix him some supper. They looked at him grudgingly, but Marianne said with a shrug, "Well, all right. We've all got to eat. I guess it doesn't make no never mind, does it?"

"I just hope," Longarm said, "that neither one of you girls are carrying any poison."

Marianne gave him a look. She said, "Honey, we're in the love business, not the killing business that you're in."

Longarm said, "Well, for the first time, we've got the

truth. You're not going to claim to be the fiancées anymore?''

She gave him a bland look. She said, "Can't fiancées be in the love business, Marshal Long?''

He shrugged. "Just fix supper. It'll be dark in about an hour and a half, and then things might get kind of hot around here.''

Longarm was amused when he got back to his rifle position to see that the Hunsackers had finished their camp. Two tents were pitched. One was nothing but a flat tarpaulin stretched out between poles and anchored with ropes. It did little more than provide shade. It was big enough that the horses could be driven up under it, and now the animals were standing in the relative coolness, eating hay and feed.

The other tent was a big, closed-sided affair, but Longarm could see it was the center of the operation. A campfire had been built. Where they had gotten the wood, Longarm had no idea, but he suspected from the wagon. So far as the wagon went, it and the mules that had drawn it had disappeared. But as he watched, he saw it coming out of a depression in the ground and reappear far off in the distance.

If he had any guess in the matter, he figured the wagon would be going back to replenish the water in the barrels and get more grub and firewood, and then turn around and come back. He swore softly to himself. He didn't much care for this situation as much as he thought he was going to. He rubbed his jaw, feeling the day's growth of whiskers. Things were not going as he had preferred, but then, he didn't know when they ever did.

He had decided that if there was going to be an attack, they would wait until the moon had set somewhere around four o'clock in the morning. It was going to be a long night, and he was the only one on duty. Longarm reckoned he'd just have to forget about sleep. He took one last look at the Hunsacker camp, and then went down the row of rocks and ducked into the cave where the girls were frying ham in a skillet and warming up some of the biscuits they had brought with them.

When it was ready, they put the meal together, but very little was said. Longarm took the occasion to warn the two young women again not to walk across the desert at night, because it could be very dangerous as the Hunsackers were probably going to shoot at any movement. He said, "Yes, you are my bait. I make no bones about it. You're what I've lured the Hunsackers with this far, and if I ain't got you, I ain't got much. But it's a long way to their camp, and a whole bunch of things could happen. Keep that in mind."

The girls hadn't bothered to answer him. He went to where he had dumped his saddle and bedroll, and took out two blankets and the slicker he carried for outdoor use. He carried them back to the two women to pitch on the floor of the cave. "That's the best I can do for you. I don't know what you've got to sleep in, but your luggage is in the buggy. I reckon you can fetch it yourself. I'm going to be kind of busy. I wouldn't be running around the rocks too frisky either, because I am going to be a little nervous and my finger on that trigger could be a little quick."

He left them and went back to his post, not at all satisfied with the way things were going. In the first place, he was good and tired out and he hadn't had much sleep for the last two or three nights. That was going to make staying awake that much harder. He couldn't decide in his mind if he expected an attack that night or not. Likely, they would try to wear him out by just sitting and eating, but when they came, they'd probably come from all sides.

It started out as a long night, and it only got longer. Sometime around ten, the moon came up and he could see the shadows of the rocks that protected him. The moonlight made strange shapes out of the Hunsacker camp. The one advantage was that it was difficult for them to move about without being clearly seen against the white of the desert floor. Fortunately, he had a handy rock that he could sit on while he gazed out through the cleft of the rock wall. His guess was that his greatest vulnerability was behind him and to his left, where the rocks were low and broken. And, of course, the biggest opening was behind him to the north.

He couldn't smoke, but he had brought the bottle of whiskey he had left, and every now and then he took a small nip. If nothing else, it helped him to keep awake. But still, the hours dragged. He looked at his watch at eleven, then at twelve, and then again at twelve-thirty. After that, he resolved that he would just tell time by the stars.

He was tired, more so than he had been in a long time. He was tired physically from running around all over the desert. But he was tired mentally of the game of being a lawman, of hunting desperados like the Hunsackers. It was a twenty-four-hour-a-day job with very few breaks in between. He was sick of this dry country, sick of this lonely country, sick of this desolate country, and especially sick of people like the Hunsackers.

He certainly wished that he was back in Denver with his lady friend who owned the dressmaking shop, back at his favorite saloon at his favorite poker table with some of his good Maryland whiskey in front of him. But unfortunately, there was this little mess to clean up before he could go back and enjoy the comfort of doing a little living for a change instead of merely existing and getting by.

The night ran on. He shifted down from the gun port between the two rocks to a seat almost on the hard floor. He was growing very sleepy, and by the depth of the darkness, he judged it to be at least two o'clock, and maybe even a little later. It didn't really make any difference what time it was. The Hunsackers were now calling the tune on the time.

He sat facing the east side of his fort, the side where the rocks were low, some no more than up to a man's chest. He expected the attack to come from there, though as dark as it was, he doubted that he could do much to defend himself if they tried it and came quietly. But the inside of the rock outcropping was a hard place to be quiet in, since it was full of all kinds of things to trip over and knock against.

In spite of himself, his eyelids were growing heavy. He hoped this would come down to a shooting match before it came down to a sleeping match. If it came down to a sleeping match, he was going to lose. His plan was to wait until daylight, until the desert turned into a frying pan, and then handcuff the girls together or tie them up and catch some sleep, not expecting the Hunsackers to come at such a time.

As he sat, nodding, struggling to hold his eyes open, he suddenly heard a tiny sound. He was instantly alert. He had slumped down against a rock, and was lying almost on his back with one of his shoulders propped up. His rifle was at his side. He let his right hand slip down to his pistol butt. Without opening his eyes, he slowly let them slit a little and looked out though his eyelashes.

Chapter 7

If anything, he smelled her before he recognized her dim form in the night. He started to speak, to ask what she was doing, but from out of the darkness of her form, a hand reached to his mouth and covered it. It was Marianne. At first, when he had caught a glimpse of the movement in the night, he'd only known by the rustle of the skirts that it was a woman. Which one, he couldn't be sure until she came close and he smelled the musky perfume of her body.

Without a word, she reached down and began to unbutton his jeans. The smell of her, the nearness of her, and now her touch brought him instantly erect. He had no idea whatsoever what she was doing or why she was doing it. All he knew was that he wasn't going to fight. He felt her take his member out of the constraints of his jeans, and then he saw her head dip, and felt a warmth go all through him as her mouth enveloped him. He gasped and thrust upward slightly. For a moment, she played with him with her tongue. He started to put his hand on her head, but as if she had anticipated that, she pushed his arm back. He lay back against the rock, panting, the passion taking him and shaking him like a terrier with a rag doll.

When he was so fiery inside that he thought he could no longer stand it, she raised her head and then rose to her knees and straddled his body. With her hands on his chest, she walked her way up until she was positioned over his throbbing penis. She reached under her skirts, and then quickly lowered herself on him. She had planned it well beforehand—she wore no underclothes.

She plunged him inside her. For the next moment, she rolled and rocked and pistoned her body up and down so that her vagina rode his length.

It was over too soon. Suddenly, the world turned bright white before his eyes. The rocks disappeared. The sky disappeared. He arched his back and stared up into the blinding whiteness, shot through with bolts of vivid color. It seemed to last forever, but all too quickly, he slumped back, gasping for breath, panting, spent.

As quickly as she had come, she was gone. Before he could realize what was happening, Marianne had risen to her feet, turned, and was running away. He could hear her gleeful laugh. Over her shoulder, she said, "Now, try and stay awake after that."

Longarm stared at her retreating form. She was right. She had done a good job on him. The first thing a man wanted after such an experience was a nap, and he had already been sleepy well before her visit. Damn her, he thought. But then, he had to smile ruefully. If the woman had thought she had done him a dirty trick, she had another think coming. He could stand those kinds of tricks all night long. With a sigh, he pulled himself back up on the rock.

He felt weak, but he knew it wouldn't be long before his strength returned, and in the meantime, he had a lovely memory to last him the rest of the night.

It was sometime later that he caught a flash of movement out of the corner of his eye. He had repositioned himself on the rock just below his firing hole, and he had seen the flicker some twenty yards to his left. It was the darkest part of the night. The moon was down, the stars were fast retreating, and the sun wouldn't be up for another hour or two. He swung his rifle to his left, holding it loosely chest-high, his eyes trying to search the dim dark recesses of the rocky layout.

He could barely make out the eastern outline of his rocky walls against the dark, black sky. He shifted his eyes back to where he had thought he had seen movement, but now he was not so sure. Vision could play tricks on you at night, especially in the desert. He took a step forward. He was almost convinced that it was either Marianne or Verlene. He said in a low voice, "Marianne?"

The words were barely out of his mouth before there was the roar of a gun and the red-hot flame of a muzzle blast. Instinctively, even as he felt something tug at his side, he dropped to one knee, bringing the hammer back on his rifle. He fired without putting the gun to his shoulder. The shot, following on the sound of the other shot, echoed loud in the thin desert air against the hard faces of the rock. It still seemed to him that he heard something like a moan or a grunt and the soft thud of a bullet striking flesh, but he couldn't be sure.

He stooped, moving as quietly as he could, trying to ignore the pain in his side, and worked his way though the rocks toward the middle of the outcropping where the buggy stood, shafts resting on the ground. He had to stay quiet and figure out the situation. Nobody moved that he could see. He took a half-dozen steps, bending low toward the buggy, and then squatted down before searching the perimeter of his fortress. As far as he could tell, he was still alone.

Finally, he reached the buggy and began a search of his fort. He hid behind one of the buggy's high wheels. Carefully, he traced the outline of the rocks with his eyes from one end to the other.

He was about to look to the west when, again, something caught his attention out of the corner of his eye. He swirled his head back just in time to see a figure standing on the rock, making ready to hop to the next rock and then down to the ground outside the outcropping. Without pause, he levered another shell into the chamber of his rifle, threw the gun to his shoulder, and fired. He saw the man jump into air, leaping to the next rock. It seemed to him that the man suddenly gained momentum, falling and pitching forward more than he jumped. Longarm could not hear the bullet strike, but he thought he had hit the man.

He had no time to speculate on such thoughts. The muzzle blast from his rifle revealed his position, and it was necessary that he move. He went quickly to a big rock about ten yards away. Then he paused and studied the ground around him. There was no motion. There was no sound. There was nothing.

It occurred to him that he would be far better off if he had to stay holed up for any span of time in the cave with the water. He had no time to consider his wound or to make any examination. If his strength began to fade, it would be better that he be hidden in the strong place when that happened.

Taking a chance, he hurriedly made his way to the southern end of the rock wall. He painstakingly searched out the cave where the spring was located. He ducked in under the low entrance and settled himself to the floor just inside the mouth. When his breathing had slowed and it was quiet, he could hear the low gurgle of the water as it came through a fissure in the rock and ran downhill behind him. He inched himself forward until his head was just outside the cave's entrance. That way, he was able to look to the left and right and survey all of the area around his little fortress.

Now, for the first time, he became conscious of his wound. It was beginning to throb. He knew the danger of being wounded so far out in the desert with no medical attention available. Even if the wound was not serious, a man could get gangrene or putrefication and die, or he could bleed to death.

Carefully, Longarm put his hand inside his shirt and felt down along his left side. He found no holes up near his ribs. The wound was just below them. It seemed to be about two inches in from his side. He worked his other hand around and felt his back. There was another hole there. It had been a through-and-through hit. The bullet had hit him in the front and gone out the back. That was lucky. It was also lucky that it hadn't hit a rib, sending broken bits of bone through his body. But his hand felt warm and sticky, and he had no doubt that he was bleeding fairly profusely.

There was no use worrying about it, not then. If he relaxed his guard, another member of the gang would no doubt be ready to take advantage. If Longarm let them start shooting into the cave, he would very shortly have slugs ricocheting all over, and one of them would be bound to hit him.

He wished he had his saddlebags, not for any change of clothes, not even for the extra cartridges that were in there, but mainly for the bottle of Maryland whiskey, standing ready to drink. If he had that whiskey, he'd take a drink and then pour a little in his wound, and then take another drink to kill the pain, and then pour a little more in his wound to kill the gangrene, and then take another drink to kill the pain with the whiskey. Between him and the hole in his side, he figured he could polish off about half of the bottle before daylight.

But that wasn't going to happen. All he could do was be very quiet, very still, and very watchful, and wait until dawn.

The pain, at least, had the effect of driving sleep away from his mind. He had no trouble staying awake and alert as the sun slowly rose beside the desert sand and tipped up into the sky. It was with considerable relief that he saw the night shadows driven from the scattered rocks by the rays of the rising sun. When it was good and up, when he was able to see it over the low rim of rocks to the east, he got carefully to his feet, feeling the sharp pain in his side. He cradled his rifle in the crook of his arm, and stepped out through the mouth of the cave into the clear sunshine. It was still cool this early in the morning.

He took the time to reach in his pocket, take out two shells, and reload them in the magazine of his rifle. He didn't expect any trouble, but then he couldn't be sure. They might still be inside the enclosure.

He stood stock-still, listening for any sound. Other than the faint stir of the wind through the cracks and crevices of the rocks, there was no sound. That was the thing about the desert—you never heard a leaf rustle, a bird sing, or the sound of a horse grunt. The desert meant heat and silence.

He set his hat firmly on his head and tugged at the brim, and then started down to the left to the cave where the young ladies were supposed to be with the horses and his saddlebags and his whiskey, and also where he calculated there should be a body that he had hit the night before. He went slowly, his hand holding his side. As he passed the cave where the girls were, he saw that Marianne was standing in the entrance. She gave him a quick look, and then her eyes settled on his bloody shirt.

She said, "You're hurt!"

He nodded. "Would you mind slipping back in there and getting me that bottle of whiskey out of my saddlebag?"

"Why should I?"

"Because it hurts me to stoop over. Is that a good enough reason, or does it make you happy I can't stoop over?"

Marianne gave him a look, and then ducked back into the dark. He could make out her dim outline and that of Verlene's, and he could smell the horses and hear them rustling around. He needed to take them to water soon.

Marianne brought the whiskey back, and he opened it and had a quick hard pull. He put the cork back in and nodded his head at Marianne, who was studying his face. He limped along by the outside wall to where he thought the shot had come from a few hours earlier. It didn't take much effort to find the body. The man was about where Longarm thought he would be. He was lying on his back with a surprised look on his face, his mouth wide open, his arms bent. The rifle he had been carrying was right beside him. Longarm didn't recognize the man. He wasn't any kin of J.J. Hunsacker that Longarm had seen before.

Longarm reached down and got the man's rifle, and then leaned over and even though it hurt, closed the man's eyes with his fingers. He straightened up, looking down in the heat. The man was going to spoil pretty quick. He could throw him over the rocks that formed the outside walls of the outcropping, but he doubted that he had the strength. Longarm wasn't going to do anything that would cause the blood to start pumping again.

He walked along, carrying the two rifles in one hand and the bottle of whiskey in the other. He went to his gun port, where he could get a good view of the Hunsacker camp. He eased himself gently down on the rock that he had been sitting on, and leaned the rifles against another rock. He looked out into the morning.

The two tents were still there, and he was not too surprised to see the wagon returning in the distance. It appeared that J.J. Hunsacker was settling in for a long siege. What J.J. didn't know, though, was the he had lost one man for sure, and maybe another one, depending on whether that other man had gotten over the wall or had been shot over. Longarm watched for a long time, trying to discern any sign of movement or purpose, but other than a few scattered figures walking around, apparently going about the business of the camp, there was no scheme or plan to be discerned.

He took the bottle of whiskey and had another pull. He slipped down from the rock and lay on his back. He pulled his shirt up in the front and craning his neck, looked down to where the wound was in his side. It was a clean hole, sure enough, and looked about the proper caliber to be at

114

least a .44 or .45. He reckoned the hole in the back was a good deal bigger than the neat little hole in the front.

Gritting his teeth, he took the bottle of whiskey and held it poised over the bloody hole. Then, looking away, he poured the whiskey with shaking hands down into the depth of his own body. He wanted to scream, to gnash his teeth, to bite on a stick. He did nothing but simply endure it. For a minute, he thought he was not going to be able to stand the pain. He poured more in, willing himself to do it. Finally, his hands started to tremble, the whiskey seemed to cauterize the wound, and the pain eased somewhat.

He sat up slowly. After the burn of the whiskey, the pain from the shot itself seemed like nothing. He took another drink out of the bottle, and then shook his head and said, "Whew!" several times out loud before putting the cork back in the bottle and climbing back up on his rock. For a moment, he just sat there quietly, watching the Hunsacker camp, not thinking about anything. He knew he had to go search for the other body, but for the moment, he was in no hurry.

Longarm stood up slowly, feeling pain in his side, and was aware of Marianne coming around the slight bulge in the rock wall, stopping to pause by the dead man, and then coming on to stand in front of him. Longarm said, "Should be lobbing some shells in here directly. I wouldn't be out walking around as free and easy, was I you. I'd get back in that cave and crouch down the best I could."

She wasn't heeding his word. Instead she stared at his bloody shirt. "Let me see that," she said.

He shook his head. His shirt was hanging outside his jeans, but he didn't think it was a sight for a woman's eyes. He said, "I reckon not."

115

Before he could stop her, she had reached over and lifted his shirt, revealing the wound. He saw her face pinch tightly. She looked first at the front and then the back. "At least it's not still lodged inside of you."

Longarm said, "No, it went clean through. It ain't as bad as it looks."

Marianne said, "It's stopped bleeding, but if you go to stirring around much, it's going to start again and you look like you've already lost a lot of blood."

Longarm said, "I reckon it'll be all right."

Without a word, she suddenly leaned over, pulled up her skirt, and ripped and tore a linen undergarment loose. He could see her white petticoat and its lace along the bottom with its smooth cloth falling into fans. Tearing a piece about six inches wide into a square, she put it around the wound at his back. She took his hand and told him, "Hold this."

He did as he was told while she wound the long bandage around him, slipping his fingers out just as she pulled it tight so that the square cloth that she had put over the wound would hold.

When she was done, she stopped back while he held his shirt. "Yes, that ought to help," she said. "Though if you get to jerking around, you'll get to bleeding again, sure as hell."

He said curiously, "Where did you get your nursing skill?"

She shrugged and gave him a look. "I guess when you've been raised in the life I was raised, you get a chance to see a lot of gunshot wounds."

"I'm sorry to hear that."

"What difference does it make?" She jerked her head

back toward the body. "Who is that back there?"

Longarm shook his head. "I don't know his name. In fact, I'm pretty sure I've never seen him before."

She motioned to Longarm's wounds. "Did he do that?"

"I would reckon so. All I saw, though, was a flash of a muzzle blast. Then it hit me. I just fired at the muzzle blast."

She glanced toward the body. It had a bullet hole dead center in the chest. "Must have been a lucky shot."

Longarm smiled slightly. "Well, it put me ahead for the time being, though you could say that we both fired at about the same time. I reckon he came off second best, at least for the time being. There's always the chance before I get out of here that we could end up tied."

Now Marianne gave him a slight smile. "I doubt, Marshal Long, that you are going to leave this desert."

Before he could answer her surprising statement, Marianne turned on her heels and walked back toward the cave, leaving him standing, staring after her. He was about to start her way, following her footsteps, when a heavy slug hit the rock near where he was standing, and then went whining off into the distance, followed almost immediately by a boom. Longarm knew what it was—Jim Stock with his Sharps heavy-caliber rifle. That was going to make moving around the compound a little chancier than it had been. Longarm ducked down and hurried toward the cave with the water. He wanted to get a good drink before he started out to find what had happened to the second man who had infiltrated their premises the night before.

Chapter 8

It didn't take long to find the body. The man had fallen down between two big rocks. Longarm located him easily enough, but had difficulty getting into a position to see the man's face. He looked familiar, and Longarm was fairly certain it was one of J.J. Hunsacker's kin, but whether he was a son or a cousin of the old man, Longarm didn't know for sure. The man looked young, in his mid-twenties maybe, and he was wearing a side arm and carrying a shotgun. Longarm was considerably surprised at the shotgun. Apparently they had expected to do some close-in work. Maybe the old man knew about the caves, and thought that was the best way to clear out one of them.

There was nothing that Longarm could do about the second dead man either. He doubted that he could manhandle both bodies over the outer outcropping of rock, even if he hadn't been hurt. As it was, there was nothing to do but leave them where they lay.

As he trudged back across the center of the circle of

rocks, there came the whizz of a heavy slug as it passed through the air, and then a boom. The bullet hit the northern wall of rocks, glanced off, and then whizzed and whined almost through the center of the camp. Longarm heard the slug strike near one of the cave's entrances. It was clear that J.J. Hunsacker had Jim Stock throwing in enough lead to keep him nervous. It was unlikely that the random shots would do much harm, but it kept the body tense, just waiting for the next one.

Longarm hurried across the floor of the little fortress, and made his way to the cave where the girls and the horses were hiding. He had left his bottle of whiskey down by his firing port when Marianne had made him the bandage. He'd also left the rifle of the first dead man. It was a slightly larger caliber than Longarm's .44 weapon. Longarm guessed it to be a .44-60, the latter number referring to the powder load. To Longarm's mind, that was a light powder load for a .44-caliber weapon, but it did give him an idea. He had taken the shotgun shells from the second dead man, but he hadn't taken the shotgun. At that moment, he had no need for the gun. For any close work that he'd ever needed done, Longarm had used his revolver.

He bypassed the cave, even though he saw Marianne's face peering out at him. He could hear the shuffle and movement of the horses and the mule. He passed the dead man again, and got back down to his firing slot. Before he did anything, he had another drag from his bottle of whiskey. It was already beginning to get hot, and the whiskey was warming up accordingly.

Longarm peered around the cleft in the rock toward the Hunsackers' camp. It had seemed to him that Jim Stock's shot had come from a little higher vantage point, and he was startled to see that Stock had taken a position on the wagon and that they had built him some kind of a perch. It didn't raise the man more than ten or twelve feet above the desert floor, but the angle was an advantage in shooting into the rock enclosure. Even as he looked, Longarm saw a white puff of smoke and heard the whizzing ricochet of the big slug that Stock was firing out of his .50-caliber rifle, followed by a boom.

Longarm stared thoughtfully, thinking about the man perched up on that high handmade stool they had built for him on the back of the wagon. He got one of the cartridges out of the magazine of the dead man's rifle, and then, with the point of the knife, he worked the slug out of the brass casing. There was a wad inside, which he carefully picked out with his knife.

After that, he set the brass casing down so that the powder wouldn't leak out, and opened a shotgun shell he had selected. He poured out the pellets, pulled out the wad, and looked down into the flecks of powder that remained. Holding the shotgun shell casing in his right hand and the rifle cartridge in the other, he slowly added some of the shell's powder into the cartridge. He added as much as he dared.

What he was about to do was a rather dangerous trick. The manufacturer decided how much powder to put in a cartridge. If you put more in, you could very well have gun blow up in your face. Longarm had seen several examples of that, and it hadn't been pretty.

When he was through adding the powder, he replaced the plug in the rifle cartridge, and then took the lead slug and rammed it home so that it was in place. Now, except for the added powder, the .44-60 cartridge was as good as new. He slid the action back on the man's rifle, and inserted the cartridge with the extra powder into the chamber. Then he rammed the mechanism closed and swung the rifle around, aiming it out the little cleft in the rocks. If he had been smart, and if he was very, very lucky, the extra powder would give the slug enough carry to reach Jim Stock, who was sitting on his perch on the wagon.

Longarm sighted carefully along the rifle's length, calculating the distance, the lack of wind, and how much the slug would drop in such a distance. He finally settled on a point about six feet over Jim Stock's head. He let out his breath, and then slowly squeezed the trigger. The rifle slammed against his shoulder, and the boom almost deafened him. For an instant, Longarm thought that the muzzle had exploded, but no such thing had happened. Even as he blinked from the severe kick of the rifle, he saw Stock suddenly throw his arms up into the air and then fall backwards. He couldn't tell if he had hit the man or not. Stock had fallen hard, but he had hit behind the wagon and Longarm couldn't see. The shot brought an instant volley of lightweight carbine fire from the Hunsacker camp. It was ineffective, some of the cartridges not even reaching the rock walls, the others glancing harmlessly away from the rock and falling into the sand.

Longarm picked up his own rifle, and then hurriedly made his way as fast as the pain in his side would let him back to the cave with the water. He got down on his hands and knees and took a long drink. It was very easy to get thirsty in such conditions, but he was more than thirsty. The plain fact of the matter was that he was worried. Longarm didn't like the way the situation was developing. It didn't matter whether he had hit Jim Stock or not. Stock's rifle would still be there, and any one of the half-dozen men left in the camp could fire it.

Longarm stood up from the springs and turned toward the entrance, wondering in his mind what steps he would take to get out of the plight he found himself in. It didn't seem that he was chasing the Hunsackers now as much as being chased. Just as he took a step toward the entrance of the cave, Marianne appeared in the lighted opening.

With the sun shining behind her, her hair looked even brighter and more golden than before. She looked at him as he came up to her, tilting her head to look up into his face. "Marshal Long, what are you going to do? I've had a look out there, and it appears to be that Mr. Hunsacker is just a little more than serious about this. The man doesn't like to be shamed and showed up in front of his woman and his kinfolks, especially his sons."

Longarm tried to act unconcerned. "Oh, I don't see where there's been any showing up on my part. It appears to me that I'm the one inside this rock jail. He's out there with all the grub and all the water and all the ammunition. Plus he's got plenty of reinforcements. I'm not expecting any myself."

Marianne said, "Maybe you think it's funny now, but you're not going to think it's so funny if you spend another night without sleep. You can't afford to sleep."

Longarm nodded his head slowly. "No, but I appreciate the way you woke me up last night."

She grimaced suddenly. "That was mean of me and I admit it," she said. "I shouldn't have done that, but Verlene and I got to talking and it seemed funny at the time. Besides that, I was very angry with you. You stopped us from a lawful pursuit, and you had no right to do that."

"Maybe I did and maybe I didn't, Miss Marianne. I can't account for what you think I have to do. What I can account for is how I do my job. That's all I've done from the very beginning. I've tried to do my job as a peace officer for the United States Government. Maybe it ain't in line with what you think I ought to be doing, but I don't answer to anybody except my boss, and he ain't here. He's back in Denver."

Marianne said, "Whether you think you're right or wrong doesn't make much difference. I'm telling you, Marshal Long . . ."

"Deputy Long, please."

"All right, if it's that important. Deputy Long. I'm telling you, Deputy, that wound looks bad. You are weakened, haven't had any sleep, and we're very low on food. Verlene and I have both taken our breakfast, and there's enough left for your breakfast and for one more meal today. I don't know what we'll do after that. You know, if that wound gets infected, you're going to be in real trouble. Now, what I think . . . well, never mind what I think."

"No, let me hear."

She looked out toward the opening at the scattered rocks at the center of the enclosure. Just then another heavy slug slammed against the rock, with the sound of another heavy boom. Apparently, Longarm thought, he hadn't silenced Jim Stock after all.

"I think you should get on your horse, take the other one with you, and ride toward Reno," said Marianne. "That miners camp is off in that direction." She pointed to the northwest. "About three miles. At least I think it is. I'm not all that certain, and I don't know what kind of a welcome you'd get. If your horses are in good shape, I think you should try for Reno. I think you need help, a doctor or something."

Longarm smiled. "That's good of you to think about me, Miss Marianne. I couldn't rightly leave you out here in the middle of this desert."

She said dryly, "Oh, I don't think we'd be alone long. But I do think it would give you time enough to get a head start where they couldn't catch you before you could get back to some sort of civilization. We would give you a good hour or so before we signaled them to come forward."

Longarm said, "Why don't you signal them anyway? That would solve all my problems. If you get them within fifty yards of this rock pile, I guarantee you all my troubles would be over. I don't know about yours."

Marianne stiffened and glared at him. "Are you insinuating that I would betray my friends?"

Longarm gave her a mocking look. "Miss Marianne, who do you think you're fooling? The Hunsackers are not friends of yours. This is all a business proposition. I know it and you know it. Why don't you admit it? Look, you're a decent enough woman—you've already showed me that side of you. Why don't you go all the way and be decent all around. I'd like to see you from the other side."

She turned on her heel and marched out of the cave. Longarm followed her, and then stopped suddenly as another slug came whining into the enclosure. It came nowhere near him, but it was unnerving. After a few moments, he walked out onto the desert floor, and then turned left and traveled a few yards to the main cave. It was time for some sort of breakfast, but before that, he wanted to get one more look at the Hunsackers to make sure they weren't up to anything.

It required a little climbing, but he took it carefully so as not to put any great strain on his side. He was able to peer out between two rocks. The sun was up good now, and in a little while, he wouldn't be able to put his bare hands on the big rocks. He would blister his palms. He could already feel the heat pounding on his back like a waterfall, but it didn't seem to be bothering J.J. Hunsacker and his brood.

They all seemed to be back, in under the big tent they had thrown up, leaving the sides off to let what breeze there was come through. The only person out in the sun was someone who had taken Jim Stock's perch high up on the little platform they had built.

As Longarm watched, he saw the man aim for a long time and then fire. He saw the flash of smoke, and then heard the whine of the bullet before the sound reached his ear. He guessed that it was a game they were going to continue to play, just to keep the women unsettled maybe.

He reckoned that Minnie Sewell would have filled J.J. Hunsacker in with all the peculiarities about Longarm's situation with the two young women. Old J.J. wouldn't be too worried about Longarm fooling around with the ladies. But that wouldn't keep him from urgently being pestered by his sons into fetching them into their beds.

Longarm studied the layout for a few moments, watching to make sure that no daylight raids were being planned. For now, it seemed that the Hunsackers were content to rest their horses under the shade of the tent, and to rest themselves and to drink whatever they had. As carefully as he could, Longarm clambered down from the rocks and then made his way into the cave, carrying his Winchester with him.

The women had found a way to heat some beans, and there was a good portion of them left. They had made a little fire from some dried wood that they'd found. He sat down beside them, and Marianne silently make him a plate of beans and dried beef. There was no bread of any kind left. He was aware of his side as he ate, but he tried to ignore it. Verlene looked at him with hard eyes, but Marianne almost seemed sympathetic as she handed him a tin cup of cold water and shook her head. "How's your wound?"

He said, "It ain't bothering me overmuch."

Verlene said, "You're a lucky old sonofabitch. You should be dead."

Longarm sighed and said, "Verlene, I'm no sonofabitch. I know that. But you ain't got to remind me that I'm old."

She said, "Go to Hell."

Marianne hadn't been far from wrong when she'd said they were going to run out of food and run out of it quick. As he ate, he reflected on the fact that J.J. Hunsacker would know how much food they had left. He should. He had been the one who'd sent it down by Minnie Sewell.

While he was eating, Verlene looked at Longarm with her hard eyes. She said, "You're a damned fool. You better run while you've got the chance. Marianne said that we'd hold up on giving the alarm to let you get a head start. She can speak for herself. I'm not sure I want to do that."

Longarm shook his head. "I didn't expect you would, Verlene. There's a lot of money to be made off that crowd, and I imagine that you'll try for every penny."

Marianne said wearily, "Don't you two start at each

other. This is a fix that none of us are enjoying. It's hot as hell. I haven't had a bath in I don't remember when. The food is horrible.'' She looked first at Longarm and then at Verlene. ''And the company is even worse.''

Longarm had expected to feel better once he had eaten, but it hadn't seemed to work. He felt as weak as he had earlier that morning. Every once in a while, a little chill would run through him and then he would feel hot. He finished his meal with a can of peaches, opening the top with his pocketknife, and then spearing the peaches with the blade and eating them straight out of the can. After that, he crinkled the can and poured the juice straight down his throat. It was sweet and good, and he hoped it would give him some strength.

He got up and said, ''Ladies, it's about time I got back to work. You be thinking about what you can do to help me get out of this fix.''

Both of the girls gave him a look that was intended to wither the shirt on his back, but he just shrugged it off. He had been joking. Apparently they hadn't been in a joking mood. He wondered what his boss, Billy Vail, would do if he were in this situation. Well, that was easy to answer. The reason Billy Vail was boss was that he didn't get himself into such situations. The way to avoid this sort of mess was to not get in it in the first place.

Longarm took a moment to look the horses over. They seemed to be fine, but the mule still looked a little down. Longarm would have to come back a little later in the morning or early afternoon, and take them back down to the cave and give them a drink of water. He gave the two young women a final nod, and then ducked through the entrance and walked slowly down to his rifle position.

The day dragged by slowly. Several times, he walked down to fill himself up with water. It seemed the sun dried him out about ten minutes faster than he could fill up. Once, he took the horse and the mule to the stream and let them drink their fill. They had been rested long enough that they could be trusted with the water. After that, he put them away and then had a drink of his whiskey.

Neither one of the young women paid him much of a mind, but it seemed to him that Marianne gave him a good looking over. Once Verlene said, "What are we supposed to do? Just sit around here and wait for them to kill you so that we can get along with our business?"

Longarm had an answer, but he just shook his head and went on out.

The sun got straight overhead at noon, and then slowly began to drop toward the west. It was very difficult for him to hold his eyes open. Occasionally, his chin would drop on his chest and he would nap for five or ten minutes at a stretch. He was the kind who could do such a thing and not wake up either dead or somebody's prisoner. If he was going to sleep, he knew it was best done during the hottest part of the day when the Hunsackers were content to stay in the comfort of their tent. But truthfully, he did not know how much longer he could last. He was nearly out of whiskey, nearly out of food, and completely out of sleep. If it had not been for the driving desire that was built into his very fiber to catch the men he'd started after, he would have abandoned the chase and gone after help.

The light chills caught him now and again. He was hot enough so it was impossible to tell if he was running any fever, but he had had infections before and he knew the symptoms. He took a look at his wounds from time to time, but they didn't seem to be any redder or any angrier than when he had first been shot. He was moving around enough to keep from getting stiff, but not enough to cause any fresh discharge of blood.

About six o'clock by his watch, he went back down to the cave and had another meal of beans and beef. It wasn't very good, but it was filling.

Marianne said, "We've just a little meat left, and the cheese and a few canned goods—tomatoes, peaches, and whatnot. After that, it's all gone."

Longarm said, "You can always go out and stand with your mouth open and let the moon shine on your tongue. I've heard moonlight was right filling."

Verlene said, "Oh, don't try and be joking, Marshal. You're not the man for the job."

Longarm said mildly, "I thought you were sort of prickly when we first met, but I do think you are getting more and more thorny. Pretty soon, a man won't be able to get within five feet of you without feeling a sharp stab."

For answer, she just looked away.

Longarm walked back to his post. There was only about an hour of daylight left. He felt pretty good at the moment, but he didn't know how much longer that would last.

It gradually grew dark, and the desert became painted with moonshine as the big orb slowly rose in the heavens. Longarm paid the Hunsackers careful attention. He would not put it past J.J. to try and pull something just when Longarm was least expecting it. He carefully counted the number of horses under the tent, and got a fair count of the number of men. It looked to be about the right number. He had no reason to believe that anyone had cut out to the east or the west to try and flank him during the night by coming up from his blind side. But then he didn't really have a blind side, not from his position. Now that the moon was up, anyone who tried to ride away from the Hunsackers' camp would be in full view. Other than a direct frontal attack, his only danger lay in falling asleep.

Longarm watched until his eyes ached. He had his whiskey with him, and he was taking little nips every now and then.

Longarm could tell that he was suffering from an infection. The chills were coming closer and closer together, and he could feel the fever building up in his body, even in the heat. Most worrisome were the red streaks running away from his wounds. He knew what that meant. The wounds had somehow gotten corrupted, and he hadn't figured out a way to get the corruption out of his body before he got too weak to help himself. The problem was that doing what was necessary would leave him even weaker.

He looked up at one point, and Marianne was standing there, studying him. She said, "You're sick, aren't you?"

He said, "No." He shook his head. He didn't think it was wise for either one of the women to know how bad off he was. "No, I'm fine." He tried to make his voice strong. "Why would you want to go and think a thing like that?"

Marianne came closer. "Because it's all over your face. That wound has done got infected, hasn't it?"

He shook his head again. "I don't know what you're talking about. I'd know if it was infected."

"Let me see it."

"Listen, dammit. It ain't none of your affair. I ain't asking for no nurse and I'm not looking to get one. Right now,

131

you're in my custody, so you do what I tell you."

She suddenly knelt by his side and lifted his shirt. She said with a low whistle, "Oh, yes. That's bad. You're going to have to open that up or you're not going to make it."

He jerked his shirt out of her hand. "Don't be tending to no business that ain't your own, Marianne. This ain't your business."

She looked at him with surprising compassion. "Deputy Long, I'm not near as bad a person as you think I am. I know you think that I'm a common whore, and I know you think I am against the law. But I don't care to see a man suffer when something can be done about it. As I've told you, I've had some hand at tending the sick, and not just because of my line of work."

He said, nodding his head toward the Hunsackers' camp, "I don't reckon we'd have much time to do surgery in here with that bunch of vultures out there waiting to swoop down."

She said as she stood up, "You might as well face it, Deputy Long. They have the upper hand. The best thing you could do would be to make the hard ride to safety. I think you can get to someplace where you would be safe and could open your wound and let it drain. You need to be well before you go after Mr. Hunsacker and his sons. You're no match for them now."

He licked his dry lips. "I reckon you're right. That would give you a chance to go on about your business. I reckon you'd like that."

She shook her head slowly. "No, I was planning on going with you to take care of you and help you with what needs to be done."

It startled him so, he couldn't speak for a moment. He

said, "Go with me? Leave this sure money?" He jerked his head again toward the Hunsackers' camp. "Ain't your fiancé over there waiting for you with a fistful of double eagles?"

She said, "It never was what you thought. There are some things that I don't charge for, and this is one of them. I think you'd better consider that we could slip away during the night. You had better think seriously about it."

He shook his head as if to clear the cobwebs. He said, "What about the other young lady? Verlene? What does she say?"

"Verlene is not very smart. Verlene is perfectly placed for what she knows. She's not very fond of you, Deputy Long. I think she'll stay here, but as soon as they come in, she'll tell them where you have gone. That's why I think we should wait until she's asleep and then slip out."

Longarm sat there, studying her for a full moment. He said, "I don't know what to make of all this. I've got to give it some thought. You're right about one thing. I do have an infection. I've got the chills and the fever and everything that goes with it."

She motioned with her hand. "It doesn't take a very sharp eye to see that you are not far from something even more serious than an infection."

"Are you talking about gangrene?"

She nodded. "What do you think? How long does it take in this heat?"

"You go on back now to the cave. I'll let you know something soon."

She nodded, and started back over the rock-strewn desert floor. Longarm let her take several steps before he called her name. She turned. He said, "Whichever way it turns out, Marianne, I want to thank you for the offer. That was mighty kind of you."

She shrugged her shoulders. "Forget it, Deputy Long. I'd do it for anyone."

He half smiled. "Well, then. I won't go getting a big head thinking that I've been treated special by a pretty lady."

It brought a half smile to her face. She said, "Yes, that's right. Don't feel special."

After it got good and dark, he changed his firing position, clambering painfully and slowly up a pile of rocks to a much higher vantage point. He was about fifteen or twenty yards above the desert floor, and he could see clearly. The moon hid behind clouds, but he could make out the dark figures around the Hunsackers' camp.

He was no more than settled with his rifle in position when, to his surprise, he saw two men swing aboard their horses and start off to the east. He could not tell where they were headed because they never veered toward him. He saw them ride over a slight rise in the desert floor, and then watched as they disappeared as if the ground had swallowed them.

After that, all he could do was sit and watch toward the direction the men had taken. There was nothing out there. There was no town, there was no well, there was nothing. It was his guess that they were going to swing far to the east and then come back, perhaps from the north or northeast, in hopes of coming through the north entrance of the enclosure.

Longarm sat, thinking about it, studying the desert, waiting to see if the men would appear at some other location. If he were to proceed on his assumption that they were going to try to flank him, he would be leaving himself unprotected from the other sides. He didn't know what else to think. He hated the idea of climbing back down the rock and then making his way across the enclosure to meet the possible threat, but he hated even worse the thought of trying to fend off an attack from his rear.

Just as he started to move, the thought came that might be exactly what Hunsacker was counting on him to think, and that the real attack would come through the western opening. He slid down as best he could to be out of sight, yet still be able to keep an eye on the Hunsacker camp. If they were coming, they should come fairly quickly. They would assume that he would take the bait and move his defense to meet them, leaving the western opening unguarded.

There was no way to know exactly what they were going to do. J.J. Hunsacker had never struck Longarm as the smartest hombre around. In the last gunfight they had had, Hunsacker had made some bad mistakes. He had sacrificed some men but, Longarm thought, had gotten away with himself and most of his close family. The men he had sacrificed had been some third cousins and hangers-on and such. It had been a bloody gunfight, but none of the blood that had been spilled had been close to J.J. Hunsacker.

Longarm wondered if the two men he had seen riding off to the east were a couple of decoys to be picked off at no cost to J.J. while the near and dear ones attacked from the west. He shook his head. It was going to be a tough, long wait and a tough decision. Two men had gotten inside the night before, and they had come from the east. More reason to think that that would be the direction they would come from again, but Longarm still doubted it.

His main problem now was where to locate himself. If a party left the Hunsacker camp and rode to the west, he would not be able to see them from his previous position. The only position from which he could see with any clarity was the high perch he was presently occupying, but it was too far from the western entrance to do him any good in a gunfight. He didn't want anybody getting inside the rock enclosure. He wanted to stop them at least a hundred yards away. He said softly, "Damn, damn, damn." It was a hell of a time to be feeling bad, but there was nothing else for him.

He cursed softly under his breath as he made his way down from the high place, almost stumbling once or twice, catching himself in time. Once on the desert floor, he walked to a place beyond his former gun position, a place where he could see to the west, although his vision was badly restricted toward the south and the Hunsacker camp. It was the best firing position he could find if the attack came from the west or the north. He knew there was no way to be sure. All he could do was go on his best instincts.

Longarm settled down and began searching the desert. The moon still hadn't come all the way up, and if anything, it was still fairly dark. He looked at his watch. The best he could see, it was somewhere around eight o'clock. In another half hour, the moon would be high. If they were going to circle him, now would be the time.

Almost as if on order, several riders suddenly appeared passing the thin cracks in the rocks to the west. They crossed his line of vision. He stood up and hurried to a place that faced south, in their direction. Once there, he took off his hat and lifted his head slightly above the boulders. He could see three men distinctly now. They were

136

swinging wide to the west, and even as he watched, they were turning back toward his fortress. They were going to attack him.

As he saw the men start to come toward his position, he heard gunfire from the east. Rifles cracked and bullets splattered into the rocks. The two men who had ridden to circle him were now positioned out in the desert, attempting to draw his attention away from the three Hunsacker men who were making a serious advance.

Longarm could see the three begin to spread out as they rode slowly toward the opening in the rock walls. Behind him, the firing continued, but he paid it no mind. As long as they wanted to stand out in the desert and shoot slugs into the rocks, that was all right by him. He was more interested in the business of the three he was watching.

He calculated they were some seven or eight hundred yards away, a half mile at the most. They had topped the rise in the desert floor and then dropped down into a depression. They kept on coming, steadily, aiming at the big break in the rock on the western side. They were riding with about ten yards distance between each man, but it was gradually narrowing down as they rode closer. They had their horses in a fast walk.

He expected them, when they were close enough, to make a dash to get inside the fort and blaze away at anything that moved and wasn't wearing a skirt. He supposed that he could go and get Verlene and use her for cover, but that hardly seemed the gentlemanly thing to do. Not that he expected the Hunsackers to act much like gentlemen either.

As he waited, he put his hand inside his shirt and felt the flesh around his bandaged wound. He could tell it was warm, as if it had fever in it, and he could also tell the skin was stretching taut. There was an infection inside him. He had not allowed the wound to heal from the inside out as he was supposed to. Instead, the holes had closed up on the outside, keeping the corruption inside. He had made a mistake. He should have put a little rag in each wound.

The drain rag was called a tent. It tickled him that they should have such a name. There were the Hunsackers out in the desert, taking shade and ease and comfort under a tent. Now, he was distinctly uncomfortable because he hadn't used a tent in his wound. He should have put one piece of rag in each opening to drain it. He was getting careless. The wound had been worse than he had originally thought. He could feel the chills and fever running through him, and he knew he could not hold his present position much longer.

Now the men were about four hundred yards away, and they were picking their horses up into a trot. Longarm assumed that they didn't want to go into a galloping charge just yet because their horses were probably not in good shape, even though they were getting plenty of water. Traveling around in the desert was hard on both a man and his horse, not to mention women.

He slid his rifle across the rock in front of him and sighted on the middle rider. He couldn't tell who it was, but he doubted it was LeeRoy or Joe or Shank, though he would have liked to eliminate Shank as early as possible. He knew for certain that it wasn't the old man. The old man wasn't going to be trotting around the desert at night with bullets aimed at him. He would be back at the camp with a bottle of good whiskey and the ministrations of Minnie Sewell. The old man was probably well on his way to getting his ashes hauled.

Longarm felt a flutter in his stomach as the men got closer. They were preparing themselves for a charge. He guessed them to be no more than 120 or 130 yards away, and any moment now, they would start their horses into a gallop, which would make his first shot that much harder. They rode fearlessly secure, he guessed, figuring that his attention was occupied on the east side of the outcropping. He drew a bead in the center of the middle man's chest. Longarm watched as the dark form got bigger and bigger in his sight. He slowly eased the hammer back on his rifle. They were less than a hundred yards away now, and he could see them lifting their horses into a lope. Longarm waited ten seconds, holding his breath. Then he fired, feeling the kick of his rifle against his shoulder. The middle man disappeared as if a giant hand had slapped him out of the saddle.

That did not deter the other two. They flung themselves further forward on their horse's necks, and kicked the animals up into a gallop, racing fast to the gate. Longarm knew that once they were inside the enclosure, there would be trouble. He tracked the man closest to him, leading him just slightly. The man was so melded into his horse that it was going to be difficult to hit the man and not the horse. Longarm fired, and saw both horse and man go down. He could see the man tumbling free. Longarm jacked another shell into the chamber of his rifle, and fired at the man just as he stood up. He saw the man stagger backwards, and then fall.

He didn't know if he had killed him or not. He had no time to wait. The third man was going to be inside any second. He levered another shell into the chamber, and rose and started toward an opening in the rock to get a head-on shot. He was late. The rider came through the gate, a pistol in his right hand. He fired at Longarm, and in that instant, Longarm fired back. They both missed. Longarm chambered another shell, fell to one knee, and fired again as the man fought to control his horse on the rocky ground. The shot took the man high up on the chest, short of his neck. He went sideways over the side of his horse. Longarm saw him almost bounce as he hit the ground. The riderless horse ran on, trailing the reins, startled and nervous by the gunfire and tripping on rocks. Longarm could hear the clank of a shod hoof as the horse tried to find a way out of the noise and violence. Longarm understood how the animal felt. He didn't care much for it himself.

There was no time to lose. Longarm went quickly to the man's side and leaned down and looked at him. He didn't know him other than he could see the Hunsacker face on him. The man was dead, there was no mistaking that. Longarm took the man's rifle and his side arm, sticking his revolver in his belt.

He walked quickly toward the east side to see what kind of threat the two other men posed. They were still wasting ammunition recklessly. He had knocked down three more of the Hunsacker gang in a short time. The odds were getting better and better. He would like it even more if he could put a dent in the two that were trying to get at him from the east.

Longarm went to the north end of the low rocks, and leaned down and peered up and over. He could just distinguish the two men against the dark sky. They were sitting on their horses some five hundred yards away and methodically pumping round after round into the enclosure. He figured it was going to take luck to score a hit on either man. He decided his best chance was to concentrate on one of the figures and fire rapidly at that one man. Perhaps he could hit the man. Perhaps he would hit the horse. It was not possible for his weapon to make an accurate shot at such a distance.

He eased the hammer back on his carbine and aimed at the man on the left, who was more heavyset than the other. Longarm thought that made him a better target. He fired, smelling the acrid powder as it blasted out from his rifle. He fired again, then three times, then four times, then five. He saw the man's horse go down. He didn't know if he had just hit the horse or the man.

Then the man stumbled free, and Longarm could see him running toward his fellow rider, running heavily across the sand floor of the desert. Longarm fired the single shot left in his rifle at the man, but he didn't break stride. His companion was coming back for him, turning his horse and reaching down to help the stout man get up behind him to ride double.

Frantically, Longarm reached into his shirt pocket and grabbed a handful of cartridges. As quickly as he could, he shoved four of them into the magazine, levered a shell into the chamber, and fired at the men and the horse as the heavyset man tried to get up behind the other man. On his third shot, Longarm saw both men suddenly fall. The second rider looked down at his companion, and Longarm snapped a shot off at him, but he knew it had gone wide. The rider paid no more attention to the man on the ground. Longarm could only guess that the fallen bandit was either badly hurt or dead. The rider spurred his horse and headed straight back for the Hunsackers' camp.

Longarm got up slowly. He walked, methodically loading his carbine. It was about time to get out of this place. If he stayed much longer, he would be dead. He noticed the riderless horse standing in the middle of the fort. He walked to the animal, which was trembling from all the shooting and the noise. He took the horse by the bridle and led him behind him. The least he could do for the animal was let him have a drink of water. The horse followed Longarm to the cave with the bubbling spring.

Longarm led him further into the cave, and watched as the horse immediately went to water. He smelled at the water for several seconds, and then Longarm watched the horse raise his head, water dripping from his jaws before plunging his mouth back in. Longarm didn't know what he was going to do with the third horse, but he didn't see any point in leaving it behind for the Hunsackers.

He led the horse out of the cave and dropped his reins, letting him stand near the wall. Longarm walked down to where the women and his other two horses were. The two girls were standing against the cave wall. They turned quickly as he came in. Marianne said, "What happened? We heard shooting!" She held her hand to her mouth.

Longarm was about to speak when Verlene said with venom in her voice, "Any chance you got shot again, Deputy Long?"

Longarm gave her half a smile. "Sorry to disappoint you, Verlene. There were some people that got shot, but I wasn't one of them this time. Reckon I just got lucky."

Marianne said, looking at him, to his surprise, with concern on her face, "You're all right then?"

He nodded. "Yes, ma'am. Thank you very much. I'm doing pretty well." He walked on to where the two horses were standing, one still bearing the saddle but with the cinch loosened, but still bridled, and the other with a halter and a lead rope. He caught up the bridles and the lead rope and turned. He said, "I reckon I'm going to have to disappoint you, ladies. I'll be pulling my freight."

Marianne said, "You leaving?"

He nodded again. "Yes, I reckon it's about time I got out of here." He gave her a look he knew she would understand. "I don't think I'm going to hold up much longer."

Verlene gave him a hard laugh. "So, you're going to run, are ya? They run you out? I knew they would. I knew all that big, brave lawman talk was just so much stuffing."

Marianne gave her an annoyed look, and said, "That's not necessary, Verlene. Leave the man alone. He's just doing his job."

Verlene looked at her with her mouth open. She said, "When did you go defending the law?"

"I'm not defending the law. The man's hurt. Can't you see that?"

"Maybe you forgot, but he's the man who has held us here against our will, draggin' us halfway around the country."

Longarm said, touching his hand to the brim of his hat, "Well, if you ladies will forgive me, I'm going to get on along. Now, Miss Verlene, I know you're right anxious for the Hunsackers to get their hands on me. But I don't think they're going to be coming up here until dawn, and I don't think it would be a very good idea for you to think about trying to get down to their camp. I might have to hit you

143

on the head with a rock, that kind of thing.''

Verlene drew herself up. "Did you hear that, Marianne? Hit me on the head with a rock!"

Marianne said, "Don't be silly, Verlene. He won't hit you with a rock." Then she turned her head toward Longarm. "I'm going with you."

Longarm frowned slightly. "Marianne, are you sure that you want to do that?"

"I don't think you can make it without me."

He grimaced. "I hate to admit that."

She said, "Somebody is going to have to open that wound up. I've never seen anybody who could open a wound in their own self."

Longarm said, "I kind of have to agree with you, though I don't see how it's going to make you any too popular with the folks back there."

Verlene broke in to say, "Marianne, are you crazy? You can't run out on this deal. There's a lot of money involved here. Minnie has already set it up. All we have to do is wait until this fool is out of here and it will be all right."

Marianne said, with a touch of anger in her voice, "Verlene, can't you ever think of anything other than cash? You don't really want to get married, do you? Besides, this deputy here has thinned out the Hunsacker bunch so that I don't think they're going to be so anxious for you and me. I think they are going to be more anxious to find *him*." She looked at Longarm when she said it. "I don't think they'll be stopping for fun. I think they'll be trailing him too fast."

Longarm nodded. "Yes, that's why I want to get as much of a start as I can." He glanced at Verlene. "That's why I don't think you better try and get down to their camp tonight. They are liable to shoot you in the dark—not knowing who you are. Or I might shoot you from this side. You might just think I've gone.''

Marianne said sternly, ''I won't have that kind of talk, Deputy Long.''

Longarm gave her a smile. ''My friends call me Long-arm.''

Marianne said, ''Well, I ain't your friend, Deputy Long. Hadn't we better get going?''

Longarm nodded. ''I reckon so.'' All he felt was weak. He led the two horses out of the cave, leaving Verlene standing there, with Marianne trailing behind him. He could hear Verlene as she implored Marianne not to do what she was about to do. He heard her say, ''Have you gone crazy in this heat?''

Marianne said, ''The man is wounded. He needs help. If they catch him, they will kill him. He needs someone to help him treat his wounds. It's part of me, Verlene. I don't expect you to understand. Maybe you haven't noticed, but I've never really been a whore. You're a whore, I'm not. I just fuck sometimes for money.''

Longarm could hear the fury in Verlene's voice. She said, ''Why, you bitch. Who the hell do you think you're talking to? You ain't so highfalutin. I've seen you work. Don't try and fool me. Don't you think I won't tell Mr. Hunsacker what you've done, and when he catches up with you and that no good lawman, you'll find out just how high and mighty you are.''

Longarm called back. ''Marianne, if you're going with me, you'd better step it up. The time's getting short.''

Marianne said to Verlene, ''I wouldn't advise you to try and get to Mr. Hunsacker. I'd let him come to you. The marshal told you that there's going to be some itchy trigger fingers around that camp. If you go to slipping up there, you're liable to get the surprise of your life, and it may be the last surprise you ever get.''

She turned and followed after Longarm as he led the two horses to where the third one was standing. There really wasn't much to take. He sent Marianne to fill the big canteen, and then he watered the other two horses even though they had just been watered a few hours earlier. They were going to be traveling across the desert, and they would need all the help they could get.

Longarm was cinching up the saddle on the big bay when Marianne came back. He'd ride the bay for as long as he could, then switch to the smaller, less durable roan. He didn't know anything about the horse he had acquired from the Hunsackers. Marianne would ride that one, and her light weight should keep the animal going at a moderate pace along with his. The horse was a good-looking buckskin, four or five years old, Longarm reckoned. The fact that he was a good-blooded horse made Longarm think that whoever had been on his back had been a son rather than a cousin to old J.J. A fine horse like that would naturally go to one of his sons.

Longarm helped Marianne up on the buckskin. She didn't need much assistance. He gave her a little lift to help her get her small slipper in the stirrup, and then she swung into the saddle with a great flurry of petticoats and skirts. She was seemingly oblivious to how her clothes and underclothes rode up around her hips. But the sight of it, even in his condition, gave Longarm an erection. He remembered how warm and soft and wet she had been.

He swung into his saddle, flinching as he did. He had

146

pulled Marianne's stirrups up, but they still seemed a little too long. He was about to say that he would get down and take them up for her, but she shook her head. "These will be just fine," she said. "I don't really pay much attention to the stirrups. I learned to ride bareback. Sitting in this saddle will be as easy as pie."

Longarm said, "Now, you know what you're doing?"

"I think so."

"This is going to be one hell of a ride over some rough country. You said that mining camp was three miles away, or it could be ten or it could be twelve or it could be fifteen. It's very easy to lose your bearings in the desert."

She shrugged. "Hadn't we better get going?"

Marianne was completely right. The moon was up full now. For a while, they would be hidden from the Hunsackers as they trailed north. The Hunsackers camp was directly south, and the rocks and eruptions would conceal him and Marianne for a time. He didn't know how long it would be before the Hunsackers caught their trail. He had no earthly idea. He had loaded his horse and Marianne's horse with two rifles and a shotgun, and he had his six-gun at hand. He could get off twenty shots in all, including the two shotgun barrels.

He nudged his bay forward. "Well, let's give it a try," he said. As his horse moved, he took the roan on lead, starting for the north gate. Marianne pulled up beside him, both of them walking their horses across the rocks on the floor of the rock outcropping. The place had served its purpose. It had given him a chance to reduce the Hunsacker gang and dim their eagerness. Maybe it had hurt them so bad they'd go to ground and lick their wounds for a while.

But he really didn't think so. He was almost certain they

would be hot on his trail when they realized he and Marianne were gone. He didn't know if he had time enough to clean up his wound. If he didn't, he would be in bad shape before they reached help. He could already feel himself getting lighter in the head.

They trailed out through the northern entrance. It seemed the great expanse of desert lit up in front of them with the big full moon shining down.

Longarm said to Marianne, "Well, good luck to both of us."

She said grimly, "I think you're the one that needs it."

Chapter 9

For the first ten minutes, neither of them spoke. The only sounds around the desert were the soft shuffle of their horses' hooves and the creaking of their saddles. Longarm kept them pointed due north to keep the rock outcropping between himself and the Hunsackers. After he had gone about three quarters of a mile, he pulled up his horse. Beside him, Marianne did the same. He turned as best as he could in the saddle with his side paining him as bad as it was. He looked back. The Hunsacker camp was still obscured by the rock formations, but he could faintly hear the sound of someone screaming riding on the desert wind.

Marianne said dryly, "That would be Verlene telling the Hunsackers that she is waiting to be fetched back to their camp."

Longarm said, "That ain't all she's telling them. We'd better get on the move."

He picked up the pace ever so slightly. It wouldn't do to wear the horses out. On foot, they would very likely be targets out in the middle of nowhere. He turned to Marianne as they made their slow way across the desert. "How's the compass working in your head?" he said. "Do you have any better idea where that mining camp is?"

She gestured to her left. "The best I can remember, it's over that way. But . . . I can't be sure."

"You were pretty specific when you were talking about it. Do you know if it's three miles, five miles, or seven miles?"

Marianne shook her head slowly, her blond hair catching the glow of the moon. "I don't know. I didn't realize it would be necessary for me to remember a thing like that. I didn't know we were coming here to get in a war."

Longarm said, "It ain't a war, Marianne. It's a law officer trying to bring criminals to justice. If you'd been one of their victims, you might not think so kindly of them."

She shrugged. "Well, I have no reason to think otherwise. I've never been their victim. They've paid me well for my services. They've been drunk and disorderly, but then so are cowboys who work on ranches."

They rode on in silence. In time, Longarm said, "You know, I guess I ought to be surprised with you, but I ain't. You said you were going to do this and I doubted you then. I didn't see any reason for you to face the hard cold facts of the matter, but you did." He looked around at the young woman riding to his right. "You're better than you think you are."

She said, "I don't look down my nose at myself, Marshal Long. That's *your* doing. Do you think I'm not capable of being kind because I'm a whore?"

Longarm shook his head. "Being a whore has nothing to do with it. Frankly, I don't think you *are* one. In your heart, that is. What I'm talking about is going up to the Hunsackers' camp under the pretense of getting married."

"How do you know we weren't?"

Longarm smiled. "Because you've come with me, that's why. For my money, I think you got talked into doing something you didn't want to do. The closer you got to it, the more you wanted out. I think I'm your chance. What do you say to that?"

In the moonlight, he almost saw her flush slightly. He supposed it was just his imagination. She said, "Don't flatter yourself. I don't need your chance. I'm coming along with you because I want to. Let it be that."

Longarm laughed softly. "Just as you say."

A little further along, she said, glancing at the sky, "What time do you suppose it is?"

Longarm looked at the rising moon. "Oh, I reckon it's a little after midnight. I could get out my watch, but it's a little too dark to see. Thank heavens for that. We're getting a few clouds helping us."

"How much time before you think they find out you're gone?"

"I don't think that Verlene's screaming is going to fetch them. I'd think they'd be a mite cautious about riding up toward those rocks. For all they know, I might have gotten Verlene, either through threat or persuasion or purchase, to set up a squall to draw them in. There's not but about four or five of them left as I counted. If they got within a hundred yards of the rocks with the moon bright, I could get them all. So, I think they'll be cautious about tonight."

He looked over at her. "In a way, I'm kind of betting my life on it. We need to get enough distance between us and them for me to open this wound up and get some of

151

this corruption out of my side. I'm hoping they don't get hot behind us."

She shrugged again. "I think you can count on the fact that Verlene won't do anything but scream."

"You don't think she'll try walking across that desert to their camp?"

"Not at night. Not as afraid as she is of the outdoors."

Longarm nodded his head at her. "You sit a horse like you're used to being outdoors."

Marianne shrugged again. "I grew up in Wyoming. There you did what you had to do in order to get by. If you couldn't ride a horse, you'd freeze walking."

Longarm said, "Yeah, that's pretty country but it can be deadly. I sure hope you are right about Verlene. If she'll sit right where she is, maybe I've got time to get to that mining camp."

Marianne looked at him. "If we can find it. Can't we go any faster?"

Longarm shook his head. "I don't know how far we've got to go, so I don't want to use these horses too hard. If it comes to it, we might have to run a spell, so I need them ready." He was glad for the coolness of the night because he could feel the fever working through his body. He knew he was getting sicker.

They rode on and on, holding a northerly course at first, and then veering off to the left, toward the west. Marianne had no sense of where the mining camp was located. She grew vaguer and vaguer in her suggestions. Finally, Longarm struck a route a few points to the left of the North Star. They plowed on through the small hours heading toward dawn, hoping desperately that they could find someplace before the Hunsackers arrived.

Time after time, turning in his saddle, Longarm looked back, but the horizon stayed clear. He guessed Marianne was right that Verlene couldn't draw the Hunsackers with her screams and that she was too afraid of the desert at night to make her own way to their camp. He knew he and Marianne would leave a clear trail on the desert floor. The sandy dirt was too loose and soft to hide their fresh tracks, which would be visible even to the untrained eye the next morning.

Once, Marianne rode up next to him and put her left hand out to his face. She said with concern in her voice, "Marshal Long, we've got to find someplace quick to do something about you. If we don't, the Hunsackers will have already killed you."

Longarm felt his face. He was sweating, even as the air grew cooler. He said, "Yeah, I know, but we can't just stop here in the middle of nothing. Hell, if we could just find an old river bottom or a ravine or a gully or a little hill. Anything. But I don't see anything. Just all this damned desert. They would see us from two miles off, sure as hell, if we pulled up. We're going to have to build a fire, and they'll damned sure see that."

"We've got to do something soon," she said.

"I know."

It was Marianne who spotted the structure first. An hour or so after she had touched his face, she said, "What's that?" Her words came sharp in the cold air.

Longarm said, "What? I don't see. . . ." His eyes scanned the horizon. He thought maybe she was seeing the first signs of daylight. He knew it shouldn't be long before dawn. The moon had been down for a good hour or so. "What are you talking about?"

She stopped her horse and pointed to the left of their line of march. In the distance, he could see the low run of foothills that stretched into the mountains. The Sierra Madres, he knew they were called.

Longarm stopped his horse also, and narrowed his eyes, but everything faded into the rounded hills that were still a good way off. He said, "I don't see anything."

Marianne poked an insistant finger out. "There to the left of that rounded hill."

He peered hard in the darkness. Sure enough, he saw a sharp corner that didn't belong to the roundness of the hill. He said, "Just there? Just yonder?"

She nodded. "Yes, it looks like a cabin."

"Well, your eyes are sharper than mine, which ain't most often the case. Let's head for it."

They urged their horses forward, and aimed a little west by northwest. As they rode, he asked her if she thought it was part of the mining camp. She shook her head. "I don't know. All I can see is just the one cabin. The mining camp has five or six, and then there was a two-story frame house where we stayed. They brought the lumber in from Reno."

Now he could see the dim outline of what she had seen earlier. It was indeed the framework of a lone cabin with nothing else around it. It appeared to be about two miles away, but then, distances were so deceptive in the desert. He said, "Well, let's get on up to it. If it's what I think it is, I don't want to be riding after dawn, and I don't reckon that's more than an hour away."

In fifteen minutes, they were approaching the cabin, and even in the darkness, Longarm could tell it wasn't much. It was built of native rock with a tin roof. It never pretended to be more than it was—a one-room miner's cabin. As they neared, Longarm could see that it was on a downslope, facing down into the foothills. By then, they were close enough that they could see a dry streambed in front of the cabin.

The yard of the place told its own story.

Long years past, some optimistic miner had built the cabin on the banks of a creek that had been flowing at that time. He'd had the water to wash his gold, but the falling-down roof of the place attested to the fact that the water hadn't lasted and neither had the miner. With the loss of the water, either through drought or the lack of snow in the mountains to make its way down to form the creek, the miner hadn't been able to water himself or his stock or his gold, and had had to pull up stakes.

But the lone cabin would do for Longarm's purposes. It would give him cover while they tended to his wound. If the Hunsackers came up on him, either while he and Marianne were draining out the corruption or while he was resting up from the operation, the outlaws would pay a dear price if they tried to approach.

Longarm led them straight to the front of the cabin. He dismounted, and then gave Marianne his shoulder as an aid as she came down from the high saddle to the ground. The cabin was in worse repair than it had seemed from a distance. Longarm reckoned that it had been falling apart for some ten years or so, not that that really mattered. If the water had stayed in the streambed, there would have been a lot of other cabins stretched out along its length.

He led the three horses through the narrow door, one at a time, into the cabin. He guessed it to be not much bigger than sixteen feet by sixteen, but he didn't want to leave the horses outside. With his strength draining out of him, he still took the time to uncinch the two saddles and take the bits out of their mouths. The horses seemed in pretty good shape. Fortunately, the walls of the cabin were high enough that they would be protected from gunfire. There were two windows, one at the back and one to the west. The door opened from the north. Longarm said, "Well, I reckon we can set up housekeeping here. What do we have for vital goods besides a canteen of water?"

Marianne shrugged. "I think there may be a can of tomatoes and a can of peaches and maybe a little piece of cheese. Other than that, I guess we're going to have to make do with sand and cactus."

Longarm said, "How are we planning on going about this?" He put his hand to his side.

Marianne said, "We're going to need a fire. I'll go and collect some wood."

"You ain't scared of the desert at night?"

She shook her head. "Anybody that's ever lived in this kind of country knows that snakes and varmints go to ground in the cold of the morning. They don't come out until the sun does."

She disappeared out the door, and Longarm sat down to wait. The horses were huddled over in a far corner, looking at him curiously. The cabin was dark, but Longarm's eyes had adjusted well enough so that he could see. It wasn't but a few moments until Marianne was back with a small bundle of dried mesquite limbs and twigs and branches off of some small greasewood bushes. They were dry, and they would burn hot and without smoke. Not, he guessed, that the Hunsackers were going to have any trouble finding where he had gone to.

Marianne put her load down, expertly built the twigs into

a pile, and added branches. Longarm struck a match, and the tinder caught almost instantly. In a matter of a few minutes, they had a bright blaze going. Marianne added bigger sticks to the fire until it spread a circle of warmth that was welcome in the cold of the coming morning.

Marianne looked at him. "I reckon you'd better get your knife out," she said.

Longarm nodded. He wasn't particularly looking forward to the proceedings, but he didn't see any way around them. He knew he was sick. He was hurting, and he knew he wasn't going to get better until certain steps were taken. Marianne went over to the saddlebags and came back with the small skillet that Longarm carried. She filled it with water and set it against the coals that were building up as the wood burned down. Then she took the jackknife that Longarm had handed her, opened the blade, and washed it in the water until she deemed it clean. She left it in the water with the handle away from the fire while the edge of the water began to tremble slightly as it heated on the coals.

She said, "The knife seems sharp enough."

Longarm was unbuttoning his shirt. He didn't have to be told what to do. He said, "I'd as soon carry an empty gun as a dull knife. It would make about as much sense." He finished stripping off his shirt, and carefully laid it on the dirt floor of the cabin beside the fire.

Before he knelt down, he untied the knot in the bandage that Marianne had put on the day before. He unwound it and dropped it on the floor. The two pads covering the front part of the wound and the back part didn't fall off. He knew they were dried to his skin by the blood. He reached for a corner of the bandage in the front, and Marianne stayed his hand. She said, "You better wait and let me work that loose. I don't want it tearing off the scab any more than it has to. I'll moisten it with some water when it gets to boiling."

Longarm slumped down next to the fire in a position where he could lay on his right side, exposing his left side to Marianne. "You're the boss," he said.

"How are you feeling?"

Longarm shook his head slightly from side to side. "I've been better, but then I've also been shot before. Generally, however, I've taken better care of myself."

She said, "I don't think it's gone too far." She reached under her skirt and tore loose another piece of petticoat. She soaked it in the now-bubbling water in the skillet, took it out, and then let it cool a little. She circled the fire before she knelt down beside Longarm. She held the moist piece of cloth against the back bandage, gradually and gently pulling at the edge. He felt it come loose. She cast the used bandage away in the corner, and then began on the bandage in the front. It hurt a little more, and Longarm was surprised. He said, "Hell, I'd have thought that big one in the back was worse off."

She said, "No, it made a bigger hole coming out. It ain't quite healed up. It looks like most of the infection is in the front."

"That's halfway good to hear."

She said, "That doesn't mean that I don't have to reopen the back."

"I thought that's what you were going to say."

She reached under her clothes and pulled off the slip she had been ripping. In spite of himself, Longarm stirred at the sight of her long bare golden legs flashing in the firelight. She took the petticoat and ripped it into long strips,

158

then put them, one by one, into the boiling water.

Longarm said, "Ain't we nearly there?"

She said, "Just about."

"Well, in my saddlebag, there's a bottle of whiskey. I'd appreciate it if you would fetch it for me."

She got up, went over to his horse, and rummaged around for a moment, and then came back with the bottle, which was still half full. She uncorked it and handed it to him. He looked at her and said, "You might as well throw that cork away. I don't reckon to have much use for it for the next couple of hours."

She silently pitched the cork out the front door, and knelt down beside him again and then took the knife by the handle. She said, "I'm going to heat this knife in the fire because I'm hoping to sear that wound when I open it up so that it won't get reinfected."

Longarm was having a long, hard pull on the bottle. He said, "Yeah, I was afraid you'd know about that. That's what you're supposed to do. I guess you also know about sticking tents in the wound."

In the dim light, he could see her nod. "Yeah," she said. "Those pieces of bandages that I've got cooking, when they get to boiling, I'll take that knife and set it in the coals and use the bandages. I'm going to have to get it hot, Marshal. You ain't going to jump or anything, are you? It'll just make it worse."

"I'll hold as steady as I can," Longarm said. "Wish I had saved that cork now."

"What for?"

"Give me something to bite on."

He could see her take the knife out of the skillet of boiling water and hold it just over the hot coals. He could see

159

the blade tint red. He had no illusions about what was coming.

She said, "We'll do the front first. It'll be the worst, Marshal. I know it's going to hurt."

"Hell, you might as well call me Longarm. That's my nickname."

"Yeah, I've heard that. I didn't know if you liked to be called that by anyone other than your friends."

He said, "Well, what do you reckon we are now? You taking advantage of me in my sleep, you running off with me, and now you're fixing to stick something in me just like I stuck something in you. Although I believe yours is going to be a little hotter. I reckon that makes us pretty close."

She smiled at him when she picked up the handle of the knife. "I'm going to be quick now." Out of the corner of his eye, he saw her make a motion.

It seemed he could smell the burning flesh before the pain really jolted him. When the hurt got to him, it arrived full-blown, like a Texas tornado. It was all he could do to snuff a groan.

She said, "My God. You wouldn't believe what's coming out of here, Longarm. I'm surprised you are still alive."

Through clenched teeth, he said, "I'm so glad to hear that."

"I've got to wash this knife off and then get it hot again for the back."

Longarm said, "I can't wait." It was all he could do to strangle down a scream.

He waited for a second thrust. It was only just a little easier than the front. Then it was over.

She said, "It wasn't built up in the back like it was in

the front. Hopefully it will drain real good. I'm going to get those tents ready so we don't have to do this again.''

Longarm had laid his head down on his arm. He felt too weak to be weary, and he didn't try to answer. Yet at the same time, he could almost feel himself getting better, as if the fever was draining out of his body along with the blood and the infection. He still didn't try to answer. He just lay quietly as he felt her working over him. He felt her poking the long strips that were soaking wet and still hot from the boiling water in both sides of his body. Then he felt her put a pad around his side that covered both of the wounds.

Marianne said, ''You look all white-faced. I'm not going to ask you to raise up so I can get this bandage around you. I think if you'll lay there for a while, you'll be best off.''

Longarm said, ''Thanks. Hand me that bottle, will you?''

She moved and put it in his hand. It had only been some six inches away, but he hadn't been able to see it. He couldn't quite lift it, so she raised it to his lips for him. He was able to raise his head enough to pull down several swallows. Then he said, ''Ahhh . . .'' and laid his head back down.

''You still with me? You gonna make it?''

He said, ''Oh, yeah. I'll be making it. You've done a good job. I'm much obliged to you.''

She said, ''I've done things I've enjoyed more, I've got to say that. That wound was a mess. I think that bullet could have splintered when it went into you. It's kind of a funny-looking entrance wound, and the back is really a mess.''

Longarm said faintly, ''That's just what I need. Another good scar.''

He could feel her move the bandage pads in the front

161

and back. She said, "I can see that some of the redness is going away, but they are still draining. I am going to let them drain a little while longer before I bandage you up."

He worked his way up to his elbow and had another pull of the whiskey. "I reckon as long as the whiskey holds out, I can stand it," he said. "But I've got to tell you, little girl, I can already feel that poison draining out of me. I'm not ready to run a footrace with an Indian, but I'm already feeling stronger."

She said, "I don't think you should get too spry just yet. Wait."

He looked around at her, kneeling by his side, studying his wounds. Her face was very beautiful in the firelight. He said, "Marianne, we can't wait too long. We're here in the desert with no water and no food for these horses. You and I can last three or four days without water. We've got water for us, but these horses can't last. They haven't got any water. We've got to get to someplace where there is help. I've got to go on whether I'm sick or not."

She said, "Just let it drain for a few more minutes."

He laid his head back down and stared into the fire as she built up the flames. The coals were still very apparent in the heavy morning. The air seemed to carry some moisture, even though it probably hadn't rained in this country in five years. Sometimes it rained in the mountains, and it nearly always snowed in the mountains. When the snow melted in the spring and summer, it ran down into little creeks that gave prospectors hope that it was a livable land. But it was a dangerous, treacherous land. The water you found today might not be there tomorrow.

It felt very comfortable lying on his side, feeling himself get better, but he was still so tired and sleepy.

He let his eyes blink a few times, and then closed them. His mind seemed far away. It felt pleasant and warm by the fire, and somehow secure within the rock walls of the broken-down cabin. It seemed only a moment later when he heard Marianne say, "I believe sunrise has come."

Relunctantly, he fluttered his eyes open. He could tell at a glance that the light in the cabin had taken on a different texture. It was no longer quilted with black. It was now much lighter, starting to show traces of sunlight.

He said, "Oh, hell. I could have wished for it to have stayed dark a little longer. At least long enough to where they couldn't track our sign before noon."

Marianne said, "You had better sit up and let me bandage those pads on your wounds. I've got the long strips I can wind around you. It needs some pressure to keep you from bleeding overmuch. I reckon you've lost all the blood you need to lose."

He put his shirt back on, but he kept it hiked up high on his chest. Now, when he sat up, he had to keep it held up as she wound the bandage around his midriff. Surprisingly, there was very little pain. He said, "You'd think a body would hurt after having a red-hot knife stuck in it a couple of places."

She tied off the knot and looked up at him and smiled. "That was about a half bottle of whiskey ago," She said. "I wouldn't think you'd be feeling anything by now."

"Normally, I drink that much before breakfast," he said. "But since we ain't going to have any breakfast, I guess it's just as well I drank it."

She got up and crossed to where the skillet sat. The canteen was right beside it. She brought it back to him and made him drink. "You need to keep plenty of water in your

163

system," she said. "They say it's good for a body."

He drank, forcing some of the water down, not all that thirsty. When he was finished, he handed her the canteen and said, "The same goes for you."

As she drank, he admired her and her slim neck and the way her breast rose against the material of her thin muslin frock. It caused a faint stirring in his loins. It seemed silly even to him. Here he was with some bad outlaws tracking him, wounded and sick, with no food, in the middle of the desert, and he was thinking about lusting for her flesh. That took some kind of optimism, he figured.

He watched her thoughtfully until she had finished drinking. She lowered the canteen and then put the top back on it.

He said, "You know, Marianne, you're quite a lady."

She gave a short laugh. "I haven't been called that very often."

"It ain't what you do for a living that makes you a lady or not a lady. It's the way you conduct yourself in the general business of living. To me, you're a grand lady."

She gave him an amused look. "I believe that's the first compliment I ever had from a lawman."

"Well, if I'm around, it won't be the last."

She cocked her head to one side and studied him. "You know, I've heard about you," she said. "I knew your nickname was Longarm. You're supposed to be this dangerous, never-give-up, chase-them-to-the-end-of-the-earth federal marshal. And yet, you don't seem quite as hard and tough as I expected you to be."

He chuckled slightly. "I don't reckon I look like much right now. I think I've lost about ten pounds in the last few days. I feel a little drawn."

She said, "You also haven't had any sleep. Why don't you catch a little nap? I'll watch carefully."

He looked at her closely, narrowing his eyes. "I recollect that it wasn't too long ago that you more or less helped me to want to sleep."

To his surprise, her cheeks reddened in a blush. She glanced down at her hands. "I wish you wouldn't remind me of that. I'd like to say that Verlene talked me into doing that, but to tell you the truth, it was my idea." She looked up at him. "And I didn't really do it to make you sleep."

He half smiled and said, "I didn't think you did."

She gave him a stern look. "Well, don't be thinking about it. A body can be curious, that's all. Now, why don't you lay your head down and I'll call you in an hour."

Longarm said, "All right," and then laid his head gratefully on his arm. His body felt as if it had been ridden a long, long way without food or rest. He closed his eyes. He supposed sleep overcame him instantly.

How long he slept, he wasn't sure of at first. Words seem to come filtering through his consciousness. At first, the words didn't make any sense. Then gradually as his mind came awake, he heard them clearly. It was Marianne. She said, "Longarm! Wake up! They're coming! Longarm! Longarm!"

He willed his eyes to open. The first thing he was aware of was the brilliant light, and the second was how warm it was in the cabin. Dawn had long since passed. He heard Marianne call to him again, and he slowly and painfully worked himself up to a sitting position. She was in the back of the cabin, peering around the corner of the window. He said, still half asleep, "What is it?"

Marianne said, "They're coming, Longarm. You'd better

get over here if you can and see what you think."

Longarm didn't dare stand up. He was fearful that as faint and weak as he was, he might fall over, so on hands and knees, he crawled over the base of the small window and raised himself up cautiously until he could see over the ledge.

He could see a trail of black dots heading directly toward them. It took a moment to separate them, but he could tell the first dots were four horsemen with a bigger dot behind them. The other dot was probably the wagon with extra horses being towed along. He turned and sat back down, propping his back against the wall. Marianne looked at him. "It's them, isn't it?" she said.

"I don't reckon it'd be anybody else."

She was a long time in asking the question, but it came with no less impact. She said, "What are you going to do?"

Chapter 10

He was equally as long in answering. Finally, he said, "I don't know."

She looked out the window again, just peering around the edge. "You better think of something quick," she said. "I don't reckon they're more than two miles off."

Longarm nodded. "That'd be about right, and at the rate they're coming, they'll be here in less than an hour."

Marianne moved away from the window, walked across the cabin to the door, and looked through it to the foothills in the distance. She said, "What about those mountains? Can't we hide in them?"

Longarm gave a small chuckle. "We? Have you joined up?"

She gave him an angry look. "Dammit, I didn't help you to stay alive just to see you shot down. Don't be sarcastic with me. I'll be sarcastic back if you start it with me."

Longarm didn't bother to apologize. He said, shaking his head, "No, we wouldn't make it to the foothills, and it wouldn't be a good place to hide. It would take me too long to get the horses ready, and as weak as I am, I'm not sure I could make it. My best chance is to hope they get discouraged in trying to take me and give up.''

She said, "But you can't hold out here very long. All we have is some water.''

He looked at her across the cabin. He said softly, "Marianne, I don't want you staying here with me. There's going to be lead flying around in here. You go to them. You've done enough for me as it is. I'm very much obliged to you.''

She said firmly, "I'm not leaving you. Get that straight.''

"But if you got to them, they won't have any reason to press home the battle against me. It could be costly rushing this place, and I can hold out for three or four days with nothing but water.''

Marianne said, "They are going to know that you are wounded.''

"How are they going to know that?''

She said, "Because there was blood in too many places in that rock fort. You dripped blood in both of the caves.''

It made him think for a moment. "Well, so what? How does that change anything?''

"It means that they'll know that you are weak and wounded and that you can't hold out very long. They'll wait one more day and then one more. That'll be the end of you. If I stay in here, they can't shoot in the cabin.''

"Hell, Marianne. I don't want you taking that chance. You're dealing with people that you don't really understand. The Hunsackers ain't very nice folks. If they don't got no further use for you, they don't really care what happens to you. I'm trying to tell you that if they're angry enough at me, they wouldn't care if you got hit by a stray bullet or not. You've got to trust me on this. I've known the Hunsackers and their kind for a lot of years. The milk of human kindness has dried up in their udders a long time ago."

She looked across the cabin. "Are you saying that you want me to go out with people like that? You want me to go and join them?"

Her eyes made him feel uncomfortable. He said, "I think it would be a hell of a lot safer."

She said, "Maybe I don't think that way. Maybe I don't want to be around people like the Hunsackers."

Longarm pursed his lips. "Well, I'm not going to shove you out the door, but I will tell you that it's liable to get a little fierce in here. There ain't too many places to hide in this square room, and we don't have enough tin on the roof to hold off rain, much less lead."

She said, "Then you'd better think of something because I'm not going out."

Longarm turned cautiously and applied his left eye to the corner of the window. The dots were no longer dots. They had turned into horsemen and a wagon being pulled by a team trailing several horses. Longarm could see big barrels of water sitting in the bed of the wagon.

It looked to him as if there were two women on the seat of the wagon. He guessed it would be Verlene and Minnie Sewell. He reckoned Minnie was driving the team. That would leave the men free to attack him from all directions.

Even as he watched, the group began veering off to the west. They weren't going to come within range of his rifle. If he was any judge of Hunsacker and his habits and his cowardly ways, the four men left would simply surround the cabin at a distance and wait for Longarm to try to make a break for it. He doubted there would be much conversation.

He turned back into the room. Marianne had crossed back over to the window, and was standing on the other side. She said, ''Well?''

Longarm shook his head. ''I don't know. I don't see any way to draw them close enough to do any good. They've brought the wagon, and that means that they're going to have plenty of provisions for both themselves and their horses. Mainly they'll have water for their horses. That's the one thing we ain't got. Beats the hell out of me what to do.''

She said, ''Maybe I can do something.''

Longarm gave her a hard look. ''Just hold up there, missy. I don't want you looking brave. I got brave when I run into that hornet's nest back there in Lodestar. I should have been much better prepared, but I was in a hurry to get home. Now it looks like I'm going to be delayed much longer than I thought.''

He glanced quickly around the corner of the window, and then came back to her side of the room. The sun was now high enough so that the rays were coming through the ruined roof. It wouldn't be long before it was hot enough to suit anyone. Longarm said, ''There's a fellow back in Denver that would get a big kick out of this. A chief marshal by the name of Billy Vail. He's always going on as to how I have it so easy. Well, I wish he could see the fix I've gotten myself into now. Maybe he wouldn't be so quick to tell me that I need to back up to the pay window.''

Marianne said as she looked around the edge, ''They're closer. They're going further around to the west.''

Longarm nodded. "They want to stay out of rifle shot."
He peered around the window and saw the caravan bearing
off to the left. They were less than a half mile away.

Longarm said, "There's nothing we can do now but
wait."

Wait, he thought, until they have us good and surrounded, and then wait as they draw the noose tighter as
the water runs out. Just then, one of his horses smelled the
Hunsackers' stock and whined loudly. The noise was loud
in the small cabin, and both Longarm and Marianne
jumped.

Marianne said, "Dammit, they'll hear that."

Longarm shrugged. "It doesn't make a damn. They
know we are in here. The signs run straight to this cabin.
As soon as they circle, they're going to know we didn't go
on, so the horse letting out a holler doesn't make any difference." He slumped down on the floor again, trying to
think of something. His weapons were so few—a derringer,
two six-guns, and two rifles. The rifles were practically useless since the Hunsackers would never come within range.
No they'd just cast their net around the cabin and pull it
in.

After a few more moments, he looked around the window ledge. He was surprised to see that the caravan was
going on toward the north. He had expected for certain that
they would deploy behind him to the east, but they were
staying together. He motioned for Marianne to go to the
door and see what she could see.

Longarm watched as she went low on the floor and
peeked around the corner of the door at the lowest level
she could get her face to. She moved slowly so that her
movement would not attract attention. She watched for a

full five minutes. Finally, she pulled back and raised up and said, ''They're gone straight to the north of us and pulled up. It looks to be Verlene and Mrs. Sewell, and the best that I can tell, it's Shank and LeeRoy and the old man. I don't recognize the fourth person. It could be Joe.''

Longarm said, ''I was hoping that Shank was dead. You say they are all there?''

She nodded. ''Yes.''

He was much surprised. They apparently did not intend to surround him, at least not yet. As painful as it was to do, he had to take a look. He sidled around the far wall so he was out of sight through the open door, then got in behind Marianne, feeling the softness of her flesh as she leaned back into him, and took a quick look around the door frame. There was no mistake. They had parked the wagon about six hundred yards away and unhitched the team. The rest of the horses were being watered. One man was doing the job, and Longarm recognized J.J. and LeeRoy and Shank as they stood, staring at the cabin.

After a moment, the old man walked forward, putting his hands to his mouth, cupping them. He yelled out, his words carrying easily through the thin air, ''Longarm, we be knowin' you're in there. Ain't no way for you to get away. You let that girl come on out and we'll give you your life. That's the best bargain you're ever going to get.''

Longarm leaned away from the door, resting his back against the cabin wall. Marianne followed him. She looked up in his face. ''What does it mean?'' she said.

Longarm half smiled. ''It means that I'm damned if I do and I'm damned if I don't.''

Marianne said, ''If I were to go to them, they'd leave you alone. Do you believe that?''

172

Longarm smiled again. "Do you believe it? What do you think?"

She said, after a moment's thought, "No, your reputation is that you never quit, that you would always be chasing them. They couldn't afford to let you live. No, I don't believe them."

"But Verlene and Mrs. Sewell are there. Wouldn't you feel better with them?"

She gave him an odd look. "You still don't really understand me, do you?"

He looked down at the dusty floor. "Marianne, we haven't exactly known each other that long. Sometimes I don't even know myself."

The voice of J.J. Hunsacker came floating through the hot air to them. "Longarm, we ain't going to give you until the cows come home to make up your mind. We could put a hail of bullets right through that open door and fix your wagon pretty good. We could get enough lead bouncing around in there that would put more holes in you than a sieve. If you're as smart as you think you are, you'd turn that girl loose and save your life."

Marianne said, looking up at him again, "There's nothing really to do."

Longarm shook his head. "All I'll do is push you out that door."

Marianne said, "You go lay down there where you were when I dressed your wounds on your bedroll."

He gave her a questioning look. "Whatever for?"

She was studying his face, looking into his eyes. "Are you a good shot?"

He frowned, wrinkling his brow. "I don't know what you mean by a good shot. I reckon I'm a fair shot, yes."

"No, I mean with a handgun in close quarters. Is your hand steady and your nerves good?"

He wrinkled his brow even more. "I don't know what you are talking about, Marianne. But yes, I reckon I'm a pretty good shot at close quarters. I wouldn't be alive otherwise. In fact, I wouldn't be alive in any kind of quarters other than being a damn good shot."

She said, "That's what I thought."

"So? What does all this mean?"

"You go lay down on your bedroll and have your guns real handy."

"What are you going to do?"

"I'm going to get them up here in range for you."

Longarm said, "Like hell you are! Marianne, I don't know what you're up to, but . . ."

He got no further. She had suddenly stepped into the opening of the door and called in a loud voice, "J.J.! LeeRoy! Come here!"

Longarm moved swiftly to lay on his bedroll. It was placed at an angle to the door so that anyone coming through it would have to look to their left to see him.

The horses were jammed against the wall. He said, "What in the hell are you doing, Marianne? You're going to get yourself hurt."

She said, without turning her head, "You be sure you can shoot straight. Is your gun loaded?"

"I told you, I don't carry dull knives or unloaded guns."

Marianne called out again. "LeeRoy, he's wounded and he's about to die. Come up. He might be able to shoot me if I try and make a run for it, but he's very weak. He can't even sit up. Hurry!"

174

From behind her, Longarm said, "Have you ever considered going on the stage, Marianne?"

"You know," she said, "this may not be right. I don't like this, Longarm. You're going to make too good of a target. Why don't you get up and get out the back window. There's nobody out there to see you."

Seeing the rightness of it, he said, "I think you're on the right path, but I ain't sure I can get out the window."

She said urgently, "You've got to. They're starting this way."

"All of them?"

"Yes, except for the women. The four men are coming."

Longarm said, "I'm trying. I'm up on all fours. I can't take my rifle. That window ledge looks about six feet high. My God, I can't believe how weak I am." Holding his hand to his side, he hobbled over to the window, and painfully eased one leg over the rock ledge. "What are they doing now?"

"They are still coming. No, wait! One is staying behind. I think it's Joe."

Longarm said, "Are you sure Joe is with them?"

Marianne said, "It might not be, but LeeRoy and Shank and J.J. are coming on."

Longarm said, "I'm about out this window and I've only got six slugs in this gun. What are you going to do when they walk through that door and don't see nobody?"

"That's your job. I'm just supposed to get them in here."

"Why don't you get some saddle blankets off those horses, and my saddlebags and the canteen and anything else that you can think of, and put them in my bedroll. Maybe they will think that it's me under there."

She didn't wait to answer. She commenced to gather up what she could under the bedroll, putting his saddle up at the top, spreading a blanket over it so that it looked like he was using the saddle for a pillow. It was not very deceiving, but then it did not have to deceive very long. Through the window, Longarm said, "How far off are they?"

Marianne stepped to the door and looked around. "About a hundred yards. No, now they've stopped."

Longarm said, "Are they armed?"

"Yes, but they don't have their guns in their hands. Well, Mr. Hunsacker is carrying a rifle, but he's just got it loose in his hand."

"Are they still coming?"

Marianne said, "No, they've stopped again. Mr. Hunsacker is yelling something."

They both listened. Hunsacker shouted, "Longarm, if you be in there, now's the time to get out. We're liable to come in there with gunplay and you're going to be mighty sorry."

Unbidden, Marianne stepped back into the door. She called out, "Mr. Hunsacker, he may be dead. I'm scared to get close to him. There's blood all over the floor and all over his blanket."

At the window, Longarm heard J.J. Hunsacker's voice clearly. "Well, I don't wish him no harm." Then the old man chuckled. "Other than a long, slow, painful death out here amongst these rattlesnakes and big spiders. Why don't you come on, girl?"

She said, "I'll get my stuff, but I need somebody to help me carry it out and help me with the horses."

Hunsacker said, "Well, that varmint of a marshal better

176

not give us no trouble or he's going to wish he'd never been born.''

Outside the window, Longarm slowly pulled the hammer back on his revolver. With his eye at the bottom of the window, he could see out through the front door. He saw a pair of legs, then a half body, and then the bodies of the three men suddenly appear, walking toward the cabin. In another minute, he saw the faces of the old man and LeeRoy and Shank. Marianne had moved to the right of the door. Longarm waited. It would be another ten seconds. He steeled his hand, as weak as it was. He was going to give them a chance to surrender if that was what they chose.

The three men stood just inside the cabin, looking around. The old man had a carbine rifle that hung loosely in his hands. At his side, LeeRoy and Shank were both holding pistols down by their sides. They looked around. LeeRoy said, ''Well, hell. There ain't nobody in here!'' He glanced over at Marianne. ''There ain't nobody in here, woman. Where is that sonofabitch?''

That instant, Longarm suddenly stood up outside the window. He said, ''Here's that sonofabitch, right here, right now!''

Their heads swiveled around toward him, turning away from Marianne. J.J. Hunsacker said, ''Why, Longarm! You low-down, sneaky sonofabitch! You got a woman to do your lying for you?''

Longarm crouched so that he made as small a target as possible. ''Throw down your guns, right now!'' he said.

J.J. looked around at Marianne. He motioned his rifle toward her.

Longarm said, ''Drop that weapon, J.J. Hunsacker, or I'll take you quick and sudden!''

LeeRoy and Shank raised their revolvers and fired, the shots coming almost together, the noise making a loud booming racket in the stone cabin. Longarm felt his face sting as the bullets hit the rock around the window opening, spraying him with splinters. In almost the same heartbeat, he had fired, taking Shank on the left with a bullet right in the chest. The slug knocked the young man backwards. He saw the man's gun slipping out of his lifeless fingers.

Without pause, Longarm was already aiming at LeeRoy, who was trying to get off a second shot. Longarm's revolver roared toward the bandit. He had tried for a throat shot, but the bullet went high and hit LeeRoy just above his mouth, blowing his nose back into his head. The shot sent him toppling backwards, almost as if the slug had struck bone.

But Longarm had no time to observe the results of his shot. Even as LeeRoy was falling to the cabin floor, Longarm was swinging on the old man, centering the sight of his revolver on J.J.'s chest.

The old man had his rifle almost to his shoulders, pointing directly at Longarm in the window.

Longarm said, "Drop it, J.J.! Put that rifle down or I'll put a hole right through you!"

For an instant, Longarm wasn't certain whether the old man was going to stop or would have to be shot. The man's hand slowed, and the butt of the rifle never reached his shoulder. Instead, he slowly lowered the weapon until the carbine was hanging by his side.

Longarm said, "Drop it all the way, old man!"

J.J. Hunsacker let go of his carbine. It clattered to the dust floor of the cabin. He stared at Longarm with hate in his face and his eyes and his voice. He said, "You dirty

178

sonofabitch. What are you doing out there? You're supposed to be in here, bad wounded or dead.''

Longarm said, "I'm out here because that's just where I am. Now, get your hands up.''

The old man's voice was husky. "You kilt my two boys, you sonofabitch," he said.

"And I'm about to kill their father if he doesn't get his hands in the air.''

The old man slowly lifted his arms. "You ain't done with me yet, Longarm. I'll still find a way to fix your wagon.''

Longarm said, 'Not today and not anytime soon, I don't reckon.''

J.J. Hunsacker jerked his head backwards. "There's still some of us out there.''

"There is one of you out there—Joe, the last son.''

"Then you know that you've still got trouble.''

Longarm shook his head slowly. "No, J.J. *You've* got trouble. Joe ain't going to be no trouble to me, not as long as I've got you.''

"What do you mean, you murdering bastard?''

Longarm said, "If there's any murdering bastard around here, it's you and we both know that. Now, you're going to tell Joe to come on up here and give himself up.''

"What if I just tell you to go to Hell? Would you shoot me down like you did my boys?''

Longarm said, "They were both given the chance to surrender, J.J. You know that. They both got off the first shots, and you know that." The heat was beginning to beat on his back, and he could still feel the weakness in his body. "I'm not going to tell you many more times. I want you to turn around and talk.''

Longarm glanced over at Marianne as he gave the old man the order. She was wide-eyed and worried-looking. She had placed herself in between the horses. He would have guessed that Old Man Hunsacker would have liked nothing better than to get a bullet at her. As Longarm caught her eye, she gave him a slow smile, the slightest quiver in her lips. She was brave enough, and more, but it took a strong man, much less a woman, to stand by unarmed while guns were roaring all around you.

Longarm looked at the two men lying on the floor. Now, they didn't seem so dangerous or so bad. One look back at the old man's face as he sat there, deliberating Longarm's instructions, was enough to remove any sense of pity in Longarm's mind. He said, "Are you going to go to the door and do what I asked, or not?"

Hunsacker said, "Go to Hell."

Longarm knew that he had to finish the play in a hurry. Even leaning in the window casing, he could feel his strength ebbing. He needed a long rest. He needed this mess cleaned up. He said, as he lowered the angle of his aim, "Well, Mr. Hunsacker, I reckon if you refuse to do what I tell you, I'm going to have to shoot you in the thigh. If I do that, I'm going to have to break the bone. Now, you wished for me a long, slow death, and I can assure you that you'll have one."

"Oh, yeah? And what are you going to do after you do that? You'll have Joe to deal with, that's what."

"I'm not too worried about dealing with Joe. Are you going to call him up here, or am I going to kill him? One way or the other—it makes no difference to me."

Before he moved, the old man glanced over at Marianne.

He said, "How much money did he promise you, you cheap little whore?"

Longarm said sharply, "Shut up, Hunsacker."

But Marianne said, "You don't have to answer for me, Deputy Long." She turned to J.J. "I didn't do this for money, Mr. Hunsacker, but I doubt if you can understand that. There's a whore in here, all right, but it's not me."

Longarm let the hammer down on his revolver and then pulled it back again—the one sound that people about to be shot find so frightening. He said, thrusting out his arm and aiming at J.J. Hunsacker's leg, only some ten feet away, "Well, what's your answer? Are you going to turn around and go to that door? I'm going to fire in less than ten seconds."

It took Hunsacker only an instant to make up his mind. As if he were spinning on a dime, he suddenly turned, showing his back to Longarm, and said, "There, I'm facing the door. What do you want me to do now?"

Longarm said, "I want you to walk up to that door with your arms down. You're going to call Joe."

Slowly, the old man lowered his arms cautiously, as if he were afraid the movement would draw Longarm's eye. He said, "Like this?"

"Yeah, that would be about right."

"Now what?"

"Now I want you to step into the opening of that door and call Joe down here."

The old man took a few steps toward the door and began to shout. As he did so, Longarm looked toward Marianne and motioned for her to come over. As she worked her way out from behind the horses, Longarm began climbing up through the window. He handed her his revolver as she

181

came near. Their eyes touched as she took the weapon, almost as if she was recognizing the trust he was placing in her. She pointed the revolver at J.J. Hunsacker's back. Longarm clambered over the sill as quietly as he could, but he was weak and it was hard work and he knew it was making his breathing heavier.

J.J. Hunsacker started to look back, and Longarm said, "Keep your eyes outside." He didn't want J.J. to know that there was a woman holding the revolver at him. It might have made him do something foolish.

The old man turned back and yelled, "Joe! Joe! Come on!"

Longarm was inside the cabin. He leaned back against the opening of the window, resting. After a second, he took the revolver from Marianne's hand and nodded. Their eyes met again. Longarm gave her a brief smile. He pushed himself away from the wall, and then walked up behind the old man, taking off his hat as he did so he was not so easily noticed from outside.

He reckoned the last Hunsacker was still a good way out in the desert, but he didn't want to take any chances. He said, "Take a step out that door, J.J. Holler and wave your arms. Tell him I'm done for. Make him come on. Tell him it's all over."

The old man said in a low voice, "I wish to hell that was the straight truth. It still might be—the day ain't out yet. We might still get a chance at you."

"I wish you'd quit wishing me in the grave, J.J. You might be giving me some ideas about you. Now, get it straight in your head, either that boy comes in or you go down. It's your choice. So put some persuasion in your voice with that in mind."

Chapter 11

It was a week later, and Longarm was lying in a bed in a hotel room in Reno. Marianne was lying beside him. He was practically well and almost healed up, even though he still wore bandages on the two wounds in his side. They had been put on by a proper doctor and looked neat, with plaster tape so they wouldn't be slipping all over the place. The doctor had complimented Marianne on the delicacy of her work with the red-hot pocket knife. He'd said, "You got the infection just at the right place, and you cauterized the wound so that it couldn't get reinfected. That was good work. You probably saved this man's life."

But it had still been a time getting from where they had been inside the cabin and into Reno, taking three hard days with two bad prisoners—four if you counted Verlene and Minnie Sewell, both very angry with Longarm for what he had done to their plans and their future. Marianne had tried to talk some sense into them. The Hunsackers had never meant to make any sort of permanent arrangement, but had simply meant to use them and cast them aside when they were no longer valuable or when there was some fast moving that needed to be done.

They had reached Reno, and Longarm had turned the remaining Hunsackers over to the local marshal and the sheriff of the county. In all, he had accounted for eight of the Hunsacker gang. He was delighted to find that his shot at Jim Stock when he was on the elevated platform in the back of the wagon had done the job. Stock had no longer been available to fire his high-powered rifle. The others had fallen as a result of Longarm's bullets as well. Now, the last two were in jail. He and Marianne had survived the mess. He had considered turning Minnie Sewell and Verlene in for any number of infractions, but in the end, he simply cut them adrift and told them both to go their own way.

He glanced over at Marianne. They were both naked, except for the bandages that Longarm was wearing. He said, "You reckon we ought to go down to the dining room and have some lunch?"

She stared up at the ceiling, her eyes lazy and languid. "Right now, I don't think I feel like moving at all. I think I could stay in this bed for another week."

"So could I if I had my way about it, but I don't." In fact, he was leaving the next morning to return to Denver and his boss Billy Vail and his dressmaker lady friend and his regular poker partners. It had been a long time since he had been in his own bed at the boardinghouse where he stayed, and eaten decently for a stretch of time. He was looking forward to it, but he also hated to leave this very interesting woman.

He turned and propped his head up on his hand so that

he could look down and along her body. Her figure was almost as perfect as any he had ever seen. He tried to commit it to memory. Her breasts were like oversized ripe golden apples, topped with dark cherries. The nipples seemed to come out of the rosettes in hard dark cylinders. Then her body fell away to a flat stomach with a tiny navel. There were tiny golden hairs along her body that narrowed down to the mound of golden fleece that rose from the hill where her legs met. Her hips flared out in a provocative way, as did the flat stomach as it gave rise to the perfectly shaped breasts. The hair of the mound was brighter than her other hair, but it seemed to have a tinge around the edges that made Longarm want to put it in his mouth and nibble at it.

They had just finished making love, and he had spent time with her legs wrapped around his head and his face pressed into that moist warm nest. He could still smell the taste of her in his mouth. It was the second time they had made love since they had awakened that morning, both times being a perfect tumble that was wet and warm and full of soaring, aching climaxes that seemed to go on and on and on. He was pretty sure that he had a couple more times in him before they went to sleep that night, but he needed to get some food down and get a little rest.

She looked over at him as if she was reading his thoughts. "You're not tiring yourself out, are you?" she said.

He said, "How can a man get tired of good whiskey, good horses, and good pussy? That doesn't happen."

She smiled and ran her hand through his hair. She said, "Longarm, you are some man. Did you know that?"

"Marianne, I've got a lot to thank you for—a great deal. I reckon you saved my life."

"Well, I can say the same to you. I don't know where I would have finally ended up if you hadn't come along."

"What do you intend to do now?"

She shrugged. "I don't know. Anything but whore. I'm all through with that. In fact, that proposition with the Hunsackers—I had already made up my mind that that would be the last. Of course, I knew we weren't going there to get married. I don't know what Verlene thought, or Minnie Sewell thought, but I knew what it was all about. Now I have no idea but maybe get some sort of job. I've got some money saved."

Longarm said gently, "I could let you have some more. I have a thousand dollars I could let loose if you need it."

She gave him a mocking smile. "I thought you wanted me to quit whoring."

He gave her a stern look. "Hell, woman. Don't twist my words. This would be between friends."

"We are square, Longarm. Get your mind settled on that."

Longarm said, "I don't see it that way, but however you figure it. I wouldn't think you would have much problem snagging a husband if you go to some part of the country where you aren't known. I imagine the young bucks at county fairs would be lining up for you."

She gave him a long, slow look. "Would you be volunteering for the job?"

He answered her seriously. "Marianne, honey, I'm a United States deputy marshal. I can't get married. It just don't go with the job, but if I wasn't what I am, your past wouldn't stop me from marrying you in a minute."

She smiled at him and colored slightly. "That may be the sweetest thing anybody's ever said to me."

Longarm looked at her. It had been one of the hardest, roughest, meanest jobs he had ever done since he had been in the Marshals Service, but he had at least had the satisfaction of coming out of it alive having cleaned out the Hunsackers' nest. Perhaps he'd also had a hand in the making of a fine woman. He didn't know when he'd ever been so taken with a woman.

But all in all, he was glad it was over. In a way, he was going to be glad to get on that train the next morning. He said to her as he bent to her lips, "Whatever you do, though, take it slow and be careful."

She curled her arm and pulled his face down to hers. Just before their lips touched, she said, "You're the one who's got to be careful."

In another moment, he understood what she meant.

Watch for

LONGARM AND THE DANISH DAMES

Eighteenth GIANT LONGARM novel

and

LONGARM AND THE COLORADO COUNTERFEITER

241st novel in the exciting LONGARM series
from Jove

Coming in January!

Robinson Crusoe

DANIEL DEFOE

Edited with an Introduction and Notes by
JOHN RICHETTI

PENGUIN CLASSICS
an imprint of
PENGUIN BOOKS

PENGUIN CLASSICS

Published by the Penguin Group
Penguin Books Ltd, 80 Strand, London WC2R 0RL, England
Penguin Group (USA) Inc., 375 Hudson Street, New York, New York 10014, USA
Penguin Group (Canada), 90 Eglinton Avenue East, Suite 700, Toronto, Ontario, Canada M4P 2Y3
(a division of Pearson Penguin Canada Inc.)
Penguin Ireland, 25 St Stephen's Green, Dublin 2, Ireland (a division of Penguin Books Ltd)
Penguin Group (Australia), 707 Collins Street, Melbourne, Victoria 3008, Australia
(a division of Pearson Australia Group Pty Ltd)
Penguin Books India Pvt Ltd, 11 Community Centre, Panchsheel Park, New Delhi – 110 017, India
Penguin Group (NZ), 67 Apollo Drive, Rosedale, Auckland 0632, New Zealand
(a division of Pearson New Zealand Ltd)
Penguin Books (South Africa) (Pty) Ltd, Block D, Rosebank Office Park,
181 Jan Smuts Avenue, Parktown North, Gauteng 2193, South Africa

Penguin Books Ltd, Registered Offices: 80 Strand, London WC2R 0RL, England

www.penguin.com

First published in 1719
This edition first published in Penguin Classics 2001
This edition published 2013
002

Editorial material © John Richetti, 2001
All rights reserved

The moral right of the editor has been asserted

Cover design Coralie Bickford-Smith

Set in 9.47/11.95 pt Ehrhardt MT
Printed in Great Britain by Clays Ltd, St Ives plc

A CIP catalogue record for this book is available from the British Library

ISBN: 978-0-141-39340-7

www.greenpenguin.co.uk

CONTENTS

CHRONOLOGY

1660 Born in London (exact date unknown), son of James Foe and Alice Foe
1662 The Act of Uniformity passed. The Foes followed the lead of their minister, Samuel Annesley, and left the Church of England to become Presbyterian dissenters
1665-6 The Plague and the Great Fire of London
c. 1671-9 Attended school of the Revd James Fisher at Dorking, Surrey, and then the Dissenting Academy of the Revd Charles Morton, Newington Green, north of London
c. 1683 Established as a hosiery merchant in London, living in Cornhill, near the Royal Exchange
1684 Married Mary Tuffley and received a dowry of £3,700
1685-92 Fought in the rebellion against King James II led by the Duke of Monmouth. Prosperous businessman dealing in hosiery, tobacco, wine and other goods. Travels extensively on business in England and also in Europe
1688 James II forced to abdicate and William of Orange becomes William III of England
1692 Declared bankrupt for £17,000 and imprisoned for debt
1694 Established a brick and tile factory at Tilbury, in Essex
1695 Began to call himself De Foe
1697 First published book, *An Essay on Projects*, a series of proposals for radical social and economic changes
1697-1701 Agent for William III in England and Scotland
1701 *The True-Born Englishman*, a poetic satire of xenophobia and a defence of the (Dutch) King William III
1702 Death of William III and the accession of Queen Anne. *The*

Shortest Way with the Dissenters, a satiric attack on High Church extremists

1703   Arrested for writing the satiric pamphlet *The Shortest Way with the Dissenters*, charged with sedition, committed to Newgate Prison and sentenced to stand in the pillory for three days. Published the poem *A Hymn to the Pillory* and an authorized collection of his writings. Released through the influence of the powerful politician Robert Harley, but his brick and tile factory fails while he is in prison. Bankrupt again

1704–13   Secret agent and political journalist for Harley and other ministers; travelled widely in England and Scotland promoting the union of the two countries. Wrote single-handedly what was first called *A Weekly Review of the Affairs of France* and later *A Review of the State of the English Nation*, a pro-government news sheet appearing as often as three times a week

1707   Union of England and Scotland

1710   Tories come to power

1713–14   Arrested several times for debt and for his political writings but released through government influence

1714   Death of Queen Anne and the accession of George I, Elector of Hanover; fall of Robert Harley and the Tory government

1715   *The Family Instructor*, the first of Defoe's conduct books

1719   *Robinson Crusoe, The Farther Adventures of Robinson Crusoe*

1720   *Memoirs of a Cavalier, Captain Singleton, Serious Reflections . . . of Robinson Crusoe*

1722   *Moll Flanders, Religious Courtship, A Journal of the Plague Year, Colonel Jack*

1724   *Roxana, A General History of the Pyrates, A Tour Thro' the Whole Island of Great Britain* (3 volumes, 1724–6)

1725   *The Complete English Tradesman* (volume II in 1727)

1726   *The Political History of the Devil*

1727   *Conjugal Lewdness, An Essay on the History and Reality of Apparitions, A New Family Instructor*

1728   *Augusta Triumphans, A Plan of the English Commerce*

1729   *The Compleat English Gentleman* (not published until 1890)

1731   Died 24 April in Ropemaker's Alley, London, in debt, hiding from creditors

INTRODUCTION

When *Robinson Crusoe* appeared in April 1719, Daniel Defoe was fifty-nine years old. Although he had begun his adult life as a businessman and ambitious entrepreneur, bankruptcy and imprisonment for debt in 1692 had forced him to turn to his pen to support his large family (he and his wife had seven children). In the first two decades of the eighteenth century, he had produced an astonishing amount of writing as poet, political and economic pamphleteer, historian, moralist and jack-of-all-trades journalist. Defoe is remembered (vaguely) by posterity as the man who wrote *Robinson Crusoe*, but that classic represents an entirely unrepresentative fraction of his voluminous literary production. As a professional writer struggling to earn a living in those years, Defoe was in the thick of new developments that look forward to modern mass print media: the emergence in London at the beginning of the eighteenth century of a substantial market-place for reading matter and a large audience hungry for print, for books, pamphlets and newspapers in unprecedented quantities. Whatever *Robinson Crusoe* has become for its millions of readers since Defoe's day, he wrote it like everything else he produced in his long career as a writer to sell in that market to that new audience in the emerging culture of printed matter. *Robinson Crusoe* must be one of the most popular books ever written, reprinted continuously and translated into many languages (one estimate is that by the end of the nineteenth century it had appeared in at least seven hundred editions, translations and imitations). Defoe's hero is instantly and universally recognized in his goatskin clothes, an archetype of modern heroic individualism and self-reliance – the man surviving alone on a deserted island. But for all that enduring and universal appeal, Defoe's book grows out of the early-eighteenth-century English world of the new market-place for print in which its author earned a precarious living.

Defoe was born in the autumn of 1660 in the parish of St Giles,

Cripplegate, just north of the old City of London. His father James Foe (as the family was known) was a tallow-chandler, a merchant who manufactured and sold candles made from animal fat, a trade at which he prospered and rose to be an eminent merchant in the City. In 1662 the Foes and the congregation they belonged to followed their pastor, Samuel Annesley, and became Dissenters, non-conforming Protestants (Presbyterians), separate from the established Church of England which had demanded what many people considered unacceptably strict adherence to its principles by the Act of Uniformity promulgated that year. The Foes belonged to the solid middle tier of the merchant class that Napoleon was thinking of a century later when he called England a nation of shopkeepers. Defoe had a privileged, quite comfortable childhood in this prosperous and pious household. The young Daniel received his higher education at one of the best of the so-called academies established for the children of prosperous Dissenters, who were by law deprived of most civil rights and therefore excluded from attending the universities at Oxford and Cambridge. Defoe entered Charles Morton's academy in Newington Green in 1674, and the excellent education provided there was probably better and certainly more useful than the traditional curriculum based largely on classical literature at the old universities. Morton was an Oxford-trained clergyman and scholar (who later became president of Harvard College), and his students were instructed in English (rather than in Latin) in the traditional subjects but also in modern languages and modern science and philosophy, including Locke's *Essay concerning Human Understanding* (1690), then banned at Oxford.

Defoe's biographers have concluded that he had serious thoughts in 1681 of becoming a clergyman, but after what seems to have been a crisis in his faith and in his commitment to such a career he decided instead to go into business. That choice, those alternative careers, will continue to resonate in all of Defoe's writing, where the sometimes conflicting (although often complementary) demands of religion and commerce, piety and secular ambition, share the stage and occupy the thoughts of both author and characters. Instead of a minister, Defoe became a wholesale merchant in stockings, a hosier, part of the expanding trade in manufactured clothing, a growth industry in those days as domestic production of wearing apparel began to give way to mass production. He dealt extensively in wine and tobacco as well, and he travelled widely in England and perhaps to the Continent during the mid 1680s. Defoe had large ambitions as a businessman, and he seems to have played recklessly for high stakes in land speculation. Legal records indicate that he was involved in eight law suits in those years. By 1692, thanks to serious losses of cargo at sea during the war with France, he was bankrupt for the immense sum of £17,000 (in modern purchasing power more than £500,000 or $750,000), and the closing years of the seventeenth century found him surviving by various odd occupations and government posts: he served as one of the trustees of the government lottery in 1695 and 1696, and from 1695 to 1699 he was accountant for the government duty on glassware and bottles. In 1694 he opened a brick and roof tile factory in Tilbury, east of London, on the Thames, which seems to have prospered and allowed him to pay off many of his debts and to set up as a substantial householder in the London suburbs. In 1697 he published his first book, *An Essay on Projects* (a collection of proposals for radical social and economic reforms such as a rational banking system, a national highway commission, improvements in social welfare and in female education). From that point on the sheer quantity of Defoe's literary production is extraordinary, thousands and thousands of pages on every conceivable subject in a wide variety of forms and formats. During the early years of the eighteenth century, he was an active political pamphleteer, defending the policies of his hero, King William III, the Dutch Prince of Orange, who had succeeded to the throne upon the forced abdication of his brother-in-law, James II, in 1688. By 1703, Defoe became virtually a full-time writer and in the years that followed one of the most prominent (for his enemies, notorious) journalists and political writers (and poets) of the time. He seems to have been employed by William's government to defend their policies, and he was certainly a paid political writer and operative by the time Queen Anne succeeded William in 1702.

A transforming event in Defoe's early life as a writer came in 1703 when he was arrested for publishing the previous year a satirical attack on conservative, High Church extremists who wished to intensify the suppression of religious nonconformity. *The Shortest Way with the Dissenters* parodies the High Church position at its most radical and violently intolerant, concluding with the exhortation to 'crucifie the Thieves . . . let the Obstinate be rul'd with the Rod of Iron'. The government saw the pamphlet as inflammatory, seditious in its effects rather than merely ironic, and Defoe was arrested and eventually sentenced to stand in the pillory (a contraption that held in place a man's head and arms and often enough exposed him to the sometimes fatal physical abuse of the spectators) for three days and to serve an indefinite jail term. He spent six months in Newgate prison, and when he emerged, thanks to a pardon obtained through the influence of Robert Harley, the Speaker of the House of Commons, his brick and tile factory had failed and he was bankrupt for the second time. He became an informant and secret agent for Harley, and his production as a writer was from then on prolific in its extent and variety. Most remarkable of all was *A Weekly Review of the Affairs of France, Purged from the Errors and Partiality of News-Writers and Petty Statesmen of all Sides*, a thrice weekly political news and commentary sheet that Defoe produced single-handedly from 1704 through 1713. In addition, he turned out in these years a stream of other journalism, more political polemics, a book-length verse treatise on government, *Jure Divino* (1706), a satirical political allegory, *The Consolidator* (1705), a long history of the recent political union of England and Scotland, *The History of the Union* (1709), and two works on what we would call economics, *An Essay upon Public Credit* and *An Essay upon Loans* (1710).

Nominally a Whig, Defoe was employed by the Tory Harley, and his support of Harley's government's efforts when it came to power in 1710 to end the war with France provoked attacks from those who saw him as a turncoat. Something like a crisis for Defoe and possibly for the nation arrived in 1713. Queen Anne had no surviving children, and by the terms of the Act of Settlement promulgated when James II was forced to abdicate, the throne was to bypass the Stuart Pretender, James (Queen Anne's brother), in exile at the French court and go to the Elector of Hanover in Germany. The Stuarts had considerable support in England, and the Jacobite (after *Jacobus*, Latin for James) threat was real and urgent as the Queen was unlikely to produce an heir. Defoe quickly wrote several inflammatory anti-Jacobite pamphlets, including *An Answer to a Question that Nobody thinks of, viz. But What If the Queen Should Die?* (1713), whose ironies were not understood or appreciated. Once again, his enemies managed to have him arrested. It took a pardon from the Queen (obtained by the ministry) to free him.

When his patron Harley (and the Tory government) fell from power in 1714 with the death of Queen Anne and the accession of George I, the German Elector of Hanover, Defoe had to scramble to survive and to find new patrons for his work as a writer. It is now known that he went to work for the new Whig government as a covert moderating influence through his political journalism on extreme Tory opinion. At the behest of the ministry, he edited the Tory monthly journal *Mercurius Politicus* from 1716 to 1720. He also in 1717 infiltrated the rabidly Tory *Mist's Weekly Journal*, although his voice was soon recognized and he was attacked by Whig pamphleteers. In later years he continued this secret undermining of the opposition in his work for other papers. What makes all this journalistic work of interest for the modern student of Defoe and especially for readers of his fictional narratives is his extraordinary capacity for disguise and impersonation, his facility for projecting himself into the personalities and ideas of other people, to ventriloquize or mimic so effectively the voices of other people.

It is perhaps no accident that the political journalist and secret agent, the government's mole in the opposition press, turned in 1719 to writing fiction, since for most of his life he had been playing roles and assuming identities distinct from his own. *The Life and Strange Surprising Adventures of Robinson Crusoe of York, Mariner*, followed a few months later by its sequel, *The Farther Adventures of Robinson Crusoe*, is the beginning of a remarkable series of fictionalized autobiographical narratives that we nowadays call novels: *Memoirs of a Cavalier, Captain Singleton* (1720); *Moll Flanders, A Journal of the Plague Year, Colonel Jack* (1722); and *Roxana* (1724). But even as he was churning out these fictions, he continued to write prolifically in other formats and genres. The list of just some of his books during these last twelve years of his life is varied and extensive: *Religious Courtship* (1722), *A New Voyage Round the World* (1724), *A Tour thro' the Whole Island of Great Britain* (3 volumes, 1724–6), *The Complete English Tradesman* (2 volumes, 1725–7), *The Political History of the Devil* (1726), *Conjugal Lewdness; or Matrimonial Whoredom. A Treatise concerning the Use and Abuse of the Marriage Bed* (1727), *An Essay on the History and Reality of Apparitions* (1727), *A Plan of the English Commerce* (1728) and *The Compleat English Gentleman* (written 1729).

Like these multifarious productions – conduct books, moral polemics, travel narratives, popular economic and theological treatises, collections of ghost stories – *Robinson Crusoe* is first and foremost a response to commercial possibilities and opportunities in the early-eighteenth-century publishing market, Defoe's effort to give the public what he thought they would buy. Capitalizing on its instant popularity, Defoe produced a sequel in that same year, in which Crusoe not only returns to his island but travels to the Far East, to China, and overland through Asia to Russia and then home to England. The subtitle of the first part appeals breathlessly to an audience envisioned as hungry for narratives of travel to exotic places, for sensational and unusual adventures and breathtaking wonder and mystery.

The germ for the book seems to have come from the experiences of an actual marooned sailor, the Scotsman Alexander Selkirk (1676–1721), who was part of a privateering expedition of several ships led by William Dampier to prey on Spanish merchant ships. In 1704, Selkirk quarrelled with his captain, Thomas Stradling, and asked to be set ashore on one of the small islands of the Juan Fernandez group some three hundred and fifty miles off the coast of Chile in the Pacific. (This island, Mas à Tierra, is now officially called Isla Robinson Crusoe, even though Defoe placed Crusoe's island thousands of miles to the north in the Caribbean!) Four and a half years later, Selkirk was picked up by an English ship under the command of Captain Woodes Rogers, who had been part of the expedition that dropped Selkirk on the island. When Selkirk returned to England in 1711, he achieved a certain fame when Richard Steele wrote about him in 1713–14 in his periodical *The Englishman*. Defoe himself may also have met Selkirk, but the sailor's story provided only the bare starting point. Selkirk's tale is a tabloid headline – SAILOR SURVIVES FOUR YEARS ON DESERTED ISLAND!, a curious anecdote of a sojourn in which, as Steele reports it, the sailor reverted to a kind of natural state, living naked as his clothes wore out, learning to do without bread and salt for his meat, catching goats by running after them on bare feet, which grew hardened with use. In the interview with Steele, Selkirk remembered his days on the island as idyllic: 'This manner of Life grew so exquisitely pleasant, that he never had a Moment heavy upon his Hands; his Nights were untroubled, and his Days joyous, from the Practice of Temperance and Exercise. It was his Manner to use stated Hours and Places for Exercises of Devotion, which he performed aloud, in order to keep up the Faculties of Speech, and to utter himself with greater Energy.'[1] So Selkirk's story celebrates the virtues of isolation: regression to a primitive or natural state accompanied by sentimental, unwordly contentment in delicious solitude. He tells Steele that he 'frequently bewailed his Return to the World, which could not, he said, with all its Enjoyments, restore him to the Tranquility of his Solitude'.[2] Defoe's narrative largely avoids those sentimental popular themes and delivers instead a detailed account of the narrator's physical survival on the island that includes a complex rendition of his psychological and religious development in an alienating, a distinctly dangerous solitude.

Literary historians have singled out *Robinson Crusoe* as perhaps the first true instance in English of what we now call the realistic novel. They mean that Defoe's book fairly consistently renders its main character and narrator as a particularized individual situated in very recent history and society in all their moral and ideological complexity. Crusoe is not simply as the title declares a 'mariner'. Thanks to the fullness and the acute particularity of the narrator and the world he evokes, Robinson is an individualized personality, an individual and not simply a type. Defoe implicitly subordinates the various moral and religious themes the book also explores to the rendering of that person in all his uniqueness and singularity. In place of Selkirk's pastoral (and clichéd) contentment, Defoe dramatizes his hero's deep ambivalence about his life and identity, his confusion, loneliness, sheer terror, self-loathing as well as growing self-knowledge and religious awareness gained through introspection that leads to confidence and to a powerful stewardship of the island and, finally, to successful mastering of the dangers that develop with the arrival of the cannibals and later of English mutineers. Crusoe's narrative in the long run offers what the novel since Defoe's time especially aspires to represent: personal growth, self-realization, development and maturation, as Robinson in his isolation overcomes his moral and physical limitations, finds solace and serenity in religious belief and material self-sufficiency and becomes master of himself as well as the lord of his island.

To be sure, for many twenty-first-century readers, Defoe's book anticipates rather than fulfils the modern realistic novel to which they are accustomed. Psychologically and ideologically, Crusoe necessarily belongs to his time and place rather than ours, and not everyone will find Crusoe's struggles with his faith in God's Providence compelling or even convincing. The immediacy that Defoe was after in Crusoe's 'Journal' doesn't really work. The journal is an awkward narrative device that ends abruptly when he runs out of ink, and the net effect of inserting that day-to-day account into the retrospective narrative is at first distracting and then insignificant. After a while, some readers will be just a bit bored by Crusoe's minute, wordy recording of his domestic arrangements on the island. Indeed, Defoe may have realized that the story of Crusoe's survival tends to drag, so he introduces some excitement with the arrival of the cannibals and the mutineers and turns the book into an adventure story and away from a psycho-religious drama of survival.

The crucial narrative feature of *Robinson Crusoe* that makes it much more than a thrilling adventure story, however, is the narrator's retrospective, intensely thoughtful perspective on his life. Robinson looks back from a wiser late middle age to his heedless and restless youthful days in which he disregarded his old father's advice to stay at home instead of going to sea. Crusoe's father counsels middle-class safety and comfort for his son as he evokes upper-class moral decadence and working-class ('the mechanick part of mankind') misery, but of course if we are to have a novel to read his son must disregard such sober advice, and these opening scenes of Crusoe's rebellion establish him in a paradoxical position that will be maintained in various senses throughout. Looking back on his life, Crusoe will evoke an ambitious and aggressive younger individual but will tell his story from the perspective of a wiser and more mature man who has learned about the limitations on individual action and ambition and who has acquired the proper sense of divine or providential arrangement in human affairs. Crusoe's divided personality returns us to the young Defoe, the pious Dissenter who wrestled with a call to the ministry but turned to the wheeling-and-dealing life of a businessman and entrepreneur in the emerging, rough and tumble proto-capitalist order of late-seventeenth-century England and Europe. On the one hand, Robinson Crusoe exemplifies the modern adventure capitalist, full of energy and resourceful ingenuity: his early years as a youthful trader to Africa (as well as a slave in Morocco) and a planter in Brazil show his determination and undaunted spirit. Crusoe is a young man ready to seek profit in the face of great risks and to manage his daring escape from slavery. On the other hand, Crusoe awakens to terror and existential confusion on his deserted island, alone and fearful of dangers all the more terrifying because they are unknown and uncertain. He avoids madness in this isolation by discovering God, by learning to read the Bible attentively and to find in his plight some signs of divine purpose and plan. Active and aggressive, independent and self-constructing, Robinson is also in time defined by his patient submission to God's will, by his pious acceptance of a mysterious fate he can't alter.

But Defoe also achieves a unique sense of another order of reality that contains the moral, social and theological realms in which Crusoe's personal drama unfolds. Realism derives from the Latin word *res* (thing, object, matter), and *Robinson Crusoe* is a pioneering work of modern novelistic realism because Defoe renders for much of the narrative the force and feel of Crusoe's material and phenomenal world with an unprecedented density and fine-grained immediacy and intricacy. Although Crusoe's narrative is necessarily much concerned with his own thoughts and feelings, Defoe manages things so that his hero, especially on the island, situates those inner subjective explorations in a precisely and often minutely observed external objective world. Looking back, Crusoe shows us how he instinctively cooperated with the sequences of natural phenomena, their movements and rhythms, and thus survived the shipwreck and the solitude. That relationship anticipates his larger strategy on the island where he learns to cooperate with the nature of things, accommodating himself to the form and feel of the natural world that he needs to cultivate and manage for his survival.

To some extent, however, that natural world resists such management, and in a larger philosophical sense opposes human ordering. For the single most moving example of this tension between the exactly observed world Crusoe renders and his own ordering and understanding, consider the following moment just after Crusoe's shipwreck:

I walk'd about on the shore, lifting up my hands, and my whole being, as I may say, wrapt up in the contemplation of my deliverance, making a thousand gestures and motions which I cannot describe, reflecting upon all my comrades that were drown'd, and that there should not be one soul sav'd but my self; for, as for them, I never saw them afterwards, or any sign of them, except three of their hats, one cap, and two shoes that were not fellows. (pp. 38–9)

'Deliverance' is a resonant moral-religious term that Crusoe will come to meditate upon during his early years on the island and learn to understand in a specific theological sense: he is delivered not simply from death but from spiritual indifference and ignorance of the workings of God's Providence. But notice how this psychological moment – Crusoe's longing for company and puzzlement over his singular fate – is inserted by the last almost casual but precise enumeration of objects in a faithfully observed world of absolutely random material happening where things manifest themselves without regard for order or human significance. That flotsam is endowed with tremendous pathos by Crusoe's lonely plight. In their irreducible and impenetrable randomness, their tenuous connections to the people who once wore them, those hats, the cap and those two shoes that don't match evoke a material world that is frighteningly arbitrary, impervious and indifferent to human emotions and ordering. These miscellaneous adjuncts of his dead comrades provide a bleak answer to

Crusoe's reflections about his survival: there is no meaning in events, just accident and chance, even in his singular fate. Like the single human footprint that Crusoe stumbles on later in the book, these objects and occurrences defy explanation and seem to exclude coherence or consolation. But for Crusoe they also provoke creative thought and transforming activity, and that is what makes him such a remarkable and resonant modern figure. In the midst of randomness and in the face of what looks like an arbitrary set of circumstances, he struggles and creates personal and satisfying order.

These are philosophical implications that Crusoe doesn't dwell on at all, and this is not a language that he or Defoe would have understood. From his first few terrified days on the island (sleeping in a tree, fearful of wild animals and even more of unknown human enemies), Robinson moves on without hesitation to the tactics for survival. Resourceful, efficient and enterprising, he quickly gets busy and sets about stripping the wrecked ship of anything useful. The heart of the book and the centre of its longest episode is Crusoe painfully establishing himself on the island, exploiting the materials and tools (crucial technological supplements to his own intelligence and resourcefulness) that he salvages from the ship, building his cave and strengthening his fortifications, exploring his habitat and categorizing its useful as well as edible flora and fauna, charting its tides and its seasons, learning to hunt and to gather, to farm, to bake bread, to domesticate animals, to make pots and baskets and furniture and to fashion rough clothing (and, eventually, that most English of artifacts, an umbrella) for himself. All this activity has proved perennially fascinating to readers ever since, and Defoe's novel has been most influential and imitated in this aspect. In edited and modernized versions, *Robinson Crusoe* is one of the most popular children's books ever written. Crusoe building his fort and playing house, as it were, may be what children respond to with most delight, although the cannibals and mutineers who come later in the adventure are also part of the book's perennial appeal.

Crusoe's efficient outer life of rational application, mastering 'mechanick' arts and steadily producing goods, is balanced by the inner anxieties that provoke it; the outer calm and control balances deep and recurrent inner turmoil that Crusoe also charts for us. He spends a good deal of his time wondering obsessively and despairingly about the meaning of his situation, wondering 'Why Providence should thus compleatly ruin its creatures, and render them so absolutely miserable, so without help abandon'd, so entirely depress'd, that it could hardly be rational to be thankful for such a life' (p. 51). After an illness that leaves him weak and disoriented, after a terrifying dream that seems to be a signal from God, Crusoe records the following internal colloquy: '*Why has God done this to me? What have I done to be thus us'd?* My conscience presently check'd me in that enquiry, as if I had blasphem'd, and methought it spoke to me like a voice; *WRETCH! dost thou ask what thou hast done!* look back upon a dreadful mis-spent life, and ask thy self *what thou hast not done?* ask, Why is it *that thou wert not long ago destroy'd?*' (pp. 74–5). His illness seems to be returning, so Crusoe takes up his Bible and finds in it at length words that seem to be meant for him and provoke an ecstatic conversion experience:

The impression of my dream reviv'd, and the words, *All these things have not brought thee to repentance*, ran seriously in my thought: I was earnestly begging of God to give me repentance, when it happen'd providentially the very day that reading the Scripture, I came to these words, *He is exalted a prince and a saviour, to give repentance, and to give remission*: I threw down the book, and with my heart as well as my hands lifted up to Heaven, in a kind of extasy of joy, I cry'd out aloud, *Jesus, thou son of* David, *Jesus, thou exalted prince and saviour, give me repentance!* (p. 77)

One scholarly school of thought has identified *Robinson Crusoe* as rooted in Puritan spiritual autobiography, and such interpretations direct us to passages like this one as central to the book's meanings. Puritans and other pious Protestants in the seventeenth and early eighteenth centuries were encouraged to keep religious diaries and to write spiritual autobiographies, accounts of how they came to feel that they were saved, records of their deepest feelings that were meant to assure themselves of God's grace and to encourage them to keep their higher spiritual destinies in mind. Defoe's novel, some of the time, fits this pattern, and Defoe himself can be said to have sanctioned this approach by publishing in 1720 *Serious Reflections during the Life and Surprising Adventures of Robinson Crusoe*, a collection of essays and religious meditations presented as Crusoe's religious reflections on the meaning of his story. He awakens from religious and spiritual indifference to a sense of God's providential hand in his life. As complex and particularized as the events of his life are, they are shaped eventually in his mind by the master narrative of Christian salvation. In J. Paul Hunter's phrase, Crusoe is a 'reluctant pilgrim'; for Defoe and his eighteenth-century audience what looks like realistic detail to us has metaphorical overtones and emblematic as well as particular significance whereby Crusoe's story primarily illustrates, as the preface puts it, 'a religious application of events to the uses to which wise men always apply them (*viz.*) to the instruction of others by this example, and to justify and honour the wisdom of Providence in all the variety of our circumstances, let them happen how they will' (p. 5).[3]

Providence, however, works in very subtle fashion, and Crusoe will not have angelic visitors or divine miracles to save him. Defoe's prose style and narrative approach with their empirical and intensely observational manner are to some extent at odds with the desires of his hero, who longs for signs of divine purpose in a world where only material phenomena can be said for certain to exist. One sequence from early in the island part of the book is especially revealing for this tension between religious longing for proof of God's operations and the absolutely secular narration of facts and phenomena. Crusoe reports that during his early months on the island he is astonished one day to discover some familiar green stalks growing, which turn out to be 'perfect green barley of the same kind as our *European*, nay, as our *English* barley'. He is much moved by this and jumps to some enthusiastic conclusions about providential intervention in his life:

I had hitherto acted upon no religious foundation at all; indeed I had very few notions of religion in my head, or had entertain'd any sense of any thing that had befallen me, otherwise than as a chance, or, as we lightly say, what pleases God; without so much as enquiring into the end of Providence in these things, or his order in governing events in the world: But after I saw barley grow there, in a climate which I know was not proper for corn, and especially that I knew not how it came there, it startled me strangely, and I began to suggest, that God had miraculously caus'd this grain to grow without any help of seed sown, and that it was so directed purely for my sustenance on that wild miserable place. (p. 63)

But Crusoe's wonder abates considerably as he realizes that this barley has grown there because of an incident he now recalls with perfect clarity; the miraculous growth is the result of an accident, his shaking out of a bag of chicken feed that he thought was empty:

all this was nothing but what was common; tho' I ought to have been as thankful for so strange and unforeseen Providence, as if it had been miraculous; for it was really the work of Providence as to me, that should order or appoint, that 10 or 12 grains of corn should remain unspoil'd, (when the rats had destroy'd all the rest), as if it had been dropt from Heaven; as also that I should throw it out in that particular place, where it being in the shade of a high rock, it sprang up immediately; whereas if I had thrown it any where else, at that time, it had been burnt up and destroy'd. (p. 64)

Providence, Crusoe concludes, cooperates with accidents, works God's will by means of the flux and flow of everyday experience, and what appear to be merely casual incidents and everyday happenings such as Crusoe records, if properly and intensely studied, yield evidence of providential purpose. God can be found in the accidental details such as realistic fiction delivers; divine arrangement is not a matter of spectacular miracles or interventions in the natural order of things but works in subtle fashion through everyday and trivial incidents. Crusoe's God is like Defoe an empiricist; he respects the drift of material phenomena and his purpose is somehow inscribed in them. But perhaps an eighteenth-century reader would have taken this incident in a slightly different way and heard biblical echoes in the details of the story, reminded of Christ's parable of the sower, whose seed fell in various places, with some falling 'among thorns; and the thorns sprung up, and choked them: But other fell into good ground, and brought forth fruit, some an hundredfold, some sixtyfold, some thirtyfold. Who hath ears to hear, let him hear' (Matthew 13:7–9). Crusoe learns, gradually, to treat his survival as a virtual miracle, and that ability to talk about his experiences as at once natural and supernatural is one key to his survival: he learns 'to give daily thanks for that daily bread, which nothing but a croud of wonders could have brought. That I ought to consider I had been fed even by miracle, even as great as that of feeding *Elijah* by ravens; nay, by a long series of miracles, and that I could hardly have nam'd a place in the unhabitable part of the world where I could have been cast more to my advantage' (p. 105).

Whatever was uppermost in the mind of some of its pious eighteenth-century audience, readers of *Robinson Crusoe* since then have seen a number of other, decidedly secular meanings in the story, so much so that the book derives a good deal of its enduring power from mythical or archetypal qualities that have taken on a life of their own quite distinct from what actually happens in the book. As Ian Watt pointed out in his essay 'Robinson Crusoe as a Myth', the myth has three aspects: Back to Nature, the Dignity of Labor and Economic Man.[4] The French eighteenth-century philosopher Jean-Jacques Rousseau saw in the island section a lesson for how to live a properly human life, an illustration of how to situate yourself fruitfully in nature. In his *Émile: ou, de l'éducation* (1762), Rousseau's tutor hero declares that *Robinson Crusoe* will be the only book his pupil, Emile, will be allowed to read. In his labours on the island, Robinson will offer Emile a model of direct participation in the arts and manual techniques to which modern life and the division of labour have made us all strangers, and in his isolation Crusoe will illustrate and enforce the necessity of radical individualism and independence, of making your own way on your own terms. Crusoe's island for Rousseau is a paradise, a virtuous retreat from social corruption. But of course for Crusoe the island is for most of his years a terrible trial, a prison, an island of despair (as he calls it), and his solitude is the occasion for constant and intense loneliness and longing for the company of others. His independence is a punishment; his individualism a desperate necessity.

For Rousseau Crusoe's island is unspoiled nature, offering peace and beauty. For Defoe and the western capitalist, imperialistic culture that he represents and glorifies, the island is an opportunity for colonial expropriation, for development and improvement (exploitation, some might say) by human technology. As Crusoe explores his island, he finds pleasure in thinking that he owns it, that it is his estate: 'the country appear'd so fresh, so green, so flourishing, every thing being in a constant verdure, or flourish of *Spring*, that it look'd like a planted garden . . . surveying it with a secret kind of pleasure, (tho' mixt with my other afflicting thoughts) to think that this was all my own, that I was king and lord of all this country indefeasibly, and had a right of possession; and if I could convey it, I might have it in inheritance, as compleatly as any lord of a manor in *England*' (p. 80). But Crusoe realizes that without the tools salvaged from the ship he would never have survived – or he would have been forced to live a primitive and even bestial existence. His fear of that alternative to civilized life is a powerful undercurrent in the narrative. Without knives and guns, he remarks, he would 'have liv'd, if I had not perish'd, like a meer savage. That if I had kill'd a goat, or a fowl, by any contrivance, I had no way to flea or open them, or part the flesh from the skin and the bowels, or to cut it up; but must gnaw it with my teeth, and pull it with my claws like a beast' (p. 104), and he laments from the start his lack of sufficient technology for other purposes. Thus, after he grows his first grain, he describes his difficulties:

When the corn was sow'd, I had no harrow, but was forced to go over it my self, and drag a great heavy bough of a tree over it, to scratch it, as it may be call'd, rather than rake or harrow it. When it was growing and grown, I have observ'd already how many things I wanted, to fence it, secure it, mow or reap it, cure and carry it home, thrash, part it from the chaff, and save it. Then I wanted a mill to grind it, sieves to dress it, yeast and salt to make it into bread, and an oven to bake it. (pp. 94–5)

Among the most fascinating parts of Crusoe's narrative, then, the moments when he seems happiest and most fulfilled, the least troubled by anxieties and fears, and totally absorbed by his work, are his own technological breakthroughs, as he painfully improvises and learns basic techniques of production, although he tends to emphasize that his products are pale imitations and awkward and laborious versions of actual manufactured goods made by trained artisans.

But Crusoe works because he must in order to survive, not because he believes in the saving power or the inherent dignity of labour, which his story has by some later readers been taken to exemplify. We need to remember that he has been shipwrecked at the head of an illegal expedition to buy slaves, and his happy ending comes when he discovers after leaving his island that his plantation in Brazil has been making money for him in his absence, that he is in fact a rich man. Crusoe is an 'adventure capitalist' as well as a slaveholder (he sells Xury, the young boy who accompanies him from his captivity in Morocco, into slavery to the Portuguese Captain); he is essentially a manager and entrepreneur (like Defoe) rather than a worker. He does, however, draw certain economic lessons from production and consumption in isolation, and in moods like the following encourages the primitivist interpretation of his story:

In a word, the nature and experience of things dictated to me upon just reflection, that all the good things of this world, are no farther good to us, than they are for our use; and that whatever we may heap up indeed to give others, we enjoy just as much as we can use, and no more . . . I had no room for desire, except it was of things which I had not, and they were but trifles, tho' indeed of great use to me. I had, as I hinted before, a parcel of money, as well gold as silver, about thirty six pounds sterling: Alas! there the nasty sorry useless stuff lay; I had no manner of business for it; and I often thought with myself, that I would have given a handful of it for a gross of tobacco-pipes, or for a hand-mill to grind my corn; nay, I would have given it all for six penny-worth of *turnip* and *carrot* seed out of *England*, or for a handful of *pease* and *beans*, and a bottle of ink: *As it was*, I had not the least advantage by it, or benefit from it; but there it lay in a drawer, and grew mouldy with the damp of the cave, in the wet season; and if I had had the drawer full of diamonds, it had been the same case; and they had been of no manner of value to me, because of no use. (p. 103)

Crusoe lives in what philosophers of the time called the state of nature, which in his case has the advantages of teaching him about the superiority of simple use values and natural subsistence living over the artificial surplus production and consumer values of society but also many disadvantages, among them the lack of essential manufactured goods and skilled services. So in spite of its virtuous simplicity, his island existence is no idyll, and its most troubling feature is its lack of civil order. In the state of nature, as the philosopher Thomas Hobbes had notoriously evoked it in his *Leviathan, or the Matter, Form, and Power of a Commonwealth, Ecclesiastical and Civil* (1651), man is also in a constant state of war with other men, fearful that they will come and kill him and take his possessions. Although Defoe was no Hobbesian, his hero lives from his arrival on the island in constant dread of unknown enemies, and in fact he has good cause for such fear, as it turns out, when cannibals do arrive and at last when the English mutineers come to his island. Defoe's narrative is a novel partly because it is attentive to this kind of complexity, with the island and so much else in the hero's experience open to contradictory and subjective interpretations. Unlike some later redactions of the Crusoe story, Defoe's novel never simplifies the meanings of the story. It is part of Defoe's genius that he resists making his tale merely an illustration of a thesis about human nature or society.

Crusoe's state of mind after he discovers the single footprint on the beach is one of the great psychological moments in all of English fiction, and it begins a new phase in the story of his survival.

It happen'd one day about noon going towards my boat, I was exceedingly surpris'd with the print of a man's naked foot on the shore, which was very plain to be seen in the sand: I stood like one thunder-struck, or as if I had seen an apparition; I listen'd, I look'd round me, I could hear nothing, nor see any thing, I went up to a rising ground to look farther, I went up the shore and down the shore, but it was all one, I could see no other impression but that one, I went to it again to see if there were any more, and to observe if it might not be my fancy; but there was no room for that, for there was exactly the very print of a foot, toes, heel, and every part of a foot; how it came thither, I knew not, nor could in the least imagine. But after innumerable fluttering thoughts, like a man perfectly confus'd and out of myself, I came home to my fortification, not feeling, as we say, the ground I went on, but terrify'd to the last degree, looking behind me at every two or three steps, mistaking every bush and tree, and fancying every stump at a distance to be a man; nor is it possible to describe how many various shapes affrighted imagination represented things to me in, how many wild ideas were found every moment in my fancy, and what strange unaccountable whimsies came into my thoughts by the way. (p. 122)

This is a brilliant narrative touch. The island has been explored and Crusoe is established and fairly serene. This single trace of another human being, whether friend or foe, marks a new crisis in Crusoe's tale and restores tension and uncertainty at a lull in the narrative movement. Reality at its most pressing in *Robinson Crusoe*, as this passage dramatizes, coincides with the hero's fantasies, his fearful imaginings of dreadful possibilities that arise from inexplicable phenomena – here, that one footprint. Notice that his first fear is of something supernatural, 'as if' he had seen an apparition. A bit later he thinks it must be the devil's doing: 'I was so embarrass'd with my own frightful ideas of the thing, that I form'd nothing but dismal imaginations to myself, even tho' I was now a great way off it. Sometimes I fancy'd it must be the Devil; and reason joyn'd in with me upon this supposition: For how should any other thing in human shape come into the place?' (pp. 122–3). But in a sense, this moment of wild surmise marks Crusoe's definitive turn away from his isolation and his search for providential structure. In the long debate with himself about the cannibals (whose occasional visits to the island to consume their prisoners of war he verifies in the years that follow), he establishes a moral and political connection to other human beings. In working out in an internal monologue that stretches over years his emotional and intellectual relationship to the cannibals, his rivals for possession of the island, he defines himself now not in religious terms but in concrete moral and historical terms, as his thoughts about the cannibals help him, paradoxically, to understand himself in a more complex way. His first reactions are personal, visceral and violent. Finding the remains of a cannibal feast on the beach, he vomits and vows to exterminate them. Obsessed at first by the cannibals ('It would take up a larger volume than this whole work is intended to be, to set down all the contrivances I hatch'd, or rather brooded upon in my thought, for the destroying these creatures' (p. 133)), Crusoe at last comes to a position which is tactically wise and historically sophisticated: 'What authority or call I had, to pretend to be judge and executioner upon these men as criminals, whom Heaven had thought fit for so many ages to suffer unpunish'd, to go on, and to be, as it were, the executioners of his judgments one upon another. How far these people were offenders against me, and what right I had to engage in the quarrel of that blood, which they shed promiscuously one upon another' (p. 135). Just as carnivorous Europeans like himself think nothing of eating pigs and oxen, so do these cannibals eat their enemies. Moreover, he reasons, to kill these men who have done him no wrong is to perpetuate the worst European imperialistic atrocities:

this wou'd justify the conduct of the *Spaniards* in all their barbarities practis'd in *America*, and where they destroyed millions of these people, who however they were idolaters and barbarians, and had several bloody and barbarous rites in their customs . . . were yet, as to the *Spaniards*, very innocent people; and that the rooting them out of the country, is spoken of with the utmost abhorrence and detestation, by even the *Spaniards* themselves, at this time; and by all other Christian nations of *Europe*. (p. 136)

To be sure, this enlightened tolerance and cultural relativism give way to rage and disgust when Crusoe surveys the remains of a cannibal feast a few years later.

Eventually, Crusoe's solution to his cannibal problem (in addition to making his residence as inconspicuous and inaccessible as possible) exemplifies his larger survival strategy on the island and summarizes his maturity as a character in this final part of the book. He follows his instincts; he observes things closely, on the lookout for opportunity, ready to intervene for profit and advantage. He has confidence that God's Providence is working for him in subtle and surprising ways. When he dreams that one of the cannibals' prisoners escapes and comes to him, he decides that he will try to capture one of these in reality: 'I resolv'd, if possible, to get one of those savages into my hands, cost what it would. My next thing then was to contrive how to do it, and this indeed was very difficult to resolve on: But as I could pitch upon no probable means for it, so I resolv'd to put myself upon the watch, to see them when they came on shore, and leave the rest to the event, taking such measures as the opportunity should present, let be what would be' (p. 158). That things happen exactly, or almost exactly, as in his dream is only a possible rather than a likely or probable event, we might say. What actually happens makes sense as it is meticulously elaborated by Crusoe, but that it should happen exactly as Crusoe dreamed it sets up a strange ambiguity. Gradually and subtly, Crusoe becomes the master of his fate who leads a charmed life, the lucky one for whom everything will fall in place, whose desires become reality as subjective and objective come together. He becomes, that is to say, an improbable hero who goes against the grain of the realistic novel committed to the mundane and the ordinary, a character readers expect will somehow triumph even in the worst of situations and against all odds. The exciting incidents that make up the last third of the novel, the acquisition of Friday, the slaughter of the cannibals, the defeat of the English mutineers and the battle with ravenous wolves in the Pyrenees, are extravagant adventures that in some sense negate the careful domestic realism of Crusoe's island survival and its slow little daily triumphs. And yet the thrilling extravagance of these incidents is balanced and certified in a sense by the same observational exactness and precision that characterizes Crusoe's establishment on the island. Cool, measured in his rage, precise and efficient in his violent movements and in his enumerations and descriptions of their results, Crusoe is the man of action and administrator all at once. Even in the breathless aftermath of bloody mayhem and slaughter of the cannibals, he gives us an exact tally, a frighteningly precise body count of who killed whom and where and how.

Crusoe's transformation from terrified and confused survivor to colonial master and avenging overlord of his island marks *Robinson Crusoe* as one of the key modern myths of English and even of European culture. Having experienced the compulsions and mysterious drivings of fate, Crusoe now acquires and indeed embodies freedom and domination of nature and of others in his powerful and confident actions. From victim to hero, Crusoe is now a man of action and commanding energy. Descending like an avenging angel on the terrified cannibals or amazing the bewildered mutineers a bit later on like a latter-day Prospero (or an anticipation of the Wizard of Oz) as the all-powerful governor of his island, Crusoe can be said to resemble the inscrutable deity he has imagined earlier: to the cannibals and the mutineers he is a mysterious and irresistible force. Crusoe controls the fates of others; he presides suddenly over a new political order on his island, even though he treats his new authority as something of a joke: 'My island was now peopled, and I thought my self very rich in subjects; and it was a merry reflection which I frequently made, how like a king I look'd. First of all, the whole country was my own meer property; so that I had an undoubted right of dominion. Secondly, my people were perfectly subjected: I was absolute lord and law-giver; they all ow'd their lives to me, and were ready to lay down their lives, *if there had been occasion of it*, for me' (p. 190).

Defoe, it turns out, was one of James Joyce's favourite writers. In a lecture ('Verismo ed idealismo nella letterature inglese') he gave on Defoe in Trieste in 1911, Joyce called Crusoe the embodiment of British imperialism. Defoe's hero is 'the true prototype of the British colonist, as Friday (the trusty savage who arrives on an unlucky day) is the symbol of the subject races'. Joyce found in Crusoe the 'whole Anglo-Saxon spirit . . . the manly independence; the unconscious cruelty; the persistence; the slow yet efficient intelligence; the sexual apathy; the practical, well-balanced religiousness; the calculating taciturnity'.[5] What we need to add to his evocation and what should be clear to anyone who actually reads *Robinson Crusoe* is the caution that Defoe's book does not simply offer that prototype as a given but rather records the development of that imperial personality in Crusoe. The book's importance as one of the earliest English novels lies in its tracing of the hero's painful and slow acquisition of that identity. Balancing critique and celebration of its hero, *Robinson Crusoe* is not simply propaganda for British imperial expansion but, also, a dramatization of the psychological origins and moral problems of the triumphant but troubling historical phenomena of western individualism and imperialism that he comes to embody.

NOTES

1 *The Englishman: being the sequel of the Guardian* (London: S. Buckley, 1714), Number 26, p. 172.

2 Ibid., p. 173.

3 *The Reluctant Pilgrim: Defoe's Emblematic Method and Quest for Form in 'Robinson Crusoe'* (Baltimore: Johns Hopkins University Press, 1966).

4 'Robinson Crusoe as a Myth', revised from *Essays in Criticism* (1951), reprinted in *Norton Critical Edition of Robinson Crusoe*, ed. Michael Shinagel (New York: Norton, 1994), p. 289.

5 'Daniel Defoe', edited from Italian manuscripts and translated by Joseph Prescott, *Buffalo Studies* 1 (December 1964), pp. 24–5.

FURTHER READING

Paul Alkon, *Defoe and Fictional Time* (Athens: University of Georgia Press, 1979). Critically sophisticated reading of Defoe's manipulations of time in his fiction.

Paula R. Backscheider, *Daniel Defoe: His Life* (Baltimore and London: Johns Hopkins University Press, 1989). Standard, definitive biography.

Ian Bell, *Defoe's Fiction* (London: Croom Helm, 1985). Valuable treatment of the novels in the context of popular narrative in the early eighteenth century.

John Bender, *Imagining the Penitentiary: Fiction and the Architecture of Mind in Eighteenth-Century England* (Chicago: University of Chicago Press, 1987). Original and penetrating study of the relationship between the development of the novel and the emergence of the modern penitentiary.

David Blewett, *Defoe's Art of Fiction* (Toronto: University of Toronto Press, 1979). Explores very thoroughly the artistic and moral dimensions of the novels.

—, *The Illustration of Robinson Crusoe 1719–1920* (Gerrards Cross: Colin Smythe, 1995). A fascinating analysis of shifting visual interpretations of the novel.

Harold Bloom (ed.), *Robinson Crusoe: Modern Critical Interpretations* (New York: Chelsea House, 1988). Collection of the most important interpretations of Defoe's novel.

Michael M. Boardman, *Defoe and the Uses of Narrative* (New Brunswick: Rutgers University Press, 1983). Perceptive discussion of the novels' formal innovations.

Homer O. Brown, 'The Displaced Self in the Novels of Daniel Defoe', *English Literary History* 38 (1971), pp. 562–90. Sees Defoe's fictions as confessions in which characters expose their lives and conceal their identities.

Leopold Damrosch, *God's Plot and Man's Stories* (Chicago: University of Chicago Press, 1983). Insightful discussion of *Robinson Crusoe* as part of Puritan tradition exemplified in the works of Bunyan and Milton.

Carol Houlihan Flynn, *The Body in Swift and Defoe* (Cambridge: Cambridge University Press, 1990). Original exploration of the somatic qualities of Defoe's explorations of physical experience.

P. N. Furbank and W. R. Owens, *The Canonisation of Daniel Defoe* (New Haven: Yale University Press, 1988). Important history of how many of Defoe's works came to be attributed to him.

—, *A Critical Bibliography of Daniel Defoe* (London: Pickering & Chatto, 1998). Revised list of Defoe's writings based on title above.

Martin Green, *Dreams of Adventure, Deeds of Empire* (New York: Basic Books, 1979). Stimulating discussion of *Robinson Crusoe* and European imperialism.

—, *The Robinson Crusoe Story* (University Park: Pennsylvania State University Press, 1990). Survey of the lingering significance and importance of Defoe's book.

J. Paul Hunter, *The Reluctant Pilgrim: Defoe's Emblematic Method and Quest for Form in 'Robinson Crusoe'* (Baltimore: Johns Hopkins University Press, 1966). Important study of the Christian foundations of Defoe's novel.

James Joyce, 'Daniel Defoe', edited from Italian manuscripts and translated by Joseph Prescott, *Buffalo Studies* 1 (December 1964), pp. 3–27.

Michael McKeon, *The Origins of the English Novel, 1600–1740* (Baltimore: Johns Hopkins University Press, 1987). Monumental and crucial study of the emergence of the novel, with a valuable chapter devoted to *Robinson Crusoe*.

A. D. McKillop, *The Early Masters of English Fiction* (Lawrence: University of Kansas Press, 1968). Informative history of the novel in the eighteenth century that features a discussion of Defoe's role.

Maximillian E. Novak, *Daniel Defoe – Master of Fictions: His Life and Works* (London: Oxford University Press, 2001). A masterful and authoritative account of Defoe's life and writings.

—, *Defoe and the Nature of Man* (London: Oxford University Press, 1963). Traces the intellectual currents of Defoe's time and his treatment of those ideas in his fiction.

—, *Realism, Myth, and History in Defoe's Fiction* (Lincoln: University of

Nebraska Press, 1983). Explores the underestimated complexities of Defoe's novels.

John Richetti, *Daniel Defoe* (Boston: Twayne Publishers, 1987). A survey of all of Defoe's writings, fictional and non-fictional.

—, *Defoe's Narratives: Situations and Structures* (Oxford: Oxford University Press, 1975). Reads the novels as explorations of cultural contradictions and expressions of individual will to power.

Pat Rogers, *Grub Street: Studies in a Subculture* (London: Methuen, 1972). Study of Defoe's milieu as a writer.

—, *Robinson Crusoe* (London: Allen & Unwin, 1979). Sensible and thorough guide to Defoe's novel.

Manuel Schonhorn, *Defoe's Politics: Parliament, Power, Kingship, and Robinson Crusoe* (Cambridge: Cambridge University Press, 1991). Persuasive political reading of Defoe's novel.

Michael Seidel, *Robinson Crusoe: Island Myths and the Novel* (Boston: Twayne Publishers, 1991). Shrewdly original treatment of the structure and cultural resonances of the novel.

Michael Shinagel, *Daniel Defoe and Middle-Class Gentility* (Cambridge: Harvard University Press, 1968). Defoe's social aspirations as a key theme in his novels and some of his non-fiction.

Lieve Spaas and Brian Stimpson (eds.), *Robinson Crusoe: Myths and Metamorphoses* (New York: St Martin's Press, 1996). Essays discussing the cultural influences of the Crusoe story on later writers and thinkers.

G. A. Starr, *Defoe and Casuistry* (Princeton: Princeton University Press, 1971). Traces insightfully the influence of the analytic case history method of moral judgement on the structure of Defoe's novels.

—, *Defoe and Spiritual Autobiography* (Princeton: Princeton University Press, 1965). Finds the origins and organizing principles of Defoe's fiction in Puritan diaries.

James Sutherland, *Daniel Defoe: A Critical Study* (Cambridge: Harvard University Press, 1971). A study of the non-fiction and its relation to the fiction.

—, *Defoe* (London: Methuen, 1937). Sensible and readable older biography.

Elsa Vickers, *Defoe and the New Sciences* (Cambridge: Cambridge University Press, 1996). Traces the influence of Baconian science on Defoe's writing, including *Robinson Crusoe*.

Ian Watt, *The Rise of the Novel: Studies in Defoe, Richardson, and Fielding* (Berkeley and Los Angeles: University of California Press, 1957).

Chapters on Defoe are crucial for understanding his importance as a realistic innovator in fiction.

—, 'Robinson Crusoe as a Myth', revised from *Essays in Criticism* (1951), reprinted in *Norton Critical Edition of Robinson Crusoe*, ed. Michael Shinagel (New York: Norton, 1994). Influential and provocative essay about the cultural meaning of the novel.

Richard West, *Daniel Defoe: The Life and Strange, Surprising Adventures* (London: Harper Collins, 1998). A journalist's appreciative and lively narrative of Defoe's life and writings.

Everett Zimmerman, *Defoe and the Novel* (Berkeley and Los Angeles: University of California Press, 1975). Cogent and powerful examination of the changes in Defoe's moral and literary values expressed in his fictions.

NOTE ON THE TEXT

The Life and Strange Surprizing Adventures of Robinson Crusoe of York, Mariner first appeared on 25 April 1719 and was instantly popular, the initial printing of 1000 quickly selling out. To meet the great demand for the book, the London printer William Taylor issued five more separate printings that year, four of these marked as new 'editions', with the third and fourth editions issued twice. Each printing corrected many errors in the first edition, but each also introduced new errors. The text for this Penguin edition is based on a photocopy of one of the first edition copies in the British Library, but I have consulted all of the 1719 printings and made some minor modifications and editorial choices to aid readability. I have retained all features of the original text except for the capitalization of common nouns, which is for modern readers an insignificant convention of eighteenth-century typography. I have also occasionally chosen for the sake of clarity one variant among eighteenth-century spellings; for example, in place of 'cloaths' in the first edition I have substituted 'clothes' from a later printing as less distracting; in place of 'ruine' from the first edition I have substituted 'ruin'. For ease of readability, I have also introduced some consistency in the spelling; for example, turning what appears at first as 'shoar' into the later spelling of 'shore', converting what is occasionally spelled 'patroon' into its normal spelling of 'patron', spelling 'surprise' and 'surprising' with the 's' rather than the 'z' that the first edition sometimes employs, preferring 'human' to the alternative spelling of 'humane', 'comrade' to 'comerade', 'cabin' to 'cabbin', and 'till' to what sometimes appears as ''til, as well as 'cannibals' to 'canibals', 'rice' to 'ryce' and 'cargo' to 'cargoe'. Except in some places where the plain sense of the text required slight alterations, I have retained the punctuation used in the first edition, and I have made no effort to remove the many inconsistencies. There is no surviving manuscript of the novel, and scholars have supposed that most of the punctuation was supplied by the printers for what must have been the lightly punctuated manuscript Defoe gave them. Otherwise, I have corrected like editors before me some obvious errors or misprints.

THE
L I F E

AND

STRANGE SURPRIZING

ADVENTURES

OF

ROBINSON CRUSOE,
Of *YORK*, MARINER:

Who lived Eight and Twenty Years,
all alone in an un-inhabited Island on the
Coast of AMERICA, near the Mouth of
the Great River of OROONOQUE;

Having been cast on Shore by Shipwreck, wherein all the Men perished but himself.

WITH

An Account how he was at last as strangely deliver'd by PYRATES.

Written by Himself.

LONDON:

Printed for W. TAYLOR at the *Ship* in *Pater-Noster-
Row.* MDCCXIX.

THE

PREFACE

If ever the story of any private man's adventures in the world were worth making publick, and were acceptable when publish'd, the editor of this account thinks this will be so.

The wonders of this man's life exceed all that (he thinks) is to be found extant; the life of one man being scarce capable of a greater variety.

The story is told with modesty, with seriousness, and with a religious application of events to the uses to which wise men always apply them (*viz.*) to the instruction of others by this example, and to justify and honour the wisdom of Providence in all the variety of our circumstances, let them happen how they will.

The editor believes the thing to be a just history of fact; neither is there any appearance of fiction in it: And whoever thinks, because all such things are dispatch'd,[1] that the improvement of it, as well to the diversion, as to the instruction of the reader, will be the same; and as such, he thinks, without farther compliment to the world, he does them a great service in the publication.

THE LIFE AND *ADVENTURES* OF
ROBINSON CRUSOE,² *&c.*

I was born in the year 1632, in the city of *York*, of a good family, tho' not of that country, my father being a foreigner of *Bremen*,³ who settled first at *Hull*: He got a good estate by merchandise, and leaving off his trade, lived afterward at *York*, from whence he had married my mother, whose relations were named *Robinson*, a very good family in that country, and from whom I was call'd *Robinson Kreutznaer*; but by the usual corruption of words in *England*, we are now call'd, nay we call our selves, and write our name *Crusoe*, and so my companions always call'd me.

I had two elder brothers, one of which was Lieutenant Collonel to an *English* regiment of foot in *Flanders*, formerly commanded by the famous Coll. *Lockhart*, and was killed at the battle near *Dunkirk* against the *Spaniards*.⁴ What became of my second brother I never knew any more than my father or mother did know what was become of me.

Being the third son of the family, and not bred to any trade, my head began to be fill'd very early with rambling thoughts: My father, who was very ancient, had given me a competent share of learning, as far as house-education, and a country free-school generally goes, and design'd me for the law; but I would be satisfied with nothing but going to sea, and my inclination to this led me so strongly against the will, nay the commands of my father, and against all the entreaties and perswasions of my mother and other friends, that there seem'd to be something fatal in that propension of Nature tending directly to the life of misery which was to befal me.

My father, a wise and grave man, gave me serious and excellent counsel against what he foresaw was my design. He called me one morning into his chamber, where he was confined by the gout, and expostulated very warmly with me upon this subject: He ask'd me what reasons more than a meer wandring inclination I had for leaving my father's house and my native country, where I might be well introduced, and had a prospect of raising my fortunes by application and industry, with a life of ease and pleasure. He told me it was for men of desperate fortunes on one hand, or of aspiring, superior fortunes on the other, who went abroad upon adventures, to rise by enterprize, and make themselves famous in undertakings of a nature out of the common road; that these things were all either too far above me, or too far below me; that mine was the middle state, or what might be called the upper station of *low life*, which he had found by long experience was the best state in the world, the most suited to human happiness, not exposed to the miseries and hardships, the labour and sufferings of the mechanick part of mankind, and not embarrass'd with the pride, luxury, ambition and envy of the upper part of mankind. He told me, I might judge of the happiness of this state, by this one thing, *viz.* That this was the state of life which all other people envied, that kings have frequently lamented the miserable consequences of being born to great things, and wish'd they had been placed in the middle of the two extremes, between the mean and the great; that the wise man gave his testimony to this as the just standard of true felicity, when he prayed to have neither poverty or riches.[5]

He bid me observe it, and I should always find, that the calamities of life were shared among the upper and lower part of mankind; but that the middle station had the fewest disasters, and was not expos'd to so many vicissitudes as the higher or lower part of mankind; nay, they were not subjected to so many distempers and uneasinesses either of body or mind, as those were who, by vicious living, luxury and extravagancies on one hand, or by hard labour, want of necessaries, and mean or insufficient diet on the other hand, bring distempers upon themselves by the natural consequences of their way of living; *that* the middle station of life was calculated for all kind of vertues and all kind of enjoyments; that peace and plenty were the hand-maids of a middle fortune; that temperance, moderation, quietness, health, society, all agreeable diversions, and all desirable pleasures, were the blessings attending the middle station of life; that this way men went silently and smoothly thro' the world, and comfortably out of it, not embarrass'd with the labours of the hands or of the head, not sold to the life of slavery for daily bread, or harrast with perplex'd circumstances, which rob the soul of peace, and the body of rest; not enrag'd with the passion of envy, or secret burning lust of ambition for great things; but in easy circumstances sliding gently thro' the world, and sensibly tasting the sweets of living, without the bitter feeling that they are happy, and learning by every day's experience to know it more sensibly.

After this, he press'd me earnestly, and in the most affectionate manner, not to play the young man, not to precipitate my self into miseries which Nature and the station of life I was born in, seem'd to have provided against; that I was under no necessity of seeking my bread; that he would do well for me, and endeavour to enter me fairly into the station of life which he had been just recommending to me; and that if I was not very easy and happy in the world, it must be my meer fate or fault that must hinder it, and that he should have nothing to answer for, having thus discharg'd his duty in warning me against measures which he knew would be to my hurt: In a word, that as he would do very kind things for me if I would stay and settle at home as he directed, so he would not have so much hand in my misfortunes, as to give me any encouragement to go away: And to close all, he told me I had my elder brother for an example, to whom he had used the same earnest perswasions to keep him from going into the Low Country wars, but could not prevail, his young desires prompting him to run into the army where he was kill'd; and tho' he said he would not cease to pray for me, yet he would venture to say to me, that if I did take this foolish step, God would not bless me, and I would have leisure hereafter to reflect upon having neglected his counsel when there might be none to assist in my recovery.

I observed in this last part of his discourse, which was truly prophetick, tho' I suppose my father did not know it to be so himself; I say, I observed the tears run down his face very plentifully, and especially when he spoke of my brother who was kill'd; and that when he spoke of my having leisure to repent, and none to assist me, he was so mov'd, that he broke off the discourse, and told me, his heart was so full, he could say no more to me.

I was sincerely affected with this discourse, as indeed who could be otherwise; and I resolv'd not to think of going abroad any more, but to settle at home according to my father's desire. But alas! a few days wore it all off; and in short, to prevent any of my father's farther importunities, in a few weeks after, I resolv'd to run quite away from him. However, I did not act so hastily neither as my first heat of resolution prompted, but I took my mother, at a time when I thought her a little pleasanter than ordinary, and told her, that my thoughts were so entirely bent upon seeing the world, that I should never settle to any thing with resolution enough to go through with it, and my father had better give me his consent than force me to go without it; that I was now eighteen years old, which was too late to go apprentice to a trade, or clerk to an attorney; that I was sure if I did, I should never serve out my time, and I should certainly run away from my master before my time was out, and go to sea; and if she would speak to my father to let me go but one voyage abroad, if I came home again and did not like it, I would go no more, and I would promise by a double diligence to recover that time I had lost.

This put my mother into a great passion: She told me, she knew it would be to no purpose to speak to my father upon any such subject; that he knew too well what was my interest to give his consent to any such thing so much for my hurt, and that she wondered how I could think of any such thing after such a discourse as I had had with my father, and such kind and tender expressions as she knew my father had us'd to me; and that in short, if I would ruin my self there was no help for me; but I might depend I should never have their consent to it: That for her part she would not have so much hand in my destruction; and I should never have it to say, that my mother was willing when my father was not.

Tho' my mother refused to move it to my father, yet as I have heard afterwards, she reported all the discourse to him, and that my father after shewing a great concern at it, said to her with a sigh, That boy might be happy if he would stay at home, but if he goes abroad, he will be the miserablest wretch that was ever born: I can give no consent to it.

It was not till almost a year after this that I broke loose, tho' in the mean time I continued obstinately deaf to all proposals of settling to business, and frequently expostulating with my father and mother, about their being so positively determin'd against what they knew my inclinations prompted me to. But being one day at *Hull*, where I went casually, and without any purpose of making an elopement that time; but I say, being there, and one of my companions being going by sea to *London*, in his father's ship, and prompting me to go with them, with the common allurement of seafaring men, *viz.* That it should cost me nothing for my passage, I consulted neither father or mother any more, nor so much as sent them word of it; but leaving them to hear of it as they might, without asking God's blessing, or my father's, without any consideration of circumstances or consequences, and in an ill hour, God knows, on the first of *September* 1651,[6] I went on board a ship bound for *London*; never any young adventurer's misfortunes, I believe, began sooner, or continued longer than mine. The ship was no sooner gotten out of the *Humber*,[7] but the wind began to blow, and the sea to rise in a most frightful manner; and as I had never been at sea before, I was most inexpressibly sick in body, and terrify'd in my mind: I began now seriously to reflect upon what I had done, and how justly I was overtaken by the judgment of Heaven for my wicked leaving my father's house, and abandoning my duty; all the good counsel of my parents, my father's tears and my mother's entreaties came now fresh into my mind, and my conscience, which was not yet come to the pitch of hardness which it has been since, reproach'd me with the contempt of advice, and the breach of my duty to God and my father.

All this while the storm encreas'd, and the sea, which I had never been upon before, went very high, tho' nothing like what I have seen many times since; no, nor like what I saw a few days after: But it was enough to affect me then, who was but a young sailor, and had never known any thing of the matter. I expected every wave would have swallowed us up, and that every time the ship fell down, as I thought, in the trough or hollow of the sea, we should never rise more; and in this agony of mind, I made many vows and resolutions, that if it would please God here to spare my life this one voyage, if ever I got once my foot upon dry land again, I would go directly home to my father, and never set it into a ship again while I liv'd; that I would take his advice, and never run my self into such miseries as these any more. Now I saw plainly the goodness of his observations about the middle station of life, how easy, how comfortably he had liv'd all his days, and never had been expos'd to tempests at sea, or troubles on shore; and I resolv'd that I would, like a true repenting Prodigal,[8] go home to my father.

These wise and sober thoughts continued all the while the storm continued, and indeed some time after; but the next day the wind was abated and the sea calmer, and I began to be a little inur'd to it: However I was very grave for all that day, being also a little sea sick still; but towards night the weather clear'd up, the wind was quite over, and a charming fine evening follow'd; the sun went down perfectly clear, and rose so the next morning; and having little or no wind, and a smooth sea, the sun shining upon it, the sight was, as I thought, the most delightful that ever I saw.

I had slept well in the night, and was now no more sea sick, but very cheerful, looking with wonder upon the sea that was so rough and terrible the day before, and could be so calm and so pleasant in so little time after. And now lest my good resolutions should continue, my companion, who had indeed entic'd me away, comes to me, *Well* Bob, says he, clapping me upon the shoulder, *How do you do after it? I warrant you were frighted, wa'n't you last night, when it blew but a cap full of wind? A cap full d'you call it?* said I, *'twas a terrible storm: A storm, you fool you*, replies he, *do you call that a storm why it was nothing at all; give us but a good ship and sea-room, and we think nothing of such a squall of wind as that; but you're but a fresh water sailor*, Bob; *come let us make a bowl of punch and we'll forget all that, d'ye see what charming weather 'tis now*. To make short this sad part of my story, we went the old way of all sailors, the punch was made, and I was made drunk with it, and in that one night's wickedness I drowned all my repentance, all my reflections upon my past conduct, and all my resolutions for my future. In a word, as the sea was returned to its smoothness of surface and settled calmness by the abatement of that storm, so the hurry of my thoughts being over, my fears and apprehensions of being swallow'd up by the sea being forgotten, and the current of my former desires return'd, I entirely forgot the vows and promises that I made in my distress. I found indeed some intervals of reflection, and the serious thoughts did, as it were, endeavour to return again sometimes, but I shook them off, and rouz'd my self from them as it were from a distemper, and applying my self to drink and company, soon master'd the return of those fits, for so I call'd them, and I had in five or six days got as compleat a victory over conscience as any young fellow that resolv'd not to be troubled with it, could desire: But I was to have another trial for it still; and Providence, as in such cases generally it does, resolv'd to leave me entirely without excuse. For if I would not take this for a deliverance, the next was to be such a one as the worst and most harden'd wretch among us would confess both the danger and the mercy.

The sixth day of our being at sea we came into *Yarmouth*[9] Roads; the wind having been contrary, and the weather calm, we had made but little way since the storm. Here we were obliged to come to anchor, and here we lay, the wind continuing contrary, *viz.* at south-west, for seven or eight days, during which time a great many ships from *Newcastle* came into the same roads, as the common harbour where the ships might wait for a wind for the river.

We had not however rid here so long, but should have tided it up the river, but that the wind blew too fresh; and after we had lain four or five days, blew very hard. However, the roads being reckoned as good as a harbour, the anchorage good, and our ground-tackle very strong, our men were unconcerned, and not in the least apprehensive of danger, but spent the time in rest and mirth, after the manner of the sea; but the eighth day in the morning, the wind encreased, and we had all hands at work to strike our top-masts, and make every thing snug and close, that the ship might ride as easy as possible. By noon the sea went very high indeed, and our ship rid *forecastle in*, shipp'd several seas, and we thought once or twice our anchor had come home; upon which our Master order'd out the sheet anchor; so that we rode with two anchors a-head, and the cables vered out to the better end.

By this time it blew a terrible storm indeed, and now I began to see terror and amazement in the faces even of the seamen themselves. The Master, tho' vigilant to the business of preserving the ship, yet as he went in and out of his cabin by me, I could hear him softly to himself say several times, *Lord be merciful to us, we shall be all lost, we shall be all undone*; and the like. During these first hurries, I was stupid, lying still in my cabin, which was in the steerage, and cannot describe my temper: I could ill re-assume the first penitence which I had so apparently trampled upon, and harden'd my self against: I thought the bitterness of death had been past, and that this would be nothing too like the first. But when the Master himself came by me, as I said just now, and said we should be all lost, I was dreadfully frighted: I got up out of my cabin, and look'd out; but such a dismal sight I never saw: The sea went mountains high, and broke upon us every three or four minutes: When I could look about, I could see nothing but distress round us: Two ships that rid near us, we found, had cut their masts by the board, being deep loaden; and our men cry'd out, that a ship which rid about a mile a-head of us was foundered. Two more ships being driven from their anchors, were run out of the roads to sea, at all adventures, and that with not a mast standing. The light ships fared the best, as not so much labouring in the sea; but two or three of them drove, and came close by us, running away with only their sprit-sail out before the wind.

Towards evening the Mate and Boat-swain begg'd the Master of our ship to let them cut away the foremast, which he was very unwilling to: But the Boat-swain protesting to him, that if he did not, the ship would founder, he consented; and when they had cut away the foremast, the main-mast stood so loose, and shook the ship so much, they were obliged to cut her away also, and make a clear deck.

Any one may judge what a condition I must be in at all this, who was but a young sailor, and who had been in such a fright before at but a little. But if I can express at this distance the thoughts I had about me at that time, I was in tenfold more horror of mind upon account of my former convictions, and the having returned from them to the resolutions I had wickedly taken at first, than I was at death it self; and these added to the terror of the storm, put me into such a condition, that I can by no words describe it. But the worst was not come yet, the storm continued with such fury, that the seamen themselves acknowledged they had never known a worse. We had a good ship, but she was deep loaden, and wallowed in the sea, that the seamen every now and then cried out, she would founder. It was my advantage in one respect, that I did not know what they meant by founder, till I enquir'd. However, the storm was so violent, that I saw what is not often seen, the Master, the Boat-swain, and some others more sensible than the rest, at their prayers, and expecting every moment when the ship would go to the bottom. In the middle of the night, and under all the rest of our distresses, one of the men that had been down on purpose to see, cried out we had sprung a leak; another said there was four foot water in the hold. Then all hands were called to the pump. At that very word my heart, as I thought, died within me, and I fell backwards upon the side of my bed where I sat, into the cabin. However, the men roused me, and told me, that I that was able to do nothing before, was as well able to pump as another; at which I stirr'd up, and went to the pump and work'd very heartily. While this was doing, the Master seeing some light colliers, who not able to ride out the storm, were oblig'd to slip and run away to sea, and would come near us, ordered to fire a gun as a signal of distress. I who knew nothing what that meant, was so surprised, that I thought the ship had broke, or some dreadful thing had happen'd. In a word, I was so surprised, that I fell down in a swoon. As this was a time when every body had his own life to think of, no body minded me, or what was become of me; but another man stept up to the pump, and thrusting me aside with his foot, let me lye, thinking I had been dead; and it was a great while before I came to my self.

We work'd on, but the water encreasing in the hold, it was apparent that the ship would founder, and tho' the storm began to abate a little, yet as it was not possible she could swim till we might run into a port, so the Master continued firing guns for help; and a light ship who had rid it out just a head of us, ventured a boat out to help us. It was with the utmost hazard the boat came near us, but it was impossible for us to get on board, or for the boat to lie near the ship side, till at last the men rowing very heartily, and venturing their lives to save ours, our men cast them a rope over the stern with a buoy to it, and then vered it out a great length, which they after great labour and hazard took hold of, and we haul'd them close under our stern and got all into their boat. It was to no purpose for them or us after we were in the boat to think of reaching to their own ship, so all agreed to let her drive, and only to pull her in towards shore as much as we could, and our Master promised them, that if the boat was stav'd upon shore he would make it good to their Master, so partly rowing and partly driving our boat went away to the norward sloaping towards the shore almost as far as *Winterton Ness*.[10]

We were not much more than a quarter of an hour out of our ship but we saw her sink, and then I understood for the first time what was meant by a ship foundering in the sea; I must acknowledge I had hardly eyes to look up when the seamen told me she was sinking; for from that moment they rather put me into the boat than that I might be said to go in, my heart was as it were dead within me, partly with fright, partly with horror of mind and the thoughts of what was yet before me.

While we were in this condition, the men yet labouring at the oar to bring the boat near the shore, we could see, when our boat mounting the waves, we were able to see the shore, a great many people running along the shore to assist us when we should come near, but we made but slow way towards the shore, nor were we able to reach the shore, till being past the light-house at *Winterton*, the shore falls off to the westward towards *Cromer*, and so the land broke off a little the violence of the wind: Here we got in, and tho' not without much difficulty got all safe on shore, and walk'd afterwards on foot to *Yarmouth*, where, as unfortunate men, we were used with great humanity, as well by the magistrates of the town, who assign'd us good quarters, as by particular merchants and owners of ships, and had money given us sufficient to carry us either to *London* or back to *Hull*, as we thought fit.

Had I now had the sense to have gone back to *Hull*, and have gone home, I had been happy, and my father, an emblem of our Blessed Saviour's parable, had even kill'd the fatted calf for me; for hearing the ship I went away in, was cast away in *Yarmouth* Road, it was a great while before he had any assurance that I was not drown'd.

But my ill fate push'd me on now with an obstinacy that nothing could resist; and tho' I had several times loud calls from my reason and my more composed judgment to go home, yet I had no power to do it. I know not what to call this, nor will I urge, that it is a secret over-ruling decree that hurries us on to be the instruments of our own destruction, even tho' it be before us, and that we rush upon it with our eyes open. Certainly nothing but some such decreed unavoidable misery attending, and which it was impossible for me to escape, could have push'd me forward against the calm reasonings and perswasions of my most retired thoughts, and against two such visible instructions as I had met with in my first attempt.

My comrade, who had help'd to harden me before, and who was the Master's son, was now less forward than I; the first time he spoke to me after we were at *Yarmouth*, which was not till two or three days, for we were separated in the town to several quarters; I say, the first time he saw me, it appear'd his tone was alter'd, and looking very melancholy, and shaking his head, ask'd me how I did, and telling his father who I was, and how I had come this voyage only for a trial, in order to go farther abroad; his father turning to me with a very grave and concern'd tone, *Young man*, says he, *you ought never to go to sea any more, you ought to take this for a plain and visible token that you are not to be a seafaring man*. Why, sir, said I, will you go to sea no more? *That is another case*, said he, *it is my calling, and therefore my duty; but as you made this voyage for a trial, you see what a taste Heaven has given you of what you are to expect if you persist; perhaps this is all befallen us on your account, like* Jonah *in the Ship of* Tarshish.[11] *Pray*, continues he, *what are you? and on what account did you go to sea?* Upon that I told him some of my story; at the end of which he burst out with a strange kind of passion, What had I done, says he, that such an unhappy wretch should come into my ship? I would not set my foot in the same ship with thee again for a thousand pounds. This indeed was, as I said, an excursion of his spirits which were yet agitated by the sense of his loss, and was farther than he could have authority to go. However he afterwards talk'd very gravely to me, exhorted me to go back to my father, and not tempt Providence to my ruin; told me I might see a visible hand of Heaven against me, *And young man*, said he, *depend upon it, if you do not go back, where ever you go, you will meet with nothing but disasters and disappointments, till your father's words are fulfilled upon you.*

We parted soon after; for I made him little answer, and I saw him no more; which way he went, I know not. As for me, having some money in my pocket, I travelled to *London* by land; and there, as well as on the road, had many struggles with my self, what course of life I should take, and whether I should go home, or go to sea.

As to going home, shame opposed the best motions that offered to my thoughts; and it immediately occurr'd to me how I should be laugh'd at among the neighbours, and should be asham'd to see, not my father and mother only, but even every body else; from whence I have since often observed, how incongruous and irrational the common temper of mankind is, especially of youth, to that reason which ought to guide them in such cases, *viz.* that they are not asham'd to sin, and yet are asham'd to repent; not asham'd of the action for which they ought justly to be esteemed fools, but are asham'd of the returning, which only can make them be esteem'd wise men.

In this state of life however I remained some time, uncertain what measures to take, and what course of life to lead. An irresistible reluctance continu'd to going home; and as I stay'd a while, the remembrance of the distress I had been in wore off; and as that abated, the little motion I had in my desires to a return wore off with it, till at last I quite laid aside the thoughts of it, and look'd out for a voyage.

That evil influence which carried me first away from my father's house, that hurried me into the wild and indigested notion of raising my fortune; and that imprest those conceits so forcibly upon me, as to make me deaf to all good advice, and to the entreaties and even command of my father: I say the same influence, whatever it was, presented the most unfortunate of all enterprises to my view; and I went on board a vessel bound to the coast of *Africa*; or, as our sailors vulgarly call it, a voyage to *Guinea*.

It was my great misfortune that in all these adventures I did not ship my self as a sailor; whereby, tho' I might indeed have workt a little harder than ordinary, yet at the same time I had learn'd the duty and office of a fore-mast man; and in time might have qualified my self for a Mate or Lieutenant, if not for a Master: But as it was always my fate to choose for the worse, so I did here; for having money in my pocket, and good clothes upon my back, I would always go on board in the habit of a gentleman; and so I neither had any business in the ship, or learn'd to do any.

It was my lot first of all to fall into pretty good company in *London*, which does not always happen to such loose and unguided young fellows as I then was; the Devil generally not omitting to lay some snare for them very early: But it was not so with me, I first fell acquainted with the Master of a ship who had been on the coast of *Guinea*; and who having had very good success there, was resolved to go again; and who taking a fancy to my conversation, which was not at all disagreeable at that time, hearing me say I had a mind to see the world, told me if I wou'd go the voyage with him I should be at no expence; I should be his mess-mate and his companion, and if I could carry any thing with me, I should have all the advantage of it that the trade would admit; and perhaps I might meet with some encouragement.

I embrac'd the offer, and entering into a strict friendship with this Captain, who was an honest and plain-dealing man, I went the voyage with him, and carried a small adventure with me, which by the disinterested honesty of my friend the Captain, I encreased very considerably; for I carried about 40*l.* in such toys and trifles as the Captain directed me to buy. This 40*l.* I had mustered together by the assistance of some of my relations whom I corresponded with, and who, I believe, got my father, or at least my mother, to contribute so much as that to my first adventure.

This was the only voyage which I may say was successful in all my adventures, and which I owe to the integrity and honesty of my friend the Captain, under whom also I got a competent knowledge of the mathematicks and the rules of navigation, learn'd how to keep an account of the ship's course, take an observation; and, in short, to understand some things that were needful to be understood by a sailor: For, as he took delight to introduce me, I took delight to learn; and, in a word, this voyage made me both a sailor and a merchant: For I brought home *L. 5. 9 ounces* of gold dust for my adventure, which yielded me in *London* at my return, almost 300*l.* and this fill'd me with those aspiring thoughts which have since so compleated my ruin.

Yet even in this voyage I had my misfortunes too; particularly, that I was continually sick, being thrown into a violent calenture by the excessive heat of the climate; our principal trading being upon the coast, from the latitude of 15 degrees, north even to the Line it self.

I was now set up for a *Guiney* trader; and my friend, to my great misfortune, dying soon after his arrival, I resolved to go the same voyage again, and I embark'd in the same vessel with one who was his Mate in the former voyage, and had now got the command of the ship. This was the unhappiest voyage that ever man made; for tho' I did not carry quite 100*l.* of my new gain'd wealth, so that I had 200 left, and which I lodg'd with my friend's widow, who was very just to me, yet I fell into terrible misfortunes in this voyage; and the first was this, *viz.* Our ship making her course towards the *Canary* Islands, or rather between those islands and the *African* shore, was surprised in the grey of the morning, by a *Turkish* rover of *Sallee*,[12] who gave chase to us with all the sail she could make. We crowded also as much canvass as our yards would spread, or our masts carry, to have got clear; but finding the pirate gain'd upon us, and would certainly come up with us in a few hours, we prepar'd to fight; our ship having 12 guns, and the rogue 18. About three in the afternoon he came up with us, and bringing to by mistake, just athwart our quarter, instead of athwart our stern,[13] as he intended, we brought 8 of our guns to bear on that side, and pour'd in a broadside upon him, which made him sheer off again, after returning our fire, and pouring in also his small shot from near 200 men which he had on board. However, we had not a man touch'd, all our men keeping close. He prepar'd to attack us again, and we to defend our selves; but laying us on board the next time upon our other quarter, he entered 60 men upon our decks, who immediately fell to cutting and hacking the decks and rigging. We ply'd them with small-shot, half-pikes, powder-chests, and such like, and clear'd our deck of them twice. However, to cut short this melancholy part of our story, our ship being disabled, and three of our men kill'd, and eight wounded, we were obliged to yield, and were carry'd all prisoners into *Sallee*, a port belonging to the *Moors*.

The usage I had there was not so dreadful as at first I apprehended, nor was I carried up the country to the Emperor's court,[14] as the rest of our men were, but was kept by the Captain of the rover, as his proper prize, and made his slave, being young and nimble, and fit for his business. At this surprising change of my circumstances, from a merchant to a miserable slave, I was perfectly over-whelmed; and now I look'd back upon my father's prophetick discourse to me, that I should be miserable, and have none to relieve me, which I thought was now so effectually brought to pass, that it could not be worse; that now the hand of Heaven had overtaken me, and I was undone without redemption. But alas! this was but a taste of the misery I was to go thro', as will appear in the sequel of this story.

As my new patron or master had taken me home to his house, so I was in hopes that he would take me with him when he went to sea again, believing that it would some time or other be his fate to be taken by a *Spanish* or *Portugal* man of war; and that then I should be set at liberty. But this hope of mine was soon taken away; for when he went to sea, he left me on shore to look after his little garden, and do the common drudgery of slaves about his house; and when he came home again from his cruise, he order'd me to lye in the cabin to look after the ship.

Here I meditated nothing but my escape; and what method I might take to effect it, but found no way that had the least probability in it: Nothing presented to make the supposition of it rational; for I had no body to communicate it to, that would embark with me, no fellow-slave, no *English-man*, *Irishman*, or *Scotsman* there but my self; so that for two years, tho' I often pleased my self with the imagination, yet I never had the least encouraging prospect of putting it in practice.

After about two years an odd circumstance presented it self, which put the old thought of making some attempt for my liberty, again in my head: My patron lying at home longer than usual, without fitting out his ship, which, as I heard, was for want of money; he used constantly, once or twice a week, sometimes oftener, if the weather was fair, to take the ship's pinnace, and go out into the road a-fishing; and as he always took me and a young *Maresco* with him to row the boat, we made him very merry, and I prov'd very dexterous in catching fish; insomuch that sometimes he would send me with a *Moor*, one of his kinsmen, and the youth the *Maresco*, as they call'd him, to catch a dish of fish for him.

It happen'd one time, that going a fishing in a stark calm morning, a fog rose so thick, that tho' we were not half a league from the shore we lost sight of it; and rowing we knew not whither or which way, we labour'd all day, and all the next night, and when the morning came we found we had pull'd off to sea instead of pulling in for the shore; and that we were at least two leagues from the shore: However we got well in again, tho' with a great deal of labour, and some danger; for the wind began to blow pretty fresh in the morning; but particularly we were all very hungry.

But our patron warn'd by this disaster, resolved to take more care of himself for the future; and having lying by him the long-boat of our *English* ship they had taken, he resolved he would not go a fishing any more without a compass and some provision; so he ordered the carpenter of his ship, who also was an *English* slave, to build a little state-room or cabin in the middle of the long-boat, like that of a barge, with a place to stand behind it to steer and hale home the main-sheet; and room before for a hand or two to stand and work the sails; she sail'd with that we call a shoulder of mutton sail; and the boom gib'd over the top of the cabin, which lay very snug and low, and had in it room for him to lye, with a slave or two, and a table to eat on, with some small lockers to put in some bottles of such liquor as he thought fit to drink in; particularly his bread, rice and coffee.

We went frequently out with this boat a fishing, and as I was most dextrous to catch fish for him, he never went without me: It happen'd that he had appointed to go out in this boat, either for pleasure or for fish, with two or three *Moors* of some distinction in that place, and for whom he had provided extraordinarily; and had therefore sent on board the boat over night, a larger store of provisions than ordinary; and had order'd me to get ready three fuzees with powder and shot, which were on board his ship; for that they design'd some sport of fowling as well as fishing.

I got all things ready as he had directed, and waited the next morning with the boat washed clean, her antient and pendants out, and every thing to accommodate his guests; when by and by my patron came on board alone, and told me his guests had put off going, upon some business that fell out, and order'd me with the man and boy, as usual, to go out with the boat and catch them some fish, for that his friends were to sup at his house; and commanded that as soon as I had got some fish I should bring it home to his house; all which I prepar'd to do.

This moment my former notions of deliverance darted into my thoughts, for now I found I was like to have a little ship at my command; and my master being gone, I prepar'd to furnish my self, not for a fishing business, but for a voyage; tho' I knew not, neither did I so much as consider whither I should steer; for any where to get out of that place was my way.

My first contrivance was to make a pretence to speak to this *Moor*, to get something for our subsistence on board; for I told him we must not presume to eat of our patron's bread; he said, that was true; so he brought a large basket of rusk or bisket of their kind, and three jars with fresh water into the boat; I knew where my patron's case of bottles stood, which it was evident by the make were taken out of some *English* prize; and I convey'd them into the boat while the *Moor* was on shore, as if they had been there before, for our master: I convey'd also a great lump of bees-wax into the boat, which weighed above half a hundred weight, with a parcel of twine or thread, a hatchet, a saw, and a hammer, all which were of great use to us afterwards; especially the wax to make candles. Another trick I try'd upon him, which he innocently came into also; his name was *Ismael*, who they call *Muly*, or *Moely*; so I call'd to him, *Moely*, said I, our patron's guns are on board the boat, can you not get a little powder and shot, it may be we may kill some *alcamies* (a fowl like our *curlieus*) for our selves, for I know he keeps the gunner's stores in the ship? Yes, *says he*, I'll bring some, and accordingly he brought a great leather pouch which held about a pound and a half of powder, or rather more; and another with shot, that had five or six pound, with some bullets; and put all into the boat: At the same time I had found some powder of my master's in the great cabin, with which I fill'd one of the large bottles in the case, which was almost empty; pouring what was in it into another: and thus furnished with every thing needful, we sail'd out of the port to fish: The castle which is at the entrance of the port knew who we were, and took no notice of us; and we were not above a mile out of the port before we hal'd in our sail, and set us down to fish: The wind blew from the N. NE. which was contrary to my desire; for had it blown southerly I had been sure to have made the coast of *Spain*, and at least reach'd to the Bay of *Cadiz*; but my resolutions were, blow which way it would, I would be gone from that horrid place where I was, and leave the rest to fate.

After we had fish'd some time and catcht nothing, for when I had fish on my hook, I would not pull them up, that he might not see them; I said to the *Moor*, this will not do, our master will not be thus serv'd, we must stand farther off: He thinking no harm agreed, and being in the head of the boat set the sails; and as I had the helm I run the boat out near a league farther, and then brought her to as if I would fish; when giving the boy the helm, I stept forward to where the *Moor* was, and making as if I stoopt for something behind him, I took him by suprise with my arm under his twist, and tost him clear over-board into the sea; he rose immediately, for he swam like a cork, and call'd to me, begg'd to be taken in, told me he would go all over the world with me; he swam so strong after the boat that he would have reach'd me very quickly, there being but little wind; upon which I stept into the cabin, and fetching one of the fowling-pieces, I presented it at him, and told him, I had done him no hurt, and if he would be quiet I would do him none; but said I, you swim well enough to reach to the shore and the sea is calm, make the best of your way to shore, and I will do you no harm, but if you come near the boat I'll shoot you thro' the head; for I am resolved to have my liberty; so he turn'd himself about and swam for the shore, and I make no doubt but he reach'd it with ease, for he was an excellent swimmer.

I could have been content to ha' taken this *Moor* with me, and ha' drown'd the boy, but there was no venturing to trust him: When he was gone I turn'd to the boy, who they call'd *Xury*, and said to him, *Xury*, if you will be faithful to me I'll make you a great man, but if you will not stroak your face to be true to me, *that is, swear by* Mahomet *and his father's beard*, I must throw you into the sea too; the boy smil'd in my face, and

20

spoke so innocently that I could not mistrust him; and swore to be faithful to me, and go all over the world with me.

While I was in view of the *Moor* that was swimming, I stood out directly to sea with the boat, rather stretching to windward, that they might think me gone towards the *Straits*-mouth[15] (as indeed any one that had been in their wits must ha' been suppos'd to do) for who wou'd ha' suppos'd we were sail'd on to the southward to the truly *barbarian* coast, where whole nations of Negroes were sure to surround us with their canoes, and destroy us; where we could ne'er once go on shore but we should be devour'd by savage beasts, or more merciless savages of human kind.

But as soon as it grew dusk in the evening, I chang'd my course, and steer'd directly south and by east, bending my course a little toward the east, that I might keep in with the shore; and having a fair fresh gale of wind, and a smooth quiet sea, I made such sail that I believe by the next day at three a clock in the afternoon, when I first made the land, I could not be less than 150 miles south of *Sallee*; quite beyond the Emperor of *Morocco's* dominions, or indeed of any other king thereabouts, for we saw no people.

Yet such was the fright I had taken at the *Moors*, and the dreadful apprehensions I had of falling into their hands, that I would not stop, or go on shore, or come to an anchor; the wind continuing fair, till I had sail'd in that manner five days: And then the wind shifting to the southward, I concluded also that if any of our vessels were in chase of me, they also would now give over; so I ventur'd to make to the coast, and came to an anchor in the mouth of a little river, I knew not what, or where; neither what latitude, what country, what nation, or what river: I neither saw, or desir'd to see any people, the principal thing I wanted was fresh water: We came into this creek in the evening, resolving to swim on shore as soon as it was dark, and discover the country; but as soon as it was quite dark, we heard such dreadful noises of the barking, roaring, and howling of wild creatures, of we knew not what kinds, that the poor boy was ready to die with fear, and beg'd of me not to go on shore till day; well *Xury*, said I, then I won't, but it may be we may see men by day, who will be as bad to us as those lyons; *then we give them the shoot gun*, says *Xury*, laughing, *make them run wey*; such *English Xury* spoke by conversing among us slaves, however I was glad to see the boy so cheerful, and I gave him a dram (out of our patron's case of bottles) to cheer him up: After all, *Xury's* advice was good, and I took it, we dropp'd our little anchor and lay still all night;

I say still, for we slept none! for in two or three hours we saw vast great creatures (we knew not what to call them) of many sorts, come down to the sea-shore and run into the water, wallowing and washing themselves for the pleasure of cooling themselves; and they made such hideous howlings and yellings, that I never indeed heard the like.

Xury was dreadfully frighted, and indeed so was I too; but we were both more frighted when we heard one of these mighty creatures come swimming towards our boat, we could not see him, but we might hear him by his blowing to be a monstrous, huge and furious beast; *Xury* said it was a lyon, and it might be so for ought I know; but poor *Xury* cried to me to weigh the anchor and row away; no, says I, *Xury*, we can slip our cable with the buoy to it and go off to sea, they cannot follow us far; I had no sooner said so, but I perceiv'd the creature (whatever it was) within two oars length, which something surprised me; however I immediately stept to the cabin-door, and taking up my gun fir'd at him, upon which he immediately turn'd about, and swam towards the shore again.

But it is impossible to describe the horrible noises, and hideous cries and howlings, that were raised as well upon the edge of the shore, as higher within the country; upon the noise or report of the gun, a thing I have some reason to believe those creatures had never heard before: This convinc'd me that there was no going on shore for us in the night upon that coast, and how to venture on shore in the day was another question too; for to have fallen into the hands of any of the savages, had been as bad as to have fallen into the hands of lyons and tygers; at least we were equally apprehensive of the danger of it.

Be that as it would, we were oblig'd to go on shore somewhere or other for water, for we had not a pint left in the boat; when or where to get to it was the point: *Xury* said, if I would let him go on shore with one of the jars, he would find if there was any water and bring some to me. I ask'd him why he would go? Why I should not go and he stay in the boat? The boy answer'd with so much affection that made me love him ever after. Says he, *If wild mans come, they eat me, you go wey*. Well, *Xury*, said I, we will both go, and if the wild mans come, we will kill them, they shall eat neither of us; so I gave *Xury* a piece of rusk-bread to eat, and a dram out of our patron's case of bottles which I mentioned before; and we hal'd the boat in as near the shore as we thought was proper, and waded on shore, carrying nothing but our arms and two jars for water.

I did not care to go out of sight of the boat, fearing the coming of canoes with *savages* down the river; but the boy seeing a low place about a mile up the country, rambled to it; and by and by I saw him come running towards me. I thought he was pursued by some savage, or frighted with some wild beast, and I run forward towards him to help him, but when I came nearer to him, I saw something hanging over his shoulders which was a creature that he had shot, like a hare, but different in colour, and longer legs, however we were very glad of it, and it was very good meat; but the great joy that poor *Xury* came with, was to tell me he had found good water and seen no wild mans.

But we found afterwards that we need not take such pains for water, for a little higher up the creek where we were, we found the water fresh when the tide was out, which flowed but a little way up; so we filled our jars and feasted on the hare we had killed, and prepared to go on our way, having seen no foot-steps of any human creature in that part of the country.

As I had been one voyage to this coast before, I knew very well that the islands of the *Canaries*, and the *Cape de Verd* Islands[16] also, lay not far off from the coast. But as I had no instruments to take an observation to know what latitude we were in, and did not exactly know, or at least remember what latitude they were in; I knew not where to look for them, or when to stand off to sea towards them; otherwise I might now easily have found some of these islands. But my hope was, that if I stood along this coast till I came to that part where the *English* traded, I should find some of their vessels upon their usual design of trade, that would relieve and take us in.

By the best of my calculation, that place where I now was, must be that country, which lying between the Emperor of *Morocco's* dominions and the *Negroes*, lies waste and uninhabited, except by wild beasts; the *Negroes* having abandon'd it, and gone farther south for fear of the *Moors*; and the *Moors* not thinking it worth inhabiting, by reason of its barrenness; and indeed both forsaking it because of the prodigious numbers of tygers, lyons, leopards, and other furious creatures which harbour there; so that the *Moors* use it for their hunting only, where they go like an army, two or three thousand men at a time; and indeed for near an hundred miles together upon this coast, we saw nothing but a waste uninhabited country, by day; and heard nothing but howlings and roaring of wild beasts, by night.

Once or twice in the day time, I thought I saw the *Pico* of *Teneriffe*, being the high top of the mountain *Teneriffe* in the *Canaries*; and had a great mind to venture out in hopes of reaching thither; but having tried twice I was forced in again by contrary winds, the sea also going too high for my little vessel, so I resolved to pursue my first design and keep along the shore.

Several times I was obliged to land for fresh water, after we had left this place; and once in particular, being early in the morning, we came to an anchor under a little point of land which was pretty high, and the tide beginning to slow, we lay still to go farther in; *Xury*, whose eyes were more about him than it seems mine were, calls softly to me, and tells me that we had best go farther off the shore; for, says he, look yonder lies a dreadful monster on the side of that hillock fast asleep: I look'd where he pointed, and saw a dreadful monster indeed, for it was a terrible great lyon that lay on the side of the shore, under the shade of a piece of the hill that hung as it were a little over him. *Xury*, says I, you shall go on shore and kill him; *Xury* look'd frighted, and said, *Me kill! he eat me at one mouth*; one mouthful he meant; however, I said no more to the boy, but bad him lye still, and I took our biggest gun, which was almost musquet-bore, and loaded it with a good charge of powder, and with two slugs, and laid it down; then I loaded another gun with two bullets, and the third, for we had three pieces, I loaded with five smaller bullets. I took the best aim I could with the first piece to have shot him into the head, but he lay so with his leg rais'd a little above his nose, that the slugs hit his leg about the knee, and broke the bone. He started up growling at first, but finding his leg broke fell down again, and then got up upon three legs and gave the most hideous roar that ever I heard; I was a little surpris'd that I had not hit him on the head; however I took up the second piece immediately, and tho' he began to move off fir'd again, and shot him into the head, and had the pleasure to see him drop, and make but little noise, but lay struggling for life. Then *Xury* took heart, and would have me let him go on shore: Well, go said I; so the boy jump'd into the water, and taking a little gun in one hand, swam to shore with the other hand, and coming close to the creature, put the muzzle of the piece to his ear, and shot him into the head again which dispatch'd him quite.

This was game indeed to us, but this was no food, and I was very sorry to lose three charges of powder and shot upon a creature that was good for nothing to us. However *Xury* said he would have some of him; so he comes on board, and ask'd me to give him the hatchet; for what, *Xury*, said I? *Me cut off his head*, said he. However *Xury* could not cut off his head, but he cut off a foot, and brought it with him, and it was a monstrous great one.

I bethought my self however, that perhaps the skin of him might one way or other be of some value to us; and I resolved to take off his skin if I could. So *Xury* and I went to work with him; but *Xury* was much the better workman at it, for I knew very ill how to do it. Indeed it took us up both the whole day, but at last we got off the hide of him, and spreading it on the top of our cabin, the sun effectually dried it in two days time, and it afterwards serv'd me to lye upon.

After this stop we made on to the southward continually for ten or twelve days, living very sparing on our provisions, which began to abate very much, and going no oftner into the shore than we were oblig'd to for fresh water; my design in this was to make the River *Gambia* or *Sennegall*,[17] that is to say, any where about the *Cape de Verd*, where I was in hopes to meet with some *European* Ship, and if I did not, I knew not what course I had to take, but to seek out for the *Islands*, or perish there among the *Negroes*. I knew that all the ships from *Europe*, which sail'd either to the Coast of *Guiney*, or to *Brasil*, or to the *East-Indies*, made this *Cape* or those *Islands*; and in a word, I put the whole of my fortune upon this single point, either that I must meet with some ship, or must perish.

When I had pursued this resolution about ten days longer, as I have said, I began to see that the land was inhabited, and in two or three places as we sailed by, we saw people stand upon the shore to look at us, we could also perceive they were quite black and stark-naked. I was once inclin'd to ha' gone on shore to them; but *Xury* was my better councellor, and said to me, *no go, no go*; however I hal'd in nearer the shore that I might talk to them, and I found they run along the shore by me a good way; I observ'd they had no weapons in their hands, except one who had a long slender stick, which *Xury* said was a lance, and that they would throw them a great way with good aim; so I kept at a distance, but talk'd with them by signs as well as I could; and particularly made signs for something to eat, they beckon'd to me to stop my boat, and they would fetch me some meat; upon this I lower'd the top of my sail, and lay by, and two of them run up into the country, and in less than half an hour came back, and brought with them two pieces of dry flesh and some corn, such as is the produce of their country, but we neither knew what the one or the other was; however we were willing to accept it, but how to come at it was our next dispute, for I was not for venturing on shore to them, and they were as much afraid of us; but they took a safe way for us all, for they brought it to the shore and laid it down, and went and stood a great way off till we fetch'd it on board, and then came close to us again.

We made signs of thanks to them, for we had nothing to make them amends; but an opportunity offer'd that very instant to oblige them wonderfully, for while we were lying by the shore, came two mighty creatures, one pursuing the other, (as we took it) with great fury, from the mountains towards the sea; whether it was the male pursuing the female, or whether they were in sport or in rage, we could not tell, any more than we could tell whether it was usual or strange, but I believe it was the latter; because in the first place, those ravenous creatures seldom appear but in the night; and in the second place, we found the people terribly frighted, especially the women. The man that had the lance or dart did not fly from them, but the rest did; however as the two creatures ran directly into the water, they did not seem to offer to fall upon any of the *Negroes*, but plung'd themselves into the sea and swam about as if they had come for their diversion; at last one of them began to come nearer our boat than at first I expected, but I lay ready for him, for I had loaded my gun with all possible expedition, and bad *Xury* load both the other; as soon as he came fairly within my reach, I fir'd, and shot him directly into the head; immediately he sunk down into the water, but rose instantly and plung'd up and down as if he was struggling for life; and so indeed he was; he immediately made to the shore, but between the wound which was his mortal hurt, and the strangling of the water, he dyed just before he reach'd the shore.

It is impossible to express the astonishment of these poor creatures at the noise and the fire of my gun; some of them were even ready to dye for fear, and fell down as dead with the very terror. But when they saw the creature dead and sunk in the water, and that I made signs to them to come to the shore; they took heart and came to the shore and began to search for the creature. I found him by his blood staining the water, and by the help of a rope which I slung round him and gave the *Negroes* to hawl, they drag'd him on shore, and found that it was a most curious leopard, spotted and fine to an admirable degree, and the *Negroes* held up their hands with admiration to think what it was I had kill'd him with.

The other creature frighted with the flash of fire and the noise of the gun swam on shore, and ran up directly to the mountains from whence they came, nor could I at that distance know what it was. I found quickly the *Negroes* were for eating the flesh of this creature, so I was willing to have them take it as a favour from me, which when I made signs to them that they might take him, they were very thankful for, immediately they fell to work with him, and tho' they had no knife, yet with a sharpen'd piece of wood they took off his skin as readily, and much more readily than we cou'd have done with a knife; they offer'd me some of the flesh, which I declined, making as if I would give it them, but made signs for the skin, which they gave me very freely, and brought me a great deal more of their provision, which tho' I did not understand, yet I accepted; then I made signs to them for some water, and held out one of my jars to them, turning it bottom upward, to shew that it was empty, and that I wanted to have it filled. They call'd immediately to some of their friends, and there came two women and brought a great vessel made of earth, and burnt as I suppose in the sun; this they set down for me, as before, and I sent *Xury* on shore with my jars, and filled them all three. The women were as stark naked as the men.

I was now furnished with roots and corn, such as it was, and water, and leaving my friendly *Negroes*, I made forward for about eleven days more, without offering to go near the shore, till I saw the land run out a great length into the sea, at about the distance of four or five leagues before me, and the sea being very calm, I kept a large offing to make this point; at length, doubling the point at about two leagues from the land, I saw plainly land on the other side to seaward; then I concluded, as it was most certain indeed, that this was the *Cape de Verd*, and those the *Islands*, call'd from thence *Cape de Verd Islands*. However they were at a great distance, and I could not well tell what I had best to do, for if I should be taken with a fresh of wind I might neither reach one or other.

In this dilemma, as I was very pensive, I stept into the cabin, and sat me down, *Xury* having the helm, when on a sudden the boy cry'd out *Master, Master, a ship with a sail*, and the foolish boy was frighted out of his wits, thinking it must needs be some of his master's ships sent to pursue us, when, I knew we were gotten far enough out of their reach. I jump'd out of the cabin, and immediately saw not only the ship, but what she was, (*viz.*) that it was a *Portuguese* ship, and as I thought was bound to the coast of *Guinea* for *Negroes*. But when I observ'd the course she steer'd, I was soon convinc'd they were bound some other way, and did not design to come any nearer to the shore; upon which I stretch'd out to sea as much as I could, resolving to speak with them if possible.

With all the sail I could make I found I should not be able to come in their way, but that they would be gone by, before I could make any signal to them; but after I had crowded to the utmost, and began to despair, they it seems saw me by the help of their perspective-glasses, and that it was some *European* boat, which as they supposed must belong to some ship that was lost, so they shortned sail to let me come up. I was encouraged with this, and as I had my patron's antient on board, I made a waft of it to them for a signal of distress, and fir'd a gun, both which they saw, for they told me they saw the smoke, tho' they did not hear the gun; upon these signals they very kindly brought to, and lay by for me, and in about three hours time I came up with them.

They ask'd me what I was, in *Portuguese*, and in *Spanish*, and in *French*, but I understood none of them; but at last a *Scots* sailor who was on board, call'd to me, and I answer'd him, and told him I was an *Englishman*, that I had made my escape out of slavery from the *Moors* at *Sallee*; then they bad me come on board, and very kindly took me in, and all my goods.

It was an inexpressible joy to me, that any one will believe, that I was thus deliver'd, as I esteem'd it, from such a miserable and almost hopeless condition as I was in, and I immediately offered all I had to the Captain of the ship, as a return for my deliverance; but he generously told me, he would take nothing from me, but that all I had should be deliver'd safe to me when I came to the *Brasils*; for, says he, *I have sav'd your life on no other terms than I would be glad to be saved my self, and it may one time or other be my lot to be taken up in the same condition; besides,* said he, *when I carry you to the* Brasils, *so great a way from your own country, if I should take from you what you have, you will be starved there, and then I only take away that life I have given. No, no, Seignor,* Inglese, says he, *Mr.* English-man, *I will carry you thither in charity, and those things will help you to buy your subsistance there, and your passage home again.*

As he was charitable in his proposal, so he was just in the performance to a tittle, for he ordered the seamen, that none should offer to touch any thing I had; then he took every thing into his own possession, and gave me back an exact inventory of them, that I might have them, even so much as my three earthen jars.

As to my boat it was a very good one, and that he saw, and told me he would buy it of me for the ship's use, and ask'd me what I would have for it? I told him he had been so generous to me in every thing, that I could not offer to make any price of the boat, but left it entirely to him, upon which he told me he would give me a note of his hand to pay me 80 Pieces of Eight for it at *Brasil*, and when it came there, if any one offer'd to give more he would make it up; he offer'd me also 60 Pieces of Eight more for my boy *Xury*, which I was loath to take, not that I was not willing to let the Captain have him, but I was very loath to sell the poor boy's liberty, who had assisted me so faithfully in procuring my own. However when I let him know my reason, he own'd it to be just, and offer'd me this medium, that he would give the boy an obligation to set him free in ten years, if he turn'd Christian; upon this, and *Xury* saying he was willing to go to him, I let the Captain have him.

We had a very good Voyage to the *Brasils*, and arriv'd in the *Bay de Todos los Santos*, or *All-Saints Bay*,[18] in about twenty-two days after. And now I was once more deliver'd from the most miserable of all conditions of life, and what to do next with my self I was now to consider.

The generous treatment the Captain gave me, I can never enough remember; he would take nothing of me for my passage, gave me twenty Ducats for the leopard's skin, and forty for the lyon's skin which I had in my boat, and caused every thing I had in the ship to be punctually deliver'd me, and what I was willing to sell he bought, such as the case of bottles, two of my guns, and a piece of the lump of bees-wax, for I had made candles of the rest; in a word, I made about 220 Pieces of Eight of all my cargo, and with this stock I went on shore in the *Brasils*.

I had not been long here, but being recommended to the house of a good honest man like himself, who had an *Ingeino* as they call it; that is, a plantation and a sugar-house. I lived with him some time, and acquainted my self by that means with the manner of their planting and making of sugar; and seeing how well the planters liv'd, and how they grew rich suddenly, I resolv'd, if I could get licence to settle there, I would turn planter among them, resolving in the mean time to find out some way to get my money which I had left in *London* remitted to me. To this purpose getting a kind of a letter of naturalization, I purchased as much land that was uncur'd, as my money would reach, and form'd a plan for my plantation and settlement, and such a one as might be suitable to the stock which I proposed to my self to receive from *England*.

I had a neighbour, a *Portuguese* of *Lisbon*, but born of *English* parents, whose name was *Wells*, and in much such circumstances as I was. I call him my neighbour, because his plantation lay next to mine, and we went on very sociably together. My stock was but low as well as his; and we rather planted for food than any thing else, for about two years. However, we began to encrease, and our land began to come into order; so that the third year we planted some tobacco, and made each of us a large piece of ground ready for planting canes in the year to come; but we both wanted help; and now I found more than before, I had done wrong in parting with my boy *Xury*.

But alas! for me to do wrong that never did right, was no great wonder: I had no remedy but to go on; I was gotten into an employment quite remote to my genius, and directly contrary to the life I delighted in, and for which I forsook my father's house, and broke thro' all his good advice; nay, I was coming into the very middle station, or upper degree of low life, which my father advised me to before; and which if I resolved to go on with, I might as well ha' staid at home, and never have fatigu'd my self in the world as I had done; and I used often to say to my self, I could ha' done this as well in *England* among my friends, as ha' gone 5000 miles off to do it among strangers and savages in a wilderness, and at such a distance, as never to hear from any part of the world that had the least knowledge of me.

In this manner I used to look upon my condition with the utmost regret. I had no body to converse with but now and then this neighbour; no work to be done, but by the labour of my hands; and I used to say, I liv'd just like a man cast away upon some desolate island, that had no body there but himself. But how just has it been, and how should all men reflect, that when they compare their present conditions with others that are worse, Heaven may oblige them to make the exchange, and be convinc'd of their former felicity, by their experience: I say, how just has it been, that the truly solitary life I reflected on in an island of meer desolation should be my lot, who had so often unjustly compar'd it with the life which I then led, in which had I continued, I had in all probability been exceeding prosperous and rich.

I was in some degree settled in my measures for carrying on the plantation, before my kind friend the Captain of the ship that took me up at sea, went back; for the ship remained there in providing his loading, and preparing for his voyage, near three months, when telling him what little stock I had left behind me in *London*, he gave me this friendly and sincere advice, *Seignor Inglese*, says he; for so he always called me, if you will give me letters, and a procuration here in form to me, with orders to the person who has your money in *London*, to send your effects to *Lisbon*, to such persons as I shall direct, and in such goods as are proper for this country, I will bring you the produce of them, God willing, at my return; but since human affairs are all subject to changes and disasters, I would have you give orders but for one hundred Pounds *Sterl.* which you say is half your stock, and let the hazard be run for the first; so that if it come safe, you may order the rest the same way; and if it miscarry, you may have the other half to have recourse to for your supply.

This was so wholesom advice, and look'd so friendly, that I could not but be convinc'd it was the best course I could take; so I accordingly prepared letters to the gentlewoman with whom I had left my money, and a procuration to the *Portuguese* Captain, as he desired.

I wrote the *English* Captain's widow a full account of all my adventures, my slavery, escape, and how I had met with the *Portugal* Captain at sea, the humanity of his behaviour, and in what condition I was now in, with all other necessary directions for my supply; and when this honest Captain came to *Lisbon*, he found means by some of the *English* merchants there, to send over not the order only, but a full account of my story to a merchant at *London*, who represented it effectually to her; whereupon, she not only delivered the money, but out of her own pocket sent the *Portugal* Captain a very handsom present for his humanity and charity to me.

The merchant in *London* vesting this hundred Pounds in *English* goods, such as the Captain had writ for, sent them directly to him at *Lisbon*, and he brought them all safe to me to the *Brasils*, among which, without my direction (for I was too young in my business to think of them) he had taken care to have all sorts of tools, iron-work, and utensils necessary for my plantation, and which were of great use to me.

When this cargo arrived, I thought my fortune made, for I was surprised with the joy of it; and my good steward the Captain had laid out the five Pounds which my friend had sent him for a present for himself, to purchase, and bring me over a servant under bond for six years service, and would not accept of any consideration, except a little tobacco, which I would have him accept, being of my own produce.

Neither was this all; but my goods being all *English* manufactures, such as cloth, stuffs, bays, and things particularly valuable and desirable in the country, I found means to sell them to a very great advantage; so that I might say, I had more than four times the value of my first cargo, and was now infinitely beyond my poor neighbour, I mean in the advancement of my plantation; for the first thing I did, I bought me a *Negro* slave, and an *European* servant also; I mean another besides that which the Captain brought me from *Lisbon*.

But as abus'd prosperity is oftentimes made the very means of our greatest adversity, so was it with me. I went on the next year with great success in my plantation: I raised fifty great rolls of tobacco on my own ground, more than I had disposed of for necessaries among my neighbours; and these fifty rolls being each of above a 100 *wt.* were well cur'd and laid by against the return of the fleet from *Lisbon*: and now increasing in business and in wealth, my head began to be full of projects and undertakings beyond my reach; such as are indeed often the ruin of the best heads in business.

Had I continued in the station I was now in, I had room for all the happy things to have yet befallen me, for which my father so earnestly recommended a quiet retired life, and of which he had so sensibly described the middle station of life to be full of; but other things attended me, and I was still to be the wilful agent of all my own miseries; and particularly to encrease my fault and double the reflections upon my self, which in my future sorrows I should have leisure to make; all these miscarriages were procured by my apparent obstinate adhering to my foolish inclination of wandring abroad, and pursuing that inclination, in contradiction to the clearest views of doing my self good in a fair and plain pursuit of those prospects and those measures of life, which Nature and Providence concurred to present me with, and to make my duty.

As I had once done thus in my breaking away from my parents, so I could not be content now, but I must go and leave the happy view I had of being a rich and thriving man in my new plantation, only to pursue a rash and immoderate desire of rising faster than the nature of the thing admitted; and thus I cast my self down again into the deepest gulph of human misery that ever man fell into, or perhaps could be consistent with life and a state of health in the world.

To come then by the just degrees, to the particulars of this part of my story; you may suppose, that having now lived almost four years in the *Brasils*, and beginning to thrive and prosper very well upon my plantation; I had not only learn'd the language, but had contracted acquaintance and friendship among my fellow-planters, as well as among the merchants at St. *Salvadore*, which was our port; and that in my discourses among them, I had frequently given them an account of my two voyages to the coast of *Guinea*, the manner of trading with the *Negroes* there, and how easy it was to purchase upon the coast, for trifles, such as beads, toys, knives, scissars, hatchets, bits of glass, and the like; not only gold dust, *Guinea* grains, elephants teeth, *&c.* but *Negroes* for the service of the *Brasils*, in great numbers.

They listened always very attentively to my discourses on these heads, but especially to that part which related to the buying *Negroes*, which was a trade at that time not only not far entred into, but as far as it was, had been carried on by the Assiento's,[19] or permission of the Kings of *Spain* and *Portugal*, and engross'd in the publick, so that few *Negroes* were brought, and those excessive dear.

It happen'd, being in company with some merchants and planters of my acquaintance, and talking of those things very earnestly, three of them came to me the next morning, and told me they had been musing very much upon what I had discoursed with them of, the last night, and they came to make a secret proposal to me; and after enjoining me secrecy, they told me, that they had a mind to fit out a ship to go to *Guinea*, that they had all plantations as well as I, and were straiten'd for nothing so much as servants; that as it was a trade that could not be carried on, because they could not publickly sell the *Negroes* when they came home, so they desired to make but one voyage, to bring the *Negroes* on shore privately, and divide them among their own plantations; and in a word, the question was, whether I would go their super-cargo in the ship to manage the trading part upon the coast of *Guinea*? And they offer'd me that I should have my equal share of the *Negroes* without providing any part of the stock.

This was a fair proposal it must be confess'd, had it been made to any one that had not had a settlement and plantation of his own to look after, which was in a fair way of coming to be very considerable, and with a good stock upon it. But for me that was thus entered and established, and had nothing to do but go on as I had begun for three or four years more, and to have sent for the other hundred Pound from *England*, and who in that time, and with that little addition, could scarce ha' fail'd of being worth three or four thousand Pounds Sterling, and that encreasing too; for me to think of such a voyage, was the most preposterous thing that ever man in such circumstances could be guilty of.

But I that was born to be my own destroyer, could no more resist the offer than I could restrain my first rambling designs, when my father's good counsel was lost upon me. In a word, I told them I would go with all my heart, if they would undertake to look after my plantation in my absence, and would dispose of it to such as I should direct if I miscarry'd. This they all engag'd to do, and entred into writings or covenants to do so; and I made a formal will, disposing of my plantation and effects, in case of my death, making the Captain of the ship that had sav'd my life as before, my universal heir, but obliging him to dispose of my effects as I had directed in my will, one half of the produce being to himself, and the other to be ship'd to *England*.

In short, I took all possible caution to preserve my effects, and keep up my plantation; had I used half as much prudence to have look'd into my own interest, and have made a judgment of what I ought to have done, and not to have done, I had certainly never gone away from so prosperous an undertaking, leaving all the probable views of a thriving circumstance, and gone upon a voyage to sea, attended with all its common hazards; to say nothing of the reasons I had to expect particular misfortunes to my self.

But I was hurried on, and obey'd blindly the dictates of my fancy rather than my reason; and accordingly the ship being fitted out, and the cargo furnished, and all things done as by agreement, by my partners in the voyage, I went on board in an evil hour, the —th of —,[20] being the same day eight year that I went from my father and mother at *Hull*, in order to act the rebel to their authority, and the fool to my own interest.

Our ship was about 120 tun burthen,[21] carried 6 guns, and 14 men, besides the Master, his boy, and my self; we had on board no large cargo of goods, except of such toys as were fit for our trade with the *Negroes*, such as beads, bits of glass, shells, and odd trifles, especially little looking-glasses, knives, scissars, hatchets, and the like.

The same day I went on board we set sail, standing away to the northward upon our own coast, with design to stretch over for the *African* coast, when they came about 10 or 12 degrees of northern latitude, which it seems was the manner of their course in those days. We had very good weather, only excessive hot, all the way upon our own coast, till we came the height of *Cape St. Augustino*, from whence keeping farther off at sea we lost sight of land, and steer'd as if we was bound for the isle *Fernand de Noronha*,[22] holding our course *N. E. by N.* and leaving those isles on the east; in this course we past the Line in about 12 days time, and were by our last observation in 7 degrees 22 min. northern latitude, when a violent tournado or hurricane took us quite out of our knowledge; it began from the south-east, came about to the north-west, and then settled into the north-east, from whence it blew in such a terrible manner, that for 12 days together we could do nothing but drive, and scudding away before it, let it carry us whither ever fate and the fury of the winds directed; and during these 12 days, I need not say, that I expected every day to be swallowed up, nor indeed did any in the ship expect to save their lives.

In this distress, we had besides the terror of the storm, one of our men died of the calenture, and one man and the boy wash'd over board; about the 12th day the weather abating a little, the Master made an observation as well as he could, and found that he was in about 11 degrees north latitude, but that he was 22 degrees of longitude difference west from *Cape* St. *Augustino*; so that he found he was gotten upon the coast of *Guinea*, or the north part of *Brasil*, beyond the River *Amazones*, toward that of the River *Oroonoko*, commonly call'd the *Great River*, and began to consult with me what course he should take, for the ship was leaky and very much disabled, and he was going directly back to the coast of *Brasil*.

I was positively against that, and looking over the charts of the sea-coast of *America* with him, we concluded there was no inhabited country for us to have recourse to, till we came within the circle of the *Carribbe-Islands*, and therefore resolved to stand away for *Barbadoes*, which by keeping off at sea, to avoid the indraft of the Bay or Gulph of *Mexico*, we might easily perform, as we hoped, in about fifteen days sail; whereas we could not possibly make our voyage to the coast of *Africa* without some assistance, both to our ship and to our selves.

With this design we chang'd our course, and steer'd away N. W. by W. in order to reach some of our *English* islands, where I hoped for relief; but our voyage was otherwise determined, for being in the latitude of 12 deg. 18 min. a second storm came upon us, which carry'd us away with the same impetuosity westward, and drove us so out of the very way of all human commerce, that had all our lives been saved, as to the sea, we were rather in danger of being devoured by savages than ever returning to our own country.

In this distress, the wind still blowing very hard, one of our men early in the morning, cry'd out, *Land*; and we had no sooner run out of the cabin to look out in hopes of seeing whereabouts in the world we were; but the ship struck upon a sand, and in a moment her motion being so stopp'd, the sea broke over her in such a manner, that we expected we should all have perish'd immediately, and we were immediately driven into our close quarters to shelter us from the very foam and sprye of the sea.

It is not easy for any one, who has not been in the like condition, to describe or conceive the consternation of men in such circumstances; we knew nothing where we were, or upon what land it was we were driven, whether an island or the main, whether inhabited or not inhabited; and as the rage of the wind was still great, tho' rather less than at first, we could not so much as hope to have the ship hold many minutes without breaking in pieces, unless the winds by a kind of miracle should turn immediately about. In a word, we sat looking one upon another, and expecting death every moment, and every man acting accordingly, as preparing for another world, for there was little or nothing more for us to do in this; that which was our present comfort, and all the comfort we had, was, that contrary to our expectation the ship did not break yet, and that the Master said the wind began to abate.

Now tho' we thought that the wind did a little abate, yet the ship having thus struck upon the sand, and sticking too fast for us to expect her getting off, we were in a dreadful condition indeed, and had nothing to do but to think of saving our lives as well as we could; we had a boat at our stern, just before the storm, but she was first stav'd by dashing against the ship's rudder, and in the next place she broke away, and either sunk or was driven off to sea, so there was no hope from her; we had another boat on board, but how to get her off into the sea, was a doubtful thing; however there was no room to debate, for we fancy'd the ship would break in pieces every minute, and some told us she was actually broken already.

In this distress, the Mate of our vessel lays hold of the boat, and with the help of the rest of the men, they got her slung over the ship's-side, and getting all into her, let go, and committed our selves being eleven in number, to God's mercy, and the wild sea; for tho' the storm was abated considerably, yet the sea went dreadful high upon the shore, and might well be call'd, *Den wild Zee*,[23] as the *Dutch* call the sea in a storm.

And now our case was very dismal indeed; for we all saw plainly, that the sea went so high, that the boat could not live, and that we should be inevitably drowned. As to making sail, we had none, nor, if we had, could we ha' done any thing with it; so we work'd at the oar towards the land, tho' with heavy hearts, like men going to execution; for we all knew, that when the boat came nearer the shore, she would be dash'd in a thousand pieces by the breach of the sea. However, we committed our souls to God in the most earnest manner, and the wind driving us towards the shore, we hasten'd our destruction with our own hands, pulling as well as we could towards land.

What the shore was, whether rock or sand, whether steep or shoal, we knew not; the only hope that could rationally give us the least shadow of expectation, was, if we might happen into some bay or gulph, or the mouth of some river, where by great chance we might have run our boat in, or got under the lee of the land, and perhaps made smooth water. But there was nothing of this appeared; but as we made nearer and nearer the shore, the land look'd more frightful than the sea.

After we had row'd, or rather driven about a league and a half, as we reckon'd it, a raging wave, mountain-like, came rowling a-stern of us, and plainly bad us expect the *coup de grace*. In a word, it took us with such a fury, that it overset the boat at once; and separating us as well from the boat, as from one another, gave us not time hardly to say, O God! for we were all swallowed up in a moment.

Nothing can describe the confusion of thought which I felt when I sunk into the water; for tho' I swam very well, yet I could not deliver my self from the waves so as to draw breath, till that wave having driven me, or rather carried me a vast way on towards the shore, and having spent it self, went back, and left me upon the land almost dry, but half-dead with the water I took in. I had so much presence of mind as well as breath left, that seeing my self nearer the main land than I expected, I got upon my feet, and endeavoured to make on towards the land as fast as I could, before another wave should return, and take me up again. But I soon found it was impossible to avoid it; for I saw the sea come after me as high as a great hill, and as furious as an enemy which I had no means or strength to contend with; my business was to hold my breath, and raise my self upon the water, if I could; and so by swimming to preserve my breathing, and pilot my self towards the shore, if possible; my greatest concern now being, that the sea, as it would carry me a great way towards the shore when it came on, might not carry me back again with it when it gave back towards the sea.

The wave that came upon me again, buried me at once 20 or 30 foot deep in its own body; and I could feel my self carried with a mighty force and swiftness towards the shore a very great way; but I held my breath, and assisted my self to swim still forward with all my might. I was ready to burst with holding my breath, when, as I felt my self rising up, so to my immediate relief, I found my head and hands shoot out above the surface of the water; and tho' it was not two seconds of time that I could keep my self so, yet it reliev'd me greatly, gave me breath and new courage. I was covered again with water a good while, but not so long but I held it out; and finding the water had spent it self, and began to return, I stroock forward against the return of the waves, and felt ground again with my feet. I stood still a few moments to recover breath, and till the water went from me, and then took to my heels, and run with what strength I had farther towards the shore. But neither would this deliver me from the fury of the sea, which came pouring in after me again, and twice more I was lifted up by the waves and carried forwards as before, the shore being very flat.

The last time of these two had well near been fatal to me; for the sea having hurried me along as before, landed me, or rather dash'd me against a piece of a rock, and that with such force, as it left me senseless, and indeed helpless, as to my own deliverance; for the blow taking my side and breast, beat the breath as it were quite out of my body; and had it returned again immediately, I must have been strangled in the water; but I recover'd a little before the return of the waves, and seeing I should be cover'd again with the water, I resolv'd to hold fast by a piece of the rock, and so to hold my breath, if possible, till the wave went back; now as the waves were not so high as at first, being nearer land, I held my hold till the wave abated, and then fetch'd another run, which brought me so near the shore, that the next wave, tho' it went over me, yet did not so swallow me up as to carry me away, and the next run I took, I got to the main land, where, to my great comfort, I clamber'd up the clifts of the shore, and sat me down upon the grass, free from danger, and quite out of the reach of the water.

I was now landed, and safe on shore, and began to look up and thank God that my life was sav'd in a case wherein there was some minutes before scarce any room to hope. I believe it is impossible to express to the life what the extasies and transports of the soul are, when it is so sav'd, as I may say, out of the very grave; and I do not wonder now at that custom, *viz.* that when a malefactor who has the halter about his neck, is tyed up, and just going to be turn'd off, and has a reprieve brought to him: I say, I do not wonder that they bring a surgeon with it, to let him blood that very moment they tell him of it, that the surprise may not drive the animal spirits from the heart, and overwhelm him:

For sudden joys, like griefs, confound at first.[24]

I walk'd about on the shore, lifting up my hands, and my whole being, as I may say, wrapt up in the contemplation of my deliverance, making a thousand gestures and motions which I cannot describe, reflecting upon all my comrades that were drown'd, and that there should not be one soul sav'd but my self; for, as for them, I never saw them afterwards, or any sign of them, except three of their hats, one cap, and two shoes that were not fellows.

I cast my eyes to the stranded vessel, when the breach and froth of the sea being so big, I could hardly see it, it lay so far off, and considered, Lord! how was it possible I could get on shore?

After I had solac'd my mind with the comfortable part of my condition, I began to look round me to see what kind of place I was in, and what was next to be done, and I soon found my comforts abate, and that in a word I had a dreadful deliverance: For I was wet, had no clothes to shift me, nor any thing either to eat or drink to comfort me, neither did I see any prospect before me, but that of perishing with hunger, or being devour'd by wild beasts; and that which was particularly afflicting to me, was, that I had no weapon either to hunt and kill any creature for my sustenance, or to defend my self against any other creature that might desire to kill me for theirs: In a word, I had nothing about me but a knife, a tobacco-pipe, and a little tobacco in a box, this was all my provision, and this threw me into terrible agonies of mind, that for a while I run about like a mad-man; night coming upon me, I began with a heavy heart to consider what would be my lot if there were any ravenous beasts in that country, seeing at night they always come abroad for their prey.

All the remedy that offer'd to my thoughts at that time, was, to get up into a thick bushy tree like a firr, but thorny, which grew near me, and where I resolv'd to set all night, and consider the next day what death I should dye, for as yet I saw no prospect of life; I walk'd about a furlong from the shore, to see if I could find any fresh water to drink, which I did, to my great joy; and having drank, and put a little tobacco in my mouth to prevent hunger, I went to the tree, and getting up into it, endeavour'd to place my self so, as that if I should sleep I might not fall; and having cut me a short stick, like a truncheon, for my defence, I took up my lodging, and having been excessively fatigu'd, I fell fast asleep, and slept as comfortably as, I believe, few could have done in my condition, and found my self the most refresh'd with it, that I think I ever was on such an occasion.

When I wak'd it was broad day, the weather clear, and the storm abated, so that the sea did not rage and swell as before: But that which surpris'd me most, was, that the ship was lifted off in the night from the sand where she lay, by the swelling of the tyde, and was driven up almost as far as the rock which I first mention'd, where I had been so bruis'd by the dashing me against it; this being within about a mile from the shore where I was, and the ship seeming to stand upright still, I wish'd my self on board, that, at least, I might save some necessary things for my use.

When I came down from my apartment in the tree, I look'd about me again, and the first thing I found was the boat, which lay as the wind and the sea had toss'd her up upon the land, about two miles on my right hand, I walk'd as far as I could upon the shore to have got to her, but found a neck or inlet of water between me and the boat, which was about half a mile broad, so I came back for the present, being more intent upon getting at the ship, where I hop'd to find something for my present subsistence.

A little after noon I found the sea very calm, and the tyde ebb'd so far out, that I could come within a quarter of a mile of the ship; and here I found a fresh renewing of my grief, for I saw evidently, that if we had kept on board, we had been all safe, that is to say, we had all got safe on shore, and I had not been so miserable as to be left entirely destitute of all comfort and company, as I now was; this forced tears from my eyes again, but as there was little relief in that, I resolv'd, if possible, to get to the ship, so I pull'd off my clothes, for the weather was hot to extremity, and took the water, but when I came to the ship, my difficulty was still greater to know how to get on board, for as she lay a ground, and high out of the water, there was nothing within my reach to lay hold of, I swam round her twice, and the second time I spy'd a small piece of a rope, which I wonder'd I did not see at first, hang down by the fore-chains so low, as that with great difficulty I got hold of it, and by the help of that rope, got up into the fore-castle of the ship, here I found that the ship was bulg'd, and had a great deal of water in her hold, but that she lay so on the side of a bank of hard sand, or rather earth, that her stern lay lifted up upon the bank, and her head low almost to the water; by this means all her quarter was free, and all that was in that part was dry; for you may be sure my first work was to search and to see what was spoil'd and what was free; and first I found that all the ship's provisions were dry and untouch'd by the water, and being very well dispos'd to eat, I went to the bread-room and fill'd my pockets with bisket, and eat it as I went about other things, for I had no time to lose; I also found some rum in the great cabin, of which I took a large dram, and which I had indeed need enough of to spirit me for what was before me: Now I wanted nothing but a boat to furnish my self with many things which I foresaw would be very necessary to me.

It was in vain to sit still and wish for what was not to be had, and this extremity rouz'd my application; we had several spare yards, and two or three large sparrs of wood, and a spare top-mast or two in the ship; I resolv'd to fall to work with these, and I flung as many of them over board as I could manage for their weight, tying every one with a rope that they might not drive away; when this was done I went down the ship's side, and pulling them to me, I ty'd four of them fast together at both ends as well as I could, in the form of a raft, and laying two or three short pieces of plank upon them cross-ways, I found I could walk upon it very well, but that it was not able to bear any great weight, the pieces being too light; so I went to work, and with the carpenter's saw I cut a spare top-mast into three lengths, and added them to my raft, with a great deal of labour and pains, but hope of furnishing my self with necessaries, encourag'd me to go beyond what I should have been able to have done upon another occasion.

My raft was now strong enough to bear any reasonable weight; my next care was what to load it with, and how to preserve what I laid upon it from the surf of the sea; but I was not long considering this, I first laid all the planks or boards upon it that I could get, and having consider'd well what I most wanted, I first got three of the seamens chests, which I had broken open and empty'd, and lower'd them down upon my raft; the first of these I fill'd with provisions, *viz.* bread, rice, three Dutch cheeses, five pieces of dry'd goat's flesh, which we liv'd much upon, and a little remainder of *European* corn which had been laid by for some fowls which we brought to sea with us, but the fowls were kill'd, there had been some barley and wheat together, but, to my great disappointment, I found afterwards that the rats had eaten or spoil'd it all; as for liquors, I found several cases of bottles belonging to our skipper, in which were some cordial waters, and in all about five or six gallons of rack, these I stow'd by themselves, there being no need to put them into the chest, nor no room for them. While I was doing this, I found the tide began to flow, tho' very calm, and I had the mortification to see my coat, shirt, and wast-coat, which I had left on shore upon the sand, swim away; as for my breeches which were only linnen and open-knee'd, I swam on board in them and my stockings: However this put me upon rummaging for clothes, of which I found enough, but took no more than I wanted for present use, for I had other things which my eye was more upon, as first tools to work with on shore, and it was after long searching that I found out the carpenter's chest, which was indeed a very useful prize to me, and much more valuable than a ship loading of gold would have been at that time; I got it down to my raft, even whole as it was, without losing time to look into it, for I knew in general what it contain'd.

My next care was for some ammunition and arms; there were two very good fowling-pieces in the great cabin, and two pistols, these I secur'd first, with some powder-horns, and a small bag of shot, and two old rusty swords; I knew there were three barrels of powder in the ship, but knew not where our gunner had stow'd them, but with much search I found them, two of them dry and good, the third had taken water, those two I got to my raft, with the arms, and now I thought my self pretty well freighted, and began to think how I should get to shore with them, having neither sail, oar, or rudder, and the least cap full of wind would have overset all my navigation.

I had three encouragements, 1. A smooth calm sea, 2. The tide rising and setting in to the shore, 3. What little wind there was blew me towards the land; and thus, having found two or three broken oars belonging to the boat, and besides the tools which were in the chest, I found two saws, an axe, and a hammer, and with this cargo I put to sea: For a mile, or thereabouts, my raft went very well, only that I found it drive a little distant from the place where I had landed before, by which I perceiv'd that there was some indraft of the water, and consequently I hop'd to find some creek or river there, which I might make use of as a port to get to land with my cargo.

As I imagin'd, so it was, there appear'd before me a little opening of the land, and I found a strong current of the tide set into it, so I guided my raft as well as I could to keep in the middle of the stream: But here I had like to have suffer'd a second shipwreck, which, if I had, I think verily would have broke my heart, for knowing nothing of the coast, my raft run a-ground at one end of it upon a shoal, and not being a-ground at the other end, it wanted but a little that all my cargo had slipp'd off towards that end that was a-float, and so fall'n into the water: I did my utmost by setting my back against the chests, to keep them in their places, but could not thrust off the raft with all my strength, neither durst I stir from the posture I was in, but holding up the chests with all my might, stood in that manner near half an hour, in which time the rising of the water brought me a little more upon a level, and a little after, the water still rising, my raft floated again, and I thrust her off with the oar I had, into the channel, and then driving up higher, I at length found my self in the mouth of a little river, with land on both sides, and a strong current or tide running up, I look'd on both sides for a proper place to get to shore, for I was not willing to be driven too high up the river, hoping in time to see some ship at sea, and therefore resolv'd to place my self as near the coast as I could.

At length I spy'd a little cove on the right shore of the creek, to which with great pain and difficulty I guided my raft, and at last got so near, as that, reaching ground with my oar, I could thrust her directly in, but here I had like to have dipt all my cargo in the sea again; for that shore lying pretty steep, that is to say sloping, there was no place to land, but where one end of my float, if it run on shore, would lie so high, and the other sink lower as before, that it would endanger my cargo again: All that I could do, was to wait till the tide was at the highest, keeping the raft with my oar like an anchor to hold the side of it fast to the shore, near a flat piece of ground, which I expected the water would flow over; and so it did: As soon as I found water enough, for my raft drew about a foot water, I thrust her on upon that flat piece of ground, and there fasten'd or mor'd her by sticking my two broken oars into the ground; one on one side near one end, and one on the other side near the other end; and thus I lay till the water ebb'd away, and left my raft and all my cargo safe on shore.

My next work was to view the country, and seek a proper place for my habitation, and where to stow my goods to secure them from whatever might happen; where I was I yet knew not, whether on the continent or on an island, whether inhabited, or not inhabited, whether in danger of wild beasts or not: There was a hill not above a mile from me, which rose up very steep and high, and which seem'd to over-top some other hills which lay as in a ridge from it northward; I took out one of the fowling pieces, and one of the pistols, and an horn of powder, and thus arm'd I travell'd for discovery up to the top of that hill, where after I had with great labour and difficulty got to the top, I saw my fate to my great affliction, (*viz.*) that I was in an island environ'd every way with the sea, no land to be seen, except some rocks which lay a great way off, and two small islands less than this, which lay about three leagues to the west.

I found also that the island I was in was barren, and, as I saw good reason to believe, un-inhabited, except by wild beasts, of whom however I saw none, yet I saw abundance of fowls, but knew not their kinds, neither when I kill'd them could I tell what was fit for food, and what not; at my coming back, I shot at a great bird which I saw sitting upon a tree on the side of a great wood, I believe it was the first gun that had been fir'd there since the creation of the world; I had no sooner fir'd, but from all the parts of the wood there arose an innumerable number of fowls of many sorts, making a confus'd screaming, and crying every one according to his usual note; but not one of them of any kind that I knew: As for the creature I kill'd, I took it to be a kind of a hawk, its colour and beak resembling it, but had no talons or claws more than common, its flesh was carrion, and fit for nothing.

Contented with this discovery, I came back to my raft, and fell to work to bring my cargo on shore, which took me up the rest of that day, and what to do with my self at night I knew not, nor indeed where to rest; for I was afraid to lie down on the ground, not knowing but some wild beast might devour me, tho', as I afterwards found, there was really no need for those fears.

However, as well as I could, I barricado'd my self round with the chests and boards that I had brought on shore, and made a kind of a hut for that night's lodging; as for food, I yet saw not which way to supply my self, except that I had seen two or three creatures like hares run out of the wood where I shot the fowl.

I now began to consider, that I might yet get a great many things out of the ship, which would be useful to me, and particularly some of the rigging, and sails, and such other things as might come to land, and I resolv'd to make another voyage on board the vessel, if possible; and as I knew that the first storm that blew must necessarily break her all in pieces, I resolved to set all other things apart, till I got every thing out of the ship that I could get; then I call'd a council, that is to say, in my thoughts, whether I should take back the raft, but this appear'd impracticable; so I resolv'd to go as before, when the tide was down, and I did so, only that I stripp'd before I went from my hut, having nothing on but a checquer'd shirt, and a pair of linnen drawers, and a pair of pumps on my feet.

I got on board the ship, as before, and prepar'd a second raft, and having had experience of the first, I neither made this so unwieldy, nor loaded it so hard, but yet I brought away several things very useful to me; as first, in the carpenter's stores I found two or three bags full of nails and spikes, a great skrew-jack, a dozen or two of hatchets, and above all, that most useful thing call'd a grind-stone; all these I secur'd together, with several things belonging to the gunner, particularly two or three iron crows, and two barrels of musquet-bullets, seven musquets, and another fowling-piece, with some small quantity of powder more; a large bag full of small shot, and a great roll of sheet lead: But this last was so heavy, I could not hoist it up to get it over the ship's side.

Besides these things, I took all the mens clothes that I could find, and a spare fore-top-sail, a hammock, and some bedding; and with this I loaded my second raft, and brought them all safe on shore to my very great comfort.

I was under some apprehensions during my absence from the land, that at least my provisions might be devour'd on shore; but when I came back, I found no sign of any visitor, only there sat a creature like a wild cat upon one of the chests, which when I came towards it, ran away a little distance, and then stood still; she sat very compos'd, and unconcern'd, and look'd full in my face, as if she had a mind to be acquainted with me, I presented my gun at her, but as she did not understand it, she was perfectly unconcern'd at it, nor did she offer to stir away; upon which I toss'd her a bit of bisket, tho' by the way I was not very free of it, for my store was not great: However, I spar'd her a bit, I say, and she went to it, smell'd of it, and ate it, and look'd (as pleas'd) for more, but I thank'd her, and could spare no more; so she march'd off.

Having got my second cargo on shore, tho' I was fain to open the barrels of powder, and bring them by parcels, for they were too heavy, being large casks, I went to work to make me a little tent with the sail and some poles which I cut for that purpose, and into this tent I brought every thing that I knew would spoil, either with rain or sun, and I piled all the empty chests and casks up in a circle round the tent, to fortify it from any sudden attempt, either from man or beast.

When I had done this I block'd up the door of the tent with some boards within, and an empty chest set up an end without, and spreading one of the beds upon the ground, laying my two pistols just at my head, and my gun at length by me, I went to bed for the first time, and slept very quietly all night, for I was very weary and heavy, for the night before I had slept little, and had labour'd very hard all day, as well to fetch all those things from the ship, as to get them on shore.

I had the biggest magazine of all kinds now that ever were laid up, I believe, for one man; but I was not satisfy'd still; for while the ship sat upright in that posture, I thought I ought to get every thing out of her that

I could; so every day at low water I went on board, and brought away some thing or other: But particularly the third time I went, I brought away as much of the rigging as I could, as also all the small ropes and rope-twine I could get, with a piece of spare canvass, which was to mend the sails upon occasion, the barrel of wet gun-powder: In a word, I brought away all the sails first and last, only that I was fain to cut them in pieces, and bring as much at a time as I could; for they were no more useful to be sails, but as meer canvass only.

But that which comforted me more still was, that at last of all, after I had made five or six such voyages as these, and thought I had nothing more to expect from the ship that was worth my medling with, I say, after all this, I found a great hogshead of bread, and three large runlets of rum or spirits, and a box of sugar, and a barrel of fine flower; this was surprising to me, because I had given over expecting any more provisions, except what was spoil'd by the water: I soon empty'd the hogshead of that bread, and wrapt it up parcel by parcel in pieces of the sails, which I cut out; and in a word, I got all this safe on shore also.

The next day I made another voyage; and now having plunder'd the ship of what was portable and fit to hand out, I began with the cables; and cutting the great cable into pieces, such as I could move, I got two cables and a hawser on shore, with all the iron-work I could get; and having cut down the spritsail-yard, and the missen-yard, and every thing I could to make a large raft, I loaded it with all those heavy goods, and came away: But my good luck began now to leave me; for this raft was so unwieldy, and so overloaden, that after I was enter'd the little cove, where I had landed the rest of my goods, not being able to guide it so handily as I did the other, it overset, and threw me and all my cargo into the water; as for my self it was no great harm, for I was near the shore; but as to my cargo, it was great part of it lost, especially the iron, which I expected would have been of great use to me: However, when the tide was out, I got most of the pieces of cable ashore, and some of the iron, tho' with infinite labour; for I was fain to dip for it into the water, a work which fatigu'd me very much: After this, I went every day on board, and brought away what I could get.

I had been now thirteen days on shore, and had been eleven times on board the ship; in which time I had brought away all that one pair of hands could well be suppos'd capable to bring, tho' I believe verily, had the calm weather held, I should have brought away the whole ship, piece by piece:

But preparing the 12th time to go on board, I found the wind begin to rise; however at low water I went on board, and tho' I thought I had rumag'd the cabin so effectually, as that nothing more could be found, yet I discover'd a locker with drawers in it, in one of which I found two or three razors, and one pair of large scissars, with some ten or a dozen of good knives and forks; in another I found about thirty six Pounds value in money, some *European* coin, some *Brasil*, some Pieces of Eight, some gold, some silver.

I smil'd to my self at the sight of this money, O drug! said I aloud, what art thou good for? Thou art not worth to me, no not the taking off of the ground, one of those knives is worth all this heap, I have no manner of use for thee, e'en remain where thou art, and go to the bottom as a creature whose life is not worth saving. However, upon second thoughts, I took it away, and wrapping all this in a piece of canvass, I began to think of making another raft, but while I was preparing this, I found the sky over-cast, and the wind began to rise, and in a quarter of an hour it blew a fresh gale from the shore; it presently occur'd to me, that it was in vain to pretend to make a raft with the wind off shore, and that it was my business to be gone before the tide of flood began, otherwise I might not be able to reach the shore at all: Accordingly I let my self down into the water, and swam cross the channel, which lay between the ship and the sands, and even that with difficulty enough, partly with the weight of the things I had about me, and partly the roughness of the water, for the wind rose very hastily, and before it was quite high water, it blew a storm.

But I was gotten home to my little tent, where I lay with all my wealth about me very secure. It blew very hard all that night, and in the morning when I look'd out, behold no more ship was to be seen; I was a little surpris'd, but recover'd my self with this satisfactory reflection, *viz.* that I had lost no time, nor abated no dilligence to get every thing out of her that could be useful to me, and that indeed there was little left in her that I was able to bring away if I had had more time.

I now gave over any more thoughts of the ship, or of any thing out of her, except what might drive on shore from her wreck, as indeed divers pieces of her afterwards did; but those things were of small use to me.

My thoughts were now wholly employ'd about securing my self against either savages, if any should appear, or wild beasts, if any were in the island; and I had many thoughts of the method how to do this, and what kind of dwelling to make, whether I should make me a cave in the earth, or a tent upon the earth: And, in short, I resolv'd upon both, the manner and description of which it may not be improper to give an account of.

I soon found the place I was in was not for my settlement, particularly because it was upon a low moorish ground near the sea, and I believ'd would not be wholesome, and more particularly because there was no fresh water near it, so I resolv'd to find a more healthy and more convenient spot of ground.

I consulted several things in my situation which I found would be proper for me, 1st. health, and fresh water, I just now mentioned, 2dly. shelter from the heat of the sun, 3dly. security from ravenous creatures, whether men or beasts, 4thly. a view to the sea, that if God sent any ship in sight, I might not lose any advantage for my deliverance, of which I was not willing to banish all my expectation yet.

In search of a place proper for this, I found a little plain on the side of a rising hill, whose front towards this little plain, was steep as a house-side, so that nothing could come down upon me from the top; on the side of this rock there was a hollow place worn a little way in like the entrance or door of a cave, but there was not really any cave or way into the rock at all.

On the flat of the green, just before this hollow place, I resolved to pitch my tent: This plain was not above an hundred yards broad, and about twice as long, and lay like a green before my door, and at the end of it descended irregularly every way down into the low grounds by the seaside. It was on the *N.N.W.* side of the hill, so that I was sheltered from the heat every day, till it came to a *W.* and by *S.* sun, or thereabouts, which in those countries is near the setting.

Before I set up my tent, I drew a half circle before the hollow place, which took in about ten yards in its semi-diameter from the rock, and twenty yards in its diameter, from its beginning and ending.

In this half circle I pitch'd two rows of strong stakes, driving them into the ground till they stood very firm like piles, the biggest end being out of the ground about five foot and a half, and sharpen'd on the top; the two rows did not stand above six inches from one another.

Then I took the pieces of cable which I had cut in the ship, and laid them in rows one upon another, within the circle between these two rows of stakes, up to the top, placing other stakes in the inside, leaning against them, about two foot and a half high, like a spurr to a post, and this fence was so strong, that neither man or beast could get into it or over it: This cost me a great deal of time and labour, especially to cut the piles in the woods, bring them to the place, and drive them into the earth.

The entrance into this place I made to be not by a door, but by a short ladder, to go over the top, which ladder, when I was in, I lifted over after me, and so I was compleatly fenced in, and fortify'd, as I thought, from all the world, and consequently slept secure in the night, which otherwise I could not have done, tho' as it appear'd afterward, there was no need of all this caution from the enemies that I apprehended danger from.

Into this fence or fortress, with infinite labour, I carry'd all my riches, all my provisions, ammunition and stores, of which you have the account above, and I made me a large tent, which, to preserve me from the rains that in one part of the year are very violent there, I made double, *viz.* one smaller tent within, and one larger tent above it, and cover'd the uppermost with a large tarpaulin which I had sav'd among the sails.

And now I lay no more for a while in the bed which I had brought on shore, but in a hammock, which was indeed a very good one, and belong'd to the Mate of the ship.

Into this tent I brought all my provisions, and every thing that would spoil by the wet, and having thus enclos'd all my goods, I made up the entrance, which till now I had left open, and so pass'd and repass'd, as I said, by a short ladder.

When I had done this, I began to work my way into the rock, and bringing all the earth and stones that I dug down out thro' my tent, I laid 'em up within my fence in the nature of a terras, that so it rais'd the ground within about a foot and a half; and thus I made me a cave just behind my tent, which serv'd me like a cellar to my house.

It cost me much labour, and many days, before all these things were brought to perfection, and therefore I must go back to some other things which took up some of my thoughts. At the same time it happen'd after I had laid my scheme for the setting up my tent and making the cave, that a storm of rain falling from a thick dark cloud, a sudden flash of lightning happen'd, and after that a great clap of thunder, as is naturally the effect of it; I was not so much surpris'd with the lightning, as I was with a thought which darted into my mind as swift as the lightning it self: O my powder! My very heart sunk within me, when I thought, that at one blast all my powder might be destroy'd, on which, not my defence only, but the providing me food, as I thought, entirely depended; I was nothing near so anxious about my own danger, tho' had the powder took fire, I had never known who had hurt me.

Such impression did this make upon me, that after the storm was over, I laid aside all my works, my building, and fortifying, and apply'd my self to make bags and boxes to separate the powder, and keep it a little and a little in a parcel, in hope, that whatever might come, it might not all take fire at once, and to keep it so apart, that it should not be possible to make one part fire another: I finish'd this work in about a fort night, and I think my powder, which in all was about 240 l. weight, was divided in not less than a hundred parcels; as to the barrel that had been wet, I did not apprehend any danger from that, so I plac'd it in my new cave, which in my fancy I call'd my kitchin, and the rest I hid up and down in holes among the rocks, so that no wet might come to it, marking very carefully where I laid it.

In the interval of time while this was doing I went out once at least every day with my gun, as well to divert my self, as to see if I could kill any thing fit for food, and as near as I could to acquaint my self with what the island produc'd. The first time I went out I presently discover'd that there were goats in the island, which was a great satisfaction to me; but then it was attended with this misfortune to me, *viz.* that they were so shy, so subtle, and so swift of foot, that it was the difficultest thing in the world to come at them: But I was not discourag'd at this, not doubting but I might now and then shoot one, as it soon happen'd, for after I had found their haunts a little, I laid wait in this manner for them: I observ'd if they saw me in the valleys, tho' they were upon the rocks, they would run away as in a terrible fright; but if they were feeding in the valleys, and I was upon the rocks, they took no notice of me, from whence I concluded, that by the position of their opticks, their sight was so directed downward, that they did not readily see objects that were above them; so afterward I took this method, I always climbed the rocks first to get above them, and then had frequently a fair mark. The first shot I made among these creatures, I kill'd a she-goat which had a little kid by her which she gave suck to, which griev'd me heartily; but when the old one fell, the kid stood stock still by her till I came and took her up, and not only so, but when I carried the old one with me upon my shoulders, the kid follow'd me quite to my enclosure, upon which I laid down the dam, and took the kid in my arms, and carried it over my pale, in hopes to have bred it up tame, but it would not eat, so I was forc'd to kill it and eat it my self; these two supply'd me with flesh a great while, for I eat sparingly; and sav'd my provisions (my bread especially) as much as possibly I could.

Having now fix'd my habitation, I found it absolutely necessary to provide a place to make a fire in, and fewel to burn; and what I did for that, as also how I enlarg'd my cave, and what conveniencies I made, I shall give a full account of in its place: But I must first give some little account of my self, and of my thoughts about living, which it may well be supposed were not a few.

I had a dismal prospect of my condition, for as I was not cast away upon that island without being driven, as is said, by a violent storm quite out of the course of our intended voyage, and a great way, *viz.* some hundreds of leagues out of the ordinary course of the trade of mankind, I had great reason to consider it as a determination of Heaven, that in this desolate place, and in this desolate manner I should end my life; the tears would run plentifully down my face when I made these reflections, and sometimes I would expostulate with my self, Why Providence should thus compleatly ruin its creatures, and render them so absolutely miserable, so without help abandon'd, so entirely depress'd, that it could hardly be rational to be thankful for such a life.

But something always return'd swift upon me to check these thoughts, and to reprove me; and particularly one day walking with my gun in my hand by the sea-side, I was very pensive upon the subject of my present condition, when reason as it were expostulated with me t'other way, thus: Well, you are in a desolate condition, 'tis true, but pray remember, Where are the rest of you? Did not you come eleven of you into the boat, where are the ten? Why were not they sav'd and you lost? Why were you singled out? Is it better to be here or there, and then I pointed to the sea? All evils are to be consider'd with the good that is in them, and with what worse attends them.

Then it occurr'd to me again, how well I was furnish'd for my subsistence, and what would have been my case if it had not happen'd, *Which was an hundred thousand to one*, that the ship floated from the place where she first struck and was driven so near to the shore that I had time to get all these things out of her: What would have been my case, if I had been to have liv'd in the condition in which I at first came on shore, without necessaries of life, or necessaries to supply and procure them? Particularly said I aloud, (tho' to my self) what should I ha' done without a gun, without ammunition, without any tools to make any thing, or to work with, without clothes, bedding, a tent, or any manner of covering, and that now I had all these to a sufficient quantity, and was in a fair way to provide my self in such a manner, as to live without my gun when my ammunition was spent; so that I had a tolerable view of subsisting without any want as long as I liv'd; for I consider'd from the beginning how I would provide for the accidents that might happen, and for the time that was to come, even not only after my ammunition should be spent, but even after my health or strength should decay.

I confess I had not entertain'd any notion of my ammunition being destroy'd at one blast, I mean my powder being blown up by lightning, and this made the thoughts of it so surprising to me when it lighten'd and thunder'd, as I observ'd just now.

And now being to enter into a melancholy relation of a scene of silent life, such perhaps as was never heard of in the world before, I shall take it from its beginning, and continue it in its order. It was, by my account, the 30th. of *Sept.* when, in the manner as above said, I first set foot upon this horrid island, when the sun being, to us, in its autumnal equinox, was almost just over my head, for I reckon'd my self, by observation, to be in the latitude of 9 degrees 22 minutes north of the Line.

After I had been there about ten or twelve days, it came into my thoughts, that I should lose my reckoning of time for want of books and pen and ink, and should even forget the Sabbath days from the working days; but to prevent this, I cut it with my knife upon a large post, in capital letters, and making it into a great cross, I set it up on the shore where I first landed, *viz. I came on shore here on the 30th of* Sept. 1659. Upon the sides of this square post, I cut every day a notch with my knife, and every seventh notch was as long again as the rest, and every first day of the month as long again as that long one; and thus I kept my kalandar, or weekly, monthly, and yearly reckoning of time.

In the next place we are to observe, that among the many things which I brought out of the ship in the several voyages, which, as above mention'd, I made to it, I got several things of less value, but not all less useful to me, which I omitted setting down before; as in particular, pens, ink, and paper, several parcels in the Captain's, Mate's, gunner's, and carpenter's keeping, three or four compasses, some mathematical instruments, dials, perspectives, charts, and books of navigation, all which I huddled together, whether I might want them or no; also I found three very good Bibles which came to me in my cargo from *England*, and which I had pack'd up among my things; some *Portugueze* books also, and among them two or three Popish prayer-books, and several other books, all which I carefully secur'd. And I must not forget, that we had in the ship a dog and two cats, of whose eminent history I may have occasion to say something in its place; for I carry'd both the cats with me; and as for the dog, he jump'd out of the ship of himself, and swam on shore to me the day after I went on shore with my first cargo, and was a trusty servant to me many years; I wanted nothing that he could fetch me, nor any company that he could make up to me, I only wanted to have him talk to me, but that would not do: As I observ'd before, I found pen, ink and paper, and I husbanded them to the utmost; and I shall shew, that while my ink lasted, I kept things very exact; but after that was gone, I could not, for I could not make any ink by any means that I could devise.

And this put me in mind that I wanted many things, notwithstanding all that I had amass'd together, and of these, this of ink was one, as also spade, pick-axe and shovel to dig or remove the earth; needles, pins, and thread; as for linnen, I soon learn'd to want that without much difficulty.

This want of tools made every work I did go on heavily, and it was near a whole year before I had entirely finished my little pale or surrounded habitation: The piles or stakes, which were as heavy as I could well lift, were a long time in cutting and preparing in the woods, and more by far in bringing home, so that I spent some times two days in cutting and bringing home one of those posts, and a third day in driving it into the ground; for which purpose I got a heavy piece of wood at first, but at last bethought myself of one of the iron crows, which however tho' I found it, yet it made driving those posts or piles very laborious and tedious work.

But what need I ha' been concerned at the tediousness of any thing I had to do, seeing I had time enough to do it in, nor had I any other employment if that had been over, at least, that I could foresee, except the ranging the island to seek for food, which I did more or less every day.

I now began to consider seriously my condition, and the circumstance I was reduc'd to, and I drew up the state of my affairs in writing, not so much to leave them to any that were to come after me, for I was like to have but few heirs, as to deliver my thoughts from daily poring upon them, and afflicting my mind; and as my reason began now to master my despondency, I began to comfort my self as well as I could, and to set the good against the evil, that I might have something to distinguish my case from worse, and I stated it very impartially, like debtor and creditor, the comforts I enjoy'd, against the miseries I suffer'd, thus,

EVIL	GOOD
I am cast upon a horrible desolate island, void of all hope of recovery.	*But I am alive, and not drown'd as all my ship's company was.*
I am singled out and separated, as it were, from all the world to be miserable.	*But I am singled out too from all the ship's crew to be spared from death; and he that miraculously saved me from death, can deliver me from this condition.*
I am divided from mankind, a solitaire, one banish'd from human society.	*But I am not starv'd and perishing on a barren place, affording no sustenance.*
I have not clothes to cover me.	*But I am in a hot climate, where if I had clothes I could hardly wear them.*
I am without any defence or means to resist any violence of man or beast.	*But I am cast on an island, where I see no wild beasts to hurt me, as I saw on the coast of* Africa: *And what if I had been shipwreck'd there?*
I have no soul to speak to, or relieve me.	*But God wonderfully sent the ship in near enough to the shore, that I have gotten out so many necessary things as will either supply my wants, or enable me to supply my self even as long as I live.*

Upon the whole, here was an undoubted testimony, that there was scarce any condition in the world so miserable, but there was something *negative* or something *positive* to be thankful for in it; and let this stand as a direction from the experience of the most miserable of all conditions in this world, that we may always find in it something to comfort our selves from, and to set in the description of good and evil, on the credit side of the accompt.

Having now brought my mind a little to relish my condition, and given over looking out to sea to see if I could spy a ship, I say, giving over these things, I began to apply my self to accommodate my way of living, and to make things as easy to me as I could.

I have already described my habitation, which was a tent under the side of a rock, surrounded with a strong pale of posts and cables, but I might now rather call it a wall, for I rais'd a kind of wall up against it of turfs, about two foot thick on the out-side, and after some time, I think it was a year and half, I rais'd rafters from it leaning to the rock, and thatch'd or cover'd it with boughs of trees, and such things as I could get to keep out the rain, which I found at some times of the year very violent.

I have already observ'd how I brought all my goods into this pale, and into the cave which I had made behind me: But I must observe too that at first this was a confus'd heap of goods, which as they lay in no order, so they took up all my place, I had no room to turn my self; so I set my self to enlarge my cave and works farther into the earth; for it was a loose sandy rock, which yielded easily to the labour I bestowed on it; and so when I found I was pretty safe as to beasts of prey, I work'd side-ways to the right hand into the rock, and then turning to the right again, work'd quite out and made me a door to come out, on the out-side of my pale or fortification.

This gave me not only egress and regress, as it were a back way to my tent and to my storehouse, but gave me room to stow my goods.

And now I began to apply my self to make such necessary things as I found I most wanted, as particularly a chair and a table, for without these I was not able to enjoy the few comforts I had in the world, I could not write, or eat, or do several things with so much pleasure without a table.

So I went to work; and here I must needs observe, that as reason is the substance and original of the mathematicks, so by stating and squaring every thing by reason, and by making the most rational judgment of things, every man may be in time master of every mechanick art. I had never handled a tool in my life, and yet in time by labour, application and contrivance, I found at last that I wanted nothing but I could have made it, especially if I had had tools; however I made abundance of things, even without tools, and some with no more tools than an adze and a hatchet, which perhaps were never made that way before, and that with infinite labour: For example, If I wanted a board, I had no other way but to cut down a tree, set it on an edge before me, and hew it flat on either side with my axe, till I had brought it to be as thin as a plank, and then dubb it smooth with my adze. It is true, by this method I could make but one board out of a whole tree, but this I had no remedy for but patience, any more than I had for the prodigious deal of time and labour which it took me up to make a plank or board: But my time or labour was little worth, and so it was as well employ'd one way as another.

However, I made me a table and a chair, as I observ'd above, in the first place, and this I did out of the short pieces of boards that I brought on my raft from the ship: But when I had wrought out some boards, as above, I made large shelves of the breadth of a foot and a half one over another, all along one side of my cave, to lay all my tools, nails, and iron-work, and in a word, to separate every thing at large in their places, that I might come easily at them; I knock'd pieces into the wall of the rock to hang my guns and all things that would hang up.

So that had my cave been to be seen, it look'd like a general magazine of all necessary things, and I had every thing so ready at my hand, that it was a great pleasure to me to see all my goods in such order, and especially to find my stock of all necessaries so great.

And now it was when I began to keep a journal of every day's employment, for indeed at first I was in too much hurry, and not only hurry as to labour, but in too much discomposure of mind, and my journal would ha' been full of many dull things. For example, I must have said thus: *Sept.* the 30th. After I got to shore and had escap'd drowning, instead of being thankful to God for my deliverance, having first vomited with the great quantity of salt water which was gotten into my stomach, and recovering my self a little, I ran about the shore, wringing my hands, and beating my head and face, exclaiming at my misery, and crying out, I was undone, undone, till tyr'd and faint I was forc'd to lye down on the ground to repose, but durst not sleep for fear of being devour'd.

Some days after this, and after I had been on board the ship, and got all that I could out of her, yet I could not forbear getting up to the top of a little mountain, and looking out to sea in hopes of seeing a ship, then fancy at a vast distance I spy'd a sail, please my self with the hopes of it, and then after looking steadily till I was almost blind, lose it quite, and sit down and weep like a child, and thus encrease my misery by my folly.

But having gotten over these things in some measure, and having settled my household-stuff and habitation, made me a table and a chair, and all as handsome about me as I could, I began to keep my journal, of which I shall here give you the copy (tho' in it will be told all these particulars over again) as long as it lasted, for having no more ink, I was forc'd to leave it off.

The JOURNAL.

September 30, 1659. I poor miserable *Robinson Crusoe*, being shipwreck'd, during a dreadful storm, in the offing, came on shore on this dismal unfortunate island, which I call'd *The Island of Despair*, all the rest of the ship's company being drown'd, and my self almost dead.

All the rest of that day I spent in afflicting my self at the dismal circumstances I was brought to, *viz.* I had neither food, house, clothes, weapon, or place to fly to, and in despair of any relief, saw nothing but death before me, either that I should be devour'd by wild beasts, murther'd by savages, or starv'd to death for want of food. At the approach of night, I slept in a tree for fear of wild creatures, but slept soundly tho' it rain'd all night.

October 1. In the morning I saw to my great surprise the ship had floated with the high tide, and was driven on shore again much nearer the island, which as it was some comfort on one hand, for seeing her sit upright, and not broken to pieces, I hop'd, if the wind abated, I might get on board, and get some food and necessaries out of her for my relief; so on the other hand, it renew'd my grief at the loss of my comrades, who I imagin'd if we had all staid on board might have sav'd the ship, or at least that they would not have been all drown'd as they were; and that had the men been sav'd, we might perhaps have built us a boat out of the ruins of the ship, to have carried us to some other part of the world. I spent great part of this day in perplexing my self on these things; but at length seeing the ship almost dry, I went upon the sand as near as I could, and then swam on board; this day also it continu'd raining, tho' with no wind at all.

From the 1st of *October*, to the 24th. All these days entirely spent in many several voyages to get all I could out of the ship, which I brought on shore, every tide of flood, upon rafts. Much rain also in these days, tho' with some intervals of fair weather: But, it seems, this was the rainy season.

Oct. 20. I overset my raft, and all the goods I had got upon it, but being in shoal water, and the things being chiefly heavy, I recover'd many of them when the tide was out.

Oct. 25. It rain'd all night and all day, with some gusts of wind, during which time the ship broke in pieces, the wind blowing a little harder than before, and was no more to be seen, except the wreck of her, and that only at low water. I spent this day in covering and securing the goods which I had sav'd, that the rain might not spoil them.

Oct. 26. I walk'd about the shore almost all day to find out a place to fix my habitation, greatly concern'd to secure my self from any attack in the night, either from wild beasts or men. Towards night I fix'd upon a proper place under a rock, and mark'd out a semi-circle for my encampment, which I resolv'd to strengthen with a work, wall, or fortification made of double piles, lin'd within with cable, and without with turf.

From the 26th to the 30th. I work'd very hard in carrying all my goods to my new habitation, tho' some part of the time it rain'd exceeding hard.

The 31st in the morning I went out into the island with my gun to see for some food, and discover the country, when I kill'd a she-goat, and her kid follow'd me home, which I afterwards kill'd also because it would not feed.

November 1. I set up my tent under a rock, and lay there for the first night, making it as large as I could with stakes driven in to swing my hammock upon.

Nov. 2. I set up all my chests and boards, and the pieces of timber which made my rafts, and with them form'd a fence round me, a little within the place I had mark'd out for my fortification.

Nov. 3. I went out with my gun, and kill'd two fowls like ducks, which were very good food. In the afternoon went to work to make me a table.

Nov. 4. This morning I began to order my times of work, of going out with my gun, time of sleep, and time of diversion, *viz.* Every morning I walk'd out with my gun for two or three hours if it did not rain, then employ'd myself to work till about eleven a-clock, then eat what I had to live on, and from twelve to two I lay down to sleep, the weather being excessive hot, and then in the evening to work again: The working part of this day and of the next were wholly employed in making my table, for I was yet but a very sorry workman, tho' time and necessity made me a compleat natural mechanick soon after, as I believe it would do any one else.

Nov. 5. This day went abroad with my gun and my dog, and kill'd a wild cat, her skin pretty soft, but her flesh good for nothing: Every creature I kill'd, I took off the skins and preserv'd them. Coming back by the sea shore, I saw many sorts of sea fowls, which I did not understand, but was surpris'd, and almost frighted with two or three seals, which, while I was gazing at, not well knowing what they were, got into the sea, and escap'd me for that time.

Nov. 6. After my morning walk I went to work with my table again, and finish'd it, tho' not to my liking; nor was it long before I learn'd to mend it.

Nov. 7. Now it began to be settled fair weather. The 7th, 8th, 9th, 10th, and part of the 12th, (for the 11th was *Sunday*) I took wholly up to make me a chair, and with much ado brought it to a tolerable shape, but never to please me, and even in the making I pull'd it in pieces several times. *Note*, I soon neglected my keeping *Sundays*, for omitting my mark for them on my post, I forgot which was which.

Nov. 13. This day it rain'd, which refresh'd me exceedingly, and cool'd the earth, but it was accompany'd with terrible thunder and lightning, which frighted me dreadfully for fear of my powder; as soon as it was over, I resolv'd to separate my stock of powder into as many little parcels as possible, that it might not be in danger.

Nov. 14, 15, 16. These three days I spent in making little square chests or boxes, which might hold about a pound or two pound, at most, of powder, and so putting the powder in, I stowed it in places as secure and remote from one another as possible. On one of these three days I kill'd a large bird that was good to eat, but I know not what to call it.

Nov. 17. This day I began to dig behind my tent into the rock to make room for my farther conveniency: *Note*, Three things I wanted exceedingly for this work, *viz.* a pick-axe, a shovel, and a wheel-barrow or basket, so I desisted from my work, and began to consider how to supply that want and make me some tools; as for a pick-axe, I made use of the iron crows, which were proper enough, tho' heavy; but the next thing was a shovel or spade, this was so absolutely necessary, that indeed I could do nothing effectually without it, but what kind of one to make I knew not.

Nov. 18. The next day in searching the woods I found a tree of that wood, or like it, which, in the *Brasils* they call the *Iron Tree*, for its exceeding hardness, of this, with great labour and almost spoiling my axe, I cut a piece, and brought it home too with difficulty enough, for it was exceeding heavy.

The excessive hardness of the wood, and having no other way, made me a long while upon this machine, for I work'd it effectually by little and little into the form of a shovel or spade, the handle exactly shap'd like ours in *England*, only that the broad part having no iron shod upon it at bottom, it would not last me so long, however it serv'd well enough for the uses which I had occasion to put it to; but never was a shovel, I believe, made after that fashion, or so long a making.

I was still deficient, for I wanted a basket or a wheel-barrow, a basket I could not make by any means, having no such things as twigs that would bend to make wicker ware, at least none yet found out; and as to a wheel-barrow, I fancy'd I could make all but the wheel, but that I had no notion of, neither did I know how to go about it; besides I had no possible way to make the iron gudgeons for the spindle or axis of the wheel to run in, so I gave it over, and so for carrying away the earth which I dug out of the cave, I made me a thing like a hodd, which the labourers carry morter in, when they serve the bricklayers.

This was not so difficult to me as the making the shovel; and yet this, and the shovel, and the attempt which I made in vain, to make a wheel-barrow, took me up no less than four days, I mean always, excepting my morning walk with my gun, which I seldom fail'd, and very seldom fail'd also bringing home something fit to eat.

Nov. 23. My other work having now stood still, because of my making these tools; when they were finish'd, I went on, and working every day, as my strength and time allow'd, I spent eighteen days entirely in widening and deepening my cave, that it might hold my goods commodiously.

Note, during all this time, I work'd to make this room or cave spacious enough to accommodate me as a warehouse or magazine, a kitchen, a dining-room, and a cellar; as for my lodging, I kept to the tent, except that some times in the wet season of the year, it rain'd so hard, that I could not keep my self dry, which caus'd me afterwards to cover all my place within my pale with long poles in the form of rafters leaning against the rock, and load them with flags and large leaves of trees like a thatch.

December 10th, I began now to think my cave or vault finished, when on a sudden, (it seems I had made it too large) a great quantity of earth fell down from the top and one side, so much, that in short it frighted me, and not without reason too; for if I had been under it I had never wanted a grave-digger: Upon this disaster I had a great deal of work to do over again; for I had the loose earth to carry out; and which was of more importance, I had the seiling to prop up, so that I might be sure no more would come down.

Dec. 11. This day I went to work with it accordingly, and got two shores or posts pitch'd upright to the top, with two pieces of boards a-cross over each post, this I finish'd the next day; and setting more posts up with boards, in about a week more I had the roof secur'd; and the posts standing in rows, serv'd me for partitions to part of my house.

Dec. 17. From this day to the twentieth I plac'd shelves, and knock'd up nails on the posts to hang every thing up that could be hung up, and now I began to be in some order within doors.

Dec. 20. Now I carry'd every thing into the cave, and began to furnish my house, and set up some pieces of boards, like a dresser, to order my victuals upon, but boards began to be very scarce with me; also I made me another table.

Dec. 24. Much rain all night and all day, no stirring out.

Dec. 25. Rain all day.

Dec. 26. No rain, and the earth much cooler than before, and pleasanter.

Dec. 27. Kill'd a young goat, and lam'd another so as that I catch'd it, and led it home in a string; when I had it home, I bound and splinter'd up its leg which was broke, *N. B.* I took such care of it, that it liv'd, and the leg grew well, and as strong as ever; but by nursing it so long it grew tame, and fed upon the little green at my door, and would not go away: This was the first time that I entertain'd a thought of breeding up some tame creatures, that I might have food when my powder and shot was all spent.

Dec. 28, 29, 30. Great heats and no breeze; so that there was no stirring abroad, except in the evening for food; this time I spent in putting all my things in order within doors.

January 1. Very hot still, but I went abroad early and late with my gun, and lay still in the middle of the day; this evening going farther into the valleys which lay towards the center of the island, I found there was plenty of goats, tho' exceeding shy and hard to come at, however I resolv'd to try if I could not bring my dog to hunt them down.

Jan. 2. Accordingly, the next day, I went out with my dog, and set him upon the goats; but I was mistaken, for they all fac'd about upon the dog, and he knew his danger too well, for he would not come near them.

Jan. 3. I began my fence or wall; which being still jealous of my being attack'd by some body, I resolv'd to make very thick and strong.

N. B. This wall being describ'd before, I purposely omit what was said in the Journal; it is sufficient to observe, that I was no less time than from the 3d of January *to the 14th of* April, *working, finishing, and perfecting this wall, tho' it*

was no more than about 24 yards in length, being a half circle from one place in the
rock to another place about eight yards from it, the door of the cave being in the
center behind it.

All this time I work'd very hard, the rains hindering me many days, nay
sometimes weeks together; but I thought I should never be perfectly secure
till this wall was finish'd; and it is scarce credible what inexpressible labour
every thing was done with, especially the bringing piles out of the woods,
and driving them into the ground, for I made them much bigger than I
need to have done.

When this wall was finish'd, and the out-side double fenc'd with a
turf-wall rais'd up close to it, I perswaded my self, that if any people were
to come on shore there, they would not perceive any thing like a habitation;
and it was very well I did so, as may be observ'd hereafter upon a very
remarkable occasion.

During this time, I made my rounds in the woods for game every day
when the rain admitted me, and made frequent discoveries in these walks
of something or other to my advantage; particularly I found a kind of wild
pidgeons, who built not as wood pidgeons in a tree, but rather as house
pidgeons, in the holes of the rocks; and taking some young ones, I endeavoured to breed them up tame, and did so; but when they grew older they
flew all away, which perhaps was at first for want of feeding them, for I
had nothing to give them; however I frequently found their nests, and got
their young ones, which were very good meat.

And now in the managing my household affairs, I found my self wanting
in many things, which I thought at first it was impossible for me to make,
as indeed as to some of them it was; *for instance*, I could never make a cask
to be hooped, I had a small runlet or two, *as I observ'd before*, but I cou'd
never arrive to the capacity of making one by them, tho' I spent many
weeks about it; I could neither put in the heads, or joint the staves so true
to one another, as to make them hold water, so I gave that also over.

In the next place, I was at a great loss for candle; so that as soon as ever
it was dark, which was generally by seven-a-clock, I was oblig'd to go to
bed: I remembred the lump of bees-wax with which I made candles in my
African adventure, but I had none of that now; the only remedy I had was,
that when I had kill'd a goat, I sav'd the tallow, and with a little dish made
of clay, which I bak'd in the sun, to which I added a wick of some oakum,
I made me a lamp; and this gave me light, tho' not a clear steady light like

a candle; in the middle of all my labours it happen'd, that rumaging my things, I found a little bag, which, as I hinted before, had been fill'd with corn for the feeding of poultry, not for this voyage, but before, as I suppose, when the ship came from *Lisbon*, what little remainder of corn had been in the bag, was all devour'd with the rats, and I saw nothing in the bag but husks and dust; and being willing to have the bag for some other use, I think it was to put powder in, when I divided it for fear of the lightning, or some such use, I shook the husks of corn out of it on one side of my fortification under the rock.

It was a little before the great rains, just now mention'd, that I threw this stuff away, taking no notice of any thing, and not so much as remembring that I had thrown any thing there; when about a month after, or thereabout, I saw some few stalks of something green, shooting out of the ground, which I fancy'd might be some plant I had not seen, but I was surpris'd and perfectly astonish'd, when, after a little longer time, I saw about ten or twelve ears come out, which were perfect green barley of the same kind as our *European*, nay, as our *English* barley.

It is impossible to express the astonishment and confusion of my thoughts on this occasion; I had hitherto acted upon no religious foundation at all, indeed I had very few notions of religion in my head, or had entertain'd any sense of any thing that had befallen me, otherwise than as a chance, or, as we lightly say, what pleases God; without so much as enquiring into the end of Providence in these things, or his order in governing events in the world: But after I saw barley grow there, in a climate which I know was not proper for corn, and especially that I knew not how it came there, it startled me strangely, and I began to suggest, that God had miraculously caus'd this grain to grow without any help of seed sown, and that it was so directed purely for my sustenance on that wild miserable place.

This touch'd my heart a little, and brought tears out of my eyes, and I began to bless my self, that such a prodigy of Nature should happen upon my account; and this was the more strange to me, because I saw near it still all along by the side of the rock, some other straggling stalks, which prov'd to be stalks of rice, and which I knew, because I had seen it grow in *Africa* when I was ashore there.

I not only thought these the pure productions of Providence for my support, but not doubting, but that there was more in the place, I went all over that part of the island, where I had been before, peering in every corner, and under every rock, to see for more of it, but I could not find any; at last it occurr'd to my thoughts, that I had shook a bag of chickens meat out in that place, and then the wonder began to cease; and I must confess, my religious thankfulness to God's Providence began to abate too upon the discovering that all this was nothing but what was common; tho' I ought to have been as thankful for so strange and unforeseen Providence, as if it had been miraculous; for it was really the work of Providence as to me, that should order or appoint, that 10 or 12 grains of corn should remain unspoil'd, (when the rats had destroy'd all the rest,) as if it had been dropt from Heaven; as also, that I should throw it out in that particular place, where it being in the shade of a high rock, it sprang up immediately; whereas, if I had thrown it any where else, at that time, it had been burnt up and destroy'd.

I carefully sav'd the ears of this corn you may be sure in their season, which was about the end of *June*; and laying up every corn, I resolv'd to sow them all again, hoping in time to have some quantity sufficient to supply me with bread; but it was not till the 4th year that I could allow my self the least grain of this corn to eat, and even then but sparingly, as I shall say afterwards in its order; for I lost all that I sow'd the first season, by not observing the proper time; for I sow'd it just before the dry season, so that it never came up at all, at least, not as it would ha' done: Of which in its place.

Besides this barley, there was, as above, 20 or 30 stalks of rice, which I preserv'd with the same care, and whose use was of the same kind or to the same purpose, (*viz*) to make me bread, or rather food; for I found ways to cook it up without baking, tho' I did that also after some time. But to return to my Journal.

I work'd excessive hard these three or four months to get my wall done; and the 14th of *April* I closed it up, contriving to go into it, not by a door, but over the wall by a ladder, that there might be no sign in the out-side of my habitation.

April 16. I finish'd the ladder, so I went up with the ladder to the top, and then pull'd it up after me, and let it down in the in-side: This was a compleat enclosure to me; for within I had room enough, and nothing could come at me from without, unless it could first mount my wall.

The very next day after this wall was finished, I had almost had all my labour overthrown at once, and my self kill'd, the case was thus, As I was busy in the inside of it, behind my tent, just in the entrance into my cave,

I was terribly frighted with a most dreadful surprising thing indeed; for all on a sudden I found the earth come crumbling down from the roof of my cave, and from the edge of the hill over my head, and two of the posts I had set up in the cave crack'd in a frightful manner; I was heartily scared, but thought nothing of what was really the cause, only thinking that the top of my cave was falling in, as some of it had done before; and for fear I shou'd be bury'd in it, I run forward to my ladder, and not thinking my self safe there neither, I got over my wall for fear of the pieces of the hill which I expected might roll down upon me: I was no sooner stepp'd down upon the firm ground, but I plainly saw it was a terrible earthquake, for the ground I stood on shook three times at about eight minutes distance, with three such shocks, as would have overturned the strongest building that could be suppos'd to have stood on the earth; and a great piece of the top of a rock, which stood about half a mile from me next the sea, fell down with such a terrible noise, as I never heard in all my life. I perceiv'd also, the very sea was put into violent motion by it; and I believe the shocks were stronger under the water than on the island.

I was so amaz'd with the thing it self, having never felt the like, or discoursed with any one that had, that I was like one dead or stupify'd; and the motion of the earth made my stomach sick, like one that was toss'd at sea; but the noise of the falling of the rock awak'd me as it were, and rousing me from the stupify'd condition I was in, fill'd me with horror, and I thought of nothing then but the hill falling upon my tent and all my household goods, and burying all at once; and this sunk my very soul within me a second time.

After the third shock was over, and I felt no more for some time, I began to take courage, and yet I had not heart enough to go over my wall again, for fear of being buried alive, but sat still upon the ground, greatly cast down and disconsolate, not knowing what to do: All this while I had not the least serious religious thought, nothing but the common, *Lord ha' mercy upon me*;[25] and when it was over, that went away too.

While I sat thus, I found the air over-cast, and grow cloudy, as if it would rain; soon after that the wind rose by little and little, so that, in less than half an hour, it blew a most dreadful hurricane: The sea was all on a sudden cover'd over with foam and froth, the shore was cover'd with the breach of the water, the trees were torn up by the roots, and a terrible storm it was; and this held about three hours, and then began to abate, and in two hours more it was stark calm, and began to rain very hard.

All this while I sat upon the ground very much terrify'd and dejected, when on a sudden it came into my thoughts, that these winds and rain being the consequence of the earthquake, the earthquake it self was spent and over, and I might venture into my cave again: With this thought my spirits began to revive, and the rain also helping to perswade me, I went in and sat down in my tent, but the rain was so violent, that my tent was ready to be beaten down with it, and I was forc'd to go into my cave, tho' very much afraid and uneasy for fear it should fall on my head.

This violent rain forc'd me to a new work, *viz.* to cut a hole thro' my new fortification like a sink to let the water go out, which would else have drown'd my cave. After I had been in my cave some time, and found still no more shocks of the earthquake follow, I began to be more compos'd; and now to support my spirits, which indeed wanted it very much, I went to my little store, and took a small sup of rum, which however I did then and always very sparingly, knowing I could have no more when that was gone.

It continu'd raining all that night, and great part of the next day, so that I could not stir abroad, but my mind being more compos'd, I began to think of what I had best do, concluding that if the island was subject to these earthquakes, there would be no living for me in a cave, but I must consider of building me some little hut in an open place which I might surround with a wall as I had done here, and so make my self secure from wild beasts or men; but concluded, if I staid where I was, I should certainly, one time or other, be bury'd alive.

With these thoughts I resolv'd to remove my tent from the place where it stood, which was just under the hanging precipice of the hill, and which, if it should be shaken again, would certainly fall upon my tent: And I spent the two next days, being the 19th and 20th of *April*, in contriving where and how to remove my habitation.

The fear of being swallow'd up alive, made me that I never slept in quiet, and yet the apprehension of lying abroad without any fence was almost equal to it; but still when I look'd about and saw how every thing was put in order, how pleasantly conceal'd I was, and how safe from danger, it made me very loath to remove.

In the mean time it occur'd to me that it would require a vast deal of time for me to do this, and that I must be contented to run the venture where I was, till I had form'd a camp for my self, and had secured it so as to remove to it: So with this resolution I compos'd my self for a time, and resolv'd that I would go to work with all speed to build me a wall with piles and cables, &c. in a circle as before, and set my tent up in it when it was finish'd, but that I would venture to stay where I was till it was finish'd and fit to remove to. This was the 21st.

April 22. The next morning I began to consider of means to put this resolve in execution, but I was at a great loss about my tools; I had three large axes and abundance of hatchets, (for we carried the hatchets for traffick with the *Indians*) but with much chopping and cutting knotty hard wood, they were all full of notches and dull, and tho' I had a grindstone, I could not turn it and grind my tools too; this cost me as much thought as a statesman would have bestow'd upon a grand point of politicks, or a judge upon the life and death of a man. At length I contriv'd a wheel with a string, to turn it with my foot, that I might have both my hands at liberty: *Note*, I had never seen any such thing in *England*, or at least not to take notice how it was done, tho' since I have observ'd it is very common there; besides that, my grindstone was very large and heavy. This machine cost me a full week's work to bring it to perfection.

April 28, 29. These two whole days I took up in grinding my tools, my machine for turning my grindstone performing very well.

April 30. Having perceiv'd my bread had been low a great while, now I took a survey of it, and reduced my self to one bisket-cake a day, which made my heart very heavy.

May 1. In the morning looking towards the sea-side, the tide being low, I saw something lye on the shore bigger than ordinary, and it look'd like a cask; when I came to it, I found a small barrel, and two or three pieces of the wreck of the ship, which were driven on shore by the late hurricane, and looking towards the wreck itself, I thought it seem'd to lye higher out of the water than it us'd to do; I examin'd the barrel which was driven on shore, and soon found it was a barrel of gunpowder, but it had taken water, and the powder was cak'd as hard as a stone, however I roll'd it farther on shore for the present, and went on upon the sands as near as I could to the wreck of the ship to look for more.

When I came down to the ship, I found it strangely remov'd; the fore-castle, which lay before bury'd in sand, was heav'd up at least six foot, and the stern which was broke to pieces and parted from the rest by the force of the sea soon after I had left rummaging her, was toss'd, as it were, up, and cast on one side, and the sand was thrown so high on that side next her stern, that whereas there was a great place of water before, so that

I could not come within a quarter of a mile of the wreck without swimming, I could now walk quite up to her when the tide was out; I was surpris'd with this at first, but soon concluded it must be done by the earthquake, and as by this violence the ship was more broken open than formerly, so many things came daily on shore, which the sea had loosen'd, and which the winds and water rolled by degrees to the land.

This wholly diverted my thoughts from the design of removing my habitation; and I busied myself mightily that day especially, in searching whether I could make any way into the ship, but I found nothing was to be expected of that kind, for that all the in-side of the ship was choak'd up with sand: However, as I had learn'd not to despair of any thing, I resolv'd to pull every thing to pieces that I could of the ship, concluding, that every thing I could get from her would be of some use or other to me.

May 3. I began with my saw, and cut a piece of a beam thro', which I thought held some of the upper part or quarter-deck together, and when I had cut it thro', I clear'd away the sand as well as I could from the side which lay highest; but the tide coming in, I was obliged to give over for that time.

May 4. I went a fishing, but caught not one fish that I durst eat of, till I was weary of my sport, when just going to leave off, I caught a young dolphin. I had made me a long line of some rope yarn, but I had no hooks, yet I frequently caught fish enough, as much as I car'd to eat; all which I dry'd in the sun, and eat them dry.

May 5. Work'd on the wreck, cut another beam asunder, and brought three great fir planks off from the decks, which I ty'd together, and made swim on shore, when the tide of flood came on.

May 6. Work'd on the wreck, got several iron bolts out of her, and other pieces of iron-work, work'd very hard, and came home very much tyr'd, and had thoughts of giving it over.

May 7. Went to the wreck again, but with an intent not to work, but found the weight of the wreck had broke itself down, the beams being cut, that several pieces of the ship seem'd to lie loose, and the in-side of the hold lay so open, that I could see into it, but almost full of water and sand.

May 8. Went to the wreck, and carry'd an iron crow to wrench up the deck, which lay now quite clear of the water or sand; I wrench'd open two planks, and brought them on shore also with the tide: I left the iron crow in the wreck for next day.

May 9, Went to the wreck, and with the crow made way into the body of the wreck, and felt several casks, and loosen'd them with the crow; but could not break them up; I felt also the roll of *English* lead, and could stir it, but it was too heavy to remove.

May 10, 11, 12, 13, 14. Went every day to the wreck, and got a great deal of pieces of timber, and boards, or plank, and 2 or 300 weight of iron.

May 15. I carry'd two hatchets to try if I could not cut a piece off of the roll of lead, by placing the edge of one hatchet, and driving it with the other; but as it lay about a foot and a half in the water, I could not make any blow to drive the hatchet.

May 16. It had blow'd hard in the night, and the wreck appear'd more broken by the force of the water; but I stay'd so long in the woods to get pidgeons for food, that the tide prevented me going to the wreck that day.

May 17. I saw some pieces of the wreck blown on shore, at a great distance, near two miles off me, but resolv'd to see what they were, and found it was a piece of the head, but too heavy for me to bring away.

May 24. Every day to this day I work'd on the wreck, and with hard labour I loosen'd some things so much with the crow, that the first blowing tide several casks floated out, and two of the seamens chests; but the wind blowing from the shore, nothing came to land that day, but pieces of timber, and a hogshead which had some *Brazil* pork in it, but the salt-water and the sand had spoil'd it.

I continu'd this work every day to the 15th of *June*, except the time necessary to get food, which I always appointed, during this part of my employment, to be when the tide was up, that I might be ready when it was ebb'd out; and by this time I had gotten timber, and plank, and iron-work enough to have built a good boat, if I had known how; and also, I got at several times, and in several pieces, near 100 weight of the sheet-lead.

June 16. Going down to the sea-side, I found a large tortoise or turtle; this was the first I had seen, which it seems was only my misfortune, not any defect of the place, or scarcity; for had I happen'd to be on the other side of the island, I might have had hundreds of them every day, as I found afterwards; but perhaps had paid dear enough for them.

June 17. I spent in cooking the turtle; I found in her threescore eggs; and her flesh was to me at that time the most savoury and pleasant that ever I tasted in my life, having had no flesh, but of goats and fowls, since I landed in this horrid place.

June 18. Rain'd all day, and I stay'd within. I thought at this time the rain felt cold, and I was something chilly, which I knew was not usual in that latitude.

June 19. Very ill, and shivering, as if the weather had been cold.

June 20. No rest all night, violent pains in my head, and feaverish.

June 21. Very ill, frighted almost to death with the apprehensions of my sad condition, to be sick, and no help: Pray'd to GOD for the first time since the storm off of *Hull*, but scarce knew what I said, or why; my thoughts being all confused.

June 22. A little better, but under dreadful apprehensions of sickness.

June 23. Very bad again, cold and shivering, and then a violent head-ach.

June 24. Much better.

June 25. An ague very violent; the fit held me seven hours, cold fit and hot, with faint sweats after it.

June 26. Better; and having no victuals to eat, took my gun, but found myself very weak; however I kill'd a she-goat, and with much difficulty got it home, and broil'd some of it, and eat; I wou'd fain have stew'd it, and made some broth, but had no pot.

June 27. The ague again so violent, that I lay a-bed all day, and neither eat or drank. I was ready to perish for thirst, but so weak, I had not strength to stand up, or to get my self any water to drink: Pray'd to God again, but was light-headed, and when I was not, I was so ignorant, that I knew not what to say; only I lay and cry'd, *Lord look upon me, Lord pity me, Lord have mercy upon me*: I suppose I did nothing else for two or three hours, till the fit wearing off, I fell asleep, and did not wake till far in the night; when I wak'd, I found my self much refresh'd, but weak, and exceeding thirsty: However, as I had no water in my whole habitation, I was forc'd to lie till morning, and went to sleep again: In this second sleep, I had this terrible dream.

I thought, that I was sitting on the ground on the out-side of my wall, where I sat when the storm blew after the earthquake, and that I saw a man descend from a great black cloud, in a bright flame of fire, and light upon the ground: He was all over as bright as a flame, so that I could but just bear to look towards him; his countenance was most inexpressibly dreadful, impossible for words to describe; when he stepp'd upon the ground with his feet, I thought the earth trembled, just as it had done before in the earthquake, and all the air look'd to my apprehension, as if it had been fill'd with flashes of fire.

He was no sooner landed upon the earth, but he mov'd forward towards me, with a long spear or weapon in his hand, to kill me; and when he came to a rising ground, at some distance, he spoke to me, or I heard a voice so terrible, that it is impossible to express the terror of it; all that I can say I understood was this, *Seeing all these things have not brought thee to repentance, now thou shalt die*: At which words, I thought he lifted up the spear that was in his hand, to kill me.

No one, that shall ever read this account, will expect that I should be able to describe the horrors of my soul at this terrible vision, I mean, that even while it was a dream, I even dreamed of those horrors; nor is it any more possible to describe the impression that remain'd upon my mind when I awak'd and found it was but a dream.

I had alas! no divine knowledge; what I had receiv'd by the good instruction of my father was then worn out by an uninterrupted series, for 8 years, of seafaring wickedness, and a constant conversation with nothing but such as were like myself, wicked and prophane to the last degree: I do not remember that I had in all that time one thought that so much as tended either to looking upwards toward God, or inwards towards a reflection upon my own ways: But a certain stupidity of soul, without desire of good, or conscience of evil, had entirely overwhelm'd me, and I was all that the most hardned, unthinking, wicked creature among our common sailors can be suppos'd to be, not having the least sense, either of the fear of God in danger, or of thankfulness to God in deliverances.

In the relating what is already past of my story, this will be the more easily believed, when I shall add, that thro' all the variety of miseries that had to this day befallen me, I never had so much as one thought of it being the hand of God, or that it was a just punishment for my sin; my rebellious behaviour against my father, or my present sins which were great; or so much as a punishment for the general course of my wicked life. When I was on the desperate expedition on the desart shores of *Africa*, I never had so much as one thought of what would become of me; or one wish to God to direct me whither I should go, or to keep me from the danger which apparently surrounded me, as well from voracious creatures as cruel savages: But I was meerly thoughtless of a God, or a Providence, acted like a meer brute from the principles of Nature, and by the dictates of common sense only, and indeed hardly that.

When I was deliver'd and taken up at sea by the *Portugal* Captain, well us'd, and dealt justly and honourably with, as well as charitably, I had not the least thankfulness on my thoughts: When again I was shipwreck'd, ruin'd, and in danger of drowning on this island, I was as far from remorse, or looking on it as a judgment; I only said to my self often, that I was *an unfortunate dog*, and born to be always miserable.

It is true, when I got on shore first here, and found all my ship's crew drown'd, and my self spar'd, I was surpris'd with a kind of extasie, and some transports of soul, which, had the grace of God assisted, might have come up to true thankfulness; but it ended where it begun, in a meer common flight of joy, or, as I may say, *being glad I was alive*, without the least reflection upon the distinguishing goodness of the hand which had preserv'd me, and had singled me out to be preserv'd, when all the rest were destroy'd; or an enquiry why Providence had been thus merciful to me; even just the same common sort of joy which seamen generally have after they are got safe ashore from a shipwreck, which they drown all in the next bowl of punch, and forget almost as soon as it is over, and all the rest of my life was like it.

Even, when I was afterwards, on due consideration, made sensible of my condition, how I was cast on this dreadful place, out of the reach of human kind, out of all hope of relief, or prospect of redemption, as soon as I saw but a prospect of living, and that I should not starve and perish for hunger, all the sense of my affliction wore off, and I begun to be very easy, apply'd my self to the works proper for my preservation and supply, and was far enough from being afflicted at my condition, as a judgment from Heaven, or as the hand of God against me; these were thoughts which very seldom enter'd into my head.

The growing up of the corn, as is hinted in my Journal, had at first some little influence upon me, and began to affect me with seriousness, as long as I thought it had something miraculous in it; but as soon as ever that part of the thought was remov'd, all the impression which was rais'd from it, wore off also, as I have noted already.

Even the earthquake, tho' nothing could be more terrible in its nature, or more immediately directing to the invisible power which alone directs such things, yet no sooner was the first fright over, but the impression it had made, went off also. I had no more sense of God or his judgments, much less of the present affliction of my circumstances being from his hand, than if I had been in the most prosperous condition of life.

But now when I began to be sick, and a leisurely view of the miseries of death came to place itself before me; when my spirits began to sink under the burden of a strong distemper, and Nature was exhausted with the violence of the feaver; conscience that had slept so long, began to awake, and I began to reproach myself with my past life, in which I had so evidently, by uncommon wickedness, provok'd the justice of God to lay me under uncommon strokes, and to deal with me in so vindictive a manner.

These reflections oppress'd me for the second or third day of my distemper, and in the violence, as well of the feaver, as of the dreadful reproaches of my conscience, extorted some words from me, like praying to God, tho' I cannot say they were either a prayer attended with desires or with hopes; it was rather the voice of meer fright and distress; my thoughts were confus'd, the convictions great upon my mind, and the horror of dying in such a miserable condition, rais'd vapours into my head with the meer apprehensions; and in these hurries of my soul, I know not what my tongue might express; but it was rather exclamation, such as, Lord! what a miserable creature am I? If I should be sick, I shall certainly die for want of help, and what will become of me! Then the tears burst out of my eyes, and I could say no more for a good while.

In this interval, the good advice of my father came to my mind, and presently his prediction, which I mentioned at the beginning of this story, *viz. that if I did take this foolish step, God would not bless me; and I would have leisure hereafter to reflect upon having neglected his counsel, when there might be none to assist in my recovery.* Now, said I aloud, my dear father's words are come to pass: God's justice has overtaken me, and I have none to help or hear me: I rejected the voice of Providence, which had mercifully put me in a posture or station of life, wherein I might have been happy and easy; but I would neither see it my self, or learn to know the blessing of it from my parents; I left them to mourn over my folly, and now I am left to mourn under the consequences of it: I refus'd their help and assistance who wou'd have lifted me into the world, and wou'd have made every thing easy to me, and now I have difficulties to struggle with, too great for even Nature itself to support, and no assistance, no help, no comfort, no advice; then I cry'd out, *Lord be my help, for I am in great distress.*

This was the first prayer, if I may call it so, that I had made for many years. But I return to my Journal.

June 28. Having been somewhat refresh'd with the sleep I had had, and the fit being entirely off, I got up; and tho' the fright and terror of my dream was very great, yet I consider'd, that the fit of the ague wou'd return again the next day, and now was my time to get something to refresh and support myself when I should be ill; and the first thing I did, I fill'd a large square case bottle with water, and set it upon my table, in reach of my bed; and to take off the chill or aguish disposition of the water, I put about a quarter of a pint of rum into it, and mix'd them together; then I got me a piece of the goat's flesh, and broil'd it on the coals, but could eat very little; I walk'd about, but was very weak, and withal very sad and heavy-hearted in the sense of my miserable condition; dreading the return of my distemper the next day; at night I made my supper of three of the turtle's eggs, which I roasted in the ashes, and eat, as we call it, in the shell; and this was the first bit of meat I had ever ask'd God's blessing to, even as I cou'd remember, in my whole life.

After I had eaten, I try'd to walk, but found my self so weak, that I cou'd hardly carry the gun, (for I never went out without that) so I went but a little way, and sat down upon the ground, looking out upon the sea, which was just before me, and very calm and smooth: As I sat here, some such thoughts as these occurred to me.

What is this earth and sea of which I have seen so much, whence is it produced, and what am I, and all the other creatures, wild and tame, human and brutal, whence are we?

Sure we are all made by some secret power, who form'd the earth and sea, the air and sky; and who is that?

Then it follow'd most naturally, It is God that has made it all: Well, but then it came on strangely, if God has made all these things, He guides and governs them all, and all things that concern them; for the power that could make all things, must certainly have power to guide and direct them.

If so, nothing can happen in the great circuit of his works, either without his knowledge or appointment.

And if nothing happens without his knowledge, he knows that I am here, and am in this dreadful condition; and if nothing happens without his appointment, he has appointed all this to befal me.

Nothing occurr'd to my thought to contradict any of these conclusions; and therefore it rested upon me with the greater force, that it must needs be, that God has appointed all this to befal me; that I was brought to this miserable circumstance by his direction, he having the sole power, not of me only, but of every thing that happen'd in the world. Immediately it follow'd,

Why has God done this to me? What have I done to be thus us'd?

My conscience presently check'd me in that enquiry, as if I had blasphem'd, and methought it spoke to me like a voice; *WRETCH! dost thou ask what thou hast done!* look back upon a dreadful mis-spent life, and ask thy self *what thou hast not done?* ask, Why is it *that thou wert not long ago destroy'd?* Why *wert thou not drown'd in* Yarmouth Roads? *Kill'd in the fight when the ship was taken by* the Sallee man of war? *Devour'd by the wild beasts on the* coast of Africa? Or *drown'd HERE, when all the crew perish'd but thy self?* Dost thou ask *What have I done?*

I was struck dumb with these reflections, as one astonish'd, and had not a word to say, no not to answer to my self, but rose up pensive and sad, walk'd back to my retreat, and went up over my wall, as if I had been going to bed, but my thoughts were sadly disturb'd, and I had no inclination to sleep; so I sat down in my chair, and lighted my lamp, for it began to be dark: Now as the apprehension of the return of my distemper terrify'd me very much, it occurr'd to my thought, that the *Brasilians* take no physick but their tobacco, for almost all distempers; and I had a piece of a roll of tobacco in one of the chests, which was quite cur'd, and some also that was green and not quite cur'd.

I went, directed by Heaven no doubt; for in this chest I found a cure, both for soul and body, I open'd the chest, and found what I look'd for, *viz.* the tobacco; and as the few books, I had sav'd, lay there too, I took out one of the Bibles which I mention'd before, and which to this time I had not found leisure, or so much as inclination to look into; I say, I took it out, and brought both that and the tobacco with me to the table.

What use to make of the tobacco, I knew not, as to my distemper, or whether it was good for it or no; but I try'd several experiments with it, as if I was resolv'd it should hit one way or other: I first took a piece of a leaf, and chew'd it in my mouth, which indeed at first almost stupify'd my brain, the tobacco being green and strong, and that I had not been much us'd to it; then I took some and steeped it an hour or two in some rum, and resolv'd to take a dose of it when I lay down; and lastly, I burnt some upon a pan of coals, and held my nose close over the smoke of it as long as I could bear it, as well for the heat as almost for suffocation.

In the interval of this operation, I took up the Bible and began to read, but my head was too much disturb'd with the tobacco to bear reading, at least that time; only having open'd the book casually, the first words that occurr'd to me were these, *Call on me in the day of trouble, and I will deliver, and thou shalt glorify me.*[26]

The words were very apt to my case, and made some impression upon my thoughts at the time of reading them, tho' not so much as they did afterwards; for as for being deliver'd, the word had no sound, *as I may say*, to me; the thing was so remote, so impossible in my apprehension of things, that I began to say as the children of *Israel* did, when they were promis'd flesh to eat, *Can God spread a table in the wilderness;*[27] so I began to say, Can God himself deliver me from this place? And as it was not for many years that any hope appear'd, this prevail'd very often upon my thoughts: But however, the words made a great impression upon me, and I mused upon them very often. It grew now late, and the tobacco had, as I said, doz'd my head so much, that I inclin'd to sleep; so I left my lamp burning in the cave, lest I should want any thing in the night, and went to bed; but before I lay down, I did what I never had done in all my life, I kneel'd down and pray'd to God to fulfil the promise to me, that if I call'd upon him in the day of trouble, he would deliver me; after my broken and imperfect prayer was over, I drunk the rum in which I had steep'd the tobacco, which was so strong and rank of the tobacco, that indeed I could scarce get it down; immediately upon this I went to bed, I found presently it flew up in my head violently, but I fell into a sound sleep, and wak'd no more, till by the sun it must necessarily be near three a-clock in the afternoon the next day; nay, to this hour I'm partly of the opinion, that I slept all the next day and night, and till almost three that day after; for otherwise I knew not how I should lose a day out of my reckoning in the days of the week, as it appear'd some years after I had done: for if I had lost it by crossing and re-crossing the Line,[28] I should have lost more than one day: But certainly I lost a day in my accompt, and never knew which way.

Be that however one way or th'other, when I awak'd I found myself exceedingly refresh'd, and my spirits lively and cheerful; when I got up, I was stronger than I was the day before, and my stomach better, for I was hungry; and in short, I had no fit the next day, but continu'd much alter'd for the better; this was the 29th.

The 30th was my well day of course, and I went abroad with my gun, but did not care to travel too far, I kill'd a sea-fowl or two, something like a brand goose, and brought them home, but was not very forward to eat them; so I eat some more of the turtle's eggs, which were very good: This evening I renew'd the medicine which I had suppos'd did me good the day before, *viz.* the tobacco steep'd in rum, only I did not take so much as before, nor did I chew any of the leaf, or hold my head over the smoke; however, I was not so well the next day, which was the first of *July*, as I hop'd I should have been; for I had a little spice of the cold fit, but it was not much.

July 2. I renew'd the medicine all the three ways, and doz'd my self with it as at first; and doubled the quantity which I drank.

[*July*] 3. I miss'd the fit for good and all, tho' I did not recover my full strength for some weeks after, while I was thus gathering strength, my thoughts run exceedingly upon this Scripture, *I will deliver thee*: and the impossibility of my deliverance lay much upon my mind in bar of my ever expecting it. But as I was discouraging my self with such thoughts, it occurr'd to my mind, that I pored so much upon my deliverance from the main affliction, that I disregarded the deliverance I had receiv'd; and I was, as it were, made to ask my self such questions as these, *viz*. Have I not been deliver'd, and wonderfully too, from sickness? from the most distressed condition that could be, and that was so frightful to me, and what notice I had taken of it: Had I done my part, *God had delivered me, but I had not glorify'd him*; that is to say, I had not own'd and been thankful for that as a deliverance, and how could I expect greater deliverance?

This touch'd my heart very much, and immediately I kneel'd down, and gave God thanks aloud for my recovery from my sickness.

July 4. In the morning I took the Bible, and beginning at the New Testament, I began seriously to read it, and impos'd upon myself to read awhile every morning and every night, not tying my self to the number of chapters, but as long as my thoughts should engage me: It was not long after I set seriously to this work, but I found my heart more deeply and sincerely affected with the wickedness of my past life: The impression of my dream reviv'd, and the words, *All these things have not brought thee to repentance*, ran seriously in my thought: I was earnestly begging of God to give me repentance, when it happen'd providentially the very day that reading the Scripture, I came to these words, *He is exalted a prince and a saviour, to give repentance, and to give remission*:[29] I threw down the book, and with my heart as well as my hands lifted up to Heaven, in a kind of extasy of joy, I cry'd out aloud, *Jesus, thou son of* David,[30] *Jesus, thou exalted prince and saviour, give me repentance!*

This was the first time that I could say, in the true sense of the words, that I pray'd in all my life; for now I pray'd with a sense of my condition, and with a true Scripture view of hope founded on the encouragement of the word of God; and from this time, I may say, I began to have hope that God would hear me.

Now I began to construe the words mentioned above, *Call on me, and I will deliver you*, in a different sense from what I had ever done before; for then I had no notion of any thing being call'd deliverance, but my being deliver'd from the captivity I was in; for tho' I was indeed at large in the place, yet the island was certainly a prison to me, and that in the worst sense in the world; but now I learn'd to take it in another sense: Now I look'd back upon my past life with such horror, and my sins appear'd so dreadful, that my soul sought nothing of God, but deliverance from the load of guilt that bore down all my comfort: As for my solitary life it was nothing; I did not so much as pray to be deliver'd from it, or think of it; it was all of no consideration in comparison to this: And I add this part here, to hint to whoever shall read it, that whenever they come to a true sense of things, they will find deliverance from sin a much greater blessing than deliverance from affliction.

But leaving this part, I return to my Journal.

My condition began now to be, tho' not less miserable as to my way of living, yet much easier to my mind; and my thoughts being directed by a constant reading the Scripture, and praying to God, to things of a higher nature: I had a great deal of comfort within, which till now I knew nothing of; also as my health and strength returned, I bestir'd my self to furnish my self with every thing that I wanted, and make my way of living as regular as I could.

From the 4th of *July* to the 14th, I was chiefly employ'd in walking about with my gun in my hand, a little and a little, at a time, as a man that was gathering up his strength after a fit of sickness: For it is hardly to be imagin'd, how low I was, and to what weakness I was reduc'd. The application which I made use of was perfectly new, and perhaps what had never cur'd an ague before, neither can I recommend it to any one to practise, by this experiment; and tho' it did carry off the fit, yet it rather contributed to weakening me; for I had frequent convulsions in my nerves and limbs for some time.

I learn'd from it also this in particular, that being abroad in the rainy season was the most pernicious thing to my health that could be, especially in those rains which came attended with storms and hurricanes of wind; for as the rain which came in the dry season was always most accompany'd with such storms, so I found that rain was much more dangerous than the rain which fell in *September* and *October*.

I had been now in this unhappy island above 10 months, all possibility of deliverance from this condition, seem'd to be entirely taken from me; and I firmly believed, that no human shape had ever set foot upon that place: Having now secur'd my habitation, as I thought, fully to my mind, I had a great desire to make a more perfect discovery of the island, and to see what other productions I might find, which I yet knew nothing of.

It was the 15th of *July* that I began to take a more particular survey of the island it self: I went up the creek first, where, as I hinted, I brought my rafts on shore; I found after I came about two miles up, that the tide did not flow any higher, and that it was no more than a little brook of running water, and very fresh and good; but this being the dry season, there was hardly any water in some parts of it, at least not enough to run in any stream, so as it could be perceiv'd.

On the bank of this brook I found many pleasant *savanna's*, or meadows, plain, smooth, and cover'd with grass; and on the rising parts of them next to the higher grounds, where the water, as it might be supposed, never overflow'd, I found a great deal of tobacco, green, and growing to a great and very strong stalk; there were divers other plants which I had no notion of, or understanding about, and might perhaps have vertues of their own, which I could not find out.

I searched for the *cassava* root, which the *Indians* in all that climate make their bread of, but I could find none. I saw large plants of alloes, but did not then understand them. I saw several sugar canes, but wild, and for want of cultivation, imperfect. I contented myself with these discoveries for this time, and came back musing with my self what course I might take to know the virtue and goodness of any of the fruits or plants which I should discover; but could bring it to no conclusion; for in short, I had made so little observation while I was in the *Brasils*, that I knew little of the plants in the field, at least very little that might serve me to any purpose now in my distress.

The next day, the 16th, I went up the same way again, and after going something farther than I had gone the day before, I found the brook, and the *savanna's* began to cease, and the country became more woody than before; in this part I found different fruits, and particularly I found mellons upon the ground in great abundance, and grapes upon the trees; the vines had spread indeed over the trees, and the clusters of grapes were just now in their prime, very ripe and rich: This was a surprising discovery, and I was exceeding glad of them; but I was warn'd by my experience to eat sparingly of them, remembring, that when I was ashore in *Barbary*, the eating of grapes kill'd several of our *English* men who were slaves there, by throwing them into fluxes and feavers: But I found an excellent use for these grapes, and that was to cure or dry them in the sun, and keep them as dry'd grapes or raisins are kept, which I thought would be, as indeed they were, as wholesome, as agreeable to eat, when no grapes might be to be had.

I spent all that evening there, and went not back to my habitation, which by the way was the first night, as I might say, I had lain from home. In the night I took my first contrivance, and got up into a tree, where I slept well, and the next morning proceeded upon my discovery, travelling near four miles, as I might judge by the length of the valley, keeping still due north, with a ridge of hills on the south and north-side of me.

At the end of this march I came to an opening, where the country seem'd to descend to the west, and a little spring of fresh water, which issued out of the side of the hill by me, run the other way, that is due east; and the country appear'd so fresh, so green, so flourishing, every thing being in a constant verdure, or flourish of *Spring*, that it it look'd like a planted garden.

I descended a little on the side of that delicious vale, surveying it with a secret kind of pleasure, (tho' mixt with my other afflicting thoughts) to think that this was all my own, that I was king and lord of all this country indefeasibly, and had a right of possession; and if I could convey it, I might have it in inheritance, as compleatly as any lord of a manor in *England*. I saw here abundance of cocoa trees, orange, and lemon, and citron trees; but all wild, and very few bearing any fruit, at least not then: However, the green limes that I gathered, were not only pleasant to eat, but very wholesome; and I mix'd their juice afterwards with water, which made it very wholesome, and very cool, and refreshing.

I found now I had business enough to gather and carry home; and I resolv'd to lay up a store, as well of grapes, as limes and lemons, to furnish my self for the wet season, which I knew was approaching.

In order to this, I gather'd a great heap of grapes in one place, and a lesser heap in another place, and a great parcel of limes and lemons in another place; and taking a few of each with me, I travell'd homeward, and resolv'd to come again, and bring a bag or sack, or what I could make, to carry the rest home.

Accordingly, having spent three days in this journey, I came home; so

I must now call my tent and my cave: But, before I got thither, the grapes were spoil'd, the richness of the fruits, and the weight of the juice having broken them, and bruis'd them, they were good for little or nothing; as to the limes, they were good, but I could bring but a few.

The next day, being the 19th, I went back, having made me two small bags to bring home my harvest: But I was surpris'd, when coming to my heap of grapes, which were so rich and fine when I gather'd them, I found them all spread about, trod to pieces, and dragg'd about, some here, some there, and abundance eaten and devour'd: By this I concluded, there were some wild creatures thereabouts, which had done this; but what they were I knew not.

However, as I found that there was no laying them up on heaps, and no carrying them away in a sack, but that one way they would be destroy'd, and the other way they would be crush'd with their own weight. I took another course; for I gather'd a large quantity of the grapes, and hung them up upon the out branches of the trees, that they might cure and dry in the sun; and as for the limes and lemons, I carry'd as many back as I could well stand under.

When I came home from this journey, I contemplated with great pleasure the fruitfulness of that valley, and the pleasantness of the situation, the security from storms on that side the water, and the wood, and concluded, that I had pitch'd upon a place to fix my abode, which was by far the worst part of the country. Upon the whole I began to consider of removing my habitation; and to look out for a place equally safe, as where I now was situate, if possible, in that pleasant fruitful part of the island.

This thought run long in my head, and I was exceeding fond of it for some time, the pleasantness of the place tempting me; but when I came to a nearer view of it, and to consider that I was now by the sea-side, where it was at least possible that something might happen to my advantage, and by the same ill fate that brought me hither, might bring some other unhappy wretches to the same place; and tho' it was scarce probable that any such thing should ever happen, yet to enclose myself among the hills and woods, in the center of the island, was to anticipate my bondage, and to render such an affair not only improbable, but impossible; and that therefore I ought not by any means to remove.

However, I was so enamour'd of this place, that I spent much of my time there for the whole remaining part of the month of *July*; and tho' upon second thoughts I resolv'd as above, not to remove, yet I built me a little kind of a bower, and surrounded it at a distance with a strong fence, being a double hedge, as high as I could reach, well stak'd, and fill'd between with *brushwood*; and here I lay very secure, sometimes two or three nights together, always going over it with a ladder, as before; so that I fancy'd now I had my country-house, and my sea-coast-house: And this work took me up to the beginning of *August*.

I had but newly finish'd my fence, and began to enjoy my labour, but the rains came on, and made me stick close to my first habitation; for tho' I had made me a tent like the other, with a piece of a sail, and spread it very well; yet I had not the shelter of a hill to keep me from storms, nor a cave behind me to retreat into, when the rains were extraordinary.

About the beginning of *August, as I said*, I had finish'd my bower, and began to enjoy my self. The third of *August*, I found the grapes I had hung up were perfectly dry'd, and indeed, were excellent good raisins of the sun; so I began to take them down from the trees, and it was very happy that I did so; for the rains which follow'd would have spoil'd them, and I had lost the best part of my winter food; for I had above two hundred large bunches of them. No sooner had I taken them all down and carry'd most of them home to my cave, but it began to rain, and from hence, which was the fourteenth of *August*, it rain'd more or less, every day, till the middle of *October*; and sometimes so violently, that I could not stir out of my cave for several days.

In this season I was much surpris'd with the encrease of my family; I had been concern'd for the loss of one of my cats, who run away from me, or as I thought had been dead, and I heard no more tale or tidings of her, till to my astonishment she came home about the end of *August*, with three *kittens*; this was the more strange to me, because tho' I had kill'd a wild cat, as I call'd it, with my gun; yet I thought it was a quite differing kind from our *European* cats; yet the young cats were the same kind of house breed like the old one; and both my cats being females, I thought it very strange: But from these three cats, I afterwards came to be so pester'd with cats, that I was forc'd to kill them like vermin, or wild beasts, and to drive them from my house as much as possible.

From the fourteenth of *August* to the twenty sixth, incessant rain, so that I could not stir, and was now very careful not to be much wet. In this confinement I began to be straitned for food, but venturing out twice, I one day kill'd a goat, and the last day, which was the twenty-sixth, found a very large tortoise, which was a treat to me, and my food was regulated thus; I eat a bunch of raisins for my breakfast, a piece of the goat's flesh, or of the turtle for my dinner broil'd; for to my great misfortune, I had no vessel to boil or stew any thing; and two or three of the turtle's eggs for my supper.

During this confinement in my cover, by the rain, I work'd daily two or three hours at enlarging my cave, and by degrees work'd it on towards one side, till I came to the out-side of the hill, and made a door or way out, which came beyond my fence or wall, and so I came in and out this way; but I was not perfectly easy at lying so open; for as I had manag'd my self before, I was in a perfect enclosure, whereas now I thought I lay expos'd, and open for any thing to come in upon me; and yet I could not perceive that there was any living thing to fear, the biggest creature that I had yet seen upon the island being a goat.

September the thirtieth, I was now come to the unhappy anniversary of my landing. I cast up the notches on my post, and found I had been on shore three hundred and sixty five days. I kept this day as a solemn fast, setting it apart to religious exercise, prostrating myself on the ground with the most serious humiliation, confessing my sins to God, acknowledging his righteous judgments upon me, and praying to him to have mercy on me, through Jesus Christ; and having not tasted the least refreshment for twelve hours, even till the going down of the sun, I then eat a bisket cake, and a bunch of grapes, and went to bed, finishing the day as I began it.

I had all this time observ'd no Sabbath-Day; for as at first I had no sense of religion upon my mind, I had after some time omitted to distinguish the weeks, by making a longer notch than ordinary for the Sabbath-Day, and so did not really know what any of the days were; but now having cast up the days, as above, I found I had been there a year; so I divided it into weeks, and set apart every seventh day for a Sabbath; tho' I found at the end of my account I had lost a day or two in my reckoning.

A little after this my ink began to fail me, and so I contented myself to use it more sparingly, and to write down only the most remarkable events of my life, without continuing a daily *memorandum* of other things.

The rainy season, and the dry season, began now to appear regular to me, and I learn'd to divide them so, as to provide for them accordingly. But I bought all my experience before I had it; and this I am going to relate, was one of the most discouraging experiments that I made at all: I have mention'd that I had sav'd the few ears of barley and rice which I had so surprisingly found spring up, as I thought, of themselves, and believe there were about thirty stalks of rice, and about twenty of barley; and now

I thought it a proper time to sow it after the rains, the sun being in its *southern* position going from me.

Accordingly I dug up a piece of ground, as well as I could with my wooden spade, and dividing it into two parts, I sow'd my grain; but as I was sowing, it casually occur'd to my thoughts, that I would not sow it all at first, because I did not know when was the proper time for it; so I sow'd about two thirds of the seed, leaving about a handful of each.

It was a great comfort to me afterwards, that I did so, for not one grain of that I sow'd this time came to any thing; for the dry months following, the earth having had no rain after the seed was sown, it had no moisture to assist its growth, and never came up at all, till the wet season had come again, and then it grew as if it had been but newly sown.

Finding my first seed did not grow, which I easily imagin'd was by the drought, I sought for a moister piece of ground to make another trial in, and I dug up a piece of ground near my new bower, and sow'd the rest of my seed in *February*, a little before the *Vernal Equinox*; and this having the rainy months of *March* and *April* to water it, sprung up very pleasantly, and yielded a very good crop; but having part of the seed left only, and not daring to sow all that I had, I had but a small quantity at last, my whole crop not amounting to above half a peck of each kind.

But by this experiment I was made master of my business, and knew exactly when the proper season was to sow; and that I might expect two seed-times, and two harvests every year.

While this corn was growing, I made a little discovery which was of use to me afterwards: As soon as the rains were over, and the weather began to settle, which was about the month of *November*, I made a visit up the country to my bower, where tho' I had not been some months, yet I found all things just as I left them. The circle or double hedge that I had made, was not only firm and entire, but the stakes which I had cut out of some trees that grew thereabouts, were all shot out and grown with long branches, as much as a willow-tree usually shoots the first year after lopping its head. I could not tell what tree to call it, that these stakes were cut from. I was surpris'd, and yet very well pleas'd, to see the young trees grow; and I prun'd them, and led them up to grow as much alike as I could; and it is scarce credible how beautiful a figure they grew into in three years; so that tho' the hedge made a circle of about twenty five yards in diameter, yet the trees, for such I might now call them, soon cover'd it; and it was a compleat shade, sufficient to lodge under all the dry season.

This made me resolve to cut some more stakes, and make me a hedge like this in a semicircle round my wall; I mean that of my first dwelling, which I did; and placing the trees or stakes in a double row, at about eight yards distance from my first fence, they grew presently, and were at first a fine cover to my habitation, and afterward serv'd for a defence also, as I shall observe in its order.

I found now, that the seasons of the year might generally be divided, not into *Summer* and *Winter*, as in *Europe*; but into the rainy seasons, and the dry seasons, which were generally thus:

Half *February*,	rainy, the *Sun* being then on, or near the *Equinox*.
March,	rainy, the *Sun* being then on, or near the *Equinox*.
Half *April*,	rainy, the *Sun* being then on, or near the *Equinox*.
Half *April*,	dry, the *Sun* being then to the *north* of the Line.
May,	dry, the *Sun* being then to the *north* of the Line.
June,	dry, the *Sun* being then to the *north* of the Line.
July,	dry, the *Sun* being then to the *north* of the Line.
Half *August*,	dry, the *Sun* being then to the *north* of the Line.
Half *August*,	rainy, the *Sun* being then come back.
September,	rainy, the *Sun* being then come back.
Half *October*,	rainy, the *Sun* being then come back.
Half *October*,	dry, the *Sun* being then to the *south* of the Line.
November,	dry, the *Sun* being then to the *south* of the Line.
December,	dry, the *Sun* being then to the *south* of the Line.
January,	dry, the *Sun* being then to the *south* of the Line.
Half *February*,	dry, the *Sun* being then to the *south* of the Line.

The rainy season sometimes held longer or shorter, as the winds happen'd to blow; but this was the general observation I made: After I had found by experience, the ill consequence of being abroad in the rain. I took care to furnish myself with provisions before hand, that I might not be oblig'd to go out; and I sat within doors as much as possible during the wet months.

This time I found much employment, (and very suitable also to the time) for I found great occasion of many things which I had no way to furnish myself with, but by hard labour and constant application; particularly, I try'd many ways to make my self a basket, but all the twigs I could get for the purpose prov'd so brittle, that they would do nothing.

It prov'd of excellent advantage to me now, that when I was a boy, I used to take great delight in standing at a *basket-makers* in the town where my father liv'd, to see them make their *wicker-ware*; and being, as boys usually are, very officious to help, and a great observer of the manner how they work'd those things, and sometimes lending a hand, I had by this means full knowledge of the methods of it, that I wanted nothing but the materials; when it came into my mind, that the twigs of that tree from whence I cut my stakes that grew, might possibly be as tough as the *sallows*, and *willows*, and *osiers* in *England*, and I resolv'd to try.

Accordingly the next day I went to my country-house, as I call'd it, and cutting some of the smaller twigs, I found them to my purpose as much as I could desire; whereupon I came the next time prepar'd with a hatchet to cut down a quantity, which I soon found, for there was great plenty of them; these I set up to dry within my circle or hedge, and when they were fit for use, I carried them to my cave, and here during the next season, I employ'd myself in making, *as well as I could*, a great many baskets, both to carry earth, or to carry or lay up any thing as I had occasion; and tho' I did not finish them very handsomly, yet I made them sufficiently serviceable for my purpose; and thus afterwards I took care never to be without them; and as my *wicker-ware* decay'd, I made more, especially I made strong deep baskets to place my corn in, instead of sacks, when I should come to have any quantity of it.

Having master'd this difficulty, and employ'd a world of time about it, I bestirr'd my self to see if possible, how to supply two wants: I had no vessels to hold any thing that was liquid, except two runlets which were almost full of rum, and some glass bottles, some of the common size, and others which were case-bottles-square, for the holding of waters, spirits, &c. I had not so much as a pot to boil any thing, except a great kettle which I sav'd out of the ship, and which was too big for such use as I desir'd it, *viz.* to make broth, and stew a bit of meat by it self. The second thing I would fain have had, was a tobacco-pipe; but it was impossible to me to make one, however, I found a contrivance for that too at last.

I employ'd myself in planting my second rows of stakes or piles, and in this *wicker* working all the summer, or dry season, when another business took me up more time than it could be imagin'd I could spare.

I mention'd before, that I had a great mind to see the whole island, and that I had travell'd up the brook, and so on to where I built my bower, and where I had an opening quite to the sea on the other side of the island; I now resolv'd to travel quite cross to the sea-shore on that side; so taking my gun, a hatchet, and my dog, and a larger quantity of powder and shot than usual, with two bisket cakes, and a great bunch of raisins in my pouch for my store, I began my journey; when I had pass'd the vale where my bower stood, as above, I came within view of the sea, to the *west*, and it being a very clear day, I fairly descry'd land, whether an island or a continent, I could not tell; but it lay very high, extending from the *west* to the *w. s. w.* at a very great distance; by my guess it could not be less than fifteen or twenty leagues off.

I could not tell what part of the world this might be, otherwise than that I know it must be part of *America*, and as I concluded by all my observations, must be near the *Spanish* dominions, and perhaps was all inhabited by savages, where if I should have landed, I had been in a worse condition than I was now; and therefore I acquiesced in the dispositions of Providence, which I began now to own, and to believe, order'd every thing for the best; I say, I quieted my mind with this, and left afflicting myself with fruitless wishes of being there.

Besides, after some pause upon this affair, I consider'd, that if this land was the *Spanish* coast, I should certainly, one time or other, see some vessel pass or re-pass one way or other; but if not, then it was the *savage* coast between the *Spanish* country and *Brasils*, which are indeed the worst of *savages*; for they are cannibals, or men-eaters, and fail not to murther and devour all the human bodies that fall into their hands.

With these considerations I walk'd very leisurely forward. I found that side of the island where I now was, much pleasanter than mine, the open or *savanna* fields sweet, adorn'd with flowers and grass, and full of very fine woods. I saw abundance of parrots, and fain I would have caught one, if possible, to have kept it to be tame, and taught it to speak to me. I did, after some pains taking, catch a young parrot, for I knock'd it down with a stick, and having recover'd it, I brought it home; but it was some years before I could make him speak: However, at last I taught him to call me by my name very familiarly: But the accident that follow'd, tho' it be a trifle, will be very diverting in its place.

I was exceedingly diverted with this journey: I found in the low grounds hares, as I thought them to be, and foxes, but they differ'd greatly from all the other kinds I had met with; nor could I satisfy my self to eat them, tho' I kill'd several: But I had no need to be venturous; for I had no want of food, and of that which was very good too; especially these three sorts, *viz.* goats, pidgeons, and turtle or tortoise; which, added to my grapes, *Leaden-hall* market[31] could not have furnish'd a table better than I, in proportion to the company; and tho' my case was deplorable enough, yet I had great cause for thankfulness, that I was not driven to any extremities for food; but rather plenty, even to dainties.

I never travell'd in this journey above two miles outright in a day, or thereabouts; but I took so many turns and returns to see what discoveries I could make, that I came weary enough to the place where I resolved to sit down for all night; and then I either repos'd myself in a tree, or surrounded myself with a row of stakes set upright in the ground, either from one tree to another, or so as no wild creature could come at me, without waking me.

As soon as I came to the sea shore, I was surprised to see that I had taken up my lot on the worst side of the island; for here indeed the shore was cover'd with innumerable turtles, whereas on the other side I had found but three in a year and half. Here was also an infinite number of fowls, of many kinds, some which I had seen, and some which I had not seen of before, and many of them very good meat; but such as I knew not the names of, except those call'd *penguins*.

I could have shot as many as I pleas'd, but was very sparing of my powder and shot; and therefore had more mind to kill a she goat, if I could, which I could better feed on; and though there were many goats here more than on my side the island, yet it was with much more difficulty that I could come near them, the country being flat and even, and they saw me much sooner than when I was on the hill.

I confess this side of the country was much pleasanter than mine, but yet I had not the least inclination to remove; for as I was fix'd in my habitation, it became natural to me, and I seem'd all the while I was here, to be as it were upon a journey, and from home: However, I travell'd along the shore of the sea, towards the *east*, I suppose about twelve miles; and then setting up a great pole upon the shore for a mark, I concluded I would go home again; and that the next journey I took should be on the other side of the island, *east* from my dwelling, and so round till I came to my post again: Of which in its place.

I took another way to come back than that I went, thinking I could easily keep all the island so much in my view, that I could not miss finding my first dwelling by viewing the country; but I found myself mistaken; for being come about two or three miles, I found myself descended into a very large valley; but so surrounded with hills, and those hills covered with wood, that I could not see which was my way by any direction but that of the sun, nor even then, unless I knew very well the position of the sun at that time of the day.

It happen'd, to my farther misfortune, that the weather prov'd hazy for three or four days, while I was in this valley; and not being able to see the sun, I wander'd about very uncomfortably, and at last was obliged to find out the sea side, look for my post, and come back the same way I went; and then by easy journies I turn'd homeward, the weather being exceeding hot, and my gun, ammunition, hatchet, and other things very heavy.

In this journey my dog surpris'd a young kid, and seiz'd upon it, and I running in to take hold of it, caught it, and sav'd it alive from the dog: I had a great mind to bring it home if I could; for I had often been musing, whether it might not be possible to get a kid or two, and so raise a breed of tame goats, which might supply me when my powder and shot should be all spent.

I made a collar to this little creature, and with a string which I made of some rope-yarn which I always carry'd about me, I led him along, tho' with some difficulty, till I came to my bower, and there I enclos'd him, and left him; for I was very impatient to be at home, from whence I had been absent above a month.

I cannot express what a satisfaction it was to me, to come into my old hutch, and lye down in my hamock-bed: This little wandring journey, without settled place of abode, had been so unpleasant to me, that my own house, as I call'd it to myself, was a perfect settlement to me, compar'd to that; and it render'd every thing about me so comfortable, that I resolv'd I would never go a great way from it again, while it should be my lot to stay on the island.

I repos'd myself here a week, to rest and regale myself after my long journey; during which, most of the time was taken up in the weighty affair of making a cage for my Poll, who began now to be a meer domestick, and to be mighty well acquainted with me. Then I began to think of the poor kid, which I had penn'd in within my little circle, and resolv'd to go and fetch it home, or give it some food; accordingly I went, and found it where I left it; for indeed it could not get out; but almost starv'd for want of food: I went and cut bows of trees, and branches of such shrubs as I could find, and threw it over, and having fed it, I ty'd it as I did before, to lead it away; but it was so tame with being hungry, that I had no need to have ty'd it; for it follow'd me like a dog; and as I continually fed it, the creature became so loving, so gentle, and so fond, that it became from that time one of my domesticks also; and would never leave me afterwards.

The rainy season of the *Autumnal Equinox* was now come, and I kept the 30th of *September* in the same solemn manner as before, being the anniversary of my landing on the island, having now been there two years, and no more prospect of being deliver'd than the first day I came there. I spent the whole day in humble and thankful acknowledgments of the many wonderful mercies which my solitary condition was attended with, and without which it might have been infinitely more miserable. I gave humble and hearty thanks that God had been pleas'd to discover to me, even that it was possible I might be more happy in this solitary condition, than I should have been in a liberty of society, and in all the pleasures of the world. That he could fully make up to me, the deficiencies of my solitary state, and the want of human society by his presence, and the communications of his grace to my soul, supporting, comforting, and encouraging me to depend upon his Providence here, and hope for his eternal presence hereafter.

It was now that I began sensibly to feel how much more happy this life I now led was, with all its miserable circumstances, than the wicked, cursed, abominable life I led all the past part of my days; and now I chang'd both my sorrows and my joys; my very desires alter'd, my affections changed their gusts, and my delights were perfectly new, from what they were at my first coming, or indeed for the two years past.

Before, as I walk'd about, either on my hunting, or for viewing the country; the anguish of my soul at my condition, would break out upon me on a sudden, and my very heart would die within me, to think of the woods, the mountains, the desarts I was in; and how I was a prisoner lock'd up with the eternal bars and bolts of the ocean, in an uninhabited wilderness, without redemption: In the midst of the greatest composures of my mind, this would break out upon me like a storm, and make me wring my hands, and weep like a child: Sometimes it would take me in the middle of my work, and I would immediately sit down and sigh, and look upon the ground for an hour or two together; and this was still worse to me; for if I could burst out into tears, or vent myself by words, it would go off, and the grief having exhausted itself, would abate.

But now I began to exercise my self with new thoughts; I daily read the word of God, and apply'd all the comforts of it to my present state: One morning being very sad, I open'd the Bible upon these words, *I will never, never leave thee, nor forsake thee*;[32] immediately it occurr'd, that these words were to me. Why else should they be directed in such a manner, just at the moment when I was mourning over my condition, as one forsaken of God and man? Well then, said I, if God does not forsake me, of what ill consequence can it be, or what matters it, tho' the world should all forsake me, seeing on the other hand, if I had all the world, and should lose the favour and blessing of God, there wou'd be no comparison in the loss.

From this moment I began to conclude in my mind, that it was possible for me to be more happy in this forsaken solitary condition, than it was probable I should ever have been in any other particular state in the world; and with this thought I was going to give thanks to God for bringing me to this place.

I know not what it was, but something shock'd my mind at that thought, and I durst not speak the words: How canst thou be such a hypocrite, (said I, even audibly) to pretend to be thankful for a condition, which however thou may'st endeavour to be contented with, thou would'st rather pray heartily to be deliver'd from; so I stopp'd there: But tho' I could not say, I thank'd God for being there; yet I sincerely gave thanks to God for opening my eyes, by whatever afflicting Providences, to see the former condition of my life, and to mourn for my wickedness, and repent. I never open'd the Bible, or shut it, but my very soul within me bless'd God for directing my friend in *England*, without any order of mine, to pack it up among my goods; and for assisting me afterwards to save it out of the wreck of the ship.

Thus, and in this disposition of mind, I began my third year; and tho' I have not given the reader the trouble of so particular account of my works this year as the first; yet in general it may be observ'd, that I was very seldom idle; but having regularly divided my time, according to the several daily employments that were before me, such as, *first*, my duty to God, and the reading the Scriptures, which I constantly set apart some time for thrice every day. *Secondly*, the going abroad with my gun for food, which generally took me up three hours in every morning, when it did not rain. *Thirdly*, the ordering, curing, preserving, and cooking what I had kill'd or catch'd for my supply; these took up great part of the day; also it is to be consider'd that the middle of the day when the sun was in the *zenith*, the violence of the heat was too great to stir out; so that about four hours in the evening was all the time I could be suppos'd to work in; with this exception, that sometimes I chang'd my hours of hunting and working, and went to work in the morning, and abroad with my gun in the afternoon.

To this short time allow'd for labour, I desire may be added the exceeding laboriousness of my work; the many hours which for want of tools, want of help, and want of skill, every thing I did, took up out of my time: For example, I was full two and forty days making me a board for a long shelf, which I wanted in my cave; whereas two sawyers with their tools, and a saw-pit, would have cut six of them out of the same tree in half a day.

My case was this; it was to be a large tree, which was to be cut down, because my board was to be a broad one. This tree I was three days a cutting down, and two more cutting off the bows, and reducing it to a log, or piece of timber. With inexpressible hacking and hewing I reduced both the sides of it into chips, till it begun to be light enough to move; then I turn'd it, and made one side of it smooth, and flat, as a board from end to end; then turning that side downward, cut the other side, till I brought the plank to be about three inches thick, and smooth on both sides. Any one may judge the labour of my hands in such a piece of work; but labour and patience carry'd me thro' that and many other things: I only observe this in particular, to shew the reason why so much of my time went away with so little work, *viz.* that what might be a little to be done with help and tools, was a vast labour, and requir'd a prodigious time to do alone, and by hand.

But notwithstanding this, with patience and labour I went thro' many things; and indeed every thing that my circumstances made necessary to me to do, as will appear by what follows.

I was now, in the months of *November* and *December*, expecting my crop of barley and rice. The ground I had manur'd or dug up for them was not great; for as I observ'd, my seed of each was not above the quantity of half a peck; for I had lost one whole crop by sowing in the dry season; but now my crop promis'd very well, when on a sudden I found I was in danger of losing it all again by enemies of several sorts, which it was scarce possible to keep from it; as first, the goats, and wild creatures which I call'd hares, who tasting the sweetness of the blade, lay in it night and day, as soon as it came up, and eat it so close, that it could get no time to shoot up into stalk.

This I saw no remedy for, but by making an enclosure about it with a hedge, which I did with a great deal of toil; and the more, because it requir'd speed. However, as my arable land was but small, suited to my crop, I got it totally well fenced in about three weeks time; and shooting some of the creatures in the day time, I set my dog to guard it in the night, tying him up to a stake at the gate, where he would stand and bark all night long; so in a little time the enemies forsook the place, and the corn grew very strong, and well, and began to ripen apace.

But as the beasts ruined me before, while my corn was in the blade; so the birds were as likely to ruin me now, when it was in the ear; for going along by the place to see how it throve, I saw my little crop surrounded with fowls of I know not how many sorts, who stood as it were watching till I should be gone: I immediately let fly among them (for I always had my gun with me.) I had no sooner shot but there rose up a little cloud of fowls, which I had not seen at all, from among the corn it self.

This touch'd me sensibly, for I foresaw, that in a few days they would devour all my hopes, that I should be starv'd, and never be able to raise a crop at all, and what to do I could not tell: However, I resolv'd not to lose my corn, if possible, tho' I should watch it night and day. In the first place, I went among it to see what damage was already done, and found they had spoil'd a good deal of it; but that as it was yet too green for them, the loss was not so great, but that the remainder was like to be a good crop if it could be sav'd.

I staid by it to load my gun, and then coming away I could easily see the thieves sitting upon all the trees about me, as if they only waited till I was gone away, and the event proved it to be so; for as I walk'd off as if I was gone, I was no sooner out of their sight, but they dropt down one by one into the corn again. I was so provok'd that I could not have patience to stay till more came on, knowing that every grain that they eat now, was, *as it might be said*, a peck-loaf to me in the consequence; but coming up to the hedge, I fir'd again, and kill'd three of them. This was what I wish'd for; so I took them up, and serv'd them as we serve notorious thieves in *England*, (*viz.*) hang'd them in chains for a terror to others; it is impossible to imagine almost, that this should have such an effect as it had; for the fowls wou'd not only not come at the corn, but in short they forsook all that part of the island, and I could never see a bird near the place as long as my scare-crows hung there.

This I was very glad of, you may be sure, and about the latter end of *December*, which was our second harvest of the year, I reap'd my crop.

I was sadly put to it for a scythe or a sicle to cut it down, and all I could do was to make one as well as I could out of one of the broad swords or cutlasses, which I sav'd among the arms out of the ship. However, as my first crop was but small I had no great difficulty to cut it down; in short, I reap'd it my way, for I cut nothing off but the ears, and carry'd it away in a great basket which I had made, and so rubb'd it out with my hands; and at the end of all my harvesting, I found that out of my half peck of seed, I had near two bushels of rice, and above two bushels and half of barley, *that is to say*, by my guess, for I had no measure at that time.

However, this was a great encouragement to me, and I foresaw that in time, it wou'd please God to supply me with bread: And yet here I was perplex'd again, for I neither knew how to grind or make meal of my corn, or indeed how to clean it and part it; nor if made into meal, how to make bread of it, and if how to make it, yet I knew not how to bake it; these things being added to my desire of having a good quantity for store, and to secure a constant supply, I resolv'd not to taste any of this crop, but to preserve it all for seed against the next season, and in the mean time to employ all my study and hours of working to accomplish this great work of providing myself with corn and bread.

It might be truly said, that now I work'd for my bread; 'tis a little wonderful, and what I believe few people have thought much upon, (*viz.*) the strange multitude of little things necessary in the providing, producing, curing, dressing, making and finishing this one article of bread.

I that was reduced to a meer state of nature, found this to my daily discouragement, and was made more and more sensible of it every hour, even after I had got the first handful of seed-corn, which, as I have said, came up unexpectedly, and indeed to a surprise.

First, I had no plow to turn up the earth, no spade or shovel to dig it. Well, this I conquer'd, by making a wooden spade, as I observ'd before; but this did my work in but a wooden manner, and tho' it cost me a great many days to make it, yet for want of iron it not only wore out the sooner, but made my work the harder, and made it be perform'd much worse.

However, this I bore with, and was content to work it out with patience, and bear with the badness of the performance. When the corn was sow'd, I had no harrow, but was forced to go over it my self, and drag a great heavy bough of a tree over it, to scratch it, as it may be call'd, rather than rake or harrow it.

When it was growing and grown, I have observ'd already how many things I wanted, to fence it, secure it, mow or reap it, cure and carry it home, thrash, part it from the chaff, and save it. Then I wanted a mill to grind it, sieves to dress it, yeast and salt to make it into bread, and an oven to bake it, and yet all these things I did without, as shall be observ'd; and yet the corn was an inestimable comfort and advantage to me too. All this, as I said, made every thing laborious and tedious to me, but that there was no help for; neither was my time so much loss to me, because as I had divided it, a certain part of it was every day appointed to these works; and as I resolv'd to use none of the corn for bread till I had a greater quantity by me, I had the next six months to apply my self wholly by labour and invention to furnish my self with utensils proper for the performing all the operations necessary for the making the corn (when I had it) fit for my use.

But first, I was to prepare more land, for I had now seed enough to sow above an acre of ground. Before I did this, I had a weeks-work at least to make me a spade, which when it was done was but a sorry one indeed, and very heavy, and requir'd double labour to work with it; however I went thro' that, and sow'd my seed in two large flat pieces of ground, as near my house as I could find them to my mind, and fenc'd them in with a good hedge, the stakes of which were all cut of that wood which I had set before, and knew it would grow, so that in one year's time I knew I should have a quick or living-hedge, that would want but little repair. This work was not so little as to take me up less than three months, because great part of that time was of the wet season, when I could not go abroad.

Within doors, *that is*, when it rained, and I could not go out, I found employment on the following occasions; always observing, that all the while I was at work I diverted myself with talking to my parrot, and teaching him to speak, and I quickly learn'd him to know his own name, and at last to speak it out pretty loud POLL, which was the first word I ever heard spoken in the island by any mouth but my own. This therefore was not my work, but an assistant to my work, for now, as I said, I had a great employment upon my hands, as follows, (*viz.*) I had long study'd by some means or other, to make myself some earthen vessels, which indeed I wanted sorely, but knew not where to come at them: However, considering the heat of the climate, I did not doubt but if I could find out any such clay, I might botch up some such pot, as might, being dry'd in the sun, be hard enough, and strong enough to bear handling, and to hold any thing that was dry, and required to be kept so; and as this was necessary in the preparing corn, meal, *&c.* which was the thing I was upon, I resolved to make some as large as I could, and fit only to stand like jars to hold what should be put into them.

It would make the reader pity me, or rather laugh at me, to tell how many awkward ways I took to raise this paste, what odd mishapen ugly things I made, how many of them fell in, and how many fell out, the clay not being stiff enough to bear its own weight; how many crack'd by the over violent heat of the sun, being set out too hastily; and how many fell in pieces with only removing, as well before as after they were dry'd; and in a word, how after having laboured hard to find the clay, to dig it, to temper it, to bring it home and work it, I could not make above two large earthen ugly things, I cannot call them jars, in about two months labour.

However, as the sun bak'd these two very dry and hard, I lifted them very gently up, and set them down again in two great wicker-baskets, which I had made on purpose for them, that they might not break, and as between the pot and the basket there was a little room to spare, I stuff'd it full of the rice and barley straw, and these two pots being to stand always dry, I thought would hold my dry corn, and perhaps the meal, when the corn was bruised.

Tho' I miscarried so much in my design for large pots, yet I made several smaller things with better success; such as little round pots, flat dishes, pitchers and pipkins, and any things my hand turn'd to, and the heat of the sun bak'd them strangely hard.

But all this would not answer my end, which was to get an earthen pot to hold what was liquid, and bear the fire, which none of these could do. It happen'd after some time, making a pretty large fire for cooking my meat, when I went to put it out after I had done with it, I found a broken piece of one of my earthen-ware vessels in the fire, burnt as hard as a stone, and red as a tile. I was agreeably surpris'd to see it, and said to my self, that certainly they might be made to burn whole, if they would burn broken.

This set me to studying how to order my fire, so as to make it burn me some pots. I had no notion of a kiln, such as the potters burn in, or of glazing them with lead, tho' I had some lead to do it with; but I plac'd three large pipkins, and two or three pots in a pile one upon another, and plac'd my fire-wood all round it with a great heap of embers under them, I ply'd the fire with fresh fuel round the out-side, and upon the top, till I saw the pots in the inside red hot quite thro', and observ'd that they did not crack at all; when I saw them clear red, I let them stand in that heat about 5 or 6 hours, till I found one of them, tho' it did not crack, did melt or run, for the sand which was mixed with the clay melted by the violence of the heat, and would have run into glass if I had gone on, so I slack'd my fire gradually, till the pots began to abate of the red colour, and watching them all night, that I might not let the fire abate too fast, in the morning I had three very good, I will not say handsome pipkins; and two other earthen pots, as hard burnt as could be desir'd; and one of them perfectly glaz'd with the running of the sand.

After this experiment, I need not say that I wanted no sort of earthen ware for my use; but I must needs say, as to the shapes of them, they were very indifferent, as any one may suppose, when I had no way of making them; but as the children make dirt-pies, or as a woman would make pies, that never learn'd to raise paste.

No joy at a thing of so mean a nature was ever equal to mine, when I found I had made an earthen pot that would bear the fire; and I had hardly patience to stay till they were cold, before I set one upon the fire again, with some water in it, to boil me some meat, which it did admirably well; and with a piece of a kid I made some very good broth, though I wanted oatmeal, and several other ingredients requisite to make it so good as I would have had it been.

My next concern was, to get me a stone mortar to stamp or beat some corn in; for as to the mill, there was no thought at arriving to that perfection of art, with one pair of hands. To supply this want I was at a great loss; for of all trades in the world I was as perfectly unqualify'd for a stone-cutter, as for any whatever; neither had I any tools to go about it with. I spent many a day to find out a great stone big enough to cut hollow, and make fit for a mortar, and could find none at all; except what was in the solid rock, and which I had no way to dig or cut out; nor indeed were the rocks in the island of hardness sufficient, but were all of a sandy crumbling stone, which would neither bear the weight of a heavy pestle, or would break the corn without filling it with sand; so after a great deal of time lost in searching for a stone, I gave it over, and resolv'd to look out for a great block of hard wood, which I found indeed much easier; and getting one as big as I had strength to stir, I rounded it, and form'd it in the out-side with my axe and hatchet, and then with the help of fire, and infinite labour, made a hollow place in it, as the *Indians* in *Brasil* make their *canoes*. After this, I made a great heavy pestle or beater, of the wood call'd the iron-wood, and this I prepared and laid by against I had my next crop of corn, when I propos'd to my self to grind, or rather pound my corn into meal to make my bread.

My next difficulty was to make a sieve, or search, to dress my meal, and to part it from the bran, and the husk, without which I did not see it possible I could have any bread. This was a most difficult thing, so much as but to think on; for to be sure I had nothing like the necessary thing to make it; I mean fine thin canvass, or stuff, to search the meal through. And here I was at a full stop for many months; nor did I really know what to do; linnen I had none left, but what was meer rags; I had goats hair, but neither knew I how to weave it, or spin it; and had I known how, here was no tools to work it with; all the remedy that I found for this, was, that at last I did remember I had among the seamens clothes which were sav'd out of the ship, some neckcloths of callicoe, or muslin; and with some pieces of these I made three small sieves, but proper enough for the work; and thus I made shift for some years; how I did afterwards, I shall shew in its place.

The baking part was the next thing to be consider'd, and how I should make bread when I came to have corn; for first I had no yeast; as to that part, as there was no supplying the want, so I did not concern my self much about it: but for an oven, I was indeed in great pain; at length I found out an experiment for that also, which was this; I made some earthen vessels very broad, but not deep; that is to say, about two foot diameter, and not above nine inches deep; these I burnt in the fire, as I had done the other, and laid them by; and when I wanted to bake, I made a great fire upon my hearth, which I had pav'd with some square tiles of my own making, and burning also; but I should not call them square.

When the fire-wood was burnt pretty much into embers, or live coals, I drew them forward upon this hearth, so as to cover it all over, and there I let them lye, till the hearth was very hot, then sweeping away all the embers, I set down my loaf, or loaves, and whelming down the earthen pot upon them, drew the embers all round the outside of the pot, to keep in, and add to the heat; and thus, as well as in the best oven in the world, I bak'd my barley-loaves, and became in little time a meer pastry-cook into the bargain; for I made myself several cakes of the rice, and puddings; indeed I made no pies, neither had I any thing to put into them, supposing I had, except the flesh either of fowls or goats.

It need not be wondred at, if all these things took me up most part of the third year of my abode here; for it is to be observ'd, that in the intervals of these things, I had my new harvest and husbandry to manage; for I reap'd my corn in its season, and carry'd it home as well as I could, and laid it up in the ear, in my large baskets, till I had time to rub it out; for I had no floor to thrash it on, or instrument to thrash it with.

And now indeed my stock of corn increasing, I really wanted to build my barns bigger. I wanted a place to lay it up in; for the encrease of the corn now yielded me so much, that I had of the barley about twenty bushels, and of the rice as much, or more; insomuch, that now I resolv'd to begin to use it freely; for my bread had been quite gone a great while; also I resolv'd to see what quantity would be sufficient for me a whole year, and to sow but once a year.

Upon the whole, I found that the forty bushels of barley and rice, was much more than I could consume in a year; so I resolv'd to sow just the same quantity every year that I sowed the last, in hopes that such a quantity would fully provide me with bread, &c.

All the while these things were doing, you may be sure my thoughts run many times upon the prospect of land which I had seen from the other side of the island, and I was not without secret wishes that I were on shore there, fancying the seeing the main land, and in an inhabited country, I might find some way or other to convey my self farther, and perhaps at last find some means of escape.

But all this while I made no allowance for the dangers of such a condition, and how I might fall into the hands of savages, and perhaps such as I might have reason to think far worse than the lyons and tygers of *Africa*. That if I once came into their power, I should run a hazard more than a thousand to one of being kill'd, and perhaps of being eaten; for I had heard that the people of the *Carribean* coast were cannibals, or man eaters; and I knew by the latitude, that I could not be far off from that shore. That suppose they were not cannibals, yet that they might kill me, as many *Europeans* who had fallen into their hands had been served, even when they had been ten or twenty together; much more I that was but one, and could make little or no defence: All these things, I say, which I ought to have consider'd well of, and did cast up in my thoughts afterwards, yet took up none of my apprehensions at first; but my head run mightily upon the thought of getting over to the shore.

Now I wish'd for my boy *Xury*, and the long boat, with the shoulder of mutton sail, with which I sail'd above a thousand miles on the coast of

Africk; but this was in vain. Then I thought I would go and look at our ship's boat, which, as I have said, was blown up upon the shore, a great way in the storm, when we were first cast away. She lay almost where she did at first, but not quite; and was turn'd by the force of the waves and the winds, almost bottom upward, against a high ridge of beachy rough sand; but no water about her as before.

If I had had hands to have refitted her, and to have launch'd her into the water, the boat would have done well enough, and I might have gone back into the *Brasils* with her easily enough; but I might have foreseen, that I could no more turn her, and set her upright upon her bottom, than I could remove the island: However, I went to the woods, and cut levers and rollers, and brought them to the boat, resolv'd to try what I could do; suggesting to myself, that if I could but turn her down, I might easily repair the damage she had receiv'd, and she would be a very good boat, and I might go to sea in her very easily.

I spar'd no pains indeed, in this piece of fruitless toil, and spent, I think, three or four weeks about it; at last finding it impossible to heave it up with my little strength, I fell to digging away the sand to undermine it, and so to make it fall down, setting pieces of wood to thrust and guide it right in the fall.

But when I had done this, I was unable to stir it up again, or to get under it, much less to move it forward towards the water; so I was forc'd to give it over; and yet, though I gave over the hopes of the boat, my desire to venture over for the main encreased, rather than decreased, as the means for it seem'd impossible.

This at length put me upon thinking, whether it was not possible to make my self a *canoe*, or *periagua*, such as the natives of those climates make, even without tools, or, as I might say, without hands, *viz.* of the trunk of a great tree. This I not only thought possible, but easy, and pleas'd myself extreamly with the thoughts of making it, and with my having much more convenience for it than any of the *Negroes* or *Indians*; but not at all considering the particular inconveniences which I lay under, more than the *Indians* did, *viz.* want of hands to move it, when it was made, into the water, a difficulty much harder for me to surmount, than all the consequences of want of tools could be to them; for what was it to me, that when I had chosen a vast tree in the woods, I might with much trouble cut it down, if after I might be able with my tools to hew and dubb the out-side into the proper shape of a boat, and burn or cut out the in-side to make it hollow, so to make a boat of it: If after all this, I must leave it just there where I found it, and was not able to launch it into the water.

One would have thought, I could not have had the least reflection upon my mind of my circumstance, while I was making this boat; but I should have immediately thought how I should get it into the sea; but my thoughts were so intent upon my voyage over the sea in it, that I never once consider'd how I should get it off of the land; and it was really in its own nature more easy for me to guide it over forty five miles of sea, than about forty five fathom of land, where it lay, to set it a float in the water.

I went to work upon this boat, the most like a fool, that ever man did, who had any of his senses awake. I pleas'd my self with the design, without determining whether I was ever able to undertake it; not but that the difficulty of launching my boat came often into my head; but I put a stop to my own enquiries into it, by this foolish answer which I gave myself, *Let's first make it, I'll warrant I'll find some way or other to get it along, when 'tis done.*

This was a most preposterous method; but the eagerness of my fancy prevail'd, and to work I went. I fell'd a cedar tree: I question much whether *Solomon* ever had such a one for the building of the Temple at *Jerusalem*.[33] It was five foot ten inches diameter at the lower part next the stump, and four foot eleven inches diameter at the end of twenty two foot, after which it lessen'd for a while, and then parted into branches: It was not without infinite labour that I fell'd this tree: I was twenty days hacking and hewing at it at the bottom. I was fourteen more getting the branches and limbs, and the vast spreading head of it cut off, which I hack'd and hew'd through with axe and hatchet, and inexpressible labour: After this, it cost me a month to shape it, and dubb it to a proportion, and to something like the bottom of a boat, that it might swim upright as it ought to do. It cost me near three months more to clear the in-side, and work it out so, as to make an exact boat of it: This I did indeed without fire, by mere mallet and chissel, and by the dint of hard labour, till I had brought it to be a very handsome *periagua*, and big enough to have carried six and twenty men, and consequently big enough to have carried me and all my cargo.

When I had gone through this work, I was extremely delighted with it. The boat was really much bigger than I ever saw a *canoe*, or *periagua*, that was made of one tree, in my life. Many a weary stroke it had cost, you may be sure; and there remained nothing but to get it into the water; and had I gotten it into the water, I make no question but I should have began the maddest voyage, and the most unlikely to be perform'd, that ever was undertaken.

But all my devices to get it into the water fail'd me; though they cost me infinite labour too. It lay about one hundred yards from the water, and not more: But the first inconvenience was, it was up hill towards the creek; well, to take away this discouragement, I resolv'd to dig into the surface of the earth, and so make a declivity: This I begun, and it cost me a prodigious deal of pains; but who grutches pains, that have their deliverance in view: But when this was work'd through, and this difficulty manag'd, it was still much at one; for I could no more stir the *canoe*, than I could the other boat.

Then I measur'd the distance of ground, and resolv'd to cut a dock, or canal, to bring the water up to the *canoe*, seeing I could not bring the *canoe* down to the water: Well, I began this work, and when I began to enter into it, and calculate how deep it was to be dug, how broad, how the stuff to be thrown out, I found, that by the number of hands I had, being none but my own, it must have been ten or twelve years before I should have gone through with it; for the shore lay high, so that at the upper end it must have been at least twenty foot deep; so at length, tho' with great reluctancy, I gave this attempt over also.

This griev'd me heartily, and now I saw, tho' too late, the folly of beginning a work before we count the cost; and before we judge rightly of our own strength to go through with it.

In the middle of this work, I finish'd my fourth year in this place, and kept my anniversary with the same devotion, and with as much comfort as ever before; for by a constant study, and serious application of the Word of God, and by the assistance of his grace, I gain'd different knowledge from what I had before. I entertain'd different notions of things. I look'd now upon the world as a thing remote, which I had nothing to do with, no expectation from, and indeed no desires about: In a word, I had nothing indeed to do with it, nor was ever like to have; so I thought it look'd as we may perhaps look upon it hereafter,[34] *viz.* as a place I had lived in, but was come out of it; and well might I say, as Father *Abraham* to *Dives, Between me and thee is a great gulph fixed.*[35]

In the first place, I was removed from all the wickedness of the world here: I had neither the *lust of the flesh, the lust of the eye, or the pride of life.*[36] I had nothing to covet; for I had all that I was now capable of enjoying: I was lord of the whole manor; or if I pleas'd, I might call my self king, or emperor over the whole country which I had possession of. There were no rivals. I had no competitor, none to dispute sovereignty or command with me. I might have rais'd ship loadings of corn; but I had no use for it; so I let as little grow as I thought enough for my occasion. I had tortoise or turtles enough; but now and then one was as much as I could put to any use. I had timber enough to have built a fleet of ships. I had grapes enough to have made wine, or to have cur'd into raisins, to have loaded that fleet when they had been built.

But all I could make use of, was, all that was valuable. I had enough to eat, and to supply my wants, and, what was all the rest to me? If I kill'd more flesh than I could eat, the dog must eat it, or the vermin. If I sow'd more corn than I could eat, it must be spoil'd. The trees that I cut down, were lying to rot on the ground. I could make no more use of them than for fewel; and that I had no occasion for, but to dress my food.

In a word, the nature and experience of things dictated to me upon just reflection, that all the good things of this world, are no farther good to us, than they are for our use; and that whatever we may heap up indeed to give others, we enjoy just as much as we can use, and no more. The most covetous griping miser in the world would have been cured of the vice of covetousness, if he had been in my case; for I possessed infinitely more than I knew what to do with. I had no room for desire, except it was of things which I had not, and they were but trifles, tho' indeed of great use to me. I had, as I hinted before, a parcel of money, as well gold as silver, about thirty six pounds sterling: Alas! there the nasty sorry useless stuff lay; I had no manner of business for it; and I often thought with myself, that I would have given a handful of it for a gross of tobacco-pipes, or for a hand-mill to grind my corn; nay, I would have given it all for six-penny-worth of *turnip* and *carrot* seed out of *England*, or for a handful of *pease* and *beans*, and a bottle of ink: *As it was*, I had not the least advantage by it, or benefit from it; but there it lay in a drawer, and grew mouldy with the damp of the cave, in the wet season; and if I had had the drawer full of diamonds, it had been the same case; and they had been of no manner of value to me, because of no use.

I had now brought my state of life to be much easier in it self than it was at first, and much easier to my mind, as well as to my body. I frequently sat down to my meat with thankfulness, and admir'd the hand of God's Providence, which had thus spread my table in the wilderness. I learn'd to look more upon the bright side of my condition, and less upon the dark side; and to consider what I enjoy'd, rather than what I wanted; and this gave me sometimes such secret comforts, that I cannot express them; and which I take notice of here, to put those discontented people in mind of it, who cannot enjoy comfortably what God has given them; because they see, and covet something that he has not given them: All our discontents about what we want, appeared to me, to spring from the want of thankfulness for what we have.

Another reflection was of great use to me, and doubtless would be so to any one that should fall into such distress as mine was; and this was, to compare my present condition with what I at first expected it should be; nay, with what it would certainly have been, if the good Providence of God had not wonderfully ordered the ship to be cast up nearer to the shore, where I not only could come at her, but could bring what I got out of her to the shore, for my relief and comfort; without which, I had wanted for tools to work, weapons for defence, or gun-powder and shot for getting my food.

I spent whole hours, I may say whole days, in representing to myself in the most lively colours, how I must have acted, if I had got nothing out of the ship; how I could not have so much as got any food, except fish and turtles; and that as it was long before I found any of them, I must have perish'd first. That I should have liv'd, if I had not perish'd, like a meer savage. That if I had kill'd a goat, or a fowl, by any contrivance, I had no way to flea or open them, or part the flesh from the skin and the bowels, or to cut it up; but must gnaw it with my teeth, and pull it with my claws like a beast.

These reflections made me very sensible of the goodness of Providence to me, and very thankful for my present condition, with all its hardships and misfortunes: And this part also I cannot but recommend to the reflection of those who are apt in their misery to say, *Is any affliction like mine!* Let them consider, how much worse the cases of some people are, and their case might have been, if Providence had thought fit.

I had another reflection which assisted me also to comfort my mind with hopes; and this was, comparing my present condition with what I had deserv'd, and had therefore reason to expect from the hand of Providence. I had liv'd a dreadful life, perfectly destitute of the knowledge and fear of God. I had been well instructed by father and mother; neither had they been wanting to me in their early endeavours, to infuse a religious awe of God into my mind, a sense of my duty, and of what the nature and end of my being requir'd of me. But alas! falling early into the sea-faring life, which of all the lives is the most destitute of the fear of God, tho' his terrors are always before them; I say, falling early into the sea-faring life, and into sea-faring company, all that little sense of religion which I had entertain'd, was laugh'd out of me by my mess mates, by a harden'd despising of dangers, and the views of death, which grew habitual to me, by my long absence from all manner of opportunities to converse with any thing but what was like myself, or to hear any thing that was good, or tended towards it.

So void was I of every thing that was good, or of the least sense of what I was, or was to be, that in the greatest deliverances I enjoy'd, such as my escape from *Sallee*; my being taken up by the *Portuguese* Master of the ship, my being planted so well in the *Brasils*; my receiving the cargo from *England*, and the like; I never had once the word *Thank God*, so much as on my mind, or in my mouth; nor in the greatest distress, had I so much as a thought to pray to him, or so much as to say, *Lord have mercy upon me*; no nor to mention the name of God, unless it was to swear by, and blaspheme it.

I had terrible reflections upon my mind for many months, as I have already observ'd, on the account of my wicked and hardned life past; and when I look'd about me, and consider'd what particular Providences[37] had attended me since my coming into this place, and how God had dealt bountifully with me; had not only punish'd me less than my iniquity had deserv'd, but had so plentifully provided for me; this gave me great hopes that my repentance was accepted, and that God had yet mercy in store for me.

With these reflections I work'd my mind up, not only to resignation to the will of God in the present disposition of my circumstances; but even to a sincere thankfulness for my condition, and that I who was yet a living man, ought not to complain, seeing I had not the due punishment of my sins; that I enjoy'd so many mercies which I had no reason to have expected in that place; that I ought never more to repine at my condition, but to rejoyce, and to give daily thanks for that daily bread, which nothing but a croud of wonders could have brought. That I ought to consider I had been fed even by miracle, even as great as that of feeding *Elijah* by ravens;[38] nay, by a long series of miracles, and that I could hardly have nam'd a place in the unhabitable part of the world where I could have been cast more to my advantage: A place, where as I had no society, which was my affliction on one hand, so I found no ravenous beasts, no furious wolves or tygers to threaten my life, no venomous creatures or poisonous, which I might feed on to my hurt, no savages to murther and devour me.

In a word, as my life was a life of sorrow one way, so it was a life of mercy, another; and I wanted nothing to make it a life of comfort, but to be able to make my sence of God's goodness to me, and care over me in this condition, be my daily consolation; and after I did make a just improvement of these things, I went away and was no more sad.

I had now been here so long, that many things which I brought on shore for my help, were either quite gone, or very much wasted and near spent.

My ink, as I observ'd, had been gone for some time, all but a very little, which I eek'd out with water a little and a little, till it was so pale it scarce left any appearance of black upon the paper: As long as it lasted, I made use of it to minuite down the days of the month on which any remarkable thing happen'd to me, and first by casting up times past: I remember that there was a strange concurrence of days, in the various Providences which befel me; and which, if I had been superstitiously inclin'd to observe days as fatal or fortunate, I might have had reason to have look'd upon with a great deal of curiosity.

First I had observ'd, that the same day that I broke away from my father and my friends, and run away to *Hull* in order to go to sea; the same day afterwards I was taken by the *Sallee* man of war, and made a slave.

The same day of the year that I escaped out of the wreck of that ship in *Yarmouth* Roads, that same day-year afterwards I made my escape from *Sallee* in the boat.

The same day of the year I was born on, (*viz.*) the 30th of *September*, the same day I had my life so miraculously saved 26 years after,[39] when I was cast on shore in this island; so that my wicked life and my solitary life begun both on a day.

The next thing to my ink's being wasted, was that of my bread, I mean the bisket which I brought out of the ship, this I had husbanded to the last degree, allowing myself but one cake of bread a day for above a year, and yet I was quite without bread for near a year before I got any corn of my own, and great reason I had to be thankful that I had any at all, the getting it being, as has been already observed, next to miraculous.

My clothes began to decay too mightily: As to linnen, I had had none a good while, except some checquer'd shirts which I found in the chests of the other seamen, and which I carefully preserv'd, because many times I could bear no other clothes on but a shirt; and it was a very great help to me that I had among all the men's clothes of the ship almost three dozen of shirts. There were also several thick watch-coats of the seamen, which were left indeed, but they were too hot to wear; and tho' it is true, that the weather was so violent hot that there was no need of clothes, yet I could not go quite naked; no, tho' I had been inclined to it, which I was not, nor could not abide the thoughts of it, tho' I was all alone.

The reason why I could not go quite naked, was, I could not bear the heat of the sun so well when quite naked, as with some clothes on; nay, the very heat frequently blister'd my skin; whereas with a shirt on, the air itself made some motion, and whistling under that shirt, was twofold cooler than without it, no more could I ever bring myself to go out in the heat of the sun without a cap or a hat; the heat of the sun beating with such violence as it does in that place, would give me the head-ach presently, by darting so directly on my head, without a cap or a hat on, so that I could not bear it, whereas, if I put on my hat, it would presently go away.

Upon those views I began to consider about putting the few rags I had, which I called clothes, into some order: I had worn out all the wast-coats I had, and my business was now to try if I could not make jackets out of the great watch-coats which I had by me, and with such other materials as I had, so I set to work a taylering, or rather indeed a botching, for I made most piteous work of it. However, I made shift to make two or three new wast-coats, which I hoped would serve me a great while; as for breeches or drawers, I made but a very sorry shift indeed, till afterward.

I have mentioned, that I saved the skins of all the creatures that I kill'd, I mean four-footed ones, and I had hung them up stretch'd out with sticks in the sun, by which means some of them were so dry and hard that they were fit for little, but others it seems were very useful. The first thing I made of these was a great cap for my head, with the hair on the outside to shoor[40] off the rain; and this I perform'd so well, that after this I made me a suit of clothes wholly of these skins, that is to say, a wast-coat and breeches open at knees, and both loose, for they were rather wanting to keep me cool than to keep me warm. I must not omit to acknowledge that they were wretchedly made; for if I was a bad *carpenter*, I was a worse *tayler*. However, they were such as I made very good shift with; and when I was abroad, if it happen'd to rain, the hair of my wast-coat and cap being outermost, I was kept very dry.

After this I spent a great deal of time and pains to make me an umbrella;

I was indeed in great want of one, and had a great mind to make one; I had seen them made in the *Brasils*, where they are very useful in the great heats which are there. And I felt the heats every jot as great here, and greater too, being nearer the Equinox; besides, as I was obliged to be much abroad, it was a most useful thing to me, as well for the rains as the heats. I took a world of pains at it, and was a great while before I could make any thing likely to hold; nay, after I thought I had hit the way, I spoil'd 2 or 3 before I made one to my mind; but at last I made one that answer'd indifferently well: The main difficulty I found was to make it to let down. I could make it to spread, but if it did not let down too, and draw in, it was not portable for me any way but just over my head, which wou'd not do. However, at last, as I said, I made one to answer, and cover'd it with skins, the hair upwards, so that it cast off the rains like a penthouse, and kept off the sun so effectually, that I could walk out in the hottest of the weather with greater advantage than I could before in the coolest, and when I had no need of it, cou'd close it and carry it under my arm.

Thus I liv'd mighty comfortably, my mind being entirely composed by resigning to the will of God, and throwing myself wholly upon the disposal of his Providence. This made my life better than sociable; for when I began to regret the want of conversation, I would ask myself, whether thus conversing mutually with my own thoughts, and, as I hope I may say, with even God himself by ejaculations, was not better than the utmost enjoyment of human society in the world.

I cannot say that after this, for five years, any extraordinary thing happen'd to me, but I liv'd on in the same course, in the same posture and place, just as before; the chief things I was employ'd in, besides my yearly labour of planting my barley and rice, and curing my raisins, of both which I always kept up just enough to have sufficient stock of one year's provisions beforehand. I say, besides this yearly labour, and my daily labour of going out with my gun, I had one labour to make me a canoe, which at last I finished. So that by digging a canal to it of six foot wide, and four foot deep, I brought it into the creek, almost half a mile. As for the first, which was so vastly big, as I made it without considering before-hand, as I ought to do, how I should be able to launch it; so never being able to bring it to the water, or bring the water to it, I was oblig'd to let it lye where it was, as a *memorandum* to teach me to be wiser next time: Indeed, the next time, tho' I could not get a tree proper for it, and in a place where I could not get the water to it, at any less distance than as I have said, near half a mile;

yet as I saw it was practicable at last, I never gave it over; and though I was near two years about it, yet I never grutch'd my labour, in hopes of having a boat to go off to sea at last.

However, though my little *periagua* was finish'd; yet the size of it was not at all answerable to the design which I had in view, when I made the first; I mean, of venturing over to the *Terra Firma*, where it was above forty miles broad; accordingly, the smallness of my boat assisted to put an end to that design, and now I thought no more of it: But as I had a boat, my next design was to make a tour round the island; for as I had been on the other side, in one place, crossing, as I have already describ'd it, over the land; so the discoveries I made in that little journey, made me very eager to see other parts of the coast; and now I had a boat, I thought of nothing but sailing round the island.

For this purpose, that I might do every thing with discretion and consideration, I fitted up a little mast to my boat, and made a sail to it out of some of the pieces of the ship's sail, which lay in store; and of which I had a great stock by me.

Having fitted my mast and sail, and try'd the boat, I found she would sail very well: Then I made little lockers, or boxes, at either end of my boat, to put provisions, necessaries and ammunition, *&c.* into, to be kept dry, either from rain, or the sprye of the sea; and a little long hollow place I cut in the in-side of the boat, where I could lay my gun, making a flap to hang down over it to keep it dry.

I fix'd my umbrella also in a step at the stern, like a mast, to stand over my head, and keep the heat of the sun off of me like an auning; and thus I every now and then took a little voyage upon the sea, but never went far out, not far from the little creek; but at last being eager to view the circumference of my little kingdom, I resolv'd upon my tour, and accordingly I victuall'd my ship for the voyage, putting in two dozen of my loaves (cakes I should rather call them) of barley bread, an earthen pot full of parch'd rice, a food I eat a great deal of, a little bottle of rum, half a goat, and powder and shot for killing more, and two large watch-coats, of those which, as I mention'd before, I had sav'd out of the seamen's chests; these I took, one to lye upon, and the other to cover me in the night.

It was the sixth of *November*, in the sixth year of my reign, or my captivity, which you please, that I set out on this voyage, and I found it much longer than I expected; for though the island itself was not very large, yet when I came to the *east* side of it, I found a great ledge of rocks lye out above two leagues into the sea, some above water, some under it; and beyond that, a shoal of sand, lying dry half a league more; so that I was oblig'd to go a great way out to sea to double the point.

When first I discover'd them, I was going to give over my enterprise, and come back again, not knowing how far it might oblige me to go out to sea; and above all, doubting how I should get back again; so I came to an anchor; for I had made me a kind of an anchor with a piece of a broken graplin, which I got out of the ship.

Having secur'd my boat, I took my gun, and went on shore, climbing up upon a hill, which seem'd to overlook that point, where I saw the full extent of it, and resolv'd to venture.

In my viewing the sea from that hill where I stood, I perceiv'd a strong, and indeed, a most furious current, which run to the *east*, and even came close to the point; and I took the more notice of it, because I saw there might be some danger; that when I came into it, I might be carry'd out to sea by the strength of it, and not be able to make the island again; and indeed, had I not gotten first up upon this hill, I believe it would have been so; for there was the same current on the other side the island, only, that it set off at a farther distance; and I saw there was a strong eddy under the shore; so I had nothing to do but to get in out of the first current, and I should presently be in an eddy.

I lay here, however, two days; because the wind blowing pretty fresh at *E. S. E.* and that being just contrary to the said current, made a great breach of the sea upon the point; so that it was not safe for me to keep too close to the shore for the breach, nor to go too far off because of the stream.

The third day in the morning, the wind having abated over night, the sea was calm, and I ventur'd; but I am a warning piece again, to all rash and ignorant pilots; for no sooner was I come to the point, when even I was not my boat's length from the shore, but I found myself in a great depth of water, and a current like the sluice of a mill: It carry'd my boat along with it with such violence, that all I could do, could not keep her so much as on the edge of it; but I found it hurry'd me farther and farther out from the eddy, which was on my left hand. There was no wind stirring to help me, and all I could do with my paddlers signify'd nothing, and now I began to give myself over for lost; for as the current was on both sides the island, I knew in a few leagues distance they must joyn again, and then I was irrecoverably gone; nor did I see any possibility of avoiding it; so that I had no prospect before me but of perishing; not by the sea, for that was calm enough, but of starving for hunger. I had indeed found a tortoise on the shore, as big almost as I could lift, and had toss'd it into the boat; and I had a great jar of fresh water, that is to say, one of my earthen pots; but what was all this to being driven into the vast ocean, where, to be sure, there was no shore, no main land, or island, for a thousand leagues at least?

And now I saw how easy it was for the Providence of God to make the most miserable condition mankind could be in *worse*. Now I look'd back upon my desolate solitary island, as the most pleasant place in the world, and all the happiness my heart could wish for, was to be but there again. I stretch'd out my hands to it with eager wishes. O happy desart, said I, I shall never see thee more! O miserable creature, said I, whither am I going: Then I reproach'd myself with my unthankful temper, and how I had repin'd at my solitary condition; and now what would I give to be on shore there again. Thus we never see the true state of our condition, till it is illustrated to us by its contraries; nor know how to value what we enjoy, but by the want of it. It is scarce possible to imagine the consternation I was now in, being driven from my beloved island (for so it appeared to me now to be) into the wide ocean, almost two leagues, and in the utmost despair of ever recovering it again. However, I work'd hard, till indeed my strength was almost exhausted, and kept my boat as much to the *northward*, that is, towards the side of the current which the eddy lay on, as possibly I could; when about noon, as the sun pass'd the meridian, I thought I felt a little breeze of wind in my face, springing up from the S. S. E. This chear'd my heart a little, and especially when in about half an hour more, it blew a pretty small gentle gale. By this time I was gotten at a frightful distance from the island, and had the least cloud or hazy weather interven'd, I had been undone another way too; for I had no compass on board, and should never have known how to have steered towards the island, if I had but once lost sight of it; but the weather continuing clear, I apply'd myself to get up my mast again, spread my sail, standing away to the *north* as much as possible, to get out of the current.

Just as I had set my mast and sail, and the boat began to stretch away, I saw even by the clearness of the water, some alteration of the current was near; for where the current was so strong, the water was foul; but perceiving the water clear, I found the current abate, and presently I found to the *east*, at about half a mile, a breach of the sea upon some rocks; these rocks I found caus'd the current to part again, and as the main stress of it ran away more *southerly*, leaving the rocks to the *north-east*; so the other return'd by the repulse of the rocks, and made a strong eddy, which ran back again to the *north-west*, with a very sharp stream.

They who know what it is to have a reprieve brought to them upon the ladder, or to be rescued from thieves just going to murther them, or who have been in such like extremities, may guess what my present surprise of joy was, and how gladly I put my boat into the stream of this eddy, and the wind also freshning, how gladly I spread my sail to it, running cheerfully before the wind, and with a strong tide or eddy under foot.

This eddy carry'd me about a league in my way back again directly towards the island, but about two leagues more to the northward than the current which carried me away at first; so that when I came near the island, I found myself open to the northern shore of it, that is to say, the other end of the island opposite to that which I went out from.

When I had made something more than a league of way by the help of this current or eddy, I found it was spent and serv'd me no farther. However, I found that being between the two great currents, (*viz.*) that on the south side, which had hurried me away, and that on the north, which lay about a league on the other side. I say, between these two, in the wake of the island, I found the water at least still and running no way, and having still a breeze of wind fair for me, I kept on steering directly for the island, tho' not making such fresh way as I did before.

About four a-clock in the evening, being then within about a league of the island, I found the point of the rocks which occasioned this disaster, stretching out, as is described before, to the southward, and casting off the current more southwardly, had of course made another eddy to the North, and this I found very strong, but not directly setting the way my course lay, which was due west, but almost full north. However having a fresh gale, I stretch'd a-cross this eddy slanting north-west, and in about an hour came within about a mile of the shore, where it being smooth water, I soon got to land.

When I was on shore I fell on my knees and gave God thanks for my deliverance, resolving to lay aside all thoughts of my deliverance by my boat, and refreshing myself with such things as I had, I brought my boat close to the shore in a little cove that I had spy'd under some trees, and lay'd me down to sleep, being quite spent with the labour and fatigue of the voyage.

I was now at a great loss which way to get home with my boat, I had run so much hazard, and knew too much the case to think of attempting it by the way I went out, and what might be at the other side (I mean the west side) I knew not, nor had I any mind to run any more ventures; so I only resolved in the morning to make my way westward along the shore and to see if there was no creek where I might lay up my frigate in safety, so as to have her again if I wanted her; in about three miles, or thereabout, coasting the shore, I came to a very good inlet or bay about a mile over, which narrowed till it came to a very little rivulet or brook, where I found a very convenient harbour for my boat and where she lay as if she had been in a little dock made on purpose for her. Here I put in, and having stow'd my boat very safe, I went on shore to look about me and see where I was.

I soon found I had but a little past by the place where I had been before, when I travell'd on foot to that shore; so taking nothing out of my boat, but my gun and my umbrella, for it was exceeding hot, I began my march: The way was comfortable enough after such a voyage as I had been upon, and I reach'd my old bower in the evening, where I found every thing standing as I left it; for I always kept it in good order, being, as I said before, my country house.

I got over the fence, and laid me down in the shade to rest my limbs; for I was very weary, and fell asleep: But judge you, if you can, that read my story, what a surprise I must be in, when I was wak'd out of my sleep by a voice calling me by my name several times, *Robin, Robin, Robin Crusoe*, poor *Robin Crusoe*, where are you *Robin Crusoe*? Where are you? Where have you been?

I was so dead asleep at first, being fatigu'd with rowing, or paddling, as it is call'd, the first part of the day, and with walking the latter part, that I did not wake thoroughly, but dozing between sleeping and waking, thought I dream'd that some body spoke to me: But as the voice continu'd to repeat, *Robin Crusoe, Robin Crusoe*, at last I began to wake more perfectly, and was at first dreadfully frighted, and started up in the utmost consternation: But no sooner were my eyes open, but I saw my *Poll* sitting on the top of the hedge; and immediately knew that it was he that spoke to me; for just in such bemoaning language I had used to talk to him, and teach him; and he had learn'd it so perfectly, that he would sit upon my finger, and lay his bill close to my face, and cry, *Poor* Robin Crusoe, *Where are you? Where have you been? How come you here?* and such things as I had taught him.

However, even though I knew it was the parrot, and that indeed it could be no body else, it was a good while before I could compose myself: First, I was amazed how the creature got thither, and then how he should just keep about the place, and no where else: But as I was well satisfied it could be no body but honest *Poll*, I got it over; and holding out my hand, and calling him by his name *Poll*, the sociable creature came to me, and sat upon my thumb, as he used to do, and continued talking to me, *Poor* Robin Crusoe, and *how did I come here?* and *where had I been?* just as if he had been overjoy'd to see me again; and so I carry'd him home along with me.

I had now had enough of rambling to sea for some time, and had enough to do for many days to sit still, and reflect upon the danger I had been in. I would have been very glad to have had my boat again on my side of the island; but I knew not how it was practicable to get it about as to the east side of the island, which I had gone round; I knew well enough there was no venturing that way; my very heart would shrink, and my very blood run chill but to think of it: And as to the other side of the island, I did not know how it might be there; but supposing the current ran with the same force against the shore at the east, as it pass'd by it on the other, I might run the same risk of being driven down the stream, and carry'd by the island, as I had been before, of being carry'd away from it; so with these thoughts I contented my self to be without any boat, tho' it had been the product of so many months labour to make it, and of so many more to get it unto the sea.

In this government of my temper I remain'd near a year, lived a very sedate retired life, as you may well suppose; and my thoughts being very much composed as to my condition, and fully comforted in resigning myself to the dispositions of Providence, I thought I liv'd really very happily in all things, except that of society.

I improv'd my self in this time in all the mechanick exercises which my necessities put me upon applying myself to, and I believe cou'd, upon occasion, have made a very good *carpenter*, especially considering how few tools I had.

Besides this, I arrived at an unexpected perfection in my earthen ware, and contrived well enough to make them with a wheel, which I found infinitely easyer and better; because I made things round and shapable, which before were filthy things indeed to look on. But I think I was never more vain of my own performance, or more joyful for any thing I found out, than for my being able to make a tobacco-pipe. And tho' it was a very ugly clumsy thing, when it was done, and only burnt red like other earthen ware, yet as it was hard and firm, and would draw the smoke, I was exceedingly comforted with it, for I had been always used to smoke, and there were pipes in the ship, but I forgot them at first, not knowing that there was tobacco in the island; and afterwards, when I search'd the ship again, I could not come at any pipes at all.

In my wicker ware also I improved much, and made abundance of necessary baskets, as well as my invention shew'd me, though not very handsome, yet they were such as were very handy and convenient for my laying things up in, or fetching things home in. For example, if I kill'd a goat abroad, I could hang it up in a tree, flea it, and dress it, and cut it in pieces, and bring it home in a basket, and the like by a turtle, I could cut it up, take out the eggs, and a piece or two of the flesh, which was enough for me, and bring them home in a basket, and leave the rest behind me. Also large deep baskets were my receivers for my corn, which I always rub'd out as soon as it was dry, and cured, and kept it in great baskets.

I began now to perceive my powder abated considerably, and this was a want which it was impossible for me to supply, and I began seriously to consider what I must do when I should have no more powder; that is to say, how I should do to kill any goat. I had, as is observ'd in the third year of my being here, kept a young kid, and bred her up tame, and I was in hopes of getting a he-goat, but I could not by any means bring it to pass, till my kid grew an old goat; and I could never find in my heart to kill her, till she dy'd at last of meer age.

But being now in the eleventh year of my residence, and, as I have said, my ammunition growing low, I set myself to study some art to trap and snare the goats, to see whether I could not catch some of them alive, and particularly I wanted a she-goat great with young.[41]

To this purpose I made snares to hamper them, and I do believe they were more than once taken in them, but my tackle was not good, for I had no wire, and I always found them broken, and my bait devour'd.

At length I resolv'd to try a pit-fall, so I dug several large pits in the earth, in places where I had observ'd the goats used to feed, and over these pits I placed hurdles of my own making too, with a great weight upon them; and several times I put ears of barley and dry rice, without setting the trap, and I could easily perceive that the goats had gone in and eaten up the corn, for I could see the mark of their feet. At length I set three traps in one night, and going the next morning I found them all standing, and yet the bait eaten and gone: This was very discouraging. However, I alter'd my trap, and, not to trouble you with particulars, going one morning to see my trap, I found in one of them a large old he-goat, and in one of the other, three kids, a male and two females.

As to the old one, I knew not what to do with him, he was so fierce I durst not go into the pit to him; that is to say, to go about to bring him away alive, which was what I wanted. I could have kill'd him, but that was not my business, nor would it answer my end. So I e'en let him out, and he ran away as if he had been frighted out of his wits: But I had forgot then what I learned afterwards, that hunger will tame a lyon. If I had let him stay there three or four days without food, and then have carry'd him some water to drink, and then a little corn, he would have been as tame as one of the kids, for they are mighty sagacious tractable creatures where they are well used.

However, for the present I let him go, knowing no better at that time; then I went to the three kids, and taking them one by one, I ty'd them with strings together, and with some difficulty brought them all home.

It was a good while before they wou'd feed, but throwing them some sweet corn, it tempted them, and they began to be tame; and now I found that if I expected to supply myself with goat-flesh when I had no powder or shot left, breeding some up tame was my only way, when perhaps I might have them about my house like a flock of sheep.

But then it presently occurr'd to me, that I must keep the tame from the wild, or else they would always run wild when they grew up, and the only way for this was to have some enclosed piece of ground, well fenc'd either with hedge or pale, to keep them in so effectually, that those within might not break out, or those without break in.

This was a great undertaking for one pair of hands, yet as I saw there was an absolute necessity of doing it, my first piece of work was to find out a proper piece of ground, *viz.* where there was likely to be herbage for them to eat, water for them to drink, and cover to keep them from the sun.

Those who understand such enclosures will think I had very little contrivance, when I pitch'd upon a place very proper for all these, being a plain open piece of meadow-land or *savanna*, (as our people call it in the western colonies,) which had two or three little drills of fresh water in it, and at one end was very woody. I say they will smile at my forecast, when I shall tell them I began my enclosing of this piece of ground in such a manner, that my hedge or pale must have been at least two mile about.

Nor was the madness of it so great as to the compass, for if it was ten mile about I was like to have time enough to do it in. But I did not consider that my goats would be as wild in so much compass, as if they had had the whole island, and I should have so much room to chase them in, that I should never catch them.

My hedge was begun and carry'd on, I believe, about fifty yards, when this thought occur'd to me; so I presently stopt short, and for the first beginning I resolv'd to enclose a piece of about 150 yards in length, and 100 yards in breadth, which as it would maintain as many as I should have in any reasonable time, so as my flock encreased, I could add more ground to my enclosure.

This was acting with some prudence, and I went to work with courage. I was about three months hedging in the first piece, and till I had done it I tether'd the three kids in the best part of it, and us'd them to feed as near me as possible to make them familiar; and very often I would go and carry them some ears of barley, or a handful of rice, and feed them out of my hand; so that after my enclosure was finished, and I let them loose, they would follow me up and down, bleating after me for a handful of corn.

This answer'd my end, and in about a year and half I had a flock of about twelve goats, kids and all; and in two years more I had three and forty, besides several that I took and killed for my food. And after that I enclosed five several pieces of ground to feed them in, with little pens to drive them into, to take them as I wanted, and gates out of one piece of ground into another.

But this was not all, for now I not only had goats flesh to feed on when I pleas'd, but milk too, a thing which indeed in my beginning I did not so much as think of, and which, when it came into my thoughts, was really an agreeable surprise. For now I set up my dairy, and had sometimes a gallon or two of milk in a day. And as Nature, who gives supplies of food to every creature, dictates even naturally how to make use of it; so I that had never milk'd a cow, much less a goat, or seen butter or cheese made, very readily and handily, tho' after a great many essays and miscarriages, made me both butter and cheese at last, and never wanted it afterwards.

How mercifully can our great Creator treat his creatures, even in those conditions in which they seem'd to be overwhelm'd in destruction. How can he sweeten the bitterest Providences, and give us cause to praise him for dungeons and prisons. What a table was here spread for me in a wilderness, where I saw nothing at first but to perish for hunger!

It would have made a Stoick smile[42] to have seen me and my little family sit down to dinner; there was my majesty the prince and lord of the whole island; I had the lives of all my subjects at my absolute command. I could hang, draw, give liberty, and take it away, and no rebels among all my subjects.

Then to see how like a King I din'd too all alone, attended by my servants, *Poll*, as if he had been my favourite, was the only person permitted to talk to me. My dog who was now grown very old and crazy, and had found no species to multiply his kind upon, sat always at my right hand, and two cats, one on one side the table, and one on the other, expecting now and then a bit from my hand, as a mark of special favour.

But these were not the two cats which I brought on shore at first, for they were both of them dead, and had been interr'd near my habitation by my own hand; but one of them having multiply'd by I know not what kind of creature, these were two which I had preserv'd tame, whereas the rest run wild in the woods, and became indeed troublesome to me at last; for they would often come into my house, and plunder me too, till at last I was obliged to shoot them, and did kill a great many; at length they left me with this attendance, and in this plentiful manner I liv'd; neither could I be said to want any thing but society, and of that in some time after this I was like to have too much.

I was something impatient, as I have observ'd, to have the use of my boat; though very loath to run any more hazards; and therefore sometimes I sat contriving ways to get her about the island, and at other times I sat my self down contented enough without her. But I had a strange uneasiness in my mind to go down to the point of the island, where, as I have said, in my last ramble, I went up the hill to see how the shore lay, and how the current set, that I might see what I had to do: This inclination increas'd upon me every day, and at length I resolv'd to travel thither by land, following the edge of the shore, I did so: But had any one in *England* been to meet such a man as I was, it must either have frighted them, or rais'd a great deal of laughter; and as I frequently stood still to look at myself, I could not but smile at the notion of my travelling through *Yorkshire* with such an equipage, and in such a dress: Be pleas'd to take a sketch of my figure as follows,

I had a great high shapeless cap, made of a goat's skin, with a flap hanging down behind, as well to keep the sun from me, as to shoot the rain off from running into my neck; nothing being so hurtful in these climates, as the rain upon the flesh under the clothes.

I had a short jacket of goat-skin, the skirts coming down to about the middle of my thighs; and a pair of open-knee'd breeches of the same, the breeches were made of the skin of an old *he-goat*, whose hair hung down such a length on either side, that like *pantaloons* it reach'd to the middle of my legs; stockings and shoes I had none, but had made me a pair of some-things, I scarce know what to call them, like buskins, to flap over my legs, and lace on either side like spatter-dashes; but of a most barbarous shape, as indeed were all the rest of my clothes.

I had on a broad belt of goat's-skin dry'd, which I drew together with two thongs of the same, instead of buckles, and in a kind of a frog on either side of this. Instead of a sword and a dagger, hung a little saw and a hatchet, one on one side, one on the other. I had another belt not so broad, and fasten'd in the same manner, which hung over my shoulder; and at the end of it, under my left arm, hung two pouches, both made of goat's-skin too; in one of which hung my powder, in the other my shot: At my back I carry'd my basket, on my shoulder my gun, and over my head a great clumsy ugly goat-skin umbrella, but which, after all, was the most necessary thing I had about me, next to my gun: As for my face, the colour of it was really not so *moletta* like as one might expect from a man not at all careful of it, and living within nineteen degrees of the *Equinox*. My beard I had once suffer'd to grow till it was about a quarter of a yard long; but as I had both scissars and razors sufficient, I had cut it pretty short, except what grew on my upper lip, which I had trimm'd into a large pair of *Mahometan* whiskers, such as I had seen worn by some *Turks*, who I saw at *Sallee*; for the *Moors* did not wear such, tho' the *Turks* did; of these muschatoes or whiskers, I will not say they were long enough to hang my hat upon them; but they were of a length and shape monstrous enough, and such as in *England* would have pass'd for frightful.

But all this is by the by; for as to my figure, I had so few to observe me, that it was of no manner of consequence; so I say no more to that part. In this kind of figure I went my new journey, and was out five or six days. I travell'd first along the sea shore, directly to the place where I first brought my boat to an anchor, to get up upon the rocks; and having no boat now to take care of, I went over the land a nearer way, to the same height that I was upon before, when looking forward to the point of the rocks which lay out, and which I was oblig'd to double with my boat, as is said above: I was surpris'd to see the sea all smooth and quiet, no ripling, no motion, no current, any more there than in other places.

I was at a strange loss to understand this, and resolv'd to spend some time in the observing it, to see if nothing from the sets of the tide had occasion'd it; but I was presently convinced how it was, *viz.* that the tide of ebb setting from the *west*, and joyning with the current of waters from some great river on the shore, must be the occasion of this current; and that according as the wind blew more forcibly from the *west*, or from the *north*, this current came nearer, or went farther from the shore; for waiting thereabouts till evening, I went up to the rock again, and then the tide of ebb being made, I plainly saw the current again as before, only, that it run farther off, being near half a league from the shore; whereas in my case, it set close upon the shore, and hurry'd me and my *canoe* along with it, which at another time it would not have done.

This observation convinc'd me, that I had nothing to do but to observe the ebbing and the flowing of the tide, and I might very easily bring my boat about the island again: But when I began to think of putting it in practice, I had such a terror upon my spirits at the remembrance of the danger I had been in, that I could not think of it again with any patience; but on the contrary, I took up another resolution which was more safe, though more laborious; and this was, that I would build, or rather make me another *periagua* or *canoe*; and so have one for one side of the island, and one for the other.

You are to understand, that now I had, as I may call it, two plantations in the island; one my little fortification or tent, with the wall about it under the rock, with the cave behind me, which by this time I had enlarg'd into several apartments, or caves, one within another. One of these, which was the dryest, and largest, and had a door out beyond my wall or fortification; that is to say, beyond where my wall joyn'd to the rock, was all fill'd up with the large earthen pots, of which I have given an account, and with fourteen or fifteen great baskets, which would hold five or six bushels each, where I laid up my stores of provision, especially my corn, some in the ear cut off short from the straw, and the other rubb'd out with my hand.

As for my wall made, *as before*, with long stakes or piles, those piles grew all like trees, and were by this time grown so big, and spread so very much, that there was not the least appearance to any one's view of any habitation behind them.

Near this dwelling of mine, but a little farther within the land, and upon lower ground, lay my two pieces of corn-ground, which I kept duly cultivated and sow'd, and which duly yielded me their harvest in its season;

and whenever I had occasion for more corn, I had more land adjoyning as fit as that.

Besides this, I had my country seat, and I had now a tolerable plantation there also; for first, I had my little bower, as I call'd it, which I kept in repair; *that is to say*, I kept the hedge which circled it in, constantly fitted up to its usual height, the ladder standing always in the inside; I kept the trees which at first were no more than my stakes, but were now grown very firm and tall; I kept them always so cut, that they might spread and grow thick and wild, and make the more agreeable shade, which they did effectually to my mind. In the middle of this I had my tent always standing, being a piece of a sail spread over poles set up for that purpose, and which never wanted any repair or renewing; and under this I had made me a squab or couch, with the skins of the creatures I had kill'd, and with other soft things, and a blanket laid on them, such as belong'd to our sea-bedding, which I had saved, and a great watch-coat to cover me; and here, whenever I had occasion to be absent from my chief seat, I took up my country habitation.

Adjoyning to this I had my enclosures for my cattle, that is to say, my goats: And as I had taken an inconceivable deal of pains to fence and enclose this ground, so I was so uneasy to see it kept entire, lest the goats should break thro', that I never left off till with infinite labour I had stuck the out-side of the hedge so full of small stakes, and so near to one another, that it was rather a pale than a hedge, and there was scarce room to put a hand thro' between them, which afterwards when those stakes grew, as they all did in the next rainy season, made the enclosure strong like a wall, indeed stronger than any wall.

This will testify for me that I was not idle, and that I spared no pains to bring to pass whatever appear'd necessary for my comfortable support; for I consider'd the keeping up a breed of tame creatures thus at my hand, would be a living magazine of flesh, milk, butter and cheese, for me as long as I liv'd in the place, if it were to be forty years; and that keeping them in my reach, depended entirely upon my perfecting my enclosures to such a degree, that I might be sure of keeping them together; which by this method indeed I so effectually secur'd, that when these little stakes began to grow, I had planted them so very thick, I was forced to pull some of them up again.

In this place also I had my grapes growing, which I principally depended on for my winter store of raisins, and which I never fail'd to preserve very carefully, as the best and most agreeable dainty of my whole diet; and indeed they were not agreeable only, but physical, wholesome, nourishing and refreshing to the last degree.

As this was also about half way between my other habitation and the place where I had laid up my boat, I generally stay'd, and lay here in my way thither; for I used frequently to visit my boat, and I kept all things about or belonging to her in very good order; sometimes I went out in her to divert my self, but no more hazardous voyages would I go, nor scarce ever above a stone's cast or two from the shore, I was so apprehensive of being hurry'd out of my knowledge again by the currents or winds, or any other accident. But now I come to a new scene of my life.

It happen'd one day about noon going towards my boat, I was exceedingly surpris'd with the print of a man's naked foot on the shore, which was very plain to be seen in the sand: I stood like one thunder-struck, or as if I had seen an apparition; I listen'd, I look'd round me, I could hear nothing, nor see any thing, I went up to a rising ground to look farther, I went up the shore and down the shore, but it was all one, I could see no other impression but that one, I went to it again to see if there were any more, and to observe if it might not be my fancy; but there was no room for that, for there was exactly the very print of a foot, toes, heel, and every part of a foot; how it came thither, I knew not, nor could in the least imagine. But after innumerable fluttering thoughts, like a man perfectly confus'd and out of myself, I came home to my fortification, not feeling, as we say, the ground I went on, but terrify'd to the last degree, looking behind me at every two or three steps, mistaking every bush and tree, and fancying every stump at a distance to be a man; nor is it possible to describe how many various shapes affrighted imagination represented things to me in, how many wild ideas were found every moment in my fancy, and what strange unaccountable whimsies came into my thoughts by the way.

When I came to my castle, for so I think I call'd it ever after this, I fled into it like one pursued; whether I went over by the ladder as first contriv'd, or went in at the hole in the rock, which I call'd a door, I cannot remember; no, nor could I remember the next morning, for never frighted hare fled to cover, or fox to earth, with more terror of mind than I to this retreat.

I slept none that night; the farther I was from the occasion of my fright, the greater my apprehensions were, which is something contrary to the nature of such things, and especially to the usual practice of all creatures in fear: But I was so embarrass'd with my own frightful ideas of the thing, that I form'd nothing but dismal imaginations to myself, even tho' I was now a great way off it. Sometimes I fancy'd it must be the Devil; and reason joyn'd in with me upon this supposition: For how should any other thing in human shape come into the place? Where was the vessel that brought them? What marks was there of any other footsteps? And how was it possible a man should come there? But then to think that *Satan* should take human shape upon him in such a place where there could be no manner of occasion for it, but to leave the print of his foot behind him, and that even for no purpose too, for he could not be sure I should see it; this was an amusement the other way; I considered that the Devil might have found out abundance of other ways to have terrify'd me than this of the single print of a foot. That as I liv'd quite on the other side of the island, he would never have been so simple to leave a mark in a place where 'twas ten thousand to one whether I should ever see it or not, and in the sand too, which the first surge of the sea upon a high wind would have defac'd entirely: All this seem'd inconsistent with the thing itself, and with all the notions we usually entertain of the subtilty of the Devil.

Abundance of such things as these assisted to argue me out of all apprehensions of its being the Devil: And I presently concluded then, that it must be some more dangerous creature, (*viz.*) that it must be some of the savages of the main land over-against me, who had wander'd out to sea in their *canoes*, and either driven by the currents, or by contrary winds, had made the island; and had been on shore, but were gone away again to sea, being as loath, perhaps, to have stay'd in this desolate island, as I would have been to have had them.

While these reflections were rowling upon my mind, I was very thankful in my thoughts, that I was so happy as not to be thereabouts at that time, or that they did not see my boat, by which they would have concluded that some inhabitants had been in the place, and perhaps have search'd farther for me: Then terrible thoughts rack'd my imagination about their having found my boat, and that there were people here; and that if so, I should certainly have them come again in greater numbers, and devour me; that if it should happen so that they should not find me, yet they would find my enclosure, destroy all my corn, carry away all my flock of tame goats, and I should perish at last for meer want.

Thus my fear banish'd all my religious hope, all that former confidence in God, which was founded upon such wonderful experience as I had had of his goodness, now vanish'd, as if he that had fed me by miracle hitherto, could not preserve by his power the provision which he had made for me by his goodness: I reproach'd my self with my easiness, that would not sow any more corn one year than would just serve me till the next season, as if no accident could intervene to prevent my enjoying the crop that was upon the ground; and this I thought so just a reproof, that I resolv'd for the future to have two or three years corn beforehand, so that whatever might come, I might not perish for want of bread.

How strange a checquer work[43] of Providence is the life of man! and by what secret differing springs are the affections hurry'd about, as differing circumstances present! To day we love what to morrow we hate; to day we seek what to morrow we shun; to day we desire what to morrow we fear; nay even tremble at the apprehensions of; this was exemplify'd in me at this time in the most lively manner imaginable; for I whose only affliction was, that I seem'd banish'd from human society, that I was alone, circum-scrib'd by the boundless ocean, cut off from mankind, and condemn'd to what I call'd silent life; that I was as one who Heaven thought not worthy to be number'd among the living, or to appear among the rest of his creatures; that to have seen one of my own species, would have seem'd to me a raising me from death to life, and the greatest blessing that Heaven it self, next to the supreme blessing of salvation, could bestow; I say, that I should now tremble at the very apprehensions of seeing a man, and was ready to sink into the ground at but the shadow, or silent appearance of a man's having set his foot in the island.

Such is the uneven state of human life: And it afforded me a great many curious speculations afterwards, when I had a little recovered my first surprise; I considered that this was the station of life, the infinitely wise and good Providence of God had determin'd for me, that as I could not foresee what the ends of divine wisdom might be in all this, so I was not to dispute his sovereignty, who, as I was his creature, had an undoubted right by creation to govern and dispose of me absolutely as he thought fit; and who, as I was a creature who had offended him, had likewise a judicial right to condemn me to what punishment he thought fit; and that it was my part to submit to bear his indignation, because I had sinn'd against him.

I then reflected, that God, who was not only righteous but omnipotent, as he had thought fit thus to punish and afflict me, so he was able to deliver me; that if he did not think fit to do it, 'twas my unquestion'd duty to resign my self absolutely and entirely to his will; and on the other hand, it was my duty also to hope in him, pray to him, and quietly to attend the dictates and directions of his daily Providence.

These thoughts took me up many hours, days, nay, I may say, weeks and months; and one particular effect of my cogitations on this occasion, I cannot omit, *viz.* one morning early, lying in my bed, and fill'd with thought about my danger from the appearance of savages, I found it discompos'd me very much, upon which those words of the Scripture came into my thoughts, *Call upon me in the day of trouble, and I will deliver, and thou shalt glorify me.*

Upon this, rising cheerfully out of my bed, my heart was not only comforted, but I was guided and encouraged to pray earnestly to God for deliverance: When I had done praying, I took up my Bible, and opening it to read, the first words that presented to me, were, *Wait on the Lord, and be of good cheer, and he shall strengthen thy heart;*[44] *wait, I say, on the Lord*: It is impossible to express the comfort this gave me. In answer, I thankfully laid down the book, and was no more sad, at least, not on that occasion.

In the middle of these cogitations, apprehensions and reflections, it came into my thought one day, that all this might be a meer chimera of my own; and that this foot might be the print of my own foot, when I came on shore from my boat: This cheer'd me up a little too, and I began to perswade myself it was all a delusion; that it was nothing else but my own foot; and why might not I come that way from the boat, as well as I was going that way to the boat; again, I consider'd also that I could by no means tell for certain where I had trod, and where I had not; and that if at last this was only the print of my own foot, I had play'd the part of those fools, who strive to make stories of spectres, and apparitions, and then are frighted at them more than any body.

Now I began to take courage, and to peep abroad again; for I had not stirr'd out of my castle for three days and nights; so that I began to starve for provision; for I had little or nothing within doors, but some barley cakes and water. Then I knew that my goats wanted to be milk'd too, which usually was my evening diversion; and the poor creatures were in great pain and inconvenience for want of it; and indeed, it almost spoil'd some of them, and almost dry'd up their milk.

Heartning myself therefore with the belief that this was nothing but the print of one of my own feet, and so I might be truly said to start at my own shadow, I began to go abroad again, and went to my country house, to milk my flock; but to see with what fear I went forward, how often I look'd behind me, how I was ready every now and then to lay down my basket, and run for my life, it would have made any one have thought I was haunted with an evil conscience, or that I had been lately most terribly frighted, and so indeed I had.

However, as I went down thus two or three days, and having seen nothing, I began to be a little bolder; and to think there was really nothing in it, but my own imagination: But I could not perswade myself fully of this, till I should go down to the shore again, and see this print of a foot, and measure it by my own, and see if there was any similitude or fitness, that I might be assur'd it was my own foot: But when I came to the place, *first*, it appeared evidently to me, that when I laid up my boat, I could not possibly be on shore any where thereabout. *Secondly*, when I came to measure the mark with my own foot, I found my foot not so large by a great deal; both these things fill'd my head with new imaginations, and gave me the vapours again to the highest degree; so that I shook with cold, like one in an ague: And I went home again, fill'd with the belief that some man or men had been on shore there; or in short, that the island was inhabited, and I might be surpris'd before I was aware; and what course to take for my security I knew not.

O what ridiculous resolutions men take, when possess'd with fear! It deprives them of the use of those means which reason offers for their relief. The first thing I propos'd to my self, was, to throw down my enclosures, and turn all my tame cattle wild into the woods, that the enemy might not find them; and then frequent the island in prospect of the same, or the like booty: Then to the simple thing of digging up my two corn-fields, that they might not find such a grain there, and still be prompted to frequent the island; then to demolish my bower, and tent, that they might not see any vestiges of habitation, and be prompted to look further, in order to find out the persons inhabiting.

These were the subject of the first night's cogitation, after I was come home again, while the apprehensions which had so over-run my mind were fresh upon me, and my head was full of vapours, as above: Thus fear of danger is ten thousand times more terrifying than danger it self, when apparent to the eyes; and we find the burthen of anxiety greater by much, than the evil which we are anxious about; and which was worse than all this, I had not that relief in this trouble from the resignation I used to practise, that I hop'd to have. I look'd, I thought, like *Saul*, who complain'd not only that the *Philistines* were upon him, but that God had forsaken him;[45] for I did not now take due ways to compose my mind, by crying to God in my distress, and resting upon his Providence, as I had done before, for my defence and deliverance; which if I had done, I had, at least, been more cheerfully supported under this new surprise, and perhaps carry'd through it with more resolution.

This confusion of my thoughts kept me waking all night; but in the morning I fell asleep, and having, by the amusement of my mind, been, as it were tyr'd, and my spirits exhausted; I slept very soundly, and wak'd much better compos'd than I had ever been before; and now I began to think sedately; and upon the utmost debate with my self, I concluded, that this island, which was so exceeding pleasant, fruitful, and no farther from the main land than as I had seen, was not so entirely abandon'd as I might imagine: That altho' there were no stated inhabitants who liv'd on the spot; yet that there might sometimes come boats off from the shore, who either with design, or perhaps never, but when they were driven by cross winds, might come to this place.

That I had liv'd here fifteen years now, and had not met with the least shadow or figure of any people yet; and that if at any time they should be driven here, it was probable they went away again as soon as ever they could, seeing they had never thought fit to fix there upon any occasion, to this time.

That the most I cou'd suggest any danger from, was, from any such casual accidental landing of straggling people from the main, who, as it was likely if they were driven hither, were here against their wills; so they made no stay here, but went off again with all possible speed, seldom staying one night on shore, lest they should not have the help of the tides, and day-light back again; and that therefore I had nothing to do but to consider of some safe retreat, in case I should see any savages land upon the spot.

Now I began sorely to repent, that I had dug my cave so large, as to bring a door through again, which door, as I said, came out beyond where my fortification joyn'd to the rock; upon maturely considering this therefore, I resolv'd to draw me a second fortification, in the same manner of a semicircle, at a distance from my wall, just where I had planted a double row of trees, about twelve years before, of which I made mention: These trees having been planted so thick before, they wanted but a few piles to be driven between them, that they should be thicker, and stronger, and my wall would be soon finish'd.

So that I had now a double wall, and my outer wall was thickned with pieces of timber, old cables, and every thing I could think of to make it strong; having in it seven little holes, about as big as I might put my arm out at: In the in-side of this, I thickned my wall to above ten foot thick, with continual bringing earth out of my cave, and laying it at the foot of the wall, and walking upon it; and through the seven holes, I contriv'd to plant the musquets, of which I took notice, that I got seven on shore out of the ship; these, I say, I planted like my cannon, and fitted them into frames that held them like a carriage, that so I could fire all the seven guns in two minutes time: This wall I was many a weary month a finishing, and yet never thought my self safe till it was done.

When this was done, I stuck all the ground without my wall, for a great way every way, as full with stakes or sticks of the *osier* like wood, which I found so apt to grow, as they could well stand; insomuch, that I believe I might set in near twenty thousand of them, leaving a pretty large space between them and my wall, that I might have room to see an enemy, and they might have no shelter from the young trees, if they attempted to approach my outer wall.

Thus in two years time I had a thick grove, and in five or six years time I had a wood before my dwelling, growing so monstrous thick and strong, that it was indeed perfectly impassable; and no men of what kind soever, would ever imagine that there was any thing beyond it, much less a habitation: As for the way which I proposed to my self to go in and out, for I left no avenue; it was by setting two ladders; one to a part of the rock which was low, and then broke in, and left room to place another ladder upon that; so when the two ladders were taken down, no man living could come down to me without mischieving himself; and if they had come down, they were still on the out-side of my outer wall.

Thus I took all the measures human prudence could suggest for my own preservation; and it will be seen at length, that they were not altogether without just reason; though I foresaw nothing at that time, more than my meer fear suggested to me.

While this was doing, I was not altogether careless of my other affairs; for I had a great concern upon me for my little herd of goats; they were not only a present supply to me upon every occasion, and began to be sufficient to me, without the expence of powder and shot; but also without the fatigue of hunting after the wild ones, and I was loath to lose the advantage of them, and to have them all to nurse up over again.

To this purpose, after long consideration, I could think of but two ways to preserve them; one was to find another convenient place to dig a cave under-ground, and to drive them into it every night; and the other was to enclose two or three little bits of land, remote from one another, and as much conceal'd as I could, where I might keep about half a dozen young goats in each place: So that if any disaster happen'd to the flock in general, I might be able to raise them again with little trouble and time: And this, tho' it would require a great deal of time and labour, I thought was the most rational design.

Accordingly I spent some time to find out the most retir'd parts of the island; and I pitch'd upon one which was as private indeed as my heart could wish for; it was a little damp piece of ground in the middle of the hollow and thick woods, where, as is observ'd, I almost lost myself once before, endeavouring to come back that way from the eastern part of the island: Here I found a clear piece of land near three acres, so surrounded with woods, that it was almost an enclosure by Nature, at least it did not want near so much labour to make it so, as the other pieces of ground I had work'd so hard at.

I immediately went to work with this piece of ground, and in less than a month's time, I had so fenc'd it round, that my flock or herd, call it which you please, who were not so wild now as at first they might be supposed to be, were well enough secur'd in it. So without any farther delay, I removed ten young she-goats and two he-goats to this piece; and when they were there, I continu'd to perfect the fence till I had made it as secure as the other, which, however, I did at more leisure, and it took me up more time by a great deal.

All this labour I was at the expence of, purely from my apprehensions on the account of the print of a man's foot which I had seen; for as yet I never saw any human creature come near the island, and I had now liv'd two years under these uneasinesses, which indeed made my life much less comfortable than it was before; as may well be imagin'd by any who know what it is to live in the constant snare of *the fear of man*; and this I must observe with grief too, that the discomposure of my mind had too great impressions also upon the religious part of my thoughts, for the dread and terror of falling into the hands of savages and cannibals, lay so upon my spirits, that I seldom found my self in a due temper for application to my maker, at least not with the sedate calmness and resignation of soul which I was wont to do; I rather pray'd to God as under great affliction and pressure of mind, surrounded with danger, and in expectation every night of being murther'd and devour'd before morning; and I must testify from my experience, that a temper of peace, thankfulness, love and affection, is much more the proper frame for prayer, than that of terror and discomposure; and that under the dread of mischief impending, a man is no more fit for a comforting performance of the duty of praying to God, than he is for repentance on a sick bed: For these discomposures affect the mind as the others do the body; and the discomposure of the mind must necessarily be as great a disability as that of the body, and much greater, praying to God being properly an act of the mind, not of the body.

But to go on; after I had thus secur'd one part of my little living stock, I went about the whole island, searching for another private place, to make such another deposit; when wandring more to the *west* point of the island than I had ever done yet, and looking out to sea, I thought I saw a boat upon the sea, at a great distance; I had found a prospective glass, or two, in one of the seamen's chests, which I sav'd out of our ship; but I had it not about me, and this was so remote, that I could not tell what to make of it; though I look'd at it till my eyes were not able to hold to look any longer; whether it was a boat, or not, I do not know; but as I descended from the hill, I could see no more of it, so I gave it over; only I resolv'd to go no more out without a prospective glass in my pocket.

When I was come down the hill, to the end of the island, where indeed I had never been before, I was presently convinc'd, that the seeing the print of a man's foot, was not such a strange thing in the island as I imagin'd; and but that it was a special Providence that I was cast upon the side of the island where the savages never came: I should easily have known, that nothing was more frequent than for the *canoes* from the main, when they happen'd to be a little too far out at sea, to shoot over to that side of the island for harbour; likewise as they often met, and fought in their *canoes*, the victors having taken any prisoners, would bring them over to this shore, where according to their dreadful customs, being all *cannibals*, they would kill and eat them; of which hereafter.

When I was come down the hill, to the shore, as I said above, being the *S. W.* point of the island, I was perfectly confounded and amaz'd; nor is it possible for me to express the horror of my mind, at seeing the shore spread with skulls, hands, feet and other bones of human bodies; and particularly I observ'd a place where there had been a fire made, and a circle dug in the earth, like a cockpit, where it is suppos'd the savage wretches had sat down to their inhuman feastings upon the bodies of their fellow-creatures.

I was so astonish'd with the sight of these things, that I entertain'd no notions of any danger to my self from it for a long while; all my apprehensions were buried in the thoughts of such a pitch of inhuman, hellish brutality, and the horror of the degeneracy of human nature; which though I had heard of often, yet I never had so near a view of before; in short, I turn'd away my face from the horrid spectacle; my stomach grew sick, and I was just at the point of fainting, when Nature discharg'd the disorder from my stomach; and having vomited with an uncommon violence, I was a little reliev'd, but could not bear to stay in the place a moment; so I gat me up the hill again with all the speed I could, and walk'd on towards my own habitation.

When I came a little out of that part of the island, I stood still a while as amaz'd; and then recovering myself, I look'd up with the utmost affection of my soul, and with a flood of tears in my eyes, gave God thanks, that had cast my first lot in a part of the world, where I was distinguish'd from such dreadful creatures as these; and that though I had esteemed my present condition very miserable, had yet given me so many comforts in it, that I had still more to give thanks for than to complain of; and this above all, that I had even in this miserable condition been comforted with the knowledge of himself, and the hope of his blessing, which was a felicity more than sufficiently equivalent to all the misery which I had suffer'd, or could suffer.

In this frame of thankfulness, I went home to my castle, and began to be much easier now, as to the safety of my circumstances, than ever I was before; for I observ'd that these wretches never came to this island in search of what they could get; perhaps not seeking, not wanting, or not expecting any thing here; and having often, no doubt, been up in the cover'd woody part of it, without finding any thing to their purpose. I knew I had been here now almost eighteen years, and never saw the least footsteps of human creature there before; and I might be here eighteen more, as entirely conceal'd as I was now, if I did not discover my self to them, which I had no manner of occasion to do, it being my only business to keep my self entirely concealed where I was, unless I found a better sort of creatures than *cannibals* to make my self known to.

Yet I entertain'd such an abhorrence of the savage wretches that I have been speaking of, and of the wretched inhuman custom of their devouring and eating one another up, that I continu'd pensive, and sad, and kept close within my own circle for almost two years after this: When I say my own circle, I mean by it, my three plantations, *viz.* my castle, my country seat, which I call'd my bower, and my enclosure in the woods; nor did I look after this for any other use than as an enclosure for my goats; for the aversion which Nature gave me to these hellish wretches, was such, that I was fearful of seeing them, as of seeing the Devil himself; nor did I so much as go to look after my boat, in all this time; but began rather to think of making me another; for I cou'd not think of ever making any more attempts to bring the other boat round the island to me, least I should meet with some of these creatures at sea, in which, if I had happen'd to have fallen into their hands, I knew what would have been my lot.

Time however, and the satisfaction I had, that I was in no danger of being discovered by these people, began to wear off my uneasiness about them; and I began to live just in the same compos'd manner as before; only with this difference, that I used more caution, and kept my eyes more about me than I did before, least I should happen to be seen by any of them; and particularly, I was more cautious of firing my gun, least any of them being on the island, should happen to hear of it; and it was therefore a very good Providence to me, that I had furnish'd myself with a tame breed of goats, that I needed not hunt any more about the woods, or shoot at them; and if I did catch any of them, after this it was by traps, and snares, as I had done before; so that for two years after this, I believe I never fir'd my gun once off, though I never went out without it; and which was more, as I had sav'd three pistols out of the ship, I always carried them out with me, or at least two of them, sticking them in my goat-skin belt; also I furbish'd up one of the great cutlashes, that I had out of the ship, and made me a belt to put it on also; so that I was now a most formidable fellow to look at, when I went abroad, if you add to the former description of myself, the particular of two pistols, and a great broad sword hanging at my side in a belt, but without a scabbard.

Things going on thus, as I have said, for some time; I seem'd, excepting these cautions, to be reduc'd to my former calm, sedate way of living, all these things tended to shewing me more and more how far my condition was from being miserable, compared to some others; nay, to many other particulars of life, which it might have pleased God to have made my lot. It put me upon reflecting, how little repining there would be among mankind, at any condition of life, if people would rather compare their condition with those that are worse, in order to be thankful, than be always comparing them with those which are better, to assist their murmurings and complainings.

As in my present condition there were not really many things which I wanted; so indeed I thought that the frights I had been in about these savage wretches, and the concern I had been in for my own preservation, had taken off the edge of my invention for my own conveniences; and I had dropt a good design, which I had once bent my thoughts too much upon; and that was, to try if I could not make some of my barley into malt, and then try to brew myself some beer: This was really a whimsical thought, and I reprov'd myself often for the simplicity of it; for I presently saw there would be the want of several things necessary to the making my beer, that it would be impossible for me to supply; as first, casks to preserve it in, which was a thing, that as I have observ'd already, I could never compass; no, though I spent not many days, but weeks, nay months, in attempting it, but to no purpose. In the next place, I had no hops to make it keep, no yeast to make it work, no copper or kettle to make it boil; and yet all these things, notwithstanding, I verily believe, had not these things interven'd, I mean the frights and terrors I was in about the savages, I had undertaken it, and perhaps brought it to pass too; for I seldom gave any thing over without accomplishing it, when I once had it in my head enough to begin it.

But my invention now run quite another way; for night and day, I could think of nothing but how I might destroy some of these monsters in their cruel bloody entertainment, and if possible, save the victim they should bring hither to destroy. It would take up a larger volume than this whole work is intended to be, to set down all the contrivances I hatch'd, or rather brooded upon in my thought, for the destroying these creatures, or at least frighting them, so as to prevent their coming hither any more; but all was abortive, nothing could be possible to take effect, unless I was to be there to do it my self; and what could one man do among them, when perhaps there might be twenty or thirty of them together, with their darts, or their bows and arrows, with which they could shoot as true to a mark, as I could with my gun?

Sometimes I contrived to dig a hole under the place where they made their fire, and put in five or six pound of gun-powder, which when they kindled their fire, would consequently take fire, and blow up all that was near it; but as in the first place I should be very loath to waste so much powder upon them, my store being now within the quantity of one barrel; so neither could I be sure of its going off at any certain time; when it might surprise them, and at best, that it would do little more than just blow the fire about their ears and fright them, but not sufficient to make them forsake the place; so I laid it aside, and then propos'd, that I would place my self in ambush, in some convenient place, with my three guns, all double loaded; and in the middle of their bloody ceremony, let fly at them, when I should be sure to kill or wound perhaps two or three at every shoot; and then falling in upon them with my three pistols, and my sword, I made no doubt, but that if there was twenty, I should kill them all: This fancy pleas'd my thoughts for some weeks, and I was so full of it, that I often dream'd of it; and sometimes that I was just going to let fly at them in my sleep.

I went so far with it in my imagination, that I employ'd my self several days to find out proper places to put my self in ambuscade, as I said, to watch for them; and I went frequently to the place it self, which was now grown more familiar to me; and especially while my mind was thus fill'd with thoughts of revenge, and of a bloody putting twenty or thirty of them to the sword, as I may call it; the horror I had at the place, and at the signals of the barbarous wretches devouring one another, abated my malice.

Well, at length I found a place in the side of the hill, where I was satisfy'd I might securely wait, till I saw any of their boats coming, and might then, even before they would be ready to come on shore, convey my self unseen into thickets of trees, in one of which there was a hollow large enough to conceal me entirely; and where I might sit and observe all their bloody doings, and take my full aim at their heads, when they were so close together, as that it would be next to impossible that I should miss my shoot, or that I could fail wounding three or four of them at the first shoot.

In this place then I resolv'd to fix my design, and accordingly I prepar'd two musquets, and my ordinary fowling piece. The two musquets I loaded with a brace of slugs each, and four or five smaller bullets, about the size of pistol bullets; and the fowling piece I loaded with near a handful of swan-shot, of the largest size; I also loaded my pistols with about four bullets each; and in this posture, well provided with ammunition for a second and third charge, I prepar'd my self for my expedition.

After I had thus laid the scheme of my design, and in my imagination put it in practice, I continually made my tour every morning up to the top of the hill, which was from my castle, as I call'd it, about three miles, or more, to see if I could observe any boats upon the sea, coming near the island, or standing over towards it; but I began to tire of this hard duty, after I had for two or three months constantly kept my watch; but came always back without any discovery, there having not in all that time been the least appearance, not only on, or near the shore but not on the whole ocean, so far as my eyes or glasses could reach every way.

As long as I kept up my daily tour to the hill to look out, so long also I kept up the vigour of my design, and my spirits seem'd to be all the while in a suitable form for so outragious an execution as the killing twenty or thirty naked savages, for an offence which I had not at all entred into a discussion of in my thoughts, any farther than my passions were at first fir'd by the horror I conceiv'd at the unnatural custom of that people of the country, who it seems had been suffer'd by Providence, in his wise disposition of the world, to have no other guide than that of their own abominable and vitiated passions; and consequently were left, and perhaps had been so for some ages, to act such horrid things, and receive such dreadful customs, as nothing but Nature entirely abandon'd of Heaven, and acted by some hellish degeneracy, could have run them into: But now when, as I have said, I began to be weary of the fruitless excursion, which I had made so long, and so far, every morning in vain, so my opinion of the action itself began to alter, and I began with cooler and calmer thoughts to consider what it was I was going to engage in. What authority or call I had, to pretend to be judge and executioner upon these men as criminals, whom Heaven had thought fit for so many ages to suffer unpunish'd, to go on, and to be, as it were, the executioners of his judgments one upon another. How far these people were offenders against me, and what right I had to engage in the quarrel of that blood, which they shed promiscuously one upon another. I debated this very often with my self thus; how do I know what God himself judges in this particular case; it is certain these people either do not commit this as a crime; it is not against their own consciences reproving, or their light reproaching them. They do not know it to be an offence, and then commit it in defiance of divine justice, as we do in almost all the sins we commit. They think it no more a crime to kill a captive taken in war, than we do to kill an ox; nor to eat human flesh, than we do to eat mutton.

When I had consider'd this a little, it follow'd necessarily, that I was certainly in the wrong in it, that these people were not murtherers in the sense that I had before condemned them, in my thoughts; any more than those Christians were murtherers, who often put to death the prisoners taken in battle; or more frequently, upon many occasions, put whole troops of men to the sword, without giving quarter, though they threw down their arms and submitted.

In the next place it occurr'd to me, that albeit the usage they thus gave one another, was thus brutish and inhuman; yet it was really nothing to me: These people had done me no injury. That if they attempted me, or I saw it necessary for my immediate preservation to fall upon them, something might be said for it; but that as I was yet out of their power, and they had really no knowledge [of] me, and consequently no design upon me; and therefore it could not be just for me to fall upon them. That this would justify the conduct of the *Spaniards* in all their barbarities practis'd in *America*, and where they destroyed millions of these people, who however they were idolaters and barbarians, and had several bloody and barbarous rites in their customs, such as sacrificing human bodies to their idols, were yet, as to the *Spaniards*, very innocent people; and that the rooting them out of the country, is spoken of with the utmost abhorrence and detestation, by even the *Spaniards* themselves, at this time; and by all other Christian nations of *Europe*, as a meer butchery, a bloody and unnatural piece of cruelty, unjustifiable either to God or man; and such, as for which the very name of a *Spaniard* is reckon'd to be frightful and terrible to all people of humanity, or of Christian compassion: As if the kingdom of *Spain* were particularly eminent for the product of a race of men, who were without principles of tenderness, or the common bowels of pity to the miserable, which is reckon'd to be a mark of generous temper in the mind.[46]

These considerations really put me to a pause, and to a kind of a full-stop; and I began by little and little to be off of my design, and to conclude, I had taken wrong measures in my resolutions to attack the savages; that it was not my business to meddle with them, unless they first attack'd me, and this it was my business if possible to prevent; but that if I were discover'd, and attack'd, then I knew my duty.

On the other hand, I argu'd with myself, that this really was the way not to deliver myself, but entirely to ruin and destroy myself; for unless I was sure to kill every one that not only should be on shore at that time, but that should ever come on shore afterwards, if but one of them escap'd, to tell their country people what had happen'd, they would come over again by thousands to revenge the death of their fellows, and I should only bring upon myself a certain destruction, which at present I had no manner of occasion for.

Upon the whole I concluded, that neither in principle or in policy, I ought one way or other to concern myself in this affair. That my business was by all possible means to conceal myself from them, and not to leave the least signal to them to guess by, that there were any living creatures upon the island; I mean of human shape.

Religion joyn'd in with this prudential, and I was convinc'd now many ways, that I was perfectly out of my duty, when I was laying all my bloody schemes for the destruction of innocent creatures, I mean innocent as to me: As to the crimes they were guilty of towards one another, I had nothing to do with them; they were national,[47] and I ought to leave them to the justice of God, who is the governour of nations, and knows how by national punishments to make a just retribution for national offences; and to bring publick judgments upon those who offend in a publick manner, by such ways as best pleases him.

This appear'd so clear to me now, that nothing was a greater satisfaction to me, than that I had not been suffer'd to do a thing which I now saw so much reason to believe would have been no less a sin, than that of wilful murther, if I had committed it; and I gave most humble thanks on my knees to God, that had thus delivered me from blood-guiltiness; beseeching him to grant me the protection of his Providence, that I might not fall into the hands of the barbarians; or that I might not lay my hands upon them, unless I had a more clear call from Heaven to do it, in defence of my own life.

In this disposition I continued, for near a year after this; and so far was I from desiring an occasion for falling upon these wretches, that in all that time I never once went up the hill to see whether there were any of them in sight, or to know whether any of them had been on shore there, or not, that I might not be tempted to renew any of my contrivances against them, or be provoked by any advantage which might present it self, to fall upon them; only this I did, I went and removed my boat, which I had on the other side the island, and carried it down to the *east* end of the whole island, where I ran it into a little cove which I found under some high rocks, and where I knew, by reason of the currents, the savages durst not, at least would not come with their boats, upon any account whatsoever.

With my boat I carry'd away every thing that I had left there belonging to her, though not necessary for the bare going thither, *viz.* a mast and sail which I had made for her, and a thing like an anchor, but indeed which could not be call'd either anchor or graplin; however, it was the best I could make of its kind: All these I removed, that there might not be the least shadow of any discovery, or any appearance of any boat, or of any human habitation upon the island.

Besides this, I kept my self, as I said, more retired than ever, and seldom went from my cell, other than upon my constant employment, *viz.* to milk my she-goats, and manage my little flock, in the wood; which as it was quite on the other part of the island, was quite out of danger; for certain it is, that these savage people who sometimes haunted this island, never came with any thoughts of finding any thing here; and consequently never wandred off from the coast; and I doubt not, but they might have been several times on shore, after my apprehensions of them had made me cautious as well as before; and indeed, I look'd back with some horror upon the thoughts of what my condition would have been, if I had chop'd upon them, and been discover'd before that, when naked and unarm'd, except with one gun, and that loaden often only with small shot, I walk'd every where peeping and peeping about the island, to see what I could get; what a surprise should I have been in, if when I discover'd the print of a man's foot, I had instead of that seen fifteen or twenty savages, and found them pursuing me, and by the swiftness of their running, no possibility of my escaping them.

The thoughts of this sometimes sunk my very soul within me, and distress'd my mind so much, that I could not soon recover it, to think what I should have done, and how I not only should not have been able to resist them, but even should not have had presence of mind enough to do what I might have done; much less, what now after so much consideration and preparation I might be able to do: Indeed, after serious thinking of these things, I should be very melancholy, and sometimes it would last a great while; but I resolv'd it at last all into thankfulness to that Providence, which had deliver'd me from so many unseen dangers, and had kept me from those mischiefs which I could no way have been the agent in delivering my self from; because I had not the least notion of any such thing depending, or the least supposition of it being possible.

This renew'd a contemplation, which often had come to my thoughts in former time, when first I began to see the merciful dispositions of Heaven, in the dangers we run through in this life. How wonderfully we are deliver'd, when we know nothing of it. How, when we are in (a *quandary*, as we call it) a doubt or hesitation, whether to go this way, or that way, a secret hint shall direct us this way, when we intended to go that way; nay, when sense, our own inclination, and perhaps business has call'd to go the other way, yet a strange impression upon the mind, from we know not what springs, and by we know not what power, shall over-rule us to go this way; and it shall afterwards appear, that had we gone that way which we should have gone, and even to our imagination ought to have gone, we should have been ruin'd and lost: Upon these, and many like reflections, I afterwards made it a certain rule with me, that whenever I found those secret hints, or pressings of my mind, to doing, or not doing any thing that presented; or to going this way, or that way, I never fail'd to obey the secret dictate; though I knew no other reason for it, than that such a pressure, or such a hint hung upon my mind: I could give many examples of the success of this conduct in the course of my life; but more especially in the latter part of my inhabiting this unhappy island; besides many occasions which it is very likely I might have taken notice of, if I had seen with the same eyes then, that I saw with now: But 'tis never too late to be wise; and I cannot but advise all considering men, whose lives are attended with such extraordinary incidents as mine, or even though not so extraordinary, not to slight such secret intimations of Providence, let them come from what invisible intelligence they will, that I shall not discuss,[48] and perhaps cannot account for; but certainly they are a proof of the converse of spirits, and the secret communication between those embody'd, and those unembody'd; and such a proof as can never be withstood: Of which I shall have occasion to give some very remarkable instances, in the remainder of my solitary residence in this dismal place.

I believe the reader of this will not think strange, if I confess that these anxieties, these constant dangers I liv'd in, and the concern that was now upon me, put an end to all invention, and to all the contrivances that I had laid for my future accommodations and conveniences. I had the care of my safety more now upon my hands, than that of my food. I car'd not to drive a nail, or chop a stick of wood now, for fear the noise I should make, should be heard; much less would I fire a gun, for the same reason; and above all, I was intolerably uneasy at making any fire, lest the smoke, which is visible at a great distance in the day, should betray me; and for this reason I remov'd that part of my business which requir'd fire; such as burning of pots and pipes, &c. into my new apartment in the woods, where after I had been some time, I found, to my unspeakable consolation, a meer natural cave in the earth, which went in a vast way, and where, I dare say, no savage had he been at the mouth of it, would be so hardy as to venture in, nor indeed, would any man else; but one who like me, wanted nothing so much as a safe retreat.

The mouth of this hollow, was at the bottom of a great rock, where by meer accident, (I would say, if I did not see abundant reason to ascribe all such things now to Providence) I was cutting down some thick branches of trees, to make charcoal; and before I go on, I must observe the reason of my making this charcoal; which was thus:

I was afraid of making a smoke about my habitation, as I said before; and yet I could not live there without baking my bread, cooking my meat, &c. so I contriv'd to burn some wood here, as I had seen done in *England*, under turf, till it became chark, or dry coal; and then putting the fire out, I preserv'd the coal to carry home; and perform the other services which fire was wanting for at home without danger of smoke.

But this is by the by: While I was cutting down some wood here, I perceiv'd that behind a very thick branch of low brushwood, or under wood, there was a kind of hollow place. I was curious to look into it, and getting with difficulty into the mouth of it, I found it was pretty large; that is to say, sufficient for me to stand upright in it, and perhaps another with me; I must confess to you, I made more haste out than I did in, when looking farther into the place, and which was perfectly dark, I saw two broad shining eyes of some creature, whether Devil or man I knew not, which twinkled like two stars, the dim light from the cave's mouth shining directly in and making the reflection.

However, after some pause, I recover'd my self, and began to call my self a thousand fools, and tell my self, that he that was afraid to see the Devil, was not fit to live twenty years in an island all alone; and that I durst to believe there was nothing in this cave that was more frightful than my self; upon this, plucking up my courage, I took up a great firebrand, and in I rush'd again, with the stick flaming in my hand; I had not gone three steps in, but I was almost as much frighted as I was before; for I heard a very loud sigh, like that of a man in some pain, and it was follow'd by a broken noise, *as if* of words half express'd, and then a deep sigh again: I stepp'd back, and was indeed struck with such a surprise, that it put me into a cold sweat; and if I had had a hat on my head, I will not answer for it, that my hair might not have lifted it off. But still plucking up my spirits as well as I could, and encouraging my self a little with considering that the power and presence of God was every where, and was able to protect me; upon this I stepp'd forward again, and by the light of the firebrand, holding it up a little over my head, I saw lying on the ground a most monstrous frightful old he-goat, just making his will, as we say, and gasping for life, and dying indeed of meer old age.

I stirr'd him a little, to see if I could get him out, and he essay'd to get up, but was not able to raise himself; and I thought with my self, he might even lie there; for if he had frighted me so, he would certainly fright any of the savages, if any of them should be so hardy as to come in there, while he had any life in him.

I was now recover'd from my surprise, and began to look round me, when I found the cave was but very small, that is to say, it might be about twelve foot over, but in no manner of shape, either round or square, no hands having ever been employ'd in making it, but those of meer Nature: I observ'd also, that there was a place at the farther side of it, that went in farther, but was so low, that it requir'd me to creep upon my hands and knees to go into it, and whither I went I knew not; so having no candle, I gave it over for some time; but resolv'd to come again the next day, provided with candles, and a tinderbox, which I had made of the lock of one of the muskets, with some wild-fire in the pan.[49]

Accordingly, the next day I came provided with six large candles of my own making; for I made very good candles now of goat's tallow; and going into this low place, I was oblig'd to creep upon all fours, *as I have said*, almost ten yards; which, by the way, I thought was a venture bold enough, considering that I knew not how far it might go, nor what was beyond it. When I was got through the strait, I found the roof rose higher up, I believe near twenty foot; but never was such a glorious sight seen in the island, I dare say, as it was, to look round the sides and roof of this vault or cave; the walls reflected a hundred thousand lights to me from my two candles; what it was in the rock, whether diamonds, or any other precious stones, or gold, which I rather suppos'd it to be, I knew not.

The place I was in, was a most delightful cavity, or grotto, of its kind, as could be expected, though perfectly dark; the floor was dry and level, and had a sort of small loose gravel upon it, so that there was no nauseous or venomous creature to be seen, neither was there any damp or wet on the sides or roof: The only difficulty in it was the entrance, which however as it was a place of security, and such a retreat as I wanted, I thought that was a convenience; so that I was really rejoyc'd at the discovery, and resolv'd without any delay, to bring some of those things which I was most anxious about to this place; particularly, I resolv'd to bring hither my magazine of powder, and all my spare arms, *viz.* two fowling-pieces, for I had three in all; and three musquets, for of them I had eight in all; so I kept at my castle only five, which stood ready mounted, like pieces of cannon, on my out-most fence; and were ready also to take out upon any expedition.

Upon this occasion of removing my ammunition, I took occasion to open the barrel of powder which I took up out of the sea, and which had been wet; and I found that the water had penetrated about three or four inches into the powder on every side, which caking and growing hard, had preserv'd the inside like a kernel in a shell; so that I had near sixty pound of very good powder in the center of the cask, and this was an agreeable discovery to me at that time; so I carry'd all away thither, never keeping above two or three pound of powder with me in my castle, for fear of a surprise of any kind: I also carry'd thither all the lead I had left for bullets.

I fancy'd my self now like one of the ancient giants, which were said to live in caves, and holes, in the rocks, where none could come at them; for I perswaded my self while I was here, if five hundred savages were to hunt me, they could never find me out; or if they did, they would not venture to attack me here.

The old goat who I found expiring, dy'd in the mouth of the cave, the next day after I made this discovery; and I found it much easier to dig a great hole there, and throw him in, and cover him with earth, than to drag him out; so I interr'd him there, to prevent the offence to my nose.

I was now in my twenty third year of residence in this island, and was so naturaliz'd to the place, and to the manner of living, that could I have but enjoy'd the certainty that no savages would come to the place to disturb me, I could have been content to have capitulated for spending the rest of my time there, even to the last moment, till I had laid me down and dy'd, like the old goat in the cave. I had also arriv'd to some little diversions and amusements, which made the time pass more pleasantly with me a great deal, than it did before; as first, I had taught my *Poll*, as I noted before, to speak; and he did it so familiarly, and talk'd so articulately and plain, that it was very pleasant to me; and he lived with me no less than six and twenty years: How long he might live afterwards, I know not; tho' I know they have a notion in the *Brasils*, that they live a hundred years; perhaps poor

Poll may be alive there still, calling after *Poor Robin Crusoe* to this day. I wish no *English* man the ill luck to come there and hear him; but if he did, he would certainly believe it was the Devil. My dog was a very pleasant and loving companion to me, for no less than sixteen years of my time, and then dy'd of meer old age; as for my cats, they multiply'd as I have observ'd to that degree, that I was oblig'd to shoot several of them at first, to keep them from devouring me and all I had; but at length, when the two old ones I brought with me were gone, and after some time continually driving them from me, and letting them have no provision with me, they all ran wild into the woods, except two or three favourites, which I kept tame; and whose young, when they had any, I always drown'd; and these were part of my family: Besides these I always kept two or three household kids about me, who I taught to feed out of my hand; and I had two more parrots which talk'd pretty well, and would all call *Robin Crusoe*; but none like my first; nor indeed did I take the pains with any of them that I had done with him. I had also several tame sea-fowls, whose names I know not, who I caught upon the shore, and cut their wings; and the little stakes which I had planted before my castle wall being now grown up to a good thick grove, these fowls all liv'd among these low trees, and bred there, which was very agreeable to me; so that as I said above, I began to be very well contented with the life I led, if it might but have been secur'd from the dread of the savages.

But it was otherwise directed; and it may not be amiss for all people who shall meet with my story, to make this just observation from it, *viz.* how frequently, in the course of our lives, the evil which in itself we seek most to shun, and which, when we are fallen into, is the most dreadful to us, is oftentimes the very means or door of our deliverance, by which alone we can be rais'd again from the affliction we are fallen into. I cou'd give many examples of this in the course of my unaccountable life; but in nothing was it more particularly remarkable, than in the circumstances of my last years of solitary residence in this island.

It was now the month of *December*, as I said above, in my twenty third year; and this being the *southern* Solstice, for winter I cannot call it, was the particular time of my harvest, and requir'd my being pretty much abroad in the fields, when going out pretty early in the morning, even before it was thorow day-light, I was surpris'd with seeing a light of some fire upon the shore, at a distance from me, of about two mile towards the end of the island, where I had observ'd some savages had been, as before;

but not on the other side; but to my great affliction, it was on my side of the island.

I was indeed terribly surpris'd at the sight, and stepp'd short within my grove, not daring to go out, least I might be surpris'd; and yet I had no more peace within, from the apprehensions I had, that if these savages in rambling over the island, should find my corn standing, or cut, or any of my works and improvements, they would immediately conclude, that there were people in the place, and would then never give over till they had found me out: In this extremity I went back directly to my castle, pull'd up the ladder after me, and made all things without look as wild and natural as I could.

Then I prepar'd my self within, putting myself in a posture of defence; I loaded all my cannon, as I call'd them; that is to say, my musquets, which were mounted upon my new fortification, and all my pistols, and resolv'd to defend my self to the last gasp, not forgetting seriously to commend my self to the divine protection, and earnestly to pray to God to deliver me out of the hands of the barbarians; and in this posture I continu'd about two hours; but began to be mighty impatient for intelligence abroad, for I had no spies to send out.

After sitting a while longer, and musing what I should do in this case, I was not able to bear sitting in ignorance any longer; so setting up my ladder to the side of the hill, where there was a flat place, as I observ'd before, and then pulling the ladder up after me, I set it up again, and mounted to the top of the hill, and pulling out my prospective glass, which I had taken on purpose, I laid me down flat on my belly, on the ground, and began to look for the place; I presently found there was no less than nine naked savages, sitting round a small fire, they had made, not to warm them; for they had no need of that, the weather being extreme hot; but as I suppos'd, to dress some of their barbarous diet, of human flesh, which they had brought with them, whether alive or dead I could not know.

They had two *canoes* with them, which they had haled up upon the shore; and as it was then tide of ebb, they seem'd to me to wait for the return of the flood, to go away again; it is not easy to imagine what confusion this sight put me into, especially seeing them come on my side the island, and so near me too; but when I observ'd their coming must be always with the current of the ebb, I began afterwards to be more sedate in my mind, being satisfy'd that I might go abroad with safety all the time of the tide of flood, if they were not on shore before: And having made this observation, I went abroad about my harvest work with the more composure.

As I expected, so it prov'd; for as soon as the tide made to the *westward*, I saw them all take boat, and row (or paddle, as we call it) all away: I should have observ'd, that for an hour and more before they went off, they went to dancing, and I could easily discern their postures and gestures by my glasses: I could not perceive by my nicest observation, but that they were stark naked, and had not the least covering upon them; but whether they were men or women, that I could not distinguish.

As soon as I saw them shipp'd, and gone, I took two guns upon my shoulders, and two pistols at my girdle, and my great sword by my side, without a scabbard, and with all the speed I was able to make, I went away to the hill, where I had discover'd the first appearance of all; and as soon as I gat thither, which was not less than two hours; for I could not go apace, being so loaden with arms as I was. I perceiv'd there had been three *canoes* more of savages in that place; and looking out farther, I saw they were all at sea together, making over for the main.

This was a dreadful sight to me, especially when going down to the shore, I could see the marks of horror which the dismal work they had been about had left behind it, *viz.* the blood, the bones, and part of the flesh of human bodies, eaten and devour'd by those wretches, with merriment and sport: I was so fill'd with indignation at the sight, that I began now to premeditate the destruction of the next that I saw there, let them be who, or how many soever.

It seem'd evident to me, that the visits which they thus make to this island, are not very frequent; for it was above fifteen months before any more of them came on shore there again; that is to say, I neither saw them, or any footsteps, or signals of them, in all that time; for as to the rainy seasons, then they are sure not to come abroad, at least not so far; yet all this while I liv'd uncomfortably, by reason of the constant apprehensions I was in of their coming upon me by surprise; from whence I observe, that the expectation of evil is more bitter than the suffering, especially if there is no room to shake off that expectation, or those apprehensions.

During all this time, I was in the murthering humour, and took up most of my hours, which should have been better employ'd, in contriving how to circumvent, and fall upon them, the very next time I should see them; especially if they should be divided, as they were the last time, into two parties; nor did I consider at all, that if I kill'd one party, suppose ten, or a dozen, I was still the next day, or week, or month, to kill another, and so another, even *ad infinitum*, till I should be at length no less a murtherer than they were in being man-eaters; and perhaps much more so.

I spent my days now in great perplexity, and anxiety of mind, expecting that I should one day or other fall into the hands of these merciless creatures; and if I did at any time venture abroad, it was not without looking round me with the greatest care and caution imaginable; and now I found to my great comfort, how happy it was that I provided for a tame flock or herd of goats; for I durst not upon any account fire my gun, especially near that side of the island where they usually came, lest I should alarm the savages; and if they had fled from me now, I was sure to have them come back again, with perhaps two or three hundred *canoes* with them in a few days, and then I knew what to expect.

However, I wore out a year and three months more, before I ever saw any more of the savages, and then I found them again, as I shall soon observe. It is true, they might have been there once, or twice; but either they made no stay, or at least I did not hear them; but in the month of *May*, as near as I could calculate, and in my four and twentieth year, I had a very strange encounter with them, of which in its place.

The perturbation of my mind, during this fifteen or sixteen months interval, was very great; I slept unquiet, dream'd always frightful dreams, and often started out of my sleep in the night: In the day great troubles overwhelm'd my mind, and in the night I dream'd often of killing the savages, and of the reasons why I might justify the doing of it; but to wave all this for a while; it was in the middle of *May*, on the sixteenth day I think, as well as my poor wooden calendar would reckon; for I markt all upon the post still; I say, it was the sixteenth of *May*, that it blew a very great storm of wind, all day, with a great deal of lightning and thunder, and a very foul night it was after it; I know not what was the particular occasion of it; but as I was reading in the Bible, and taken up with very serious thoughts about my present condition, I was surpris'd with a noise of a gun as I thought fir'd at sea.

This was to be sure a surprise of a quite different nature from any I had met with before; for the notions this put into my thoughts were quite of another kind. I started up in the greatest haste imaginable, and in a trice clapt my ladder to the middle place of the rock, and pull'd it after me, and mounting it the second time, got to the top of the hill, the very moment, that a flash of fire bid me listen for a second gun, which accordingly, in about half a minute I heard; and by the sound, knew that it was from that part of the sea where I was driven down the current in my boat.

I immediately consider'd that this must be some ship in distress, and that they had some comrade, or some other ship in company, and fir'd these guns for signals of distress, and to obtain help: I had this presence of mind at that minute, as to think that though I could not help them, it may be they might help me; so I brought together all the dry wood I could get at hand, and making a good handsome pile, I set it on fire upon the hill; the wood was dry, and blaz'd freely; and though the wind blew very hard, yet it burnt fairly out; that I was certain, if there was any such thing as a ship, they must needs see it, and no doubt they did; for as soon as ever my fire blaz'd up, I heard another gun, and after that several others, all from the same quarter; I ply'd my fire all night long, till day broke; and when it was broad day, and the air clear'd up, I saw something at a great distance at sea, full *east* of the island, whether a sail, or a hull, I could not distinguish, no not with my glasses, the distance was so great, and the weather still something hazy also; at least it was so out at sea.

I look'd frequently at it all that day, and soon perceiv'd that it did not move; so I presently concluded that it was a ship at an anchor; and being eager, you may be sure, to be satisfy'd, I took my gun in my hand, and run toward the *south* side of the island, to the rocks where I had formerly been carry'd away with the current, and getting up there, the weather by this time being perfectly clear, I could plainly see to my great sorrow, the wreck of a ship cast away in the night, upon those concealed rocks which I found when I was out in my boat; and which rocks, as they check'd the violence of the stream, and made a kind of counter-stream, or eddy, were the occasion of my recovering from the most desperate hopeless condition that ever I had been in, in all my life.

Thus what is one man's safety, is another man's destruction; for it seems these men, whoever they were, being out of their knowledge, and the rocks being wholly under water, had been driven upon them in the night, the wind blowing hard at *E.* and *E. N. E.* Had they seen the island, as I must necessarily suppose they did not, they must, as I thought, have endeavour'd to have sav'd themselves on shore by the help of their boat; but their firing of guns for help, especially when they saw, as I imagin'd, my fire, fill'd me with many thoughts: First, I imagin'd that upon seeing my light, they might have put themselves into their boat, and have endeavour'd to make the shore; but that the sea going very high, they might have been cast away; other times I imagin'd, that they might have lost their boat before, as might be the case many ways; as particularly by the breaking of the sea upon their ship, which many times obliges men to stave, or take in pieces their boat; and sometimes to throw it over-board with their own hands: Other times I imagin'd, they had some other ship, or ships in company, who upon the signals of distress they had made, had taken them up, and carry'd them off: Other whiles I fancy'd, they were all gone off to sea in their boat, and being hurry'd away by the current that I had been formerly in, were carry'd out into the great ocean, where there was nothing but misery and perishing; and that perhaps they might by this time think of starving, and of being in a condition to eat one another.

As all these were but conjectures at best; so in the condition I was in, I could do no more than look on upon the misery of the poor men, and pity them, which had still this good effect on my side, that it gave me more and more cause to give thanks to God, who had so happily and comfortably provided for me in my desolate condition; and that of two ships companies who were now cast away upon this part of the world, not one life should be spar'd but mine: I learn'd here again to observe, that it is very rare that the Providence of God casts us into any condition of life so low, or any misery so great, but we may see something or other to be thankful for; and may see others in worse circumstances than our own.

Such certainly was the case of these men, of whom I could not so much as see room to suppose any of them were sav'd; nothing could make it rational, so much as to wish or expect that they did not all perish there, except the possibility only of their being taken up by another ship in company, and this was but meer possibility indeed; for I saw not the least signal or appearance of any such thing.

I cannot explain, by any possible energy of words, what a strange longing or hankering of desires I felt in my soul upon this sight; breaking out sometimes thus; O that there had been but one or two; nay, or but one soul sav'd out of this ship, to have escap'd to me, that I might but have had one companion, one fellow-creature to have spoken to me, and to have convers'd with! In all the time of my solitary life, I never felt so earnest, so strong a desire after the society of my fellow-creatures, or so deep a regret at the want of it.

There are some secret moving springs in the affections, which when they are set a going by some object in view, or be it some object, though not in view, yet render'd present to the mind by the power of imagination, that motion carries out the soul by its impetuosity to such violent eager embracings of the object, that the absence of it is insupportable.

Such were these earnest wishings, that but one man had been sav'd! *O that it had been but one!* I believe I repeated the words, *O that it had been but one!* a thousand times; and the desires were so mov'd by it, that when I spoke the words, my hands would clinch together, and my fingers press the palms of my hands, that if I had had any soft thing in my hand, it would have crush'd it involuntarily; and my teeth in my head would strike together, and set against one another so strong, that for some time I could not part them again.

Let the naturalists explain these things, and the reason and manner of them; all I can say to them, is, to describe the fact, which was even surprising to me when I found it; though I knew not from what it should proceed; it was doubtless the effect of ardent wishes, and of strong ideas form'd in my mind, realizing the comfort, which the conversation of one of my fellow-Christians would have been to me.

But it was not to be; either their fate or mine, or both, forbid it; for till the last year of my being on this island, I never knew whether any were sav'd out of that ship or no; and had only the affliction some days after, to see the corps of a drownded boy come on shore, at the end of the island, which was next the shipwreck: He had on no clothes, but a seaman's wast-coat, a pair of open knee'd linnen drawers, and a blew linnen shirt; but nothing to direct me so much as to guess what nation he was of: He had nothing in his pocket but two Pieces of Eight, and a tobacco pipe; the last was to me of ten times more value than the first.

It was now calm, and I had a great mind to venture out in my boat, to this wreck; not doubting but I might find something on board, that might be useful to me; but that did not altogether press me so much, as the possibility that there might be yet some living creature on board, whose life I might not only save, but might by saving that life, comfort my own to the last degree; and this thought clung so to my heart, that I could not be quiet, night nor day, but I must venture out in my boat on board this wreck; and committing the rest to God's Providence, I thought the impression was so strong upon my mind, that it could not be resisted, that it must come from some invisible direction, and that I should be wanting to my self if I did not go.

Under the power of this impression, I hasten'd back to my castle, prepar'd every thing for my voyage, took a quantity of bread, a great pot for fresh water, a compass to steer by, a bottle of rum; for I had still a great deal of that left; a basket full of raisins: And thus loading my self with every thing necessary, I went down to my boat, got the water out of her, and got her afloat, loaded all my cargo in her, and then went home again for more; my second cargo was a great bag full of rice, the umbrella to set up over my head for shade; another large pot full of fresh water, and about two dozen of my small loaves, or barley cakes, more than before, with a bottle of goat's-milk, and a cheese; all which, with great labour and sweat, I brought to my boat; and praying to God to direct my voyage, I put out, and rowing or padling the canoe along the shore, I came at last to the utmost point of the island on that side, (*viz.*) *N. E.* And now I was to launch out into the ocean, and either to venture, or not to venture. I look'd on the rapid currents which ran constantly on both sides of the island, at a distance, and which were very terrible to me, from the remembrance of the hazard I had been in before, and my heart began to fail me; for I foresaw that if I was driven into either of those currents, I should be carry'd a vast way out to sea, and perhaps out of my reach, or sight of the island again; and that then, as my boat was but small, if any little gale of wind should rise, I should be inevitably lost.

These thoughts so oppress'd my mind, that I began to give over my enterprize, and having haled my boat into a little creek on the shore, I stept out, and sat me down upon a little rising bit of ground, very pensive and anxious, between fear and desire about my voyage; when as I was musing, I could perceive that the tide was turn'd, and the flood came on, upon which my going was for so many hours impracticable; upon this presently it occurr'd to me, that I should go up to the highest piece of ground I could find, and observe, if I could, how the sets of the tide, or currents lay, when the flood came in, that I might judge whether if I was driven one way out, I might not expect to be driven another way home, with the same rapidness of the currents: This thought was no sooner in my head, but I cast my eye upon a little hill, which sufficiently over-look'd the sea both ways, and from whence I had a clear view of the currents, or sets of the tide, and which way I was to guide my self in my return; here I found, that as the current of the ebb set out close by the south point of the island, so the current of the flood set in close by the shore of the north side, and that I had nothing to do but to keep to the north of the island in my return, and I should do well enough.

Encourag'd with this observation, I resolv'd the next morning to set out with the first of the tide; and reposing myself for the night in the canoe, under the great watch-coat, I mentioned, I launch'd out: I made first a little out to sea full north, till I began to feel the benefit of the current, which set eastward, and which carry'd me at a great rate, and yet did not so hurry me as the southern side current had done before, and so as to take from me all government of the boat; but having a strong steerage with my paddle, I went at a great rate, directly for the wreck, and in less than two hours I came up to it.

It was a dismal sight to look at: The ship, which by its building was *Spanish*, stuck fast, jaum'd in between two rocks; all the stern and quarter of her was beaten to pieces, with the sea; and as her forecastle, which stuck in the rocks, had run on with great violence, her mainmast and foremast were brought by the board; that is to say, broken short off; but her boltsprit was sound, and the head and bow appear'd firm; when I came close to her, a dog appear'd upon her, who seeing me coming, yelp'd and cry'd; and as soon as I call'd him, jump'd into the sea, to come to me, and I took him into the boat; but found him almost dead for hunger and thirst: I gave him a cake of my bread, and he eat it like a ravenous wolf that had been starving a fortnight in the snow: I then gave the poor creature some fresh water, with which, if I would have let him, he would have burst himself.

After this I went on board; but the first sight I met with, was two men drown'd, in the cookroom, or forecastle of the ship, with their arms fast about one another: I concluded, as is indeed probable, that when the ship struck, it being in a storm, the sea broke so high, and so continually over her, that the men were not able to bear it, and were strangled with the constant rushing in of the water, as much as if they had been under water. Besides the dog, there was nothing left in the ship that had life, nor any goods that I could see, but what was spoil'd by the water. There were some casks of liquor, whether wine or brandy, I knew not, which lay lower in the hold; and which, the water being ebb'd out, I could see; but they were too big to meddle with: I saw several chests, which I believe belong'd to some of the seamen, and I got two of them into the boat, without examining what was in them.

Had the stern of the ship been fix'd, and the forepart broken off, I am persuaded I might have made a good voyage; for by what I found in these two chests, I had room to suppose, the ship had a great deal of wealth on board; and if I may guess by the course she steer'd, she must have been bound from the *Buenos Ayres*, or the *Rio de la Plata*, in the south part of

America, beyond the *Brasils*, to the *Havana*, in the Gulph of *Mexico*, and so perhaps to *Spain*: She had no doubt a great treasure in her; but of no use at that time to any body; and what became of the rest of her people, I then knew not.

I found, besides these chests, a little cask full of liquor, of about twenty gallons, which I got into my boat with much difficulty; there were several musquets in a cabin, and a great powder-horn, with about 4 pounds of powder in it; as for the musquets, I had no occasion for them; so I left them, but took the powder-horn: I took a fire-shovel and tongs, which I wanted extremely; as also two little brass kettles, a copper pot to make chocolate, and a gridiron; and with this cargo, and the dog, I came away, the tide beginning to make home again; and the same evening, about an hour within night, I reach'd the island again, weary and fatigu'd to the last degree.

I repos'd that night in the boat, and in the morning I resolv'd to harbour what I had gotten in my new cave, not to carry it home to my castle. After refreshing myself, I got all my cargo on shore, and began to examine the particulars: The cask of liquor I found to be a kind of rum, but not such as we had at the *Brasils*; and in a word, not at all good; but when I came to open the chests, I found several things of great use to me: For example, I found in one a fine case of bottles, of an extraordinary kind, and fill'd with cordial waters, fine, and very good; the bottles held about three pints each, and were tipp'd with silver: I found two pots of very good succades, or sweetmeats, so fasten'd also on top, that the salt water had not hurt them; and two more of the same, which the water had spoil'd: I found some very good shirts, which were very welcome to me; and about a dozen and half of linnen white handkerchiefs, and colour'd neckcloths; the former were also very welcome, being exceeding refreshing to wipe my face in a hot day; besides this, when I came to the till in the chest, I found there three great bags of Pieces of Eight, which held out about eleven hundred Pieces in all; and in one of them, wrapt up in a paper, six Doubloons of gold, and some small bars or wedges of gold; I suppose they might all weigh near a pound.

The other chest I found had some clothes in it, but of little value; but by the circumstances it must have belong'd to the gunner's Mate; though there was no powder in it, but about two pound of fine glaz'd powder, in three small flasks, kept, I suppose, for charging their fowling-pieces on occasion: Upon the whole, I got very little by this voyage, that was of any use to me; for as to the money, I had no manner of occasion for it: 'twas to me as the dirt under my feet; and I would have given it all for three or four pair of *English* shoes and stockings, which were things I greatly wanted, but had not had on my feet now for many years: I had indeed gotten two pair of shoes now, which I took off of the feet of the two drown'd men, who I saw in the wreck; and I found two pair more in one of the chests, which were very welcome to me; but they were not like our *English* shoes, either for ease or service; being rather what we call pumps, than shoes: I found in this seaman's chest, about fifty Pieces of Eight in Royals, but no gold; I suppose this belong'd to a poorer man than the other, which seem'd to belong to some officer.

Well, however, I lugg'd this money home to my cave, and laid it up, as I had done that before, which I brought from our own ship; but it was great pity, as I said, that the other part of this ship had not come to my share; for I am satisfy'd I might have loaded my *canoe* several times over with money, which if I had ever escap'd to *England*, would have lain here safe enough, till I might have come again and fetch'd it.

Having now brought all my things on shore, and secur'd them, I went back to my boat, and row'd, or paddled her along the shore, to her old harbour, where I laid her up, and made the best of my way to my old habitation, where I found every thing safe and quiet; so I began to repose my self, live after my old fashion, and take care of my family affairs; and for a while, I lived easy enough, only that I was more vigilant than I used to be, look'd out oftner, and did not go abroad so much; and if at any time I did stir with any freedom, it was always to the *east* part of the island, where I was pretty well satisfy'd the savages never came, and where I could go without so many precautions, and such a load of arms and ammunition, as I always carry'd with me, if I went the other way.

I liv'd in this condition near two years more; but my unlucky head, that was always to let me know it was born to make my body miserable, was all the two years fill'd with projects and designs, how, if it were possible, I might get away from this island; for sometimes I was for making another voyage to the wreck, though my reason told me that there was nothing left there worth the hazard of my voyage: Sometimes for a ramble one way, sometimes another; and I believe verily, if I had had the boat that I went from *Sallee* in, I should have ventur'd to sea, bound any where I knew not whither.

I have been, in all my circumstances, a *memento* to those who are touch'd with the general plague of mankind, whence, for ought I know, one half of their miseries flow; I mean, that of not being satisfy'd with the station wherein God and Nature hath plac'd them; for not to look back upon my primitive condition, and the excellent advice of my father, the opposition to which, was, *as I may call it*, my ORIGINAL SIN; my subsequent mistakes of the same kind had been the means of my coming into this miserable condition; for had that Providence, which so happily had seated me at the *Brasils*, as a planter, bless'd me with confin'd desires, and I could have been contented to have gone on gradually, I might have been by this time, *I mean, in the time of my being in this island*, one of the most considerable planters in the *Brasils*, nay, I am perswaded, that by the improvements I had made in that little time I liv'd there, and the encrease I should probably have made, if I had stay'd, I might have been worth an hundred thousand *Moydors*; and what business had I to leave a settled fortune, a well stock'd plantation, improving and encreasing, to turn *supra-cargo* to *Guinea*, to fetch Negroes; when patience and time would have so encreas'd our stock at home, that we could have bought them at our own door, from those whose business it was to fetch them; and tho' it had cost us something more, yet the difference of that price was by no means worth saving, at so great a hazard.

But as this is ordinarily the fate of young heads, so reflection upon the folly of it, is as ordinarily the exercise of more years, or of the dear-bought experience of time; and so it was with me now; and yet so deep had the mistake taken root in my temper, that I could not satisfy myself in my station, but was continually poring upon the means, and possibility of my escape from this place; and that I may with the greater pleasure to the reader, bring on the remaining part of my story, it may not be improper, to give some account of my first conceptions on the subject of this foolish scheme for my escape; and how, and upon what foundation I acted.

I am now to be suppos'd retired into my castle, after my late voyage to the wreck, my frigate laid up, and secur'd under water, as usual, and my condition restor'd to what it was before: I had more wealth indeed than I had before, but was not at all the richer; for I had no more use for it, than the *Indians* of *Peru* had, before the *Spaniards* came there.

It was one of the nights in the rainy season in *March*, the four and twentieth year of my first setting foot in this island of solitariness; I was lying in my bed, or hammock, awake, very well in health, had no pain, no distemper, no uneasiness of body; no, nor any uneasiness of mind, more than ordinary; but could by no means close my eyes; that is, so as to sleep; no, not a wink all night long, otherwise than as follows:

It is as impossible, as needless, to set down the innumerable crowd of thoughts that whirl'd through that great thorow-fare of the brain, the memory, in this night's time: I ran over the whole history of my life in miniature, or by abridgment, *as I may call it*, to my coming to this island; and also of the part of my life, since I came to this island. In my reflections upon the state of my case, since I came on shore on this island, I was comparing the happy posture of my affairs, in the first years of my habitation here, compar'd to the life of anxiety, fear, and care, which I had liv'd ever since I had seen the print of a foot in the sand; not that I did not believe the savages had frequented the island even all the while, and might have been several hundreds of them at times on shore there; but I had never known it, and was incapable of any apprehensions about it; my satisfaction was perfect, tho' my danger was the same; and I was as happy in not knowing my danger, as if I had never really been expos'd to it. This furnish'd my thoughts with many very profitable reflections, and particularly this one, How infinitely good that Providence is, which has provided in its government of mankind, such narrow bounds to his sight and knowledge of things; and tho' he walks in the midst of so many thousand dangers, the sight of which, if discover'd to him, would distract his mind, and sink his spirits; he is kept serene, and calm, by having the events of things hid from his eyes, and knowing nothing of the dangers which surround him.

After these thoughts had for some time entertain'd me, I came to reflect seriously upon the real danger I had been in, for so many years in this very island; and how I had walk'd about in the greatest security, and with all possible tranquillity; even when perhaps nothing but a brow of a hill, a great tree, or the casual approach of night, had been between me and the worst kind of destruction, *viz.* that of falling into the hands of cannibals, and savages, who would have seiz'd on me with the same view, as I did of a goat, or a turtle; and have thought it no more a crime to kill and devour me, than I did of a pidgeon, or a curlieu: I would unjustly slander my self, if I should say I was not sincerely thankful to my great preserver, to whose singular protection I acknowledg'd, with great humility, that all these unknown deliverances were due; and without which, I must inevitably have fallen into their merciless hands.

When these thoughts were over, my head was for some time taken up in considering the nature of these wretched creatures; I mean, the savages; and how it came to pass in the world, that the wise governour of all things should give up any of his creatures to such inhumanity; nay, to something so much below, even brutality it self, as to devour its own kind; but as this ended in some (at that time fruitless) speculations, it occurr'd to me to enquire, what part of the world these wretches liv'd in; how far off the coast was from whence they came; what they ventur'd over so far from home for; what kind of boats they had; and why I might not order my self, and my business so, that I might be as able to go over thither, as they were to come to me.

I never so much as troubl'd my self, to consider what I should do with my self, when I came thither; what would become of me, if I fell into the hands of the savages; or how I should escape from them, if they attempted me; no, nor so much as how it was possible for me to reach the coast, and not be attempted by some or other of them, without any possibility of delivering my self; and if I should not fall into their hands, what I should do for provision, or whither I should bend my course; none of these thoughts, I say, so much as came in my way; but my mind was wholly bent upon the notion of my passing over in my boat, to the main land: I look'd back upon my present condition, as the most miserable that could possibly be, that I was not able to throw myself into any thing but death, that could be call'd worse; that if I reach'd the shore of the main, I might perhaps meet with relief, or I might coast along as I did on the shore of *Africk*, till I came to some inhabited country, and where I might find some relief; and after all, perhaps I might fall in with some Christian ship that might take me in; and if the worse came to the worst, I could but die, which would put an end to all these miseries at once. Pray note, all this was the fruit of a disturb'd mind, an impatient temper, made as it were desperate by the long continuance of my troubles, and the disappointments I had met in the wreck, I had been on board of; and where I had been so near the obtaining what I so earnestly long'd for, *viz.* some-body to speak to, and to learn some knowledge from of the place where I was, and of the probable means of my deliverance; I say, I was agitated wholly by these thoughts. All my calm of mind in my resignation to Providence, and waiting the issue of the dispositions of Heaven, seem'd to be suspended; and I had, as it were, no power to turn my thoughts to any thing, but to the project of a voyage to the main, which came upon me with such force, and such an impetuosity of desire, that it was not to be resisted.

When this had agitated my thoughts for two hours, or more, with such violence, that it set my very blood into a ferment, and my pulse beat as high as if I had been in a feaver, meerly with the extraordinary fervour of my mind about it; Nature, as if I had been fatigued and exhausted with the very thought of it, threw me into a sound sleep; one would have thought, I should have dream'd of it: But I did not, nor of any thing relating to it; but I dream'd, that as I was going out in the morning as usual from my castle, I saw upon the shore, two *canoes*, and eleven savages coming to land, and that they brought with them another savage, who they were going to kill, in order to eat him; when on a sudden, the savage that they were going to kill, jumpt away, and ran for his life; and I thought in my sleep, that he came running into my little thick grove, before my fortification, to hide himself; and that I seeing him alone, and not perceiving that the other sought him that way, show'd my self to him, and, smiling upon him, encourag'd him; that he kneel'd down to me, seeming to pray me to assist him; upon which I shew'd my ladder, made him go up, and carry'd him into my cave, and he became my servant; and that as soon as I had gotten this man, I said to my self, now I may certainly venture to the main land; for this fellow will serve me as a pilot, and will tell me what to do, and whither to go for provisions; and whither not to go for fear of being devoured, what places to venture into, and what to escape: I wak'd with this thought, and was under such inexpressible impressions of joy at the prospect of my escape in my dream, that the disappointments which I felt upon coming to my self, and finding it was no more than a dream, were equally extravagant the other way, and threw me into a very great dejection of spirit.

Upon this however, I made this conclusion, that my only way to go about an attempt for an escape, was, if possible, to get a savage into my possession; and, if possible, it should be one of their prisoners, who they had condemn'd to be eaten, and should bring thither to kill; but these thoughts still were attended with this difficulty, that it was impossible to effect this, without attacking a whole caravan of them, and killing them all; and this was not only a very desperate attempt, and might miscarry; but, on the other hand, I had greatly scrupled the lawfulness of it to me; and my heart trembled at the thoughts of shedding so much blood, tho' it was for my deliverance. I need not repeat the arguments which occurr'd to me against this, they being the same mention'd before; but tho' I had other reasons to offer now (*viz.*) that those men were enemies to my life, and would devour me, if they could; that it was self-preservation in the highest degree, to deliver my self from this death of a life, and was acting in my own defence, as much as if they were actually assaulting me, and the like. I say, tho' these things argued for it, yet the thoughts of shedding human blood for my deliverance, were very terrible to me, and such as I could by no means reconcile my self to, a great while.

However at last, after many secret disputes with myself, and after great perplexities about it, for all these arguments one way and another struggled in my head a long time; the eager prevailing desire of deliverance at length master'd all the rest; and I resolv'd, if possible, to get one of those savages into my hands, cost what it would. My next thing then was to contrive how to do it, and this indeed was very difficult to resolve on: But as I could pitch upon no probable means for it, so I resolv'd to put myself upon the watch, to see them when they came on shore, and leave the rest to the event, taking such measures as the opportunity should present, let be what would be.

With these resolutions in my thoughts, I set myself upon the scout, as often as possible, and indeed so often till I was heartily tir'd of it, for it was above a year and half that I waited, and for great part of that time went out to the *west* end, and to the *south west* corner of the island, almost every day, to see for canoes, but none appear'd. This was very discouraging, and began to trouble me much, tho' I cannot say that it did in this case, as it had done some time before that, (*viz.*) wear off the edge of my desire to the thing. But the longer it seem'd to be delay'd, the more eager I was for it; in a word, I was not at first so careful to shun the sight of these savages, and avoid being seen by them, as I was now eager to be upon them.

Besides, I fancied myself able to manage one, nay, two or three savages, if I had them so as to make them entirely slaves to me, to do whatever I should direct them, and to prevent their being able at any time to do me any hurt. It was a great while, that I pleas'd my self with this affair, but nothing still presented; all my fancies and schemes came to nothing, for no savages came near me for a great while.

About a year and half after I had entertain'd these notions, and by long musing, had as it were resolv'd them all into nothing, for want of an occasion to put them in execution, I was surpris'd one morning early, with seeing no less than five *canoes* all on shore together on my side the island; and the people who belong'd to them all landed, and out of my sight: The number of them broke all my measures, for seeing so many, and knowing that they always came four or six, or sometimes more in a boat, I could not tell what to think of it, or how to take my measures, to attack twenty or thirty men single handed; so I lay still in my castle, perplexed and discomforted: However I put my self into all the same postures for an attack, that I had formerly provided, and was just ready for action, if any thing had presented; having waited a good while, listening to hear if they made any noise; at length being very impatient, I set my guns at the foot of my ladder, and clamber'd up to the top of the hill, by my two stages as usual; standing so however that my head did not appear above the hill, so that they could not perceive me by any means; here I observ'd, by the help of my perspective glass, that they were no less than thirty in number, that they had a fire kindled, that they had had meat dress'd. How they had cook'd it, that I knew not, or what it was; but they were all dancing in I know not how many barbarous gestures and figures, their own way, round the fire.

While I was thus looking on them, I perceiv'd by my perspective, two miserable wretches dragg'd from the boats, where it seems they were laid by, and were now brought out for the slaughter. I perceiv'd one of them immediately fell, being knock'd down, I suppose with a club or wooden sword, for that was their way, and two or three others were at work immediately cutting him open for their cookery, while the other victim was left standing by himself, till they should be ready for him. In that very moment this poor wretch seeing himself a little at liberty, Nature inspir'd him with hopes of life, and he started away from them, and ran with incredible swiftness along the sands directly towards me, I mean, towards that part of the coast where my habitation was.

I was dreadfully frighted, (that I must acknowledge) when I perceived him to run my way; and especially, when as I thought I saw him pursued by the whole body, and now I expected that part of my dream was coming to pass, and that he would certainly take shelter in my grove; but I could not depend by any means upon my dream for the rest of it, (*viz.*) that the other savages would not pursue him thither, and find him there. However I kept my station, and my spirits began to recover, when I found that there was not above three men that follow'd him; and still more was I encourag'd, when I found that he outstript them exceedingly in running, and gain'd ground of them, so that if he could but hold it for half an hour, I saw easily he would fairly get away from them all.

There was between them and my castle, the creek which I mention'd often at the first part of my story, when I landed my cargoes out of the ship; and this I saw plainly, he must necessarily swim over, or the poor wretch would be taken there: But when the savage escaping came thither, he made nothing of it, tho' the tide was then up, but plunging in, swam thro' in about thirty strokes or thereabouts, landed and ran on with exceeding strength and swiftness; when the three persons came to the creek, I found that two of them could swim, but the third could not, and that standing on the other side, he look'd at the other, but went no farther; and soon after went softly back again, which as it happen'd, was very well for him in the main.

I observ'd, that the two who swam, were yet more than twice as long swimming over the creek, as the fellow was, that fled from them: It came now very warmly upon my thoughts, and indeed irresistibly, that now was my time to get me a servant, and perhaps a companion or assistant; and that I was call'd plainly by Providence to save this poor creature's life; I immediately run down the ladders with all possible expedition, fetch'd my two guns, for they were both but at the foot of the ladders, as I observ'd above; and getting up again, with the same haste, to the top of the hill, I cross'd toward the sea; and having a very short cut, and all down hill, clapp'd myself in the way, between the pursuers, and the pursu'd; hollowing aloud to him that fled, who looking back, was at first perhaps as much frighted at me, as at them; but I beckon'd with my hand to him, to come back, and in the mean time I slowly advanc'd towards the two that follow'd; then rushing at once upon the foremost, I knock'd him down with the stock of my piece; I was loath to fire, because I would not have the rest hear; though at that distance it would not have been easily heard, and being out of sight of the smoke too, they would not have easily known what to make of it: Having knock'd this fellow down, the other who pursu'd with him stopp'd, as if he had been frighted; and I advanc'd a-pace towards him; but as I came nearer, I perceiv'd presently he had a bow and arrow, and was fitting it to shoot at me; so I was then necessitated to shoot at him first, which I did, and kill'd him at the first shoot; the poor savage who fled, but had stopp'd; though he saw both his enemies fallen, and kill'd, as he thought; yet was so frighted with the fire, and noise of my piece; that he stood stock still, and neither came forward or went backward, tho' he seem'd rather enclin'd to fly still, than to come on; I hollow'd again to him, and made signs to come forward, which he easily understood, and came a little way, then stopp'd again, and then a little farther, and stopp'd again, and I cou'd then perceive that he stood trembling, as if he had been taken prisoner, and had just been to be kill'd,[50] as his two enemies were; I

beckon'd him again to come to me, and gave him all the signs of encouragement that I could think of, and he came nearer and nearer, kneeling down
every ten or twelve steps, in token of acknowledgement for my saving his
life: I smil'd at him, and look'd pleasantly, and beckon'd to him to come
still nearer; at length he came close to me, and then he kneel'd down again,
kiss'd the ground, and laid his head upon the ground, and taking me by
the foot, set my foot upon his head; this, it seems, was in token of swearing
to be my slave for ever; I took him up, and made much of him, and
encourag'd him all I could. But there was more work to do yet, for I
perceiv'd the savage who I knock'd down, was not kill'd, but stunn'd with
the blow, and began to come to himself; so I pointed to him, and showing
him the savage, that he was not dead; upon this he spoke some words to
me, and tho' I could not understand them, yet I thought they were pleasant
to hear, for they were the first sound of a man's voice that I had heard, *my
own excepted*, for above twenty five years. But there was no time for such
reflections now the savage, who was knock'd down recover'd himself so
far, as to sit up upon the ground, and I perceiv'd that my savage began to
be afraid; but when I saw that, I presented my other piece at the man, as
if I would shoot him; upon this my savage, *for so I call him now*, made a
motion to me to lend him my sword, which hung naked in a belt by my
side; so I did; he no sooner had it, but he runs to his enemy, and at one
blow cut off his head as cleaverly, no executioner in *Germany*, could have
done it sooner or better; which I thought very strange, for one who I had
reason to believe never saw a sword in his life before, except their own
wooden swords; however it seems, as I learn'd afterwards, they make their
wooden swords so sharp, so heavy, and the wood is so hard, that they will
cut off heads even with them, ay and arms, and that at one blow too; when
he had done this, he comes laughing to me in sign of triumph, and brought
me the sword again, and with abundance of gestures which I did not
understand, laid it down with the head of the savage that he had kill'd,
just before me.

But that which astonish'd him most, was to know how I had kill'd the
other *Indian* so far off, so, pointing to him, he made signs to me to let him
go to him, so I bad him go, as well as I could; when he came to him, he
stood like one amaz'd, looking at him, turn'd him first on one side, then
on t'other, look'd at the wound the bullet had made, which, it seems, was
just in his breast, where it had made a hole, and no great quantity of blood
had follow'd, but he had bled inwardly, for he was quite dead; he took up

his bow and arrows, and came back, so I turn'd to go away, and beckon'd to him to follow me, making signs to him, that more might come after them.

Upon this he sign'd to me, that he should bury them with sand, that they might not be seen by the rest if they follow'd; and so I made signs again to him to do so; he fell to work, and in an instant he had scrap'd a hole in the sand, with his hands, big enough to bury the first in, and then dragg'd him into it, and cover'd him, and did so also by the other; I believe he had bury'd them both in a quarter of an hour; then calling him away, I carry'd him not to my castle, but quite away to my cave, on the farther part of the island; so I did not let my dream come to pass in that part, *viz.* That he came into my grove for shelter.

Here I gave him bread, and a bunch of raisins to eat, and a draught of water, which I found he was indeed in great distress for, by his running; and having refresh'd him, I made signs for him to go lie down and sleep; pointing to a place where I had laid a great parcel of rice straw, and a blanket upon it, which I used to sleep upon my self sometimes; so the poor creature laid down, and went to sleep.

He was a comely handsome fellow, perfectly well made, with straight strong limbs, not too large; tall and well shap'd, and, as I reckon, about twenty six years of age. He had a very good countenance, not a fierce and surly aspect, but seem'd to have something very manly in his face, and yet he had all the sweetness and softness of an *European* in his countenance too, especially when he smil'd. His hair was long and black, not curl'd like wool; his forehead very high, and large, and a great vivacity and sparkling sharpness in his eyes. The colour of his skin was not quite black, but very tawny; and yet not of an ugly yellow nauseous tawny, as the *Brasilians*, and *Virginians*, and other natives of *America* are; but of a bright kind of a dun olive colour, that had in it something very agreeable, tho' not very easy to describe. His face was round and plump; his nose small, not flat like the Negroes, a very good mouth, thin lips, and his fine teeth well set, and white as ivory. After he had slumber'd, rather than slept, about half an hour, he wak'd again, and comes out of the cave to me; for I had been milking my goats which I had in the enclosure just by: When he espy'd me, he came running to me, laying himself down again upon the ground, with all the possible signs of an humble thankful disposition, making a many antick gestures to shew it: At last he lays his head flat upon the ground, close to my foot, and sets my other foot upon his head, as he had done before; and after this, made all the signs to me of subjection, servitude, and submission imaginable, to let me know how, he would serve me as long as he liv'd; I understood him in many things, and let him know, I was very well pleas'd with him; in a little time I began to speak to him, and teach him to speak to me; and first, I made him know his name should be *Friday*, which was the day I sav'd his life; I call'd him so for the memory of the time; I likewise taught him to say *Master*, and then let him know that was to be my name; I likewise taught him to say, *Yes*, and *No*, and to know the meaning of them; I gave him some milk, in an earthen pot, and let him see me drink it before him, and sop my bread, in it; and I gave him a cake of bread, to do the like, which he quickly comply'd with, and made signs that it was very good for him.

I kept there with him all that night; but as soon as it was day, I beckon'd to him to come with me, and let him know I would give him some clothes, at which he seem'd very glad, for he was stark naked: As we went by the place where he had bury'd the two men, he pointed exactly to the place, and shew'd me the marks that he had made to find them again, making signs to me, that we should dig them up again, and eat them; at this I appear'd very angry, express'd my abhorrence of it, made as if I would vomit at the thoughts of it, and beckon'd with my hand to him to come away, which he did immediately, with great submission. I then led him up to the top of the hill, to see if his enemies were gone; and pulling out my glass, I look'd and saw plainly the place where they had been, but no appearance of them, or of their *canoes*; so that it was plain that they were gone, and had left their two comrades behind them, without any search after them.

But I was not content with this discovery; but having now more courage, and consequently more curiosity, I takes my man *Friday* with me, giving him the sword in his hand, with the bow and arrows at his back, which I found he could use very dextrously, making him carry one gun for me, and I two for myself, and away we march'd to the place, where these creatures had been; for I had a mind now to get some fuller intelligence of them: When I came to the place, my very blood ran chill in my veins, and my heart sunk within me at the horror of the spectacle: Indeed it was a dreadful sight, at least it was so to me, tho' *Friday* made nothing of it: The place was cover'd with human bones, the ground dy'd with their blood, great pieces of flesh left here and there, half eaten, mangled and scorch'd; and, in short, all the tokens of the triumphant feast they had been making there, after a victory over their enemies: I saw three skulls, five hands, and the bones of three or four legs and feet, and abundance of other parts of the bodies; and *Friday*, by his signs, made me understand, that they brought over four prisoners to feast upon; that three of them were eaten up, and that he, pointing to himself, was the fourth: That there had been a great battle between them, and their next king, whose subjects it seems he had been one of; and that they had taken a great number of prisoners, all which were carry'd to several places by those that had taken them in the fight, in order to feast upon them, as was done here by these wretches upon those they brought hither.

I caus'd *Friday* to gather all the skulls, bones, flesh, and whatever remain'd, and lay them together on a heap, and make a great fire upon it, and burn them all to ashes: I found *Friday* had still a hankering stomach after some of the flesh, and was still a cannibal in his nature; but I discover'd so much abhorrence at the very thoughts of it, and at the least appearance of it, that he durst not discover it; for I had, by some means let him know, that I would kill him if he offer'd it.

When we had done this, we came back to our castle, and there I fell to work for my man *Friday*; and first of all, I gave him a pair of linnen drawers, which I had out of the poor gunner's chest I mention'd, and which I found in the wreck; and which, with a little alteration fitted him very well; then I made him a jerkin of goat's-skin, as well as my skill would allow; and I was now grown a tolerable good taylor; and I gave him a cap, which I had made of a hare-skin, very convenient, and fashionable enough; and thus he was cloth'd for the present, tolerably well, and was mighty well pleas'd to see himself almost as well cloth'd as his master: It is true, he went awkwardly in these things at first; wearing the drawers was very awkward to him, and the sleeves of the wast-coat gall'd his shoulders, and the inside of his arms; but a little easing them, where he complain'd they hurt him, and using himself to them, at length he took to them very well.

The next day after I came home to my hutch with him, I began to consider where I should lodge him, and that I might do well for him, and yet be perfectly easy myself; I made a little tent for him in the vacant place between my two fortifications, in the inside of the last, and in the outside of the first; and as there was a door, or entrance there into my cave, I made a formal fram'd door case, and a door to it of boards, and set it up in the passage, a little within the entrance; and causing the door to open on the inside, I barr'd it up in the night, taking in my ladders too; so that *Friday* could no way come at me in the inside of my innermost wall, without making so much noise in getting over, that it must needs waken me; for my first wall had now a compleat roof over it of long poles, covering all my tent, and leaning up to the side of the hill, which was again laid cross with smaller sticks instead of laths, and then thatch'd over a great thickness, with the rice straw, which was strong like reeds; and at the hole or place which was left to go in or out by the ladder, I had plac'd a kind of trap-door, which if it had been attempted on the outside, would not have open'd at all, but would have fallen down, and made a great noise; and as to weapons, I took them all in to my side every night.

But I needed none of all this precaution; for never man had a more faithful, loving, sincere servant than *Friday* was to me; without passions, sullenness, or designs, perfectly oblig'd and engag'd; his very affections were ty'd to me, like those of a child to a father; and I dare say, he would have sacrific'd his life for the saving mine, upon any occasion whatsoever; the many testimonies he gave me of this, put it out of doubt, and soon convinc'd me, that I needed to use no precautions, as to my safety on his account.

This frequently gave me occasion to observe, and that with wonder, that however it had pleas'd God, in his Providence, and in the government of the works of his hands, to take from so great a part of the world of his creatures, the best uses to which their faculties, and the powers of their souls are adapted; yet that he has bestow'd upon them the same powers, the same reason, the same affections, the same sentiments of kindness and obligation, the same passions and resentments of wrongs; the same sense of gratitude, sincerity, fidelity, and all the capacities of doing good, and receiving good, that he has given to us; and that when he pleases to offer to them occasions of exerting these, they are as ready, nay, more ready to apply them to the right uses for which they were bestow'd, than we are. And this made me very melancholy sometimes, in reflecting as the several occasions presented, how mean a use we make of all these, even though we have these powers enlighten'd by the great lamp of instruction, the spirit of God, and by the knowledge of his Word, added to our understanding; and why it has pleas'd God to hide the like saving knowledge from so many millions of souls, who if I might judge by this poor savage, would make a much better use of it than we did.

From hence I sometimes was led too far to invade the sovereignty of *Providence*, and as it were arraign the justice of so arbitrary a disposition of things, that should hide that light from some, and reveal it to others, and yet expect a like duty from both: But I shut it up, and check'd my thoughts with this conclusion, (1st) that we did not know by what light and law these should be condemn'd; but that as God was necessarily, and by the nature of his being, infinitely holy and just, so it could not be, but that if these creatures were all sentenc'd to absence from himself, it was on account of sinning against that light which, as the Scripture says, was a law to themselves,[51] and by such rules as their consciences would acknowledge to be just, tho' the foundation was not discover'd to us: And (2d) that still as we are all the clay in the hand of the potter, no vessel could say to him, Why hast thou form'd me thus?[52]

But to return to my new companion; I was greatly delighted with him, and made it my business to teach him every thing that was proper to make him useful, handy, and helpful; but especially to make him speak, and understand me when I spake, and he was the aptest scholar that ever was, and particularly was so merry, so constantly diligent, and so pleas'd, when he could but understand me or make me understand him, that it was very pleasant to me to talk to him; and now my life began to be so easy, that I began to say to my self, that could I but have been safe from more savages, I cared not if I was never to remove from the place while I liv'd.

After I had been two or three days return'd to my castle, I thought that, in order to bring *Friday* off from his horrid way of feeding, and from the relish of a cannibal's stomach, I ought to let him taste other flesh; so I took him out with me one morning to the woods: I went indeed intending to kill a kid out of my own flock, and bring him home and dress it. But as I was going, I saw a she goat lying down in the shade, and two young kids sitting by her; I catch'd hold of *Friday*, hold, says I, stand still; and made signs to him not to stir, immediately I presented my piece, shot and kill'd one of the kids. The poor creature who had at a distance indeed seen me kill the savage, his enemy, but did not know, or could imagine how it was done, was sensibly surpris'd, trembled, and shook, and look'd so amaz'd, that I thought he would have sunk down. He did not see the kid I had shot at, or perceive I had kill'd it, but ripp'd up his wast-coat to feel if he was not wounded, and as I found, presently thought I was resolv'd to kill him; for he came and kneel'd down to me, and embracing my knees, said a great many things I did not understand; but I could easily see that the meaning was to pray me not to kill him.

I soon found a way to convince him that I would do him no harm, and taking him up by the hand laugh'd at him, and pointed to the kid which I had kill'd, beckon'd to him to run and fetch it, which he did; and while he was wondering and looking to see how the creature was kill'd, I loaded my gun again, and by and by I saw a great fowl like a hawk sit upon a tree within shot; so to let *Friday* understand a little what I would do, I call'd him to me again, pointed at the fowl which was indeed a parrot, tho' I thought it had been a hawk, I say, pointing to the parrot, and to my gun, and to the ground under the parrot, to let him see I would make it fall, I made him understand that I would shoot and kill that bird; accordingly I fir'd, and bad him look, and immediately he saw the parrot fall, he stood like one frighted again, notwithstanding all I had said to him; and I found he was the more amaz'd, because he did not see me put anything into the gun; but thought that there must be some wonderful fund of death and destruction in that thing, able to kill man, beast, bird, or anything, near or far off; and the astonishment this created in him was such, as could not wear off for a long time; and I believe, if I would have let him, he would have worshipp'd me and my gun: As for the gun itself, he would not so much as touch it for several days after; but would speak to it, and talk to it, as if it had answer'd him, when he was by himself; which, as I afterwards learn'd of him, was to desire it not to kill him.

Well, after his astonishment was a little over at this, I pointed to him to run and fetch the bird I had shot, which he did, but stay'd some time; for the parrot not being quite dead, was flutter'd away a good way off from the place where she fell; however, he found her, took her up, and brought her to me; and as I had perceiv'd his ignorance about the gun before, I took this advantage to charge the gun again, and not let him see me do it, that I might be ready for any other mark that might present; but nothing more offer'd at that time; so I brought home the kid, and the same evening took the skin off, and cut it out as well as I could; and having a pot for that purpose, I boil'd or stew'd some of the flesh, and made some very good broth; and after I had begun to eat some, I gave some to my man, who seem'd very glad of it, and lik'd it very well; but that which was strangest to him, was, to see me eat salt with it; he made a sign to me, that the salt was not good to eat, and putting a little into his own mouth, he seem'd to nauseate it, and would spit and sputter at it, washing his mouth with fresh water after it; on the other hand, I took some meat in my mouth without salt, and I pretended to spit and sputter for want of salt, as fast as he had done at the salt; but it would not do, he would never care for salt with his meat, or in his broth; at least, not a great while, and then but a very little.

Having thus fed him with boil'd meat and broth, I was resolv'd to feast him the next day with roasting a piece of the kid; this I did by hanging it before the fire, in a string, as I had seen many people do in *England*, setting two poles up, one on each side the fire, and one cross on the top, and tying the string to the cross-stick, letting the meat turn continually: This *Friday* admir'd very much; but when he came to taste the flesh, he took so many ways to tell me how well he lik'd it, that I could not but understand him; and at last he told me he would never eat man's flesh any more, which I was very glad to hear.

The next day I set him to work to beating some corn out, and sifting it in the manner I used to do, as I observ'd before; and he soon understood how to do it as well as I, especially after he had seen what the meaning of it was, and that it was to make bread of; for after that I let him see me make my bread, and bake it too, and in a little time *Friday* was able to do all the work for me, as well as I could do it myself.

I begun now to consider, that having two mouths to feed, instead of one, I must provide more ground for my harvest, and plant a larger quantity of corn than I used to do; so I mark'd out a larger piece of land, and began the fence in the same manner as before, in which *Friday* not only work'd very willingly, and very hard; but did it very cheerfully, and I told him what it was for, that it was for corn to make more bread, because he was now with me, and that I might have enough for him and myself too: He appear'd very sensible of that part, and let me know that he thought I had much more labour upon me on his account, than I had for my self; and that he would work the harder for me, if I would tell him what to do.

This was the pleasantest year of all the life I led in this place; *Friday* began to talk pretty well, and understand the names of almost every thing I had occasion to call for, and of every place I had to send him to, and talk'd a great deal to me; so that in short I began now to have some use for my tongue again, which indeed I had very little occasion for before; that is to say, *about speech*; besides the pleasure of talking to him, I had a singular satisfaction in the fellow himself; his simple unfeign'd honesty appear'd to me more and more every day, and I began really to love the creature; and on his side, I believe he lov'd me more than it was possible for him ever to love any thing before.

I had a mind once to try if he had any hankering inclination to his own country again, and having learn'd him *English* so well that he could answer me almost any questions, I ask'd him whether the nation that he belong'd to never conquer'd in battle? At which he smil'd, and said, Yes, yes, we always fight the better; that is, he meant always get the better in fight; and so we began the following discourse: You always fight the better, said I, How came you to be taken prisoner then, *Friday*?

Friday, My nation beat much, for all that.

Master, How beat; if your nation beat them, how come you to be taken?

Friday, They more many than my nation in the place where me was; they take one, two, three, and me; my nation over beat them in the yonder place, where me no was; there my nation take one, two, great thousand.

Master, But why did not your side recover you from the hands of your enemies then?

Friday, They run one, two, three, and me, and make go in the canoe; my nation have no canoe that time.

Master, Well, *Friday*, and what does your nation do with the men they take, do they carry them away, and eat them, as these did?

Friday, Yes, my nation eat man's too, eat all up.

Master, Where do they carry them?

Friday, Go to other place where they think.

Master, Do they come hither?

Friday, Yes, yes, they come hither; come other else place.

Master, Have you been here with them?

Friday, Yes, I been here; [*points to the* N. W. *side of the island,* which it seems was their side.]

By this I understood, that my man *Friday* had formerly been among the savages, who us'd to come on shore on the farther part of the island, on the same man eating occasions that he was now brought for; and some time after, when I took the courage to carry him to that side, being the same I formerly mention'd, he presently knew the place, and told me, he was there once when they eat up twenty men, two women, and one child; he could not tell twenty in *English*; but he numbered them by laying so many stones on a row, and pointing to me to tell them over.

I have told this passage, because it introduces what follows; that after I had had this discourse with him, I ask'd him how far it was from our island to the shore, and whether the *canoes* were not often lost; he told me, there was no danger, no *canoes* ever lost; but that after a little way out to the sea, there was a current, and a wind, always one way in the morning, the other in the afternoon.

This I understood to be no more than the sets of the tide, as going out, or coming in; but I afterwards understood, it was occasion'd by the great draft and reflux of the mighty river *Oroonooko*; in the mouth, or the gulph of which river, as I found afterwards, our island lay; and this land which I perceiv'd to the W. and N. W. was the great island *Trinidad*, on the *north* point of the mouth of the river: I ask'd *Friday* a thousand questions about the country, the inhabitants, the sea, the coast, and what nation were near; he told me all he knew with the greatest openness imaginable; I ask'd him the names of the several nations of his sort of people; but could get no other name than *Caribs*; from whence I easily understood, that these were the *Caribbees*,[53] which our maps place on that part of *America* which reaches from the mouth of the river *Oroonooko* to *Guiana*, and onwards to *St. Martha*:[54] He told me, that up a great way beyond the moon, that was, beyond the setting of the moon, which must be *W.* from their country, there dwelt white bearded men, like me, and pointed to my great whiskers, which I mention'd before; and that they had kill'd *much mans*, that was his word; by all which I understood, he meant the *Spaniards*, whose cruelties in *America* had been spread over the whole countries, and was remember'd by all the nations from father to son.

I enquir'd if he could tell me how I might come from this island, and get among those white men; he told me, yes, yes, I might go in *two canoe*; I could not understand what he meant, or make him describe to me what he meant by *two canoe*, till at last with great difficulty, I found he meant it must be in a large great boat, as big as *two canoes*.

This part of *Friday's* discourse began to relish with me very well, and from this time I entertain'd some hopes, that one time or other, I might find an opportunity to make my escape from this place; and that this poor savage might be a means to help me to do it.

During the long time that *Friday* had now been with me, and that he began to speak to me, and understand me, I was not wanting to lay a foundation of religious knowledge in his mind; particularly I ask'd him one time who made him? The poor creature did not understand me at all, but thought I had ask'd who was his father; but I took it by another handle, and ask'd him who made the sea, the ground we walk'd on, and the hills and woods; he told me it was one old *Benamuckee*, that liv'd beyond all: He could describe nothing of this great person, but that he was very old; much older he said than the sea, or the land; than the moon, or the stars: I ask'd him then, if this old person had made all things, why did not all things worship him? He look'd very grave, and with a perfect look of innocence, said, *All things do say O to him*: I ask'd him if the people, who die in his country, went away any where; he said, yes, they all went to *Benamuckee*; then I ask'd him whether these they eat up went thither too, he said yes.

From these things, I began to instruct him in the knowledge of the true God: I told him that the great maker of all things liv'd up there, pointing up towards Heaven: That he governs the world by the same power and Providence by which he had made it: That he was omnipotent, could do every thing for us, give every thing to us, take every thing from us; and thus by degrees I open'd his eyes. He listen'd with great attention, and receiv'd with pleasure the notion of *Jesus Christ* being sent to redeem us, and of the manner of making our prayers to God, and his being able to hear us, even into Heaven; he told me one day, that if our God could hear us up beyond the Sun, he must needs be a greater God than their *Benamuckee*, who liv'd but a little way off, and yet could not hear, till they went up to the great mountains where he dwelt, to speak to him; I ask'd him if ever he went thither, to speak to him; He said no, they never went that were young men; none went thither but the old men, who he call'd their *Oowocakee*, that is, as I made him explain it to me, their religious, or clergy, and that they went to say *O*, (so he call'd saying prayers) and then came back, and told them what *Benamuckee* said: By this I observ'd, that there is *priestcraft*, even amongst the most blinded ignorant pagans in the world; and the policy of making a secret religion, in order to preserve the veneration of the people to the clergy, is not only to be found in the *Roman*, but perhaps among all religions in the world, even among the most brutish and barbarous savages.

I endeavour'd to clear up this fraud, to my man *Friday*, and told him, that the pretence of their old men going up to the mountains to say *O* to their God *Benamuckee*, was a cheat, and their bringing word from thence what he said, was much more so; that if they met with any answer, or spake with any one there, it must be with an evil spirit: And then I enter'd into a long discourse with him about the Devil, the original of him, his rebellion against God, his enmity to man, the reason of it, his setting himself up in the dark parts of the world to be worship'd instead of God, and as God;[55] and the many stratagems he made use of to delude mankind to his ruin; how he had a secret access to our passions, and to our affections, to adapt his snares so to our inclinations, as to cause us even to be our own tempters, and to run upon our destruction by our own choice.

I found it was not so easy to imprint right notions in his mind about the Devil, as it was about the being of a God. Nature assisted all my arguments to evidence to him, even the necessity of a great first cause[56] and over-ruling governing power; a secret directing Providence, and of the equity and justice of paying homage to him that made us, and the like. But there appear'd nothing of all this in the notion of an evil spirit, of his original, his being, his nature, and above all, of his inclination to do evil, and to draw us in to do so too; and the poor creature puzzl'd me once in such a manner, by a question meerly natural and innocent, that I scarce knew what to say to him. I had been talking a great deal to him of the power of God, his omnipotence, his dreadful aversion to sin, his being a consuming fire[57] to the workers of iniquity;[58] how, as he had made us all, he could destroy us and all the world in a moment; and he listen'd with great seriousness to me all the while.

After this, I had been telling him how the Devil was God's enemy in the hearts of men, and used all his malice and skill to defeat the good designs of Providence, and to ruin the kingdom of Christ in the world, and the like. Well, says *Friday*, but you say, God is so strong, so great, is he not much strong, much might as the Devil? Yes, yes, says I, *Friday*, God is stronger than the Devil, God is above the Devil, and therefore we pray to God to tread him down under our feet, and enable us to resist his temptations, and quench his fiery darts.[59] *But*, says he again, *if God much strong, much might as the Devil, why God no kill the Devil, so make him no more do wicked?*

I was strangely surpris'd at his question, and after all, tho' I was now an old man, yet I was but a young doctor, and ill enough qualify'd for a casuist, or a solver of difficulties: And at first I could not tell what to say, so I pretended not to hear him, and ask'd him what he said? But he was too earnest for an answer to forget his question; so that he repeated it in the very same broken words, as above. By this time I had recovered myself a little, and I said, *God will at last punish him severely; he is reserv'd for the judgment, and is to be cast into the bottomless-pit, to dwell with everlasting fire.*[60] This did not satisfie *Friday*, but he returns upon me, repeating my words, RESERVE, AT LAST, *me no understand; but, why not kill the Devil now, not kill great ago?* You may as well ask me, *said I*, why God does not kill you and I, when we do wicked things here that offend him? We are preserv'd to repent and be pardon'd: He muses a while at this; *well, well,* says he, mighty affectionately, *that well; so you, I, Devil, all wicked, all preserve, repent, God pardon all*. Here I was run down again by him to the last degree, and it was a testimony to me, how the meer notions of Nature, though they will guide reasonable creatures to the knowledge of a God, and of a worship or homage due to the supreme being, of God as the consequence of our nature; yet nothing but divine Revelation can form the knowledge of *Jesus Christ*, and of a redemption purchas'd for us, of a mediator of the new covenant,[61] and of an intercessor, at the foot-stool of God's throne;[62] I say, nothing but a revelation from Heaven, can form these in the soul, and that therefore the Gospel of our Lord and Saviour *Jesus Christ*; I mean, the Word of God, and the Spirit of God promis'd for the guide and sanctifier of his people, are the absolutely necessary instructors of the souls of men, in the saving knowledge of God, and the means of salvation.

I therefore diverted the present discourse between me and my man, rising up hastily, as upon some sudden occasion of going out; then sending him for something a good way off, I seriously pray'd to God, that he would enable me to instruct savingly this poor savage, assisting by his spirit the heart of the poor ignorant creature, to receive the light of the knowledge of God in *Christ*, reconciling him to himself, and would guide me to speak so to him from the Word of God, as his conscience might be convinc'd, his eyes open'd, and his soul sav'd. When he came again to me, I entred into a long discourse with him upon the subject of the redemption of man by the Saviour of the world, and of the doctrine of the Gospel preach'd from Heaven, *viz.* of repentance towards God, and faith in our blessed Lord *Jesus*. I then explain'd to him, as well as I could, why our Blessed Redeemer took not on him the nature of angels, but the seed of *Abraham*,[63] and how for that reason the fallen angels had no share in the redemption; that he came only to the lost sheep of the house of *Israel*,[64] and the like.

I had, *God knows*, more sincerity than knowledge, in all the methods I took for this poor creature's instruction, and must acknowledge what I believe all that act upon the same principle will find, that in laying things open to him, I really inform'd and instructed myself in many things, that either I did not know, or had not fully consider'd before; but which occurr'd naturally to my mind, upon my searching into them, for the information of this poor savage; and I had more affection in my enquiry after things upon this occasion, than ever I felt before; so that whether this poor wild wretch was the better for me, or no, I had great reason to be thankful that ever he came to me: My grief set lighter upon me, my habitation grew comfortable to me beyond measure; and when I reflected that in this solitary life, which I had been confin'd to, I had not only been mov'd myself to look up to Heaven, and to seek to the hand that had brought me there; but was now to be made an instrument under Providence to save the life, and *for ought I knew*, the soul of a poor savage, and bring him to the true knowledge of religion, and of the Christian doctrine, that he might know Christ Jesus, *to know whom is life eternal*.[65] I say, when I reflected upon all these things, a secret joy run through every part of my soul, and I frequently rejoyc'd that ever I was brought to this place, which I had so often thought the most dreadful of all afflictions that could possibly have befallen me.

In this thankful frame I continu'd all the remainder of my time, and the conversation which employ'd the hours between *Friday* and I, was such, as made the three years which we liv'd there together perfectly and compleatly happy, *if any such thing as compleat happiness can be form'd in a sublunary state*. The savage was now a good Christian, a much better than I; though I have reason to hope, and bless God for it, that we were equally penitent, and comforted restor'd penitents; we had here the Word of God to read, and no farther off from his spirit to instruct, than if we had been in *England*.

I always apply'd myself to reading the Scripture, to let him know, as well as I could, the meaning of what I read; and he again, by his serious enquiries and questioning, made me, *as I said before*, a much better scholar in the Scripture knowledge, than I should ever have been by my own private meer reading. Another thing I cannot refrain from observing here also from experience, in this retir'd part of my life, *viz.* how infinite and inexpressible a blessing it is, that the knowledge of God, and of the doctrine of salvation by *Christ Jesus*, is so plainly laid down in the Word of God, so easy to be receiv'd and understood: That as the bare reading the Scripture made me capable of understanding enough of my duty, to carry me directly on to the great work of sincere repentance for my sins, and laying hold of a Saviour for life and salvation, to a stated reformation in practice, and obedience to all God's commands, and this without any teacher or instructer; I mean, human; so the same plain instruction sufficiently serv'd to the enlightning this savage creature, and bringing him to be such a Christian, as I have known few equal to him in my life.

As to all the disputes, wranglings, strife, and contention, which has happen'd in the world about religion, whether niceties in doctrines, or schemes of church government, they were all perfectly useless to us, as for ought I can yet see, they have been to all the rest in the world: We had the *sure guide* to Heaven, *viz.* the Word of God; and we had, *blessed be God*, comfortable views of the spirit of God, teaching and instructing us by his Word, *leading us into all truth*,[66] and making us both willing and obedient to the instruction of his Word; and I cannot see the least use that the greatest knowledge of the disputed points in religion, which have made such confusions in the world, would have been to us, if we could have obtain'd it; but I must go on with the historical part of things, and take every part in its order.

After *Friday* and I became more intimately acquainted, and that he could understand almost all I said to him, and speak fluently, tho' in broken *English*, to me; I acquainted him with my own story, or at least so much of it as related to my coming into the place, how I had liv'd there, and how long. I let him into the mystery, for such it was to him, of gunpowder, and bullet, and taught him how to shoot: I gave him a knife, which he was wonderfully delighted with, and I made him a belt, with a frog hanging to it, such as in *England* we wear hangers in; and in the frog, instead of a hanger, I gave him a hatchet, which was not only as good a weapon in some cases, but much more useful upon other occasions.

I describ'd to him the country of *Europe*, and particularly *England*, which I came from; how we liv'd, how we worshipp'd God, how we behav'd to one another; and how we traded in ships to all parts of the world: I gave him an account of the wreck which I had been on board of, and shew'd him, as near as I could, the place where she lay; but she was all beaten in pieces before, and gone.

I shew'd him the ruins of our boat, which we lost when we escap'd, and which I could not stir with my whole strength then, but was now fallen almost all to pieces: Upon seeing this boat, *Friday* stood musing a great while, and said nothing; I ask'd him what it was he study'd upon; at last, says he, *me see such boat like come to place at my nation.*

I did not understand him a good while; but at last, when I had examin'd farther into it, I understood by him, that a boat, such as that had been, came on shore upon the country where he liv'd; that is, as he explain'd it, was driven thither by stress of weather: I presently imagin'd, that some *European* ship must have been cast away upon their coast, and the boat might get loose, and drive ashore; but was so dull, that I never once thought of men making escape from a wreck thither, much less whence they might come; so I only enquir'd after a description of the boat.

Friday describ'd the boat to me well enough; but brought me better to understand him, when he added with some warmth, *we save the white mans from drown*: Then I presently ask'd him, if there was any white mans, as he call'd them, in the boat; *yes*, he said, *the boat full white mans*: I ask'd him how many; he told upon his fingers seventeen: I ask'd him then what became of them; he told me, *they live, they dwell at my nation*.

This put new thoughts into my head; for I presently imagin'd, that these might be the men belonging to the ship that was cast away in sight of *my island*, as I now call it; and who after the ship was struck on the rock, and they saw her inevitably lost, had sav'd themselves in their boat, and were landed upon that wild shore among the savages.

Upon this, I enquir'd of him more critically what was become of them? He assur'd me they liv'd still there; that they had been there about four years; that the savages let them alone, and gave them victuals to live. I ask'd him, how it came to pass they did not kill them and eat them? He said, *No, they make brother with them*; that is, as I understood him, a truce: And then he added, *they no eat mans but when make the war fight*; that is to say, they never eat any men but such as come to fight with them, and are taken in battle.

It was after this some considerable time, that being on the top of the hill, at the *east* side of the island, from whence, as I have said, I had in a clear day discover'd the main, or continent of *America*; *Friday*, the weather being very serene, looks very earnestly towards the main land, and in a kind of surprise, falls a jumping and dancing, and calls out to me, for I was at some distance from him: I ask'd him what was the matter? *O, joy!* says he, *O glad! There see my country, there my nation!*

I observ'd an extraordinary sense of pleasure appear'd in his face, and his eyes sparkled, and his countenance discover'd a strange eagerness, as if he had a mind to be in his own country again; and this observation of mine, put a great many thoughts into me, which made me at first not so easy about my new man *Friday* as I was before; and I made no doubt, but that if *Friday* could get back to his own nation again, he would not only forget all his religion, but all his obligation to me; and would be forward enough to give his countrymen an account of me, and come back perhaps, with a hundred or two of them, and make a feast upon me, at which he might be as merry as he used to be with those of his enemies, when they were taken in war.

But I wrong'd the poor honest creature very much, for which I was very sorry afterwards. However, as my jealousy increas'd, and held me some weeks, I was a little more circumspect, and not so familiar and kind to him as before; in which I was certainly in the wrong too, the honest grateful creature having no thought about it, but what consisted with the best principles, both as a religious Christian, and as a grateful friend, as appear'd afterwards to my full satisfaction.

While my jealousy of him lasted, you may be sure I was every day pumping him, to see if he would discover any of the new thoughts, which I suspected were in him; but I found every thing he said was so honest, and so innocent, that I could find nothing to nourish my suspicion; and, in spite of all my uneasiness he made me at last entirely his own again, nor did he in the least perceive that I was uneasy, and therefore I could not suspect him of deceit.

One day walking up the same hill, but the weather being hazy at sea, so that we could not see the continent, I call'd to him, and said, *Friday*, do not you wish yourself in your own country, your own nation? *Yes*, he said, *I be much O glad to be at my own nation*. What would you do there, said I, would you turn wild again, eat mens flesh again, and be a savage as you were before. He lookt full of concern, and shaking his head, said, *No, no*, Friday *tell them to live good, tell them to pray God, tell them to eat corn bread, cattle flesh, milk, no eat man again*: Why then, said I to him, *They will kill you*. He look'd grave at that, and then said, *No, they no kill me, they willing love learn*: He meant by this, they would be willing to learn. He added, they learn'd much of the bearded mans that come in the boat. Then I ask'd him if he would go back to them? He smil'd at that, and told me he could not swim so far. I told him I would make a *canoe* for him. He told me, he would go if I would go with him. I go! says I, why, they will eat me if I come there? *No, no*, says he, *me make they no eat you, me make they much love you*. He meant, he would tell them how I had kill'd his enemies, and sav'd his life, and so he would make them love me; then he told me, as well as he could, how kind they were to seventeen white men, or bearded men, as he call'd them, who came on shore there in distress.

From this time I confess I had a mind to venture over, and see if I could possibly join with these bearded men, who I made no doubt were *Spaniards* or *Portuguese*; not doubting but if I could we might find some method to escape from thence, being upon the continent, and a good company together, better than I could from an island 40 miles off the shore, and alone without help. So, after some days, I took *Friday* to work again, by way of discourse, and told him I would give him a boat to go back to his own nation; and accordingly I carry'd him to my frigate which lay on the other side of the island, and having clear'd it of water, for I always kept it sunk in the water; I brought it out, shew'd it him, and we both went into it.

I found he was a most dextrous fellow at managing it, would make it go almost as swift and fast again as I could; so when he was in, I said to him, Well now, *Friday*, shall we go to your nation? He look'd very dull at my saying so, which, it seems, was, because he thought the boat too small to go so far. I told him then I had a bigger; so the next day I went to the place where the first boat lay which I had made, but which I could not get into water: He said that was big enough; but then, as I had taken no care of it, and it had lain two or three and twenty years there, the sun had split and dry'd it, that it was in a manner rotten. *Friday* told me, such a boat would do very well, and would carry *much enough vittle, drink, bread*, that was his way of talking.

Upon the whole, I was by this time so fix'd upon my design of going over with him to the continent, that I told him we would go and make one as big as that, and he should go home in it. He answer'd not one word, but look'd very grave and sad: I ask'd him what was the matter with him? He ask'd me again thus; *Why, you angry mad with* Friday, *what me done?* I ask'd him what he meant; I told him I was not angry with him at all. *No angry! No angry!* says he, repeating the words several times, *Why send* Friday *home away to my nation?* Why, says I, *Friday*, did you not say you wish'd you were there? *Yes, yes*, says he, *wish be both there, no wish* Friday *there, no Master there*. In a word, he would not think of going there without me; I go there, *Friday*, says I, what shall I do there? He turn'd very quick upon me at this: *You do great deal much good*, says he, *you teach wild mans be good sober tame mans; you tell them know God, pray God, and live new life. Alas! Friday*, (says I), *thou knowest not what thou sayest, I am but an ignorant man my self. Yes, yes*, says he, *you teachee me good, you teachee them good. No, no*, Friday, says I, *you shall go without me, leave me here to live by my self, as I did before*. He look'd confus'd again at that word, and running to one of the hatchets which he used to wear, he takes it up hastily, comes and gives it me, *What must I do with this?* says I to him. *You take, kill*

Friday; (says he.) *What must I kill you for?* said I again. He returns very quick, *What you send* Friday *away for? take, kill* Friday, *no send* Friday *away*. This he spoke so earnestly, that I saw tears stand in his eyes: In a word, I so plainly discover'd the utmost affection in him to me, and a firm resolution in him, that I told him then, and often after, that I would never send him away from me, if he was willing to stay with me.

Upon the whole, as I found by all his discourse a settled affection to me, and that nothing should part him from me, so I found all the foundation of his desire to go to his own country, was laid in his ardent affection to the people, and his hopes of my doing them good; a thing which as I had no notion of my self, so I had not the least thought, or intention, or desire of undertaking it. But still I found a strong inclination to my attempting an escape as above, founded on the supposition gather'd from the discourse, (*viz.*) That there were seventeen bearded men there; and therefore, without any more delay, I went to work with *Friday* to find out a great tree proper to fell, and make a large periagua or canoe to undertake the voyage. There were trees enough in the island to have built a little fleet, not of periaguas and canoes, but even of good large vessels. But the main thing I look'd at, was to get one so near the water that we might launch it when it was made, to avoid the mistake I committed at first.

At last, *Friday* pitch'd upon a tree, for I found he knew much better than I what kind of wood was fittest for it; nor can I tell, to this day, what wood to call the tree we cut down, except that it was very like the tree we call *Fustic*, or between that and the *Nicaragua* Wood, for it was much of the same colour and smell. *Friday* was for burning the hollow or cavity of this tree out to make it for a boat. But I shew'd him how rather to cut it out with tools; which, after I had shew'd him how to use, he did very handily, and in about a month's hard labour, we finish'd it, and made it very handsome, especially when with our axes, which I shew'd him how to handle, we cut and hew'd the out-side into the true shape of a boat; after this, however, it cost us near a fortnight's time to get her along as it were inch by inch upon great rolwlers into the water. But when she was in, she would have carry'd twenty men with great ease.

When she was in the water, and tho' she was so big, it amaz'd me to see with what dexterity and how swift my man *Friday* would manage her, turn her, and paddle her along; so I ask'd him if he would, and if we might venture over in her; *Yes*, he said, *he venture over in her very well, tho' great blow wind*. However, I had a farther design that he knew nothing of, and that was to make a mast and sail, and to fit her with an anchor and cable: As to a mast, that was easy enough to get; so I pitch'd upon a strait young cedar-tree, which I found near the place, and which there was great plenty of in the island; and I set *Friday* to work to cut it down, and gave him directions how to shape and order it. But as to the sail, that was my particular care; I knew I had old sails, or rather pieces of old sails enough; but as I had had them now six and twenty years by me, and had not been very careful to preserve them, not imagining that I should ever have this kind of use for them, I did not doubt but they were all rotten, and indeed most of them were so; however, I found two pieces which appear'd pretty good, and with these I went to work, and with a great deal of pains, and awkward tedious stitching (you may be sure) for want of needles, I at length made a three-corner'd ugly thing, like what we call in *England*, a shoulder of mutton sail, to go with a boom at bottom, and a little short sprit at the top, such as usually our ship's long-boats sail with, and such as I best knew how to manage; because it was such a one as I had to the boat, in which I made my escape from *Barbary*, as related in the first part of my story.

I was near two months performing this last work, *viz.* rigging and fitting my mast and sails; for I finish'd them very compleat, making a small stay, and a sail, or foresail to it, to assist, if we should turn to windward; and which was more than all, I fix'd a rudder to the stern of her, to steer with; and though I was but a bungling shipwright, yet as I knew the usefulness, and even necessity of such a thing, I apply'd myself with so much pains to do it, that at last I brought it to pass, though considering the many dull contrivances I had for it that fail'd, I think it cost me almost as much labour as making the boat.

After all this was done too, I had my man *Friday* to teach as to what belong'd to the navigation of my boat; for tho' he knew very well how to paddle a *canoe*, he knew nothing what belong'd to a sail, and a rudder; and was the most amaz'd when he saw me work the boat too and again in the sea by the rudder, and how the sail gyb'd, and fill'd this way, or that way, as the course we sail'd chang'd; I say, when he saw this, he stood like one astonish'd, and amaz'd: However, with a little use, I made all these things familiar to him; and he became an expert sailor, except that as to the compass, I could make him understand very little of that. On the other hand, as there was very little cloudy weather, and seldom or never any fogs in those parts, there was the less occasion for a compass, seeing the stars were always to be seen by night, and the shore by day, except in the rainy seasons, and then no body cared to stir abroad, either by land or sea.

I was now entered on the seven and twentieth year of my captivity in this place; tho' the three last years that I had this creature with me, ought rather to be left out of the account, my habitation being quite of another kind than in all the rest of the time. I kept the anniversary of my landing here with the same thankfulness to God for his mercies, as at first; and if I had such cause of acknowledgment at first, I had much more so now, having such additional testimonies of the care of Providence over me, and the great hopes I had of being effectually and speedily deliver'd; for I had an invincible impression upon my thoughts, that my deliverance was at hand, and that I should not be another year in this place: However, I went on with my husbandry, digging, planting, fencing, as usual; I gather'd and cur'd my grapes, and did every necessary thing as before.

The rainy season was in the mean time upon me, when I kept more within doors than at other times; so I had stow'd our new vessel as secure as we could, bringing her up into the creek, where, as I said, in the beginning, I landed my rafts from the ship, and haling her up to the shore, at high water mark, I made my man *Friday* dig a little dock, just big enough to hold her, and just deep enough to give her water enough to float in; and then, when the tide was out, we made a strong dam cross the end of it, to keep the water out; and so she lay dry, as to the tide, from the sea; and to keep the rain off, we laid a great many boughs of trees, so thick, that she was as well thatch'd as a house; and thus we waited for the month of *November* and *December*, in which I design'd to make my adventure.

When the settled season began to come in, as the thought of my design return'd with the fair weather, I was preparing daily for the voyage; and the first thing I did, was to lay by a certain quantity of provisions, being the stores for our voyage; and intended in a week or a fortnight's time, to open the dock, and launch out our boat. I was busy one morning upon some thing of this kind, when I call'd to *Friday*, and bid him go to the sea shore, and see if he could find a turtle, or tortoise, a thing which we generally got once a week, for the sake of the eggs, as well as the flesh: *Friday* had not been long gone, when he came running back, and flew over my outer wall, or fence, like one that felt not the ground, or the steps he set his feet on; and before I had time to speak to him, he cries out to me, *O Master! Master! O sorrow! O bad!* What's the matter, *Friday*, says I; *O yonder, there*, says he, *one, two, three canoe! one, two, three!* By his way of speaking, I concluded there were six; but on enquiry, I found it was but three: Well, *Friday*, says I, do not be frighted; so I heartned him up as well as I could: However, I saw the poor fellow was most terribly scar'd; for nothing ran in his head but that they were come to look for him, and would cut him in pieces, and eat him; and the poor fellow trembled so, that I scarce knew what to do with him: I comforted him as well as I could, and told him I was in as much danger as he, and that they would eat me as well as him; but, says I, *Friday, we must resolve to fight them; Can you fight*, Friday? *Me shoot*, says he, *but there come many great number*. No matter for that, said I again, our guns will fright them that we do not kill; so I ask'd him, Whether if I resolv'd to defend him, he would defend me, and stand by me, and do just as I bid him? He said, *me die, when you bid die, Master*; so I went and fetch'd a good dram of rum, and gave him; for I had been so good a husband of my rum, that I had a great deal left: When he had drank it, I made him take the two fowling-pieces, which we always carry'd, and load them with large swan-shot, as big as small pistol bullets; then I took four musquets, and loaded them with two slugs, and five small bullets each; and my two pistols I loaded with a brace of bullets each; I hung my great sword as usual, naked by my side, and gave *Friday* his hatchet.

When I had thus prepar'd my self, I took my perspective-glass, and went up to the side of the hill, to see what I could discover; and I found quickly, by my glass, that there were one and twenty savages, three prisoners, and three canoes; and that their whole business seem'd to be the triumphant banquet upon these three human bodies, (a barbarous feast indeed) but nothing more than as I had observ'd was usual with them.

I observ'd also, that they were landed not where they had done, when *Friday* made his escape; but nearer to my creek, where the shore was low, and where a thick wood came close almost down to the sea: This, with the abhorrence of the inhuman errand these wretches came about, fill'd me with such indignation, that I came down again to *Friday*, and told him, I was resolv'd to go down to them, and kill them all; and ask'd him, if he would stand by me? He was now gotten over his fright, and his spirits being a little rais'd with the dram I had given him, he was very cheerful, and told me, as before, *he would die, when I bid die*.

In this fit of fury, I took first and divided the arms which I had charg'd, as before, between us; I gave *Friday* one pistol to stick in his girdle, and three guns upon his shoulder; and I took one pistol, and the other three my self; and in this posture we march'd out: I took a small bottle of rum in my pocket, and gave *Friday* a large bag, with more powder and bullet; and, as to orders, I charg'd him to keep close behind me, and not to stir, or shoot, or do any thing, till I bid him; and in the mean time, not to speak a word: In this posture I fetch'd a compass to my right hand of near a mile, as well to get over the creek, as to get into the wood; so that I might come within shot of them before I should be discover'd, which I had seen by my glass, it was easy to do.

While I was making this march, my former thoughts returning, I began to abate my resolution; I do not mean, that I entertain'd any fear of their number; for as they were naked, unarm'd wretches, 'tis certain I was superior to them; nay, though I had been alone; but it occurr'd to my thoughts, What call? What occasion? much less, What necessity I was in to go and dip my hands in blood, to attack people, who had neither done, or intended me any wrong? Who, as to me, were innocent, and whose barbarous customs were their own disaster, being in them a token indeed of God's having left them, with the other nations of that part of the world, to such stupidity and to such inhuman courses; but did not call me to take upon me to be a judge of their actions, much less an executioner of his justice; that whenever he thought fit, he would take the cause into his own hands, and by national vengeance punish them as a people for national crimes; but that in the meantime, it was none of my business; that it was true, *Friday* might justify it, because he was a declar'd enemy, and in a state of war with those very particular people; and it was lawful for him to attack them; but I could not say the same with respect to me. These things were so warmly press'd upon my thoughts, all the way as I went, that I resolv'd I would only go and place myself near them, that I might observe their barbarous feast, and that I would act then as God should direct; but that unless something offer'd that was more a call to me than yet I knew of, I would not meddle with them.

With this resolution I enter'd the wood, and with all possible wariness and silence, *Friday* following close at my heels, I march'd till I came to the skirt of the wood, on the side which was next to them; only that one corner of the wood lay between me and them; here I call'd softly to *Friday*, and shewing him a great tree, which was just at the corner of the wood, I bad him go to the tree, and bring me word if he could see there plainly what they were doing; he did so, and came immediately back to me, and told me they might be plainly view'd there; that they were all about their fire, eating the flesh of one of their prisoners; and that another lay bound upon the sand, a little from them, which he said they would kill next, and which fir'd all the very soul within me; he told me it was not one of their nation; but one of the bearded men, who he had told me of, that came to their country in the boat: I was fill'd with horror at the very naming the white-bearded man, and going to the tree, I saw plainly, by my glass, a white man who lay upon the beach of the sea, with his hands and his feet ty'd, with flags, or things like rushes; and that he was an *European*, and had clothes on.

There was another tree, and a little thicket beyond it, about fifty yards nearer to them than the place where I was, which by going a little way about, I saw I might come at undiscover'd, and that then I should be within half shot of them; so I with-held my passion, though I was indeed enrag'd to the highest degree, and going back about twenty paces, I got behind some bushes, which held all the way, till I came to the other tree; and then I came to a little rising ground, which gave me a full view of them, at the distance of about eighty yards.

I had now not a moment to lose; for nineteen of the dreadful wretches sat upon the ground, all close huddled together, and had just sent the other two to butcher the poor *Christian*, and bring him perhaps limb by limb to their fire, and they were stoop'd down to untie the bands, at his feet; I turn'd to *Friday*, now *Friday*, said I, do as I bid thee; *Friday* said he would; then, *Friday*, says I, do exactly as you see me do, fail in nothing; so I set down one of the musquets, and the fowling-piece, upon the ground, and *Friday* did the like by his; and with the other musquet, I took my aim at the savages, bidding him do the like; then asking him if he was ready? He said, yes, then fire at them, said I; and the same moment I fir'd also.

Friday took his aim so much better than I, that on the side that he shot, he kill'd two of them, and wounded three more; and on my side, I kill'd one and wounded two. They were, you may be sure, in a dreadful consternation; and all of them, who were not hurt, jump'd up upon their feet, but did not immediately know which way to run, or which way to look; for they knew not from whence their destruction came: *Friday* kept his eyes close upon me, that as I had bid him, he might observe what I did; so as soon as the first shot was made, I threw down the piece, and took up the fowling-piece, and *Friday* did the like; he saw me cock, and present, he did the same again; are you ready, *Friday*? said I; yes, says he; let fly then, says I, in the name of God, and with that I fir'd again among the amaz'd wretches, and so did *Friday*; and as our pieces were now loaden with what I call'd swan shot, or small pistol bullets, we found only two drop; but so many were wounded, that they ran about yelling and skreaming like mad creatures, all bloody, and miserably wounded, most of them; whereof three more fell quickly after, though not quite dead.

Now *Friday*, says I, laying down the discharg'd pieces, and taking up the musquet, which was yet loaden; follow me, says I, which he did, with a great deal of courage; upon which I rush'd out of the wood, and shew'd myself, and *Friday* close at my foot; as soon as I perceiv'd they saw me, I shouted as loud as I could, and bad *Friday* do so too; and running as fast as I could, *which, by the way, was not very fast, being loaden with arms as I was*, I made directly towards the poor victim, who was, as I said, lying upon the beach, or shore, between the place where they sat, and the sea; the two butchers, who were just going to work with him, had left him, at the surprise of our first fire, and fled in a terrible fright to the sea side, and had jump'd into a *canoe*, and three more of the rest made the same way; I turn'd to *Friday*, and bid him step forwards, and fire at them; he understood me immediately, and running about forty yards to be near them, he shot at them, and I thought he had kill'd them all; for I saw them all fall of a heap into the boat; though I saw two of them up again quickly: However, he kill'd two of them, and wounded the third; so that he lay down in the bottom of the boat, as if he had been dead.

While my man *Friday* fir'd at them, I pull'd out my knife, and cut the flags that bound the poor victim, and loosing his hands, and feets, I lifted him up, and ask'd him, in the *Portuguese* tongue, what he was? He answer'd in *Latin, Christianus*; but was so weak, and faint, that he could scarce stand, or speak; I took my bottle out of my pocket, and gave it him, making signs that he should drink, which he did; and I gave him a piece of bread, which he eat; then I ask'd him, what countryman he was? And he said, *Espagniole*; and being a little recover'd, let me know by all the signs he could possibly make, how much he was in my debt for his deliverance; *Seignior*, said I, with as much *Spanish* as I could make up, we will talk afterwards; but we must fight now; if you have any strength left, take this pistol, and sword, and lay about you; he took them very thankfully, and no sooner had he the arms in his hands, but as if they had put new vigour into him, he flew upon his murtherers, like a fury, and had cut two of them in pieces in an instant; for the truth is, as the whole was a surprise to them; so the poor creatures were so much frighted with the noise of our pieces, that they fell down for meer amazement and fear; and had no more power to attempt their own escape, than their flesh had to resist our shot; and that was the case of those five that *Friday* shot at in the boat; for as three of them fell with the hurt they receiv'd; so the other two fell with the fright.

I kept my piece in my hand still, without firing, being willing to keep my charge ready; because I had given the *Spaniard* my pistol, and swords; so I call'd to *Friday*, and bad him run up to the tree, from whence we first fir'd, and fetch the arms which lay there, that had been discharg'd, which he did with great swiftness; and then giving him my musquet, I sat down myself to load all the rest again, and bad them come to me when they wanted: While I was loading these pieces, there happen'd a fierce engagement between the *Spaniard*, and one of the savages, who made at him with one of their great wooden swords, the same weapon that was to have kill'd him before, if I had not prevented it: The *Spaniard*, who was as bold, and as brave as could be imagin'd, though weak, had fought this *Indian* a good while, and had cut him two great wounds on his head; but the savage being a stout lusty fellow, closing in with him, had thrown him down (being faint) and was wringing my sword out of his hand, when the *Spaniard*, tho' undermost wisely quitting the sword, drew the pistol from his girdle, shot the savage through the body, and kill'd him upon the spot; before I, who was running to help him, could come near him.

Friday being now left to his liberty, pursu'd the flying wretches with no weapon in his hand but his hatchet; and with that he dispatch'd those three, who, as I said before, were wounded at first and fallen, and all the rest he could come up with, and the *Spaniard* coming to me for a gun, I gave him one of the fowling-pieces, with which he pursu'd two of the savages, and wounded them both; but as he was not able to run, they both got from him into the wood, where *Friday* pursu'd them, and kill'd one of them; but the other was too nimble for him, and tho' he was wounded, yet had plung'd himself into the sea, and swam with all his might off to those two who were left in the *canoe*, which three in the *canoe*, with one wounded, who we know not whether he dy'd or no, were all that escap'd our hands of one and twenty: The account of the rest is as follows:

3 Kill'd at our first shot from the tree.
2 Kill'd at the next shot.
2 Kill'd by *Friday* in the boat.
2 Kill'd by *ditto*, of those at first wounded.

1 Kill'd by *ditto*, in the wood.

3 Kill'd by the *Spaniard*.

4 Kill'd, being found dropp'd here and there of their wounds, or
 kill'd by *Friday* in his chase of them.

4 Escap'd in the boat, whereof one wounded if not dead.
___
21 In all.

Those that were in the *canoe*, work'd hard to get out of gun-shot; and
though *Friday* made two or three shot at them, I did not find that he hit
any of them. *Friday* would fain have had me take one of their *canoes*, and
pursu'd them; and indeed I was very anxious about their escape, least
carrying the news home to their people, they should come back, perhaps,
with two or three hundred of their *canoes*, and devour us by meer multitude;
so I consented to pursue them by sea, and running to one of their *canoes*,
I jump'd in, and bad *Friday* follow me; but when I was in the *canoe*, I was
surpris'd to find another poor creature lye there alive, bound hand and
foot, as the *Spaniard* was, for the slaughter, and almost dead with fear, not
knowing what the matter was; for he had not been able to look up over the
side of the boat, he was ty'd so hard, neck and heels, and had been ty'd so
long, that he had really but little life in him.

I immediately cut the twisted flags, or rushes, which they had bound
him with, and would have helped him up; but he could not stand, or speak,
but groan'd most piteously, believing it seems still that he was only
unbound in order to be kill'd.

When *Friday* came to him, I bad him speak to him, and tell him of his
deliverance, and pulling out my bottle, made him give the poor wretch a
dram, which, with the news of his being deliver'd, reviv'd him, and he sat
up in the boat; but when *Friday* came to hear him speak, and look in his
face, it would have mov'd any one to tears, to have seen how *Friday* kiss'd
him, embrac'd him, hugg'd him, cry'd, laugh'd, hollow'd, jump'd about,
danc'd, sung, then cry'd again, wrung his hands, beat his own face and
head, and then sung, and jump'd about again, like a distracted creature: It
was a good while before I could make him speak to me, or tell me what
was the matter; but when he came a little to himself, he told me, that it
was his father.

It is not easy for me to express how it mov'd me to see what extasy and
filial affection had work'd in this poor *savage*, at the sight of his father, and
of his being deliver'd from death; nor indeed can I describe half the

extravagancies of his affection after this; for he went into the boat and out of the boat a great many times: When he went in to him, he would sit down by him, open his breast, and hold his father's head close to his bosom half an hour together, to nourish it; then he took his arms and ankles, which were numb'd and stiff with the binding, and chaffed and rubbed them with his hands; and I perceiving what the case was, gave him some rum out of my bottle to rub them with, which did them a great deal of good.

This action put an end to our pursuit of the canoe, with the other *savages*, who were now gotten almost out of sight; and it was happy for us that we did not; for it blew so hard within two hours after, and before they could be gotten a quarter of their way, and continued blowing so hard all night, and that from the *north-west*, which was against them, that I could not suppose their boat could live, or that they ever reach'd to their own coast.

But to return to *Friday*, he was so busy about his father, that I could not find in my heart to take him off for some time: But after I thought he could leave him a little, I call'd him to me, and he came jumping and laughing, and pleas'd to the highest extream; then I ask'd him, If he had given his father any bread? He shook his head, and said, *None*: *Ugly dog eat all up self*; so I gave him a cake of bread out of a little pouch I carry'd on purpose; I also gave him a dram for himself, but he would not taste it, but carry'd it to his father: I had in my pocket also two or three bunches of my raisins, so I gave him a handful of them for his father. He had no sooner given his father these raisins, but I saw him come out of the boat, and run away as if he had been bewitch'd, he ran at such a rate; for he was the swiftest fellow of his foot that ever I saw; I say, he run at such a rate, that he was out of sight, as it were, in an instant; and though I call'd, and hollow'd too, after him, it was all one, away he went, and in a quarter of an hour, I saw him come back again, though not so fast as he went; and as he came nearer, I found his pace was slacker, because he had something in his hand.

When he came up to me, I found he had been quite home for an earthen jugg or pot to bring his father some fresh water, and that he had got two more cakes, or loaves of bread: The bread he gave me, but the water he carry'd to his father: However, as I was very thirsty too, I took a little sup of it. This water reviv'd his father more than all the rum or spirits I had given him; for he was just fainting with thirst.

When his father had drank, I call'd to him to know if there was any water left; he said, yes; and I bad him give it to the poor *Spaniard*, who was in as much want of it as his father; and I sent one of the cakes, that *Friday* brought, to the *Spaniard* too, who was, indeed, very weak, and was reposing himself upon a green place under the shade of a tree; and whose limbs were also very stiff, and very much swell'd with the rude bandage he had been ty'd with. When I saw that, upon *Friday's* coming to him with the water, he sat up and drank, and took the bread, and began to eat, I went to him, and gave him a handful of raisins; he look'd up in my face with all the tokens of gratitude and thankfulness that could appear in any countenance; but was so weak, notwithstanding he had so exerted himself in the fight, that he could not stand upon his feet; he try'd to do it two or three times, but was really not able, his ankles were so swell'd and so painful to him; so I bad him sit still, and caused *Friday* to rub his ankles, and bathe them with rum, as he had done his father's.

I observ'd the poor affectionate creature every two minutes, or perhaps less, all the while he was here, turn'd his head about, to see if his father was in the same place and posture, as he left him sitting; and at last he found he was not to be seen; at which he started up, and without speaking a word, flew with that swiftness to him, that one could scarce perceive his feet to touch the ground, as he went: But when he came, he only found he had laid himself down to ease his limbs; so *Friday* came back to me presently, and I then spoke to the *Spaniard* to let *Friday* help him up if he could, and lead him to the boat, and then he should carry him to our dwelling, where I would take care of him: But *Friday*, a lusty strong fellow, took the *Spaniard* quite up upon his back, and carry'd him away to the boat, and set him down softly upon the side or gunnel of the canoe, with his feet in the inside of it, and then lifted him quite in, and set him close to his father, and presently stepping out again, launch'd the boat off, and paddled it along the shore faster than I could walk, though the wind blew pretty hard too; so he brought them both safe into our creek, and leaving them in the boat, runs away to fetch the other canoe. As he pass'd me, I spoke to him, and ask'd him, whither he went, he told me, *Go fetch more boat*; so away he went like the wind; for sure never man or horse run like him, and he had the other canoe in the creek almost as soon as I got to it by land; so he wafted me over, and then went to help our new guests out of the boat, which he did; but they were neither of them able to walk; so that poor *Friday* knew not what to do.

To remedy this, I went to work in my thought, and calling to *Friday* to bid them sit down on the bank while he came to me, I soon made a kind of hand-barrow to lay them on, and *Friday* and I carry'd them up both together upon it between us: But when we had got them to the outside of our wall or fortification, we were at a worse loss than before; for it was impossible to get them over; and I was resolv'd not to break it down: So I set to work again; and *Friday* and I, in about two hours time, made a very handsome tent, cover'd with old sails, and above that with boughs of trees, being in the space without our outward fence, and between that and the grove of young wood which I had planted: And here we made them two beds of such things as I had (*viz.*) of good rice-straw, with blankets laid upon it, to lye on, and another to cover them on each bed.

My island was now peopled, and I thought my self very rich in subjects; and it was a merry reflection which I frequently made, how like a king I look'd. First of all, the whole country was my own meer property; so that I had an undoubted right of dominion. Secondly, my people were perfectly subjected: I was absolute lord and law-giver; they all ow'd their lives to me, and were ready to lay down their lives, *if there had been occasion of it*, for me. It was remarkable too, we had but three subjects, and they were of three different religions. My man *Friday* was a Protestant, his father was a pagan and a *cannibal*, and the *Spaniard* was a Papist: However, I allow'd liberty of conscience throughout my dominions: But this is by the way.

As soon as I had secur'd my two weak rescued prisoners, and given them shelter, and a place to rest them upon, I began to think of making some provision for them: And the first thing I did, I order'd *Friday* to take a yearling goat, betwixt a kid and a goat, out of my particular flock, to be kill'd, when I cut off the hinder quarter, and chopping it into small pieces, I set *Friday* to work to boiling and stewing, and made them a very good dish, I assure you, of flesh and broth, having put some barley and rice also into the broth; and as I cook'd it without doors, for I made no fire within my inner wall, so I carry'd it all into the new tent; and having set a table there for them, I sat down and eat my own dinner also with them, and, as well as I could, cheer'd them and encourag'd them; *Friday* being my interpreter, especially to his father, and indeed to the *Spaniard* too; for the *Spaniard* spoke the language of the *savages* pretty well.

After we had dined, or rather supped, I order'd *Friday* to take one of the canoes, and go and fetch our musquets and other fire-arms, which for want of time we had left upon the place of battle, and the next day I order'd him to go and bury the dead bodies of the savages, which lay open to the sun, and would presently be offensive; and I also order'd him to bury the horrid remains of their babarous feast, which I knew were pretty much, and which I could not think of doing my self; nay, I could not bear to see them, if I went that way: All which he punctually perform'd, and defac'd the very appearance of the *savages* being there; so that when I went again, I could scarce know where it was, otherwise than by the corner of the wood pointing to the place.

I then began to enter into a little conversation with my two new subjects; and first I set *Friday* to enquire of his father, what he thought of the escape of the *savages* in that canoe, and whether we might expect a return of them with a power too great for us to resist. His first opinion was, that the savages in the boat never could live out the storm which blew that night they went off, but must of necessity be drown'd or driven *south* to those other shores, where they were as sure to be devour'd as they were to be drown'd if they were cast away; but as to what they would do if they came safe on shore, he said he knew not; but it was his opinion that they were so dreadfully frighted with the manner of their being attack'd, the noise and the fire, that he believ'd they would tell their people they were all kill'd by thunder and lightning, not by the hand of man, and that the two which appear'd, (*viz.*) *Friday* and me, were two heavenly spirits or furies, come down to destroy them and not men with weapons: This he said he knew, because he heard them all cry out so in their language to one another, for it was impossible to them to conceive that a man could dart fire, and speak thunder, and kill at a distance without lifting up the hand, as was done now: And this old savage was in the right; for, as I understood since by other hands, the savages never attempted to go over to the island afterwards; they were so terrified with the accounts given by those four men, (for it seems they did escape the sea) that they believ'd whoever went to that enchanted island would be destroy'd with fire from the gods.

This however I knew not, and therefore was under continual apprehensions for a good while, and kept always upon my guard, me and all my army; for as we were now four of us, I would have ventur'd upon a hundred of them fairly in the open field at any time.

In a little time, however, no more canoes appearing, the fear of their coming wore off, and I began to take my former thoughts of a voyage to the main into consideration, being likewise assur'd by *Friday's* father, that

I might depend upon good usage from their nation on his account, if I would go.

But my thoughts were a little suspended, when I had a serious discourse with the *Spaniard*, and when I understood that there were sixteen more of his countrymen and *Portuguese*, who having been cast away, and made their escape to that side, liv'd there at peace indeed with the savages, but were very sore put to it for necessaries, and indeed for life: I ask'd him all the particulars of their voyage, and found they were a *Spanish* ship bound from the *Rio de la Plata* to the *Havana*, being directed to leave their loading there, which was chiefly hides and silver, and to bring back what *European* goods they could meet with there; that they had five *Portuguese* seamen on board, whom they took out of another wreck; that five of their own men were drowned when the first ship was lost, and that these escaped thro' infinite dangers and hazards, and arriv'd almost starv'd on the *cannibal* coast, where they expected to have been devour'd every moment.

He told me, they had some arms with them, but they were perfectly useless, for that they had neither powder or ball, the washing of the sea having spoil'd all their powder but a little, which they used at their first landing to provide themselves some food.

I ask'd him what he thought would become of them there, and if they had form'd no design of making any escape? He said, They had many consultations about it, but that having neither vessel, or tools to build one, or provisions of any kind, their counsels always ended in tears and despair.

I ask'd him how he thought they would receive a proposal from me, which might tend towards an escape? And whether, if they were all here, it might not be done? I told him with freedom, I fear'd mostly their treachery and ill usage of me, if I put my life in their hands; for that gratitude was no inherent virtue in the nature of man; nor did men always square their dealings by the obligations they had receiv'd, so much as they did by the advantages they expected. I told him, it would be very hard, that I should be the instrument of their deliverance, and that they should afterwards make me their prisoner in *New Spain*, where an *English* man was certain to be made a sacrifice, what necessity, or what accident soever brought him thither: And that I had rather be deliver'd up to the *savages*, and be devour'd alive, than fall into the merciless claws of the priests, and be carry'd into the *Inquisition*. I added, that otherwise I was perswaded, if they were all here, we might, with so many hands, build a bark large enough to carry us all away, either to the *Brasils* south-ward, or to the islands or *Spanish* coast north-ward: But that if in requital they should, when I had put weapons into their hands, carry me by force among their own people, I might be ill used for my kindness to them, and make my case worse than it was before.

He answer'd with a great deal of candor and ingenuity, that their condition was so miserable, and they were so sensible of it, that he believed they would abhor the thought of using any man unkindly that should contribute to their deliverance; and that, if I pleased, he would go to them with the old man, and discourse with them about it, and return again, and bring me their answer: That he would make conditions with them upon their solemn oath, that they should be absolutely under my leading, as their commander and captain; and that they should swear upon the Holy Sacraments and the Gospel, to be true to me, and to go to such Christian country as that I should agree to, and no other; and to be directed wholly and absolutely by my orders, till they were landed safely in such country as I intended; and that he would bring a contract from them under their hands for that purpose.

Then he told me, he would first swear to me himself, That he would never stir from me as long as he liv'd, till I gave him orders; and that he would take my side to the last drop of his blood, if there should happen the least breach of faith among his country-men.

He told me, they were all of them very civil honest men, and they were under the greatest distress imaginable, having neither weapons or clothes, nor any food, but at the mercy and discretion of the *savages*; out of all hopes of ever returning to their own country; and that he was sure, if I would undertake their relief, they would live and die by me.

Upon these assurances, I resolv'd to venture to relieve them, if possible, and to send the old *savage* and this *Spaniard* over to them to treat: But when we had gotten all things in a readiness to go, the *Spaniard* himself started an objection, which had so much prudence in it on one hand, and so much sincerity on the other hand, that I could not but be very well satisfy'd in it; and, by his advice, put off the deliverance of his comrades for at least half a year. The case was thus:

He had been with us now about a month; during which time, I had let him see in what manner I had provided, with the assistance of Providence, for my support; and he saw evidently what stock of corn and rice I had laid up; which, as it was more than sufficient for my self, so it was not sufficient, at least without good husbandry, for my family; now it was encreas'd to number four: But much less would it be sufficient, if his country-men, who were, as he said, fourteen still alive, should come over. And least of all would it be sufficient to victual our vessel, if we should build one, for a voyage to any of the Christian colonies of *America*. So he told me, he thought it would be more advisable, to let him and the two other, dig and cultivate some more land, as much as I could spare seed to sow; and that we should wait another harvest, that we might have a supply of corn for his country-men when they should come; for want might be a temptation to them to disagree, or not to think themselves delivered, otherwise than out of one difficulty into another. You know, says he, the children of *Israel*, though they rejoyc'd at first for their being deliver'd out of *Egypt*, yet rebell'd even against God himself that deliver'd them, when they came to want bread in the wilderness.[67]

His caution was so seasonable, and his advice so good, that I could not but be very well pleased with his proposal, as well as I was satisfy'd with his fidelity. So we fell to digging all four of us, as well as the wooden tools we were furnish'd with permitted; and in about a month's time, by the end of which it was seed time, we had gotten as much land cur'd and trimm'd up, as we sowed 22 bushels of barley on, and 16 jars of rice, which was in short all the seed we had to spare; nor indeed did we leave our selves barley sufficient for our own food, for the six months that we had to expect our crop, that is to say, reckoning from the time we set our seed aside for sowing; for it is not to be supposed it is six months in the ground in the country.

Having now society enough, and our number being sufficient to put us out of fear of the *savages*, if they had come, unless their number had been very great, we went freely all over the island, where-ever we found occasion; and as here we had our escape or deliverance upon our thoughts, it was impossible, *at least for me*, to have the means of it out of mine; to this purpose, I mark'd out several trees which I thought fit for our work, and I set *Friday* and his father to cutting them down; and then I caused the *Spaniard* to whom I imparted my thought on that affair, to oversee and direct their work. I shew'd them with what indefatigable pains I had hewed a large tree into single planks, and I caused them to do the like, till they had made about a dozen large planks of good oak, near two foot broad, 35 foot long, and from 2 inches to 4 inches thick: What prodigious labour it took up, any one may imagine.

At the same time I contriv'd to encrease my little flock of tame goats as much as I could; and to this purpose, I made *Friday* and the *Spaniard* go out one day, and myself with *Friday* the next day, for we took our turns: And by this means we got above 20 young kids to breed up with the rest; for whenever we shot the dam, we saved the kids, and added them to our flock: But above all, the season for curing the grapes coming on, I caused such a prodigious quantity to be hung up in the sun, that I believe, had we been at *Alicant*,[68] where the raisins of the sun are cur'd, we could have fill'd 60 or 80 barrels; and these with our bread was a great part of our food, and very good living too, I assure you; for it is an exceeding nourishing food.

It was now harvest, and our crop in good order; it was not the most plentiful increase I had seen in the island, but however it was enough to answer our end; for from our 22 bushels of barley, we brought in and thrashed out above 220 bushels; and the like in proportion of the rice, which was store enough for our food to the next harvest, tho' all the 16 *Spaniards* had been on shore with me; or if we had been ready for a voyage, it would very plentifully have victualled our ship, to have carry'd us to any part of the world, that is to say, of *America*.

When we had thus hous'd and secur'd our magazine of corn, we fell to work to make more wicker work, (*viz.*) great baskets in which we kept it; and the *Spaniard* was very handy and dexterous at this part, and often blam'd me that I did not make some things for defence, of this kind of work; but I saw no need of it.

And now having a full supply of food for all the guests I expected, I gave the *Spaniard* leave to go over to the *main*, to see what he could do with those he had left behind him there. I gave him a strict charge in writing, not to bring any man with him, who would not first swear in the presence of himself and of the old *savage*, that he would no way injure, fight with, or attack the person he should find in the island, who was so kind to send for them in order to their deliverance; but that they would stand by and defend him against all such attempts, and where-ever they went, would be entirely under and subjected to his commands; and that this should be put in writing, and sign'd with their hands: How we were to have this done, when I knew they had neither pen or ink; that indeed was a question which we never ask'd.

Under these instructions, the *Spaniard*, and the old *savage* (the father of *Friday*) went away in one of the canoes, which they might be said to come in, or rather were brought in, when they came as prisoners to be devour'd by the *savages*.

I gave each of them a musquet with a firelock on it, and about eight charges of powder and ball, charging them to be very good husbands of both, and not to use either of them but upon urgent occasion.

This was a cheerful work, being the first measures used by me in view of my deliverance for now 27 years and some days. I gave them provisions of bread, and of dry'd grapes, sufficient for themselves for many days, and sufficient for all their country-men for about eight days time; and wishing them a good voyage, I saw them go, agreeing with them about a signal they should hang out at their return, by which I should know them again, when they came back, at a distance, before they came on shore.

They went away with a fair gale on the day that the moon was at full by my account, in the month of *October*: But as for an exact reckoning of days, after I had once lost it, I could never recover it again, nor had I kept even the number of years so punctually, as to be sure that I was right, tho', as it prov'd, when I afterwards examin'd my account, I found I had kept a true reckoning of years.

It was no less than eight days I had waited for them, when a strange and unforeseen accident interven'd, of which the like has not perhaps been heard of in history. I was fast asleep in my hutch one morning, when my man *Friday* came running in to me, and call'd aloud, Master, Master, they are come, they are come.

I jump'd up, and, regardless of danger, I went out as soon as I could get my clothes on, thro' my little grove, which (by the way) was by this time grown to be a very thick wood; I say, regardless of danger, I went without my arms, which was not my custom to do; but I was surpris'd, when turning my eyes to the sea, I presently saw a boat at about a league and half's distance, standing in for the shore, with a *shoulder of mutton sail*, as they call it; and the wind blowing pretty fair to bring them in; also I observ'd presently, that they did not come from that side which the shore lay on, but from the southermost end of the island: Upon this, I call'd *Friday* in, and bid him lie close, for these were not the people we look'd for, and that we might not know yet whether they were friends or enemies.

In the next place, I went in to fetch my perspective glass, to see what I could make of them; and having taken the ladder out, I climb'd up to the top of the hill, as I used to do when I was apprehensive of anything, and to take my view the plainer without being discover'd.

I had scarce set my foot on the hill, when my eye plainly discover'd a ship lying at an anchor, at about two leagues and a half's distance from me south-south-east, but not above a league and an half from the shore. By my observation it appear'd plainly to be an *English* ship, and the boat appear'd to be an *English* long-boat.

I cannot express the confusion I was in, tho' the joy of seeing a ship, and one who I had reason to believe was mann'd by my own country-men, and consequently friends, was such as I cannot describe; but yet I had some secret doubts hung about me, I cannot tell from whence they came, bidding me keep upon my guard. In the first place, it occurr'd to me to consider what business an *English* ship could have in that part of the world, since it was not the way to or from any part of the world where the *English* had any traffick; and I knew there had been no storms to drive them in there, as in distress; and that if they were *English* really, it was most probable that they were here upon no good design; and that I had better continue as I was, than fall into the hands of thieves and murtherers.

Let no man despise the secret hints and notices of danger which sometimes are given him, when he may think there is no possibility of its being real. That such hints and notices are given us, I believe few that have made any observations of things can deny; that they are certain discoveries of an invisible world, and a converse of spirits, we cannot doubt, and if the tendency of them seems to be to warn us of danger, why should we not suppose they are from some friendly agent, whether supreme, or inferior and subordinate, is not the question; and that they are given for our good?

The present question abundantly confirms me in the justice of this reasoning; for had I not been made cautious by this secret admonition, come it from whence it will, I had been undone inevitably, and in a far worse condition than before, as you will see presently.

I had not kept myself long in this posture, but I saw the boat draw near the shore, as if they look'd for a creek to thrust in at for the convenience of landing; however, as they did not come quite far enough, they did not see the little inlet where I formerly landed my rafts; but ran their boat on shore upon the beach, at about half a mile from me, which was very happy for me; for otherwise, they would have landed just as I may say at my door, and would soon have beaten me out of my castle, and perhaps have plunder'd me of all I had.

When they were on shore, I was fully satisfy'd that they were *English* men; at least, most of them; one or two I thought were *Dutch*; but it did not prove so: There were in all eleven men, whereof three of them I found were unarm'd, and, as I thought, bound; and when the first four or five of them were jump'd on shore, they took those three out of the boat as prisoners: One of the three I could perceive using the most passionate gestures of entreaty, affliction and despair, even to a kind of extravagance; the other two I could perceive lifted up their hands sometimes, and appear'd concern'd indeed, but not to such a degree as the first.

I was perfectly confounded at the sight, and knew not what the meaning of it should be. *Friday* call'd out to me in *English*, as well as he could, *O Master! You see* English *mans eat prisoner as well as* savage *mans.* Why, says I, *Friday*, do you think they are a going to eat them then? *Yes*, says Friday, *They will eat them*: No, no, says I, *Friday, I am afraid they will murther them, indeed, but you may be sure they will not eat them.*

All this while I had no thought of what the matter really was; but stood trembling with the horror of the sight, expecting every moment when the three prisoners should be kill'd; nay, once I saw one of the villains lift up his arm with a great cutlash, (as the seamen call it) or sword, to strike one of the poor men; and I expected to see him fall every moment, at which all the blood in my body seem'd to run chill in my veins.

I wish'd heartily now for my *Spaniard*, and the savage that was gone with him; or that I had any way to have come undiscover'd within shot of them, that I might have rescu'd the three men; for I saw no fire arms they had among them; but it fell out to my mind another way.

After I had observ'd the outragious usage of the three men by the insolent seamen, I observ'd the fellows run scattering about the land, as if they wanted to see the country: I observ'd that the three other men had liberty to go also where they pleas'd; but they sat down all three upon the ground very pensive, and look'd like men in despair.

This put me in mind of the first time when I came on shore, and began to look about me; how I gave my self over for lost: How wildly I look'd round me, what dreadful apprehensions I had: And how I lodg'd in the tree all night for fear of being devour'd by wild beasts.

As I knew nothing that night of the supply I was to receive by the providential driving of the ship nearer the land, by the storms and tide, by which I have since been so long nourish'd and supported; so these three poor desolate men knew nothing how certain of deliverance and supply they were, how near it was to them, and how effectually and ready they were in a condition of safety, at the same time that they thought themselves lost, and their case desperate.

So little do we see before us in the world, and so much reason have we to depend cheerfully upon the great Maker of the world, that he does not leave his creatures so absolutely destitute, but that in the worst circumstances they have always something to be thankful for, and sometimes are nearer their deliverance than they imagine; nay, are even brought to their deliverance by the means by which they seem to be brought to their destruction.

It was just at the top of high-water when these people came on shore, and while partly they stood parlying with the prisoners they brought, and partly while they rambled about to see what kind of a place they were in, they had carelessly staid till the tide was spent, and the water was ebb'd considerably away, leaving their boat a-ground.

They had left two men in the boat, who as I found afterwards, having drank a little too much brandy, fell a-sleep; however, one of them waking sooner than the other, and finding the boat too fast a-ground for him to stir it, hollow'd for the rest who were straggling about, upon which they all soon came to the boat; but it was past all their strength to launch her, the boat being very heavy, and the shore on that side being a soft ousy sand, almost like a quick-sand.

In this condition, like true seamen who are perhaps the least of all mankind given to fore-thought, they gave it over, and away they stroll'd about the country again; and I heard one of them say aloud to another, calling them off from the boat, *Why, let her alone*, Jack, *can't ye, she will float next tide*; by which I was fully confirm'd in the main enquiry, of what country-men they were.

All this while I kept my self very close, not once daring to stir out of my castle, any farther than to my place of observation, near the top of the hill; and very glad I was, to think how well it was fortify'd: I knew it was no less than ten hours before the boat could be on float again, and by that time it would be dark, and I might be at more liberty to see their motions, and to hear their discourse, if they had any.

In the mean time, I fitted my self up for a battle as before, though with more caution, knowing I had to do with another kind of enemy than I had at first. I order'd *Friday* also, who I had made an excellent marksman with his gun, to load himself with arms: I took myself two fowling-pieces, and I gave him three musquets; my figure indeed was very fierce; I had my formidable goat-skin coat on, with the great cap I have mention'd, a naked sword by my side, two pistols in my belt, and a gun upon each shoulder.

It was my design, as I said above, not to have made any attempt till it was dark: But about two a clock, being the heat of the day, I found that in short they were all gone straggling into the woods, and, as I thought, were laid down to sleep. The three poor distressed men, too anxious for their condition to get any sleep, were however set down under the shelter of a great tree, at about a quarter of a mile from me, and, as I thought, out of sight of any of the rest.

Upon this I resolv'd to discover my self to them, and learn something of their condition: Immediately I march'd in the figure as above, my man *Friday* at a good distance behind me, as formidable for his arms as I, but not making quite so staring a *spectre-like* figure as I did.

I came as near them undiscover'd as I could, and then before any of them saw me, I call'd aloud to them in *Spanish*, *What are ye gentlemen?*

They started up at the noise, but were ten times more confounded when they saw me, and the uncouth figure that I made. They made no answer at all; but I thought I perceiv'd them just going to fly from me, when I spoke to them in *English*, Gentlemen, said I, do not be surpris'd at me; perhaps you may have a friend near you when you did not expect it. He must be sent directly from Heaven then, *said one of them very gravely to me, and pulling off his hat at the same time to me,* for our condition is past the help of man. All help is from Heaven, *sir, said I.* But can you put a stranger in the way how to help you, for you seem to me to be in some great distress? I saw you when you landed, and when you seem'd to make application to the brutes that came with you, I saw one of them lift up his sword to kill you.

The poor man, with tears running down his face, and trembling, looking like one astonish'd, return'd, *Am I talking to God, or man! Is it a real man, or an angel!* Be in no fear about that, sir, *said I,* if God had sent an angel to relieve you, he would have come better cloth'd, and arm'd after another manner than you see me in; pray lay aside your fears, I am a man, an *English* man, and dispos'd to assist you, you see; I have one servant only; we have arms and ammunition; tell us freely, Can we serve you?—What is your case?

Our case, said he, sir, is too long to tell you, while our murtherers are so near; but, in short, sir, I was commander of that ship, my men have mutinied against me; they have been hardly prevail'd on not to murther me, and at last have set me on shore in this desolate place, with these two men with me, one my Mate, the other a passenger, where we expected to perish, believing the place to be uninhabited, and know not yet what to think of it.

Where are those brutes, your enemies, said I, do you know where they are gone? *There they lye*, sir, said he, pointing to a thicket of trees; *my heart trembles for fear they have seen us, and heard you speak; if they have, they will certainly murther us all.*

Have they any fire-arms, *said I?* He answer'd, they had only two pieces, and one which they left in the boat. Well then, said I, leave the rest to me; I see they are all asleep, it is an easy thing to kill them all; but shall we rather take them prisoners? He told me, there were two desperate villains among them that it was scarce safe to shew any mercy to; but if they were secur'd, he believ'd all the rest would return to their duty. I ask'd him, which they were? He told me, he could not at that distance describe them; but he would obey my orders in any thing I would direct. Well, says I, let us retreat out of their view or hearing, lest they awake, and we will resolve farther; so they willingly went back with me, till the woods cover'd us from them.

Look you, sir, said I, if I venture upon your deliverance, are you willing to make two conditions with me; he anticipated my proposals, by telling me, that both he and the ship, if recover'd, should be wholly directed and commanded by me in every thing; and if the ship was not recover'd, he would live and die with me in what part of the world soever I would send him; and the two other men said the same.

Well, says I, *my conditions are but two.* 1. That while you stay on this island with me, you will not pretend to any authority here; and if I put arms into your hands, you will upon all occasions give them up to me, and do no prejudice to me or mine, upon this island, and in the mean time be govern'd by my orders.

2. That if the ship is, or may be recover'd, you will carry me and my man to *England* passage-free.

He gave me all the assurances that the invention and faith of man could devise, that he would comply with these most reasonable demands, and besides would owe his life to me, and acknowledge it upon all occasions as long as he liv'd.

Well then, *said I*, here are three musquets for you, with powder and ball; tell me next what you think is proper to be done. He shew'd all the testimony of his gratitude that he was able; but offer'd to be wholly guided by me. I told him, I thought it was hard venturing any thing; but the best method I could think of was to fire upon them at once, as they lay; and if any was not kill'd at the first volley, and offered to submit, we might save them, and so put it wholly upon God's Providence to direct the shot.

He said very modestly, that he was loath to kill them, if he could help it, but that those two were incorrigible villains, and had been the authors of all the mutiny in the ship, and if they escaped, we should be undone still; for they would go on board, and bring the whole ship's company, and destroy us all. *Well then*, says I, *necessity* legitimates my advice; for it is the only way to save our lives. However, seeing him still cautious of shedding blood, I told him they should go themselves, and manage as they found convenient.

In the middle of this discourse, we heard some of them awake, and soon after, we saw two of them on their feet, I ask'd him, if either of them were the men who he had said were the heads of the mutiny? He said, *No*: Well then, said I, you may let them escape, and Providence seems to have wakened them on purpose to save themselves. Now, says I, if the rest escape you, *it is your fault*.

Animated with this, he took the musquet, I had given him, in his hand, and a pistol in his belt, and his two comerades with him, with each man a piece in his hand. The two men who were with him going first, made some noise, at which one of the seamen who was awake, turn'd about, and seeing them coming, cry'd out to the rest; but it was too late then; for the moment he cry'd out, they fir'd; *I mean the two men*, the Captain wisely reserving his own piece: They had so well aim'd their shot at the men they knew, that one of them was kill'd on the spot, and the other very much wounded; but not being dead, he started up upon his feet, and call'd eagerly for help to the other; but the Captain stepping to him, told him, 'twas too late to cry for help, he should call upon God to forgive his villainy, and with that word knock'd him down with the stock of his musket, so that he never spoke more: There were three more in the company, and one of them was also slightly wounded: By this time I was come, and when they saw their danger, and that it was in vain to resist, they begg'd for mercy: The Captain told them he would spare their lives, if they would give him any assurance of their abhorrence of the treachery they had been guilty of, and would swear to be faithful to him in recovering the ship, and afterwards in carrying her back to *Jamaica*, from whence they came: They gave him all the protestations of their sincerity that could be desir'd, and he was willing to believe them, and spare their lives, which I was not against; only I oblig'd him to keep them bound hand and foot while they were upon the island.

While this was doing, I sent *Friday* with the Captain's Mate to the boat, with orders to secure her, and bring away the oars, and sail, which they did; and by and by, three straggling men that were (happily for them) parted from the rest, came back upon hearing the guns fir'd, and seeing their Captain, who before was their prisoner, now their conqueror, they submitted to be bound also; and so our victory was compleat.

It now remain'd, that the Captain and I should enquire into one another's circumstances: I began first, and told him my whole history, which he heard with an attention even to amazement; and particularly, at the wonderful manner of my being furnish'd with provisions and ammunition; and indeed, as my story is a whole collection of wonders, it affected him deeply; but when he reflected from thence upon himself, and how I seem'd to have been preserv'd there, on purpose to save his life, the tears ran down his face, and he could not speak a word more.

After this communication was at an end, I carry'd him and his two men into my apartment, leading them in, just where I came out, *viz.* at the top of the house, where I refresh'd them with such provisions as I had, and shew'd them all the contrivances I had made, during my long, long, inhabiting that place.

All I shew'd them, all I said to them, was perfectly amazing; but above all, the Captain admir'd my fortification, and how perfectly I had conceal'd my retreat with a grove of trees, which having been now planted near twenty years, and the trees growing much faster than in *England*, was become a little wood, and so thick, that it was unpassable in any part of it, but at that one side, where I had reserv'd my little winding passage into it: I told him, this was my castle, and my residence; but that I had a seat in the country, as most princes have, whither I could retreat upon occasion, and I would shew him that too another time; but at present, our business was to consider how to recover the ship: He agreed with me as to that; but told me, he was perfectly at a loss what measures to take; for that there were still six and twenty hands on board, who having entred into a cursed conspiracy, by which they had all forfeited their lives to the law, would be harden'd in it now by desperation; and would carry it on, knowing that if they were reduc'd, they should be brought to the gallows, as soon as they came to *England*, or to any of the *English* colonies; and that therefore there would be no attacking them with so small a number as we were.

I mus'd for some time upon what he had said, and found it was a very rational conclusion; and that therefore something was to be resolv'd on very speedily, as well to draw the men on board into some snare for their surprise, as to prevent their landing upon us, and destroying us; upon this it presently occurr'd to me, that in a little while the ship's crew wondring what was become of their comrades, and of the boat, would certainly come on shore in their other boat, to see for them, and that then perhaps they might come arm'd, and be too strong for us; this he allow'd was rational.

Upon this, I told him the first thing we had to do, was to stave the boat, which lay upon the beach, so that they might not carry her off; and taking every thing out of her, leave her so far useless as not to be fit to swim; accordingly we went on board, took the arms which were left on board, out of her, and whatever else we found there, which was a bottle of brandy, and another of rum, a few bisket cakes, a horn of powder, and a great lump of sugar, in a piece of canvas; the sugar was five or six pounds; all which was very welcome to me, especially the brandy and sugar, of which I had had none left for many years.

When we had carry'd all these things on shore (the oars, mast, sail, and rudder of the boat, were carry'd away before, as above) we knock'd a great hole in her bottom, that if they had come strong enough to master us, yet they could not carry off the boat.

Indeed, it was not much in my thoughts, that we could be able to recover the ship; but my view was that if they went away without the boat, I did not much question to make her sit again, to carry us away to the *Leeward* Islands, and call upon our friends, the *Spaniards*, in my way, for I had them still in my thoughts.

While we were thus preparing our designs, and had first, by main strength, heav'd the boat up upon the beach, so high that the tide would not fleet her off at high-water-mark; and besides, had broke a hole in her bottom, too big to be quickly stopp'd, and were sat down musing what we should do; we heard the ship fire a gun, and saw her make a waft with her antient, as a signal for the boat to come on board; but no boat stirr'd; and they fir'd several times, making other signals for the boat.

At last, when all their signals and firings prov'd fruitless, and they found the boat did not stir, we saw them by the help of my glasses, hoist another boat out, and row towards the shore; and we found as they approach'd, that there was no less than ten men in her, and that they had fire-arms with them.

As the ship lay almost two leagues from the shore, we had a full view of them as they came, and a plain sight of the men, even of their faces, because the tide having set them a little to the *east* of the other boat, they row'd up under shore, to come to the same place, where the other had landed, and where the boat lay.

By this means, I say, we had a full view of them, and the Captain knew the persons and characters of all the men in the boat, of whom he said, that there were three very honest fellows, who he was sure were led into this conspiracy by the rest, being over-power'd and frighted.

But that as for the Boat-swain, who it seem was the chief officer among them, and all the rest, they were as outragious as any of the ship's crew, and were no doubt made desperate in their new enterprize, and terribly apprehensive he was, that they would be too powerful for us.

I smil'd at him, and told him, that men in our circumstances were past the operation of fear: That seeing almost every condition that could be was better than that which we were suppos'd to be in, we ought to expect that the consequence, whether death or life, would be sure to be a deliverance: I ask'd him, what he thought of the circumstances of my life? And, whether a deliverance were not worth venturing for? And where, sir, said I, is your belief of my being preserv'd here on purpose to save your life, which elevated you a little while ago? For my part, said I, there seems to be but one thing amiss in all the prospect of it; *What's that?* says he; why, said I, 'tis, that as you say, there are three or four honest fellows among them, which should be spar'd; had they been all of the wicked part of the crew, I should have thought God's Providence had singled them out to deliver them into your hands; for depend upon it, every man of them that comes a-shore are our own, and shall die, or live, as they behave to us.

As I spoke this with a rais'd voice and cheerful countenance, I found it greatly encourag'd him; so we set vigorously to our business: We had upon the first appearance of the boat's coming from the ship, consider'd of separating our prisoners, and had indeed secur'd them effectually.

Two of them, of whom the Captain was less assur'd than ordinary, I sent with *Friday*, and one of the three (deliver'd men) to my cave, where they were remote enough, and out of danger of being heard or discover'd, or of finding their way out of the woods, if they could have deliver'd themselves: Here they left them bound, but gave them provisions, and promis'd them if they continued there quietly, to give them their liberty in a day or two; but that if they attempted their escape, they should be put to death without mercy: They promis'd faithfully to bear their confinement with patience, and were very thankful that they had such good usage, as to have provisions, and a light left them; for *Friday* gave them candles (such as we made our selves) for their comfort; and they did not know but that he stood sentinel over them at the entrance.

The other prisoners had better usage; two of them were kept pinion'd indeed, because the Captain was not free to trust them; but the other two were taken into my service upon their Captain's recommendation, and upon their solemnly engaging to live and die with us; so with them and the three honest men, we were seven men, well arm'd; and I made no doubt we shou'd be able to deal well enough with the ten that were a coming, considering that the Captain had said, there were three or four honest men among them also.

As soon as they got to the place where their other boat lay, they run their boat in to the beach, and came all on shore, hailing the boat up after them, which I was glad to see; for I was afraid they would rather have left the boat at an anchor, some distance from the shore, with some hands in her, to guard her; and so we should not be able to seize the boat.

Being on shore, the first thing they did, they ran all to their other boat, and it was easy to see that they were under a great surprise, to find her stripp'd as above, of all that was in her, and a great hole in her bottom.

After they had mus'd a while upon this, they set up two or three great shouts, hollowing with all their might, to try if they could make their companions hear; but all was to no purpose: Then they came all close in a ring, and fir'd a volley of their small arms, which indeed we heard, and the echoes made the woods ring; but it was all one, those in the cave we were sure could not hear, and those in our keeping, though they heard it well enough, yet durst give no answer to them.

They were so astonish'd at the surprise of this, that as they told us afterwards, they resolv'd to go all on board again to their ship, and let them know there, that the men were all murther'd, and the long-boat stav'd; accordingly they immediately launch'd their boat again, and gat all of them on board.

The Captain was terribly amaz'd, and even confounded at this, believing they would go on board the ship again, and set sail, giving their comrades for lost, and so he should still lose the ship, which he was in hopes we should have recover'd; but he was quickly as much frighted the other way.

They had not been long put off with the boat, but we perceiv'd them all coming on shore again; but with this new measure in their conduct, which it seems they consulted together upon, *viz.* to leave three men in the boat, and the rest to go on shore, and go up into the country to look for their fellows.

This was a great disappointment to us; for now we were at a loss what to do; for our seizing those seven men on shore would be no advantage to us, if we let the boat escape; because they would then row away to the ship, and then the rest of them would be sure to weigh and set sail, and so our recovering the ship would be lost.

However, we had no remedy, but to wait and see what the issue of things might present; the seven men came on shore, and the three who remain'd in the boat, put her off to a good distance from the shore, and came to an anchor to wait for them; so that it was impossible for us to come at them in the boat.

Those that came on shore, kept close together, marching towards the top of the little hill, under which my habitation lay; and we could see them plainly, though they could not perceive us: We could have been very glad they would have come nearer to us, so that we might have fir'd at them, or that they would have gone farther off, that we might have come abroad.

But when they were come to the brow of the hill, where they could see a great way into the valleys and woods, which lay towards the *north-east* part, and where the island lay lowest, they shouted, and hollow'd till they were weary; and not caring it seems to venture far from the shore, nor far from one another, they sat down together under a tree, to consider of it: Had they thought fit to have gone to sleep there, as the other party of them had done, they had done the jobb for us; but they were too full of apprehensions of danger, to venture to go to sleep, tho' they could not tell what the danger was they had to fear neither.

The Captain made a very just proposal to me, upon this consultation of theirs, *viz.* that perhaps they would all fire a volley again, to endeavour to make their fellows hear, and that we should all sally upon them, just at the juncture when their pieces were all discharg'd, and they would certainly yield, and we should have them without blood-shed: I lik'd the proposal, provided it was done while we were near enough to come up to them, before they could load their pieces again.

But this event did not happen, and we lay still a long time, very irresolute what course to take; at length I told them, there would be nothing to be done in my opinion till night, and then if they did not return to the boat, perhaps we might find a way to get between them and the shore, and so might use some stratagem with them in the boat to get them on shore.

We waited a great while, though very impatient for their removing; and were very uneasy, when, after long consultations, we saw them start all up, and march down toward the sea: It seems they had such dreadful apprehensions upon them of the danger of the place, that they resolv'd to go on board the ship again, give their companions over for lost, and so go on with their intended voyage with the ship.

As soon as I perceiv'd them go towards the shore, I imagin'd it to be as it really was, that they had given over their search, and were for going back again; and the Captain, as soon as I told him my thoughts, was ready to sink at the apprehensions of it; but I presently thought of a stratagem to fetch them back again, and which answer'd my end to a tittle.

I order'd *Friday*, and the Captain's Mate, to go over the little creek *westward*, towards the place where the *savages* came on shore, when *Friday* was rescu'd; and as soon as they came to a little rising ground, at about half a mile distance, I bad them hollow, as loud as they could, and wait till they found the seamen heard them; that as soon as ever they heard the seamen answer them, they should return it again, and then keeping out of sight, take a round, always answering when the other hollow'd, to draw them as far into the island, and among the woods, as possible, and then wheel about again to me, by such ways as I directed them.

They were just going into the boat, when *Friday* and the Mate hollow'd, and they presently heard them, and answering, run along the shore *westward*, towards the voice they heard, when they were presently stopp'd by the creek, where the water being up, they could not get over, and call'd for the boat to come up, and set them over, as indeed I expected.

When they had set themselves over, I observ'd, that the boat being gone up a good way into the creek, and as it were, in a harbour within the land, they took one of the three men out of her to go along with them, and left only two in the boat, having fastned her to the stump of a little tree on the shore.

This was what I wish'd for, and immediately leaving *Friday* and the Captain's Mate to their business, I took the rest with me, and crossing the creek out of their sight, we surpris'd the two men before they were aware; one of them lying on shore, and the other being in the boat; the fellow on shore, was between sleeping and waking, and going to start up, the Captain who was foremost, ran in upon him, and knock'd him down, and then call'd out to him in the boat to yield, or he was a dead man.

There needed very few arguments to perswade a single man to yield, when he saw five men upon him, and his comrade knock'd down; besides, this was it seems one of the three who were not so hearty in the mutiny as the rest of the crew, and therefore was easily perswaded, not only to yield, but afterwards to joyn very sincerely with us.

In the mean time, *Friday* and the Captain's Mate so well manag'd their business with the rest, that they drew them by hollowing and answering, from one hill to another; and from one wood to another, till they not only heartily tyr'd them, but left them, where they were very sure they could not reach back to the boat, before it was dark; and indeed they were heartily tyr'd themselves also by the time they came back to us.

We had nothing now to do, but to watch for them, in the dark, and to fall upon them, so as to make sure work with them.

It was several hours after *Friday* came back to me, before they came back to their boat; and we could hear the foremost of them long before they came quite up, calling to those behind to come along, and could also hear them answer and complain how lame and tyr'd they were, and not able to come any faster, which was very welcome news to us.

At length they came up to the boat; but 'tis impossible to express their confusion, when they found the boat fast a-ground in the creek, the tide ebb'd out, and their two men gone: We could hear them call to one another in a most lamentable manner, telling one another they were gotten into an inchanted island; that either there were inhabitants in it, and they should all be murther'd, or else there were devils and spirits in it, and they should be all carry'd away, and devour'd.

They hollow'd again, and call'd their two comrades by their names, a great many times, but no answer. After some time, we could see them, by the little light there was, run about wringing their hands like men in despair; and that sometimes they would go and sit down in the boat to rest themselves, then come ashore again, and walk about again, and so over the same thing again.

My men would fain have me given them leave to fall upon them at once in the dark; but I was willing to take them at some advantage, so to spare them, and kill as few of them as I could; and especially I was unwilling to hazard the killing any of our own men, knowing the other were very well armed. I resolved to wait to see if they did not separate; and therefore to make sure of them, I drew my ambuscade nearer, and order'd *Friday* and the Captain, to creep upon their hands and feet as close to the ground as they could, that they might not be discover'd, and get as near them as they could possibly, before they offered to fire.

They had not been long in that posture, but that the Boat-swain, who was the principal ringleader of the mutiny, and had now shewn himself the most dejected and dispirited of all the rest, came walking towards them with two more of their crew; the Captain was so eager, as having this principal rogue so much in his power, that he could hardly have patience to let him come so near, as to be sure of him; for they only heard his tongue before: But when they came nearer, the Captain and *Friday* starting up on their feet, let fly at them.

The Boat-swain was kill'd upon the spot, the next man was shot into the body, and fell just by him, tho' he did not die till an hour or two after; and the third run for it.

At the noise of the fire, I immediately advanc'd with my whole army, which was now 8 men, *viz.* my self *Generalissimo*, *Friday* my Lieutenant-General, the Captain and his two men, and the three prisoners of war, who we had trusted with arms.

We came upon them indeed in the dark, so that they could not see our number; and I made the man we had left in the boat, who was now one of us, call to them by name, to try if I could bring them to a parly, and so might perhaps reduce them to terms, which fell out just as we desir'd: For indeed it was easy to think, as their condition then was, they would be very willing to capitulate; so he calls out as loud as he could, to one of them, *Tom Smith, Tom Smith; Tom Smith* answer'd immediately, *Who's that*, Robinson? for it seems he knew his voice: T'other answer'd, *Ay, ay; for God's sake*, Tom Smith, *throw down your arms, and yield*, or, *you are all dead men this moment.*

Who must we yield to? where are they? (says *Smith* again;) *Here they are*, says he, here's our Captain, and fifty men with him, have been hunting you this two hours; the Boat-swain is kill'd, *Will Frye* is wounded, and I am a prisoner; and if you do not yield, you are all lost.

Will they give us quarter then, (says *Tom Smith*) *and we will yield? I'll go and ask, if you promise to yield*, says *Robinson*; so he ask'd the Captain, and the Captain then calls himself out, You *Smith*, you know my voice, if you lay down your arms immediately, and submit, you shall have your lives all but *Will. Atkins.*

Upon this, *Will. Atkins* cry'd out, *For God's sake, Captain, give me quarter, what have I done? They have been all as bad as I*, which by the way was not true neither; for it seems this *Will. Atkins* was the first man that laid hold of the Captain, when they first mutiny'd, and used him barbarously, in tying his hands, and giving him injurious language. However, the Captain told him he must lay down his arms at discretion, and trust to the Governour's mercy, by which he meant me; for they all call'd me Governour.

In a word, they all laid down their arms, and begg'd their lives; and I sent the man that had parly'd with them, and two more, who bound them all; and then my great army of 50 men, which particularly with those three, were all but eight, came up and seiz'd upon them all, and upon their boat, only that I kept my self and one more out of sight, for reasons of state.

Our next work was to repair the boat, and think of seizing the ship; and as for the Captain, now he had leisure to parly with them: He expostulated with them upon the villany of their practices with him, and at length upon the farther wickedness of their design, and how certainly it must bring them to misery and distress in the end, and perhaps to the gallows.

They all appear'd very penitent, and begg'd hard for their lives; as for that, he told them they were none of his prisoners, but the Commander of the island; that they thought they had set him on shore in a barren uninhabited island, but it had pleased God so to direct them, that the island was inhabited, and that the Governour was an *English* man; that he might hang them all there, if he pleased; but as he had given them all quarter, he supposed he would send them to *England* to be dealt with there, as justice requir'd, except *Atkins*, who he was commanded by the Governour to advise to prepare for death; for that he would be hang'd in the morning.

Though this was all a fiction of his own, yet it had its desired effect; *Atkins* fell upon his knees to beg the Captain to intercede with the Governour for his life; and all the rest begg'd of him for God's sake, that they might not be sent to *England*.

It now occurr'd to me, that the time of our deliverance was come, and that it would be a most easy thing to bring these fellows in, to be hearty in getting possession of the ship; so I retir'd in the dark from them, that they might not see what kind of a Governour they had, and call'd the Captain to me; when I call'd, as at a good distance, one of the men was order'd to speak again, and say to the Captain, *Captain, the Commander calls for you*; and presently the Captain reply'd, *Tell his Excellency I am just a coming*: This more perfectly amused them; and they all believed that the Commander was just by with his fifty men.

Upon the Captain's coming to me, I told him my project for seizing the ship, which he lik'd of wonderfully well, and resolv'd to put it in execution the next morning.

But in order to execute it with more art, and secure of success, I told him, we must divide the prisoners, and that he should go and take *Atkins* and two more of the worst of them, and send them pinion'd to the cave where the others lay: This was committed to *Friday* and the two men who came on shore with the Captain.

They convey'd them to the cave, as to a prison; and it was indeed a dismal place, especially to men in their condition.

The other I order'd to my *bower*, as I call'd it, of which I have given a full description; and as it was fenc'd in, and they pinion'd, the place was secure enough, considering they were upon their behaviour.

To these in the morning I sent the Captain, who was to enter into a parly with them, in a word to try them, and tell me, whether he thought they might be trusted or no, to go on board and surprise the ship. He talk'd to them of the injury done him, of the condition they were brought to; and that though the Governour had given them quarter for their lives, as to the present action, yet that if they were sent to *England*, they would all be hang'd in chains, to be sure; but that if they would join in so just an attempt, as to recover the ship, he would have the Governour's engagement for their pardon.

Any one may guess how readily such a proposal would be accepted by men in their condition; they fell down on their knees to the Captain, and promised with the deepest imprecations, that they would be faithful to him to the last drop, and that they should owe their lives to him, and would go with him all over the world, that they would own him for a father to them as long as they liv'd.

Well, says the Captain, I must go and tell the Governour what you say, and see what I can do to bring him to consent to it: So he brought me an account of the temper he found them in; and that he verily believ'd they would be faithful.

However, that we might be very secure, I told him he should go back again, and choose out those five, and tell them, they might see that he did not want men, that he would take out those five to be his assistants, and that the Governour would keep the other two, and the three that were sent prisoners to the castle, (*my cave*) as hostages, for the fidelity of those five; and that if they prov'd unfaithful in the execution, the five hostages should be hang'd in chains alive upon the shore.

This look'd severe, and convinc'd them that the Governour was in earnest; however they had no way left them, but to accept it; and it was now the business of the prisoners, as much as of the Captain, to perswade the other five to do their duty.

Our strength was now thus ordered for the expedition: 1. The Captain, his Mate, and passenger. 2. Then the two prisoners of the first gang, to whom having their characters from the Captain, I had given their liberty, and trusted them with arms. 3. The other two who I had kept till now, in my apartment, pinion'd; but upon the Captain's motion, had now releas'd. 4. The single man taken in the boat. 5. These five releas'd at last: So that they were thirteen in all, besides five we kept prisoners in the cave, and the two hostages.

I ask'd the Captain, if he was willing to venture with these hands on board the ship; for as for me and my man *Friday*, I did not think it was proper for us to stir, having seven men left behind; and it was employment enough for us to keep them asunder, and supply them with victuals.

As to the five in the cave, I resolv'd to keep them fast, but *Friday* went in twice a day to them, to supply them with necessaries; and I made the other two carry provisions to a certain distance, where *Friday* was to take it.

When I shew'd my self to the two hostages, it was with the Captain, who told them, I was the person the Governour had order'd to look after them, and that it was the Governour's pleasure they should not stir any where, but by my direction; that if they did, they should be fetch'd into the castle, and be lay'd in irons; so that as we never suffered them to see me as Governour, so I now appear'd as another person, and spoke of the Governour, the garrison, the castle, and the like, upon all occasions.

The Captain now had no difficulty before him, but to furnish his two boats, stop the breach of one, and man them. He made his passenger captain of one, with four other men; and himself, and his Mate, and five more went in the other: And they contriv'd their business very well; for they came up to the ship about midnight: As soon as they came within call of the ship, he made *Robinson* hale them, and tell them they had brought off the men and the boat, but that it was a long time before they had found them, and the like; holding them in a chat till they came to the ship's side; when the Captain and the Mate entring first with their arms, immediately knock'd down the second Mate and Carpenter with the but-end of their musquets, being very faithfully seconded by their men, they secur'd all the rest that were upon the main and quarter decks, and began to fasten the hatches to keep them down who were below, when the other boat and their men entring at the fore chains, secur'd the fore-castle of the ship, and the scuttle which went down into the cookroom, making three men they found there, prisoners.

When this was done, and all safe upon deck, the Captain order'd the Mate with three men to break into the round-house, where the new rebel Captain lay, and having taken the alarm, was gotten up, and with two men and a boy had gotten fire arms in their hands, and when the Mate with a crow split open the door, the new Captain and his men fir'd boldly among them, and wounded the Mate with a musquet ball, which broke his arm, and wounded two more of the men, but kill'd no body.

The Mate calling for help, rush'd however into the round-house, wounded as he was, and with his pistol shot the new Captain thro' the head, the bullet entring at his mouth, and came out again behind one of his ears; so that he never spoke a word; upon which the rest yielded, and the ship was taken effectually, without any more lives lost.

As soon as the ship was thus secur'd, the Captain order'd seven guns to be fir'd, which was the signal agreed upon with me, to give me notice of his success, which you may be sure I was very glad to hear, having sat watching upon the shore for it till near two of the clock in the morning.

Having thus heard the signal plainly, I laid me down; and it having been a day of great fatigue to me, I slept very sound, till I was something surpris'd with the noise of a gun; and presently starting up, I heard a man call me by the name of Governour, Governour, and presently I knew the Captain's voice, when climbing up to the top of the hill, there he stood, and pointing to the ship, he embrac'd me in his arms, *My dear friend and deliverer*, says he, *there's your ship, for she is all yours, and so are we and all that belong to her.* I cast my eyes to the ship, and there she rode within little more than half a mile of the shore; for they had weighed her anchor as soon as they were masters of her; and the weather being fair, had brought her to an anchor just against the mouth of the little creek; and the tide being up, the Captain had brought the pinnace in near the place where I at first landed my rafts, and so landed just at my door.

I was at first ready to sink down with the surprise. For I saw my deliverance indeed visibly put into my hands, all things easy, and a large ship just ready to carry me away whither I pleased to go. At first, for some time, I was not able to answer him one word; but as he had taken me in his arms, I held fast by him, or I should have fallen to the ground.

He perceived the surprise, and immediately pulls a bottle out of his pocket, and gave me a dram of cordial, which he had brought on purpose for me; after I had drank it, I sat down upon the ground; and though it brought me to my self, yet it was a good while before I could speak a word to him.

All this while the poor man was in as great an extasy as I, only not under any surprise, as I was; and he said a thousand kind tender things to me, to compose me and bring me to my self; but such was the flood of joy in my breast, that it put all my spirits into confusion; at last it broke out into tears, and in a little while after, I recovered my speech.

Then I took my turn, and embrac'd him as my deliverer; and we rejoyc'd together. I told him, I look'd upon him as a man sent from Heaven to deliver me, and that the whole transaction seemed to be a chain of wonders; that such things as these were the testimonies we had of a secret hand of Providence governing the world, and an evidence, that the eyes of an infinite power could search into the remotest corner of the world, and send help to the miserable whenever he pleas'd.

I forgot not to lift up my heart in thankfulness to Heaven, and what heart could forbear to bless him, who had not only in a miraculous manner provided for one in such a wilderness, and in such a desolate condition, but from whom every deliverance must always be acknowledged to proceed.

When we had talk'd a while, the Captain told me he had brought me some little refreshment, such as the ship afforded, and such as the wretches that had been so long his masters had not plunder'd him of: Upon this he call'd aloud to the boat, and bid his men bring the things ashore that were for the Governour; and indeed it was a present, as if I had been one not that was to be carry'd away along with them, but as if I had been to dwell upon the island still, and they were to go without me.

First he had brought me a case of bottles full of excellent cordial waters, six large bottles of *Madera* wine; the bottles held two quarts a-piece; two pound of excellent good tobacco, twelve good pieces of the ship's beef, and six pieces of pork, with a bag of pease, and about a hundred weight of bisket.

He brought me also a box of sugar, a box of flower, a bag full of lemons, and two bottles of lime-juice, and abundance of other things: But besides these, and what was a thousand times more useful to me, he brought me six clean new shirts, six very good neckclothes, two pair of gloves, one pair of shoes, a hat, and one pair of stockings, and a very good suit of clothes of his own, which had been worn but very little: In a word, he clothed me from head to foot.

It was a very kind and agreeable present, as any one may imagine, to one in my circumstances: But never was any thing in the world of that kind so unpleasant, awkward, and uneasy, as it was to me to wear such clothes at their first putting on.

After these ceremonies past, and after all his good things were brought into my little apartment, we began to consult what was to be done with the prisoners we had; for it was worth considering, whether we might venture to take them away with us or no, especially two of them, who we knew to be incorrigible and refractory to the last degree; and the Captain said, he knew they were such rogues, that there was no obliging them, and if he did carry them away, it must be in irons, as malefactors to be delivered over to justice at the first *English* colony he should come at; and I found that the Captain himself was very anxious about it.

Upon this, I told him, that if he desir'd it, I durst undertake to bring the two men he spoke of, to make it their own request that he should leave them upon the island: *I should be very glad of that*, says the Captain, *with all my heart*.

Well, says I, I will send for them up, and talk with them for you; so I caused *Friday* and the two hostages, for they were now discharg'd, their comrades having perform'd their promise; I say, I caused them to go to the cave, and bring up the five men pinion'd, as they were, to the bower, and keep them there till I came.

After some time, I came thither dress'd in my new habit, and now I was call'd Governour again; being all met, and the Captain with me, I caused the men to be brought before me, and I told them, I had had a full account of their villainous behaviour to the Captain, and how they had run away with the ship, and were preparing to commit farther robberies, but that Providence had ensnar'd them in their own ways, and that they were fallen into the pit which they had digged for others.

I let them know, that by my direction the ship had been seiz'd, that she lay now in the road; and they might see by and by, that their new Captain had receiv'd the reward of his villainy; for that they might see him hanging at the yard-arm.

That as to them, I wanted to know what they had to say, why I should not execute them as pirates taken in the fact, as by my commission they could not doubt I had authority to do.

One of them answer'd in the name of the rest, that they had nothing to say but this, that when they were taken the Captain promis'd them their lives, and they humbly implor'd my mercy; but I told them, I knew not what mercy to shew them; for as for my self, I had resolv'd to quit the island with all my men, and had taken passage with the Captain to go for *England*: And as for the Captain, he could not carry them to *England* other than as prisoners in irons to be try'd for mutiny, and running away with the ship; the consequence of which, they must needs know, would be the gallows; so that I could not tell which was best for them, unless they had a mind to take their fate in the island; if they desir'd, that I did not care, as I had liberty to leave it, I had some inclination to give them their lives, if they thought they could shift on shore.

They seem'd very thankful for it, said they would much rather venture to stay there, than to be carry'd to *England* to be hang'd, so I left it on that issue.

However, the Captain seem'd to make some difficulty of it, as if he durst not leave them there: Upon this I seem'd a little angry with the Captain, and told him, that they were my prisoners, not his; and that seeing I had offer'd them so much favour, I would be as good as my word; and that if he did not think fit to consent to it, I would set them at liberty, as I found them; and if he did not like it, he might take them again if he could catch them.

Upon this they appeared very thankful, and I accordingly set them at liberty, and bad them retire into the woods to the place whence they came, and I would leave them some fire arms, some ammunition, and some directions how they should live very well, if they thought fit.

Upon this I prepar'd to go on board the ship, but told the Captain, that I would stay that night to prepare my things, and desir'd him to go on board in the mean time, and keep all right in the ship, and send the boat on shore the next day for me; ordering him in the mean time to cause the new Captain, who was kill'd, to be hang'd at the yard-arm, that these men might see him.

When the Captain was gone, I sent for the men up to me to my apartment, and entred seriously into discourse with them of their circumstances. I told them, I thought they had made a right choice; that if the Captain carry'd them away, they would certainly be hanged. I shewed them the new Captain, hanging at the yard-arm of the ship, and told them they had nothing less to expect.

When they had all declar'd their willingness to stay, I then told them, I would let them into the story of my living there, and put them into the way of making it easy to them: Accordingly I gave them the whole history of the place, and of my coming to it; shew'd them my fortifications, the way I made my bread, planted my corn, cured my grapes; and in a word, all that was necessary to make them easy: I told them the story also of the sixteen *Spaniards* that were to be expected; for whom I left a letter, and made them promise to treat them in common with themselves.

I left them my fire arms, *viz.* five musquets, three fowling pieces, and three swords. I had above a barrel and half of powder left; for after the first year or two, I used but little, and wasted none. I gave them a description of the way I manag'd the goats, and directions to milk and fatten them, and to make both butter and cheese.

In a word, I gave them every part of my own story; and I told them, I would prevail with the Captain to leave them two barrels of gun-powder more, and some garden-seeds, which I told them I would have been very glad of; also I gave them the bag of pease which the Captain had brought me to eat, and bade them be sure to sow and encrease them.

Having done all this, I left them the next day, and went on board the ship: We prepared immediately to sail, but did not weigh that night: The next morning early, two of the five men came swimming to the ship's side, and making a most lamentable complaint of the other three, begged to be taken into the ship, for God's sake, for they should be murthered, and begg'd the Captain to take them on board, tho' he hang'd them immediately.

Upon this the Captain pretended to have no power without me; but after some difficulty, and after their solemn promises of amendment, they were taken on board, and were some time after soundly whipp'd and pickl'd;[69] after which, they prov'd very honest and quiet fellows.

Some time after this, the boat was order'd on shore, the tide being up, with the things promised to the men, to which the Captain, at my intercession, caused their chests and clothes to be added, which they took, and were very thankful for; I also encourag'd them, by telling them, that if it lay in my way to send any vessel to take them in, I would not forget them.

When I took leave of this island, I carry'd on board for reliques the great goat's-skin-cap I had made, my umbrella, and my parrot; also I forgot not to take the money I formerly mention'd, which had lain by me so long useless, that it was grown rusty, or tarnish'd, and could hardly pass for silver, till it had been a little rubb'd, and handled; as also the money I found in the wreck of the *Spanish* ship.

And thus I left the island, the nineteenth of *December*, as I found by the ship's account, in the year 1686, after I had been upon it eight and twenty years, two months, and 19 days; being deliver'd from this second captivity, the same day of the month that I first made my escape in the *barco-longo*, from among the *Moors* of *Sallee*.

In this vessel, after a long voyage, I arriv'd in *England* the eleventh of *June*, in the year 1687, having been thirty and five years absent.

When I came to *England*, I was as perfect a stranger to all the world, as if I had never been known there. My benefactor and faithful steward, who I had left in trust with my money, was alive; but had had great misfortunes in the world; was become a widow the second time, and very low in the world: I made her easy as to what she ow'd me, assuring her, I would give her no trouble; but on the contrary, in gratitude to her former care and faithfulness to me, I reliev'd her, as my little stock would afford, which at that time would indeed allow me to do but little for her; but I assur'd her, I would never forget her former kindness to me; nor did I forget her, when I had sufficient to help her, as shall be observ'd in its place.

I went down afterwards into *Yorkshire*; but my father was dead, and my mother, and all the family extinct, except that I found two sisters, and two of the children of one of my brothers, and as I had been long ago given over for dead, there had been no provision made for me; so that in a word, I found nothing to relieve, or assist me; and that little money I had, would not do much for me, as to settling in the world.

I met with one piece of gratitude indeed, which I did not expect; and this was, that the Master of the ship, who I had so happily deliver'd, and by the same means sav'd the ship and cargo, having given a very handsome account to the owners, of the manner how I had sav'd the lives of the men, and the ship, they invited me to meet them, and some other merchants concern'd, and all together made me a very handsome compliment upon the subject, and a present of almost two hundred pounds sterling.

But after making several reflections upon the circumstances of my life, and how little way this would go towards settling me in the world, I resolv'd to go to *Lisbon*, and see if I might not come by some information of the state of my plantation in the *Brasils*, and of what was become of my partner, who I had reason to suppose had some years now given me over for dead.

With this view I took shipping for *Lisbon*, where I arriv'd in *April* following; my man *Friday* accompanying me very honestly in all these ramblings, and proving a most faithful servant upon all occasions.

When I came to *Lisbon*, I found out by enquiry, and to my particular satisfaction, my old friend the Captain of the ship, who first took me up at sea, off of the shore of *Africk*: He was now grown old, and had left off the sea, having put his son, who was far from a young man, into his ship; and who still used the *Brasil* trade. The old man did not know me, and indeed I hardly knew him; but I soon brought him to my remembrance, and as soon brought my self to his remembrance, when I told him who I was.

After some passionate expressions of the old acquaintance, I enquir'd, you may be sure, after my plantation and my partner: The old man told me he had not been in the *Brasils* for about nine years; but that he could assure me, that when he came away my partner was living, but the trustees, who I had join'd with him to take cognizance of my part, were both dead; that however, he believ'd that I would have a very good account of the improvement of the plantation; for that upon the general belief of my being cast away, and drown'd, my trustees had given in the account of the produce of my part of the plantation, to the Procurator Fiscal, who had appropriated it, in case I never came to claim it; one third to the King, and two thirds to the monastery of St. *Augustine*, to be expended for the benefit of the poor, and for the conversion of the *Indians* to the Catholick faith; but that if I appear'd, or any one for me, to claim the inheritance, it should be restor'd; only that the improvement, or annual production, being distributed to charitable uses, could not be restor'd; but he assur'd me, that the steward of the King's revenue (from lands) and the Proviedore, or Steward of the monastery, had taken great care all along, that the incumbent, that is to say, my partner, gave every year a faithful account of the produce, of which they receiv'd duly my moiety.

I ask'd him if he knew to what height of improvement he had brought the plantation? And, whether he thought it might be worth looking after? Or, whether on my going thither, I should meet with no obstruction to my possessing my just right in the moiety?

He told me, he could not tell exactly to what degree the plantation was improv'd; but this he knew, that my partner was grown exceeding rich upon the enjoying but one half of it; and that to the best of his remembrance, he had heard, that the King's third of my part, which was it seems granted away to some other monastery, or religious house, amounted to above two hundred Moidores a year; that as to my being restor'd to a quiet possession of it, there was no question to be made of that, my partner being alive to witness my title, and my name being also enrolled in the register of the country; also he told me, that the survivors of my two trustees were very fair honest people, and very wealthy; and he believ'd I would not only have their assistance for putting me in possession, but would find a very considerable sum of money in their hands, for my account; being the produce of the farm while their fathers held the trust, and before it was given up as above, which as he remember'd, was for about twelve years.

I shew'd my self a little concern'd, and uneasy at this account, and enquir'd of the old Captain, how it came to pass, that the trustees should thus dispose my effects, when he knew that I had made my will, and had made him, the *Portuguese* Captain, my universal heir, *&c.*

He told me, that was true; but that as there was no proof of my being dead, he could not act as executor, until some certain account should come of my death, and that besides, he was not willing to intermeddle with a thing so remote; that it was true he had register'd my will, and put in his claim; and could he have given any account of my being dead or alive, he would have acted by procuration, and taken possession of the *Ingenio*, so they call'd the sugar-house, and had given his son, who was now at the *Brasils*, order to do it.

But, says the old man, I have one piece of news to tell you, which perhaps may not be so acceptable to you as the rest, and that is, that believing you were lost, and all the world believing so also, your partner and trustees did offer to accompt to me in your name, for six or eight of the first years of profits, which I receiv'd; but there being at that time, says he, great disbursements for encreasing the works, building an *Ingenio*, and buying slaves, it did not amount to near so much as afterwards it produced: However, says the old man, I shall give you a true account of what I have received in all, and how I have disposed of it.

After a few days farther conference with this ancient friend, he brought me an account of the six first years income of my plantation, sign'd by my partner and the merchants trustees, being always deliver'd in goods, *viz.* tobacco in roll, and sugar in chests, besides rum, molossus, *&c.* which is the consequence of a sugar work; and I found by this account, that every year the income considerably encreased; but as above, the disbursement being large, the sum at first was small: However, the old man let me see, that he was debtor to me 470 Moidores of gold, besides 60 chests of sugar, and 15 double rolls of tobacco which were lost in his ship; he having been ship-wreck'd coming home to *Lisbon* about 11 years after my leaving the place.

The good man then began to complain of his misfortunes, and how he had been oblig'd to make use of my money to recover his losses, and buy him a share in a new ship: However, my old friend, says he, you shall not want a supply in your necessity; and as soon as my son returns, you shall be fully satisfy'd.

Upon this, he pulls out an old pouch, and gives me 160 *Portugal* Moidores in gold; and giving me the writing of his title to the ship, which his son was gone to the *Brasils* in, of which he was a quarter part owner, and his son another, he puts them both into my hands for security of the rest.

I was too much mov'd with the honesty and kindness of the poor man, to be able to bear this; and remembring what he had done for me, how he had taken me up at sea, and how generously he had used me on all occasions, and particularly, how sincere a friend he was now to me, I could hardly refrain weeping at what he said to me: Therefore first I asked him, if his circumstances admitted him to spare so much money at that time, and if it would not straiten him? He told me, he could not say but it might straiten him a little; but however it was my money, and I might want it more than he.

Every thing the good man said was full of affection, and I could hardly refrain from tears while he spoke: In short, I took 100 of the Moidores, and call'd for a pen and ink to give him a receipt for them; then I returned him the rest, and told him, If ever I had possession of the plantation, I would return the other to him also, as indeed I afterwards did; and that as to the bill of sale of his part in his son's ship, I would not take it by any means; but that if I wanted the money, I found he was honest enough to pay me; and if I did not, but came to receive what he gave me reason to expect, I would never have a penny more from him.

When this was pass'd, the old man began to ask me, If he should put me into a method to make my claim to my plantation? I told him, I thought to go over to it my self: He said, I might do so if I pleas'd; but that if I did not, there were ways enough to secure my right, and immediately to appropriate the profits to my use; and as there were ships in the River of *Lisbon*,[70] just ready to go away to *Brasil*, he made me enter my name in a publick register, with his affidavit, affirming upon oath that I was alive, and that I was the same person who took up the land for the planting the said plantation at first.

This being regularly attested by a notary, and a procuration affix'd, he directed me to send it with a letter of his writing, to a merchant of his acquaintance at the place, and then propos'd my staying with him till an account came of the return.

Never any thing was more honourable, than the proceedings upon this procuration; for in less than seven months I receiv'd a large packet from the survivors of my trustees the merchants, for whose account I went to sea, in which were the following particular letters and papers enclos'd.

First, there was the account current of the produce of my farm, or plantation, from the year when their fathers had ballanc'd with my old *Portugal* Captain, being for six years; the ballance appear'd to be 1174 Moidores in my favour.

Secondly, there was the account of four years more while they kept the effects in their hands, before the government claim'd the administration, as being the effects of a person not to be found, which they call *civil death*; and the ballance of this, the value of the plantation encreasing, amounted to 38892 Cruisadoes,[71] which made 3241 Moidores.

Thirdly, there was the Prior of the *Augustin's* account, who had receiv'd the profits for above fourteen years; but not being to account for what was dispos'd to the hospital, very honestly declar'd he had 872 Moidores not distributed, which he acknowledged to my account; as to the King's part, that refunded nothing.

There was a letter of my partner's, congratulating me very affectionately upon my being alive, giving me an account how the estate was improv'd, and what it produced a year, with a particular of the number of squares or acres that it contain'd; how planted, how many slaves there were upon it, and making two and twenty crosses for blessings, told me he had said so many *Ave Marias* to thank the Blessed Virgin that I was alive; inviting me very passionately to come over and take possession of my own; and in the mean time to give him orders to whom he should deliver my effects, if I did not come my self; concluding with a hearty tender of his friendship, and that of his family, and sent me, as a present, seven fine leopard's skins, which he had it seems received from *Africa*, by some other ship which he had sent thither, and who it seems had made a better voyage than I: He sent me also five chests of excellent sweet-meats, and an hundred pieces of gold uncoin'd, not quite so large as Moidores.

By the same fleet, my two merchant trustees shipp'd me 1200 chests of sugar, 800 rolls of tobacco, and the rest of the whole accompt in gold.

I might well say, now indeed, that the latter end of *Job* was better than the beginning.[72] It is impossible to express here the flutterings of my very heart, when I look'd over these letters, and especially when I found all my wealth about me; for as the *Brasil* ships come all in fleets, the same ships which brought my letters, brought my goods; and the effects were safe in the river before the letters came to my hand. In a word, I turned pale, and grew sick; and had not the old man run and fetch'd me a cordial, I believe the sudden surprise of joy had overset Nature, and I had dy'd upon the spot.

Nay after that, I continu'd very ill, and was so some hours, till a physician being sent for, and something of the real cause of my illness being known, he order'd me to be let blood; after which, I had relief, and grew well: But I verily believe, if it had not been eas'd by a vent given in that manner to the spirits, I should have dy'd.

I was now master, all on a sudden, of above 5000 *l. Sterling* in money, and had an estate, as I might well call it, in the *Brasils*, of above a thousand pounds a year, as sure as an estate of lands in *England*:[73] And in a word, I was in a condition which I scarce knew how to understand, or how to compose my self, for the enjoyment of it.

The first thing I did, was to recompense my original benefactor, my good old Captain, who had been first charitable to me in my distress, kind to me in my beginning, and honest to me at the end: I shew'd him all that was sent me, I told him, that next to the Providence of Heaven, which disposes all things, it was owing to him; and that it now lay on me to reward him, which I would do a hundred fold: So I first return'd to him the hundred Moidores I had receiv'd of him, then I sent for a notary, and caused him to draw up a general release or discharge for the 470 Moidores, which he had acknowledg'd he ow'd me in the fullest and firmest manner possible; after which, I caused a procuration to be drawn, impowering him to be my receiver of the annual profits of my plantation, and appointing my partner to accompt to him, and make the returns by the usual fleets to him in my name; and a clause in the end, being a grant of 100 Moidores a year to him, during his life, out of the effects, and 50 Moidores a year to his son after him, for his life: And thus I requited my old man.

I was now to consider which way to steer my course next, and what to do with the estate that Providence had thus put into my hands; and indeed

I had more care upon my head now, than I had in my silent state of life in the island, where I wanted nothing but what I had, and had nothing but what I wanted: Whereas I had now a great charge upon me, and my business was how to secure it. I had ne'er a cave now to hide my money in, or a place where it might lye without lock or key, till it grew mouldy and tarnish'd before any body would meddle with it: On the contrary, I knew not where to put it, or who to trust with it. My old patron, the Captain, indeed was honest, and that was the only refuge I had.

In the next place, my interest in the *Brasils* seem'd to summon me thither, but now I could not tell how to think of going thither, till I had settled my affairs, and left my effects in some safe hands behind me. At first I thought of my old friend the widow, who I knew was honest, and would be just to me; but then she was in years, and but poor, and for ought I knew, might be in debt; so that in a word, I had no way but to go back to *England* my self, and take my effects with me.

It was some months however before I resolved upon this; and therefore, as I had rewarded the old Captain fully, and to his satisfaction, who had been my former benefactor, so I began to think of my poor widow, whose husband had been my first benefactor, and she, while it was in her power, my faithful steward and instructor. So the first thing I did, I got a merchant in *Lisbon* to write to his correspondent in *London*, not only to pay a bill, but to go find her out, and carry her in money an hundred pounds from me, and to talk with her, and comfort her in her poverty, by telling her she should, if I liv'd, have a farther supply: At the same time I sent my two sisters in the country, each of them an hundred pounds, they being, though not in want, yet not in very good circumstances; one having been marry'd, and left a widow; and the other having a husband not so kind to her as he should be.

But among all my relations, or acquaintances, I could not yet pitch upon one, to whom I durst commit the gross of my stock, that I might go away to the *Brasils*, and leave things safe behind me; and this greatly perplex'd me.

I had once a mind to have gone to the *Brasils*, and have settled my self there; for I was, as it were, naturaliz'd to the place; but I had some little scruple in my mind about religion, which insensibly drew me back, of which I shall say more presently. However, it was not religion that kept me from going there for the present; and as I had made no scruple of being openly of the religion of the country, all the while I was among them, so neither did I yet; only that now and then having of late thought more of it, (than formerly) when I began to think of living and dying among them, I began to regret my having profess'd my self a Papist, and thought it might not be the best religion to die with.

But, as I have said, this was not the main thing that kept me from going to the *Brasils*, but that really I did not know with whom to leave my effects behind me; so I resolv'd at last to go to *England* with it, where, if I arrived, I concluded I should make some acquaintance, or find some relations that would be faithful to me; and accordingly I prepar'd to go for *England* with all my wealth.

In order to prepare things for my going home, I first, the *Brasil* fleet being just going away, resolved to give answers suitable to the just and faithful account of things I had from thence; and first to the Prior of St. *Augustin* I wrote a letter full of thanks for their just dealings, and the offer of the 872 Moidores, which was indisposed of, which I desir'd might be given 500 to the monastery, and 372 to the poor, as the Prior should direct, desiring the good *Padres* prayers for me, and the like.

I wrote next a letter of thanks to my two trustees, with all the acknowledgment that so much justice and honesty call'd for; as for sending them any present, they were far above having any occasion of it.

Lastly, I wrote to my partner, acknowledging his industry in the improving the plantation, and his integrity in encreasing the stock of the works, giving him instructions for his future government of my part, according to the powers I had left with my old patron, to whom I desir'd him to send whatever became due to me, till he should hear from me more particularly; assuring him that it was my intention, not only to come to him, but to settle my self there for the remainder of my life: To this I added a very handsom present of some *Italian* silks for his wife, and two daughters, for such the Captain's son inform'd me he had; with two pieces of fine *English* broad cloth, the best I could get in *Lisbon*, five pieces of black bays, and some *Flanders* lace of a good value.

Having thus settled my affairs, sold my cargo, and turn'd all my effects into good bills of exchange, my next difficulty was, which way to go to *England*: I had been accustom'd enough to the sea, and yet I had a strange aversion to going to *England* by sea at that time; and though I could give no reason for it, yet the difficulty encreas'd upon me so much, that though I had once shipp'd my baggage, in order to go, yet I alter'd my mind, and that not once, but two or three times.

It is true, I had been very unfortunate by sea, and this might be some of the reasons: But let no man slight the strong impulses of his own thoughts in cases of such moment: Two of the ships which I had singled out to go in, I mean, more particularly singled out than any other, that is to say, so as in one of them to put my things on board, and in the other to have agreed with the Captain; I say, two of these ships miscarry'd, *viz.* one was taken by the *Algerines*, and the other was cast away on the *Start* near *Torbay*,[74] and all the people drown'd except three; so that in either of those vessels I had been made miserable; and in which most, it was hard to say.

Having been thus harass'd in my thoughts, my old pilot, to whom I communicated every thing, press'd me earnestly not to go by sea, but either to go by land to the *Groyne*,[75] and cross over the Bay of *Biscay* to *Rochell*, from whence it was but an easy and safe journey by land to *Paris*, and so to *Calais* and *Dover*; or to go up to *Madrid*, and so all the way by land thro' *France*.

In a word, I was so prepossess'd against my going by sea at all, except from *Calais* to *Dover*, that I resolv'd to travel all the way by land; which as I was not in haste, and did not value the charge, was by much the pleasanter way; and to make it more so, my old Captain brought an *English* gentleman, the son of a merchant in *Lisbon*, who was willing to travel with me: After which, we pick'd up two more *English* merchants also, and two young *Portuguese* gentlemen, the last going to *Paris* only; so that we were in all six of us, and five servants; the two merchants and the two *Portuguese*, contenting themselves with one servant between two, to save the charge; and as for me, I got an *English* sailor to travel with me as a servant, besides my man *Friday*, who was too much a stranger to be capable of supplying the place of a servant on the road.

In this manner I set out from *Lisbon*; and our company being all very well mounted and armed, we made a little troop, whereof they did me the honour to call me Captain, as well because I was the oldest man, as because I had two servants, and indeed was the original of the whole journey.

As I have troubled you with none of my sea-journals, so I shall trouble you now with none of my land-journal: But some adventures that happen'd to us in this tedious and difficult journey, I must not omit.

When we came to *Madrid*, we being all of us strangers to *Spain*, were willing to stay some time to see the court of *Spain*, and to see what was worth observing; but it being the latter part of the summer, we hasten'd away, and set out from *Madrid* about the middle of *October*: But when we came to the edge of *Navarre*, we were alarm'd at several towns on the way, with an account, that so much snow was fallen on the *French* side of the mountains, that several travellers were obliged to come back to *Pampeluna*,[76] after having attempted at an extream hazard to pass on.

When we came to *Pampeluna* it self, we found it so indeed; and to me that had been always used to a hot climate, and indeed to countries where we could scarce bear any clothes on, the cold was insufferable; nor indeed was it more painful than it was surprising, to come but ten days before out of the *Old Castile*,[77] where the weather was not only warm, but very hot, and immediately to feel a wind from the *Pyrenean* Mountains, so very keen, so severely cold, as to be intolerable, and to endanger benumbing and perishing of our fingers and toes.

Poor *Friday* was really frighted when he saw the mountains all cover'd with snow, and felt cold weather, which he had never seen or felt before in his life.

To mend the matter, when we came to *Pampeluna*, it continued snowing with so much violence, and so long, that the people said, winter was come before its time, and the roads which were difficult before, were now quite impassable: For in a word, the snow lay in some places too thick for us to travel; and being not hard frozen, as is the case in northern countries: There was no going without being in danger of being bury'd alive every step. We stay'd no less than twenty days at *Pampeluna*; when seeing the winter coming on, and no likelihood of its being better; for it was the severest winter all over *Europe* that had been known in the memory of man. I propos'd that we should all go away to *Fontarabia*,[78] and there take shipping for *Bourdeaux*, which was a very little voyage.

But while we were considering this, there came in four *French* gentlemen, who having been stopp'd on the *French* side of the passes, as we were on the *Spanish*, had found out a guide, who traversing the country near the head of *Languedoc*,[79] had brought them over the mountains by such ways, that they were not much incommoded with the snow; and where they met with snow in any quantity, they said it was frozen hard enough to bear them and their horses.

We sent for this guide, who told us, he would undertake to carry us the same way with no hazard from the snow, provided we were armed sufficiently to protect our selves from wild beasts; for he said, upon these great snows, it was frequent for some wolves to show themselves at the foot of the mountains, being made ravenous for want of food, the ground being covered with snow: We told him, we were well enough prepar'd for such creatures as they were, if he would ensure us from a kind of two-legged wolves, which we were told we were in most danger from, especially on the *French* side of the mountains.

He satisfy'd us there was no danger of that kind in the way that we were to go; so we readily agreed to follow him, as did also twelve other gentlemen, with their servants, some *French*, some *Spanish*; who, as I said, had attempted to go, and were oblig'd to come back again.

Accordingly, we all set out from *Pampeluna*, with our guide, on the fifteenth of *November*; and indeed, I was surpris'd, when instead of going forward, he came directly back with us, on the same road that we came from *Madrid*, above twenty miles; when being pass'd two rivers, and come into the plain country, we found our selves in a warm climate again, where the country was pleasant, and no snow to be seen; but on a sudden, turning to his left, he approach'd the mountains another way; and though it is true, the hills and precipices look'd dreadful, yet he made so many tours, such meanders, and led us by such winding ways, that we were insensibly pass'd the height of the mountains, without being much incumbred with the snow; and all on a sudden, he shew'd us the pleasant fruitful provinces of *Languedoc* and *Gascoign*,[80] all green and flourishing; tho' indeed it was at a great distance, and we had some rough way to pass yet.

We were a little uneasy however, when we found it snow'd one whole day, and a night, so fast, that we could not travel; but he bid us be easy, we should soon be past it all: We found indeed, that we began to descend every day, and to come more *north* than before; and so depending upon our guide, we went on.

It was about two hours before night, when our guide being something before us, and not just in sight, out rushed three monstrous wolves, and after them a bear, out of a hollow way, adjoyning to a thick wood; two of the wolves flew upon the guide, and had he been half a mile before us, he had been devour'd indeed, before we could have help'd him: One of them fastned upon his horse, and the other attack'd the man with that violence, that he had not time, or not presence of mind enough to draw his pistol, but hollow'd and cry'd out to us most lustily; my man *Friday* being next to me, I bid him ride up, and see what was the matter; as soon as *Friday* came in sight of the man, he hollow'd as loud as t'other, *O Master! O Master!* But like a bold fellow, rode directly up to the poor man, and with his pistol shot the wolf that attack'd him into the head.

It was happy for the poor man, that it was my man *Friday*; for he having been us'd to that kind of creature in his country, had no fear upon him; but went close up to him, and shot him as above; whereas any of us, would have fir'd at a farther distance, and have perhaps either miss'd the wolf, or endanger'd shooting the man.

But it was enough to have terrify'd a bolder man than I, and indeed it alarm'd all our company, when with the noise of *Friday's* pistol, we heard on both sides the dismallest howling of wolves, and the noise redoubled by the echo of the mountains, that it was to us as if there had been a prodigious multitude of them; and perhaps indeed there was not such a few, as that we had no cause of apprehensions.

However, as *Friday* had kill'd this wolf, the other that had fastned upon the horse, left him immediately, and fled; having happily fastned upon his head, where the bosses of the bridle had stuck in his teeth; so that he had not done him much hurt: The man indeed was most hurt; for the raging creature had bit him twice, once on the arm, and the other time a little above his knee; and he was just as it were tumbling down by the disorder of his horse, when *Friday* came up and shot the wolf.

It is easy to suppose, that at the noise of *Friday's* pistol, we all mended our pace, and rid up as fast as the way (which was very difficult) would give us leave, to see what was the matter; as soon as we came clear of the trees, which blinded us before, we saw clearly what had been the case, and how *Friday* had disengag'd the poor guide; though we did not presently discern what kind of creature it was he had kill'd.

But never was a fight manag'd so hardily, and in such a surprising manner, as that which follow'd between *Friday* and the bear, which gave us all (though at first we were surpris'd and afraid for him) the greatest diversion imaginable: As the bear is a heavy, clumsey creature, and does not gallop as the wolf does, who is swift, and light; so he has two particular qualities, which generally are the rule of his actions; first, as to men, who are not his proper prey; I say, not his proper prey; because tho' I can't say what excessive hunger might do, which was now their case, the ground being all cover'd with snow; but as to men, he does not usually attempt them, unless they first attack him: On the contrary, if you meet him in the woods, if you don't meddle with him, he won't meddle with you; but then you must take care to be very civil to him, and give him the road; for he is a very nice gentleman, he won't go a step out of his way for a prince; nay, if you are really afraid, your best way is to look another way, and keep going on; for sometimes if you stop, and stand still, and look steadily at him, he takes it for an affront; but if you throw or toss any thing at him, and it hits him, though it were but a bit of a stick, as big as your finger, he takes it for an affront, and sets all his other business aside to pursue his revenge; for he will have satisfaction in point of honour; that is his first quality: The next is, that if he be once affronted, he will never leave you, night or day, till he has his revenge; but follows at a good round rate, till he overtakes you.

My man *Friday* had deliver'd our guide, and when we came up to him, he was helping him off from his horse; for the man was both hurt and frighted, and indeed the last more than the first; when on the sudden, we spy'd the bear come out of the wood, and a vast monstrous one it was, the biggest by far that ever I saw. We were all a little surpris'd when we saw him; but when *Friday* saw him, it was easy to see joy and courage in the fellow's countenance; *O! O! O!* says *Friday*, three times, pointing to him; *O Master; You give me te leave, me shakee te hand with him: Me make you good laugh.*

I was surpris'd to see the fellow so pleas'd; *You fool you*, says I, *he will eat you up! Eatee me up! Eatee me up!* says *Friday*, twice over again; *Me eatee him up: Me make you good laugh: You all stay here, me show you good laugh*; so down he sits, and gets his boots off in a moment, and put on a pair of pumps, (as we call the flat shoes they wear) and which he had in his pocket, gives my other servant his horse, and with his gun away he flew swift like the wind.

The bear was walking softly on, and offer'd to meddle with no body, till *Friday* coming pretty near, calls to him, as if the bear could understand him; *Hark ye, hark ye*, says *Friday*, *me speakee wit you*: We follow'd at a distance; for now being come down on the *Gascoign* side of the mountains, we were entred a vast great forest, where the country was plain, and pretty open, though many trees in it scatter'd here and there.

Friday, who had as we say, the heels of the bear, came up with him quickly, and takes up a great stone, and throws at him, and hit him just on the head; but did him no more harm, than if he had thrown it against a wall; but it answer'd *Friday's* end; for the rogue was so void of fear, that he did it purely to make the bear follow him, and shew us some laugh, as he call'd it.

As soon as the bear felt the stone, and saw him, he turns about, and comes after him, taking devilish long strides, and shuffling along at a strange rate, so as would have put a horse to a middling gallop; away runs *Friday*, and takes his course, as if he run towards us for help; so we all resolv'd to fire at once upon the bear, and deliver my man; though I was angry at him heartily, for bringing the bear back upon us, when he was going about his own business another way; and especially I was angry that he had turn'd the bear upon us, and then run away; and I call'd out, *You dog*, said I, *is this your making us laugh? Come away, and take your horse, that we may shoot the creature*; he hears me, and cries out, *No shoot, no shoot, stand still, you get much laugh*: And as the nimble creature run two foot for the beast's one, he turn'd on a sudden, on one side of us, and seeing a great oak-tree, fit for his purpose, he beckon'd to us to follow, and doubling his pace, he gets nimbly up the tree, laying his gun down upon the ground, at about five or six yards from the bottom of the tree.

The bear soon came to the tree, and we follow'd at a distance; the first thing he did, he stopp'd at the gun, smelt to it, but let it lye, and up he scrambles into the tree, climbing like a cat, though so monstrously heavy: I was amaz'd at the folly, as I thought it, of my man, and could not for my life see any thing to laugh at yet, till seeing the bear get up the tree, we all rode nearer to him.

When we came to the tree, there was *Friday* got out to the small end of a large limb of the tree, and the bear got about half way to him; as soon as the bear got out to that part where the limb of the tree was weaker, *Ha*, says he to us, *now you see me teachee the bear dance*; so he falls a jumping and shaking the bough, at which the bear began to totter, but stood still, and began to look behind him, to see how he should get back; then indeed we did laugh heartily: But *Friday* had not done with him by a great deal; when he sees him stand still, he calls out to him again, as if he had suppos'd the bear could speak *English*; *What, you no come farther? Pray you come farther*; so he left jumping and shaking the trees; and the bear, just as if he had understood what he said, did come a little farther, then he fell a jumping again, and the bear stopp'd again.

We thought now was a good time to knock him on the head, and I call'd to *Friday* to stand still, and we would shoot the bear; but he cry'd out earnestly, *O pray! O pray! No shoot, me shoot, by and then*; he would have said, *by and by*: However, to shorten the story, *Friday* danc'd so much, and the bear stood so ticklish, that we had laughing enough indeed, but still could not imagine what the fellow would do; for first we thought he depended upon shaking the bear off; and we found the bear was too cunning for that too; for he would not go out far enough to be thrown down, but clings fast with his great broad claws and feet, so that we could not imagine what would be the end of it, and where the jest would be at last.

But *Friday* put us out of doubt quickly; for seeing the bear cling fast to the bough, and that he would not be perswaded to come any farther; *Well, well,* says *Friday, you no come farther, me go, me go; you no come to me, me go come to you*; and upon this, he goes out to the smallest end of the bough, where it would bend with his weight, and gently let himself down by it, sliding down the bough, till he came near enough to jump down on his feet, and away he run to his gun, takes it up, and stands still.

Well, said I to him, *Friday*, What will you do now? Why don't you shoot him? *No shoot,* says *Friday, no yet, me shoot now, me no kill; me stay, give you one more laugh*; and indeed so he did, as you will see presently; for when the bear sees his enemy gone, he comes back from the bough where he stood, but did it mighty leisurely, looking behind him every step, and coming backward till he got into the body of the tree; then with the same hinder end foremost, he came down the tree, grasping it with his claws, and moving one foot at a time, very leisurely; at this juncture, and just before he could set his hind feet upon the ground, *Friday* stept up close to him, clapt the muzzle of his piece into his ear, and shot him dead as a stone.

Then the rogue turn'd about, to see if we did not laugh, and when he saw we were pleas'd by our looks, he falls a laughing himself very loud; *so we kill bear in my country,* says *Friday*; so you kill them, says I, why you have no guns: *No,* says he, *no gun, but shoot, great much long arrow.*

This was indeed a good diversion to us; but we were still in a wild place, and our guide very much hurt, and what to do we hardly knew; the howling of wolves run much in my head; and indeed, except the noise I once heard on the shore of *Africa*, of which I have said something already, I never heard any thing that filled me with so much horrour.

These things, and the approach of night, called us off, or else, as *Friday* would have had us, we should certainly have taken the skin of this monstrous creature off, which was worth saving; but we had three leagues to go, and our guide hasten'd us, so we left him, and went forward on our journey.

The ground was still cover'd with snow, tho' not so deep and dangerous as on the mountains, and the ravenous creatures, as we heard afterwards, were come down into the forest and plain country, press'd by hunger to seek for food; and had done a great deal of mischief in the villages, where they surpris'd the country people, kill'd a great many of their sheep and horses, and some people too.

We had one dangerous place to pass, which our guide told us, if there were any more wolves in the country, we should find them there; and this was in a small plain, surrounded with woods on every side, and a long narrow defile or lane, which we were to pass to get through the wood, and then we should come to the village where we were to lodge.

It was within half an hour of sun-set when we entred the first wood; and a little after sun-set, when we came into the plain, we met with nothing in the first wood, except that in a little plain within the wood, which was not above two furlongs over, we saw five great wolves cross the road, full speed one after another, as if they had been in chase of some prey, and had it in view, they took no notice of us, and were gone, and out of our sight in a few moments.

Upon this our guide, who by the way was a wretched faint-hearted fellow, bid us keep in a ready posture; for he believed there were more wolves a coming.

We kept our arms ready, and our eyes about us, but we saw no more wolves, till we came thro' that wood, which was near half a league, and entred the plain; as soon as we came into the plain, we had occasion enough to look about us: The first object we met with, was a dead horse; that is to say, a poor horse which the wolves had kill'd, and at least a dozen of them at work; we could not say eating of him, but picking of his bones rather; for they had eaten up all the flesh before.

We did not think fit to disturb them at their feast, neither did they take much notice of us: *Friday* would have let fly at them, but I would not suffer him by any means; for I found we were like to have more business upon our hands than we were aware of. We were not gone half over the plain, but we began to hear the wolves howl in the wood on our left, in a frightful manner, and presently after we saw about a hundred coming on directly towards us, all in a body, and most of them in a line, as regularly as an army drawn up by experienc'd officers. I scarce knew in what manner to receive them; but found to draw our selves in a close line was the only way: so we form'd in a moment: But that we might not have too much interval, I order'd, that only every other man should fire, and that the others who had not fir'd should stand ready to give them a second volley immediately, if they continued to advance upon us, and that then those who had fir'd at first, should not pretend to load their fusees again, but stand ready with every one a pistol; for we were all arm'd with a fusee, and a pair of pistols each man; so we were by this method able to fire six volleys, half of us at a time; however, at present we had no necessity; for upon firing the first volley, the enemy made a full stop, being terrify'd as well with the noise, as with the fire; four of them being shot into the head, dropp'd, several others were wounded, and went bleeding off, as we could see by the snow: I found they stopp'd, but did not immediately retreat; whereupon remembring that I had been told, that the fiercest creatures were terrify'd at the voice of a man, I caus'd all our company to hollow as loud as we could; and I found the notion not altogether mistaken; for upon our shout, they began to retire, and turn about; then I order'd a second volley to be fir'd, in their rear, which put them to the gallop, and away they went to the woods.

This gave us leisure to charge our pieces again, and that we might lose no time, we kept going; but we had but little more than loaded our fusees, and put our selves into a readiness, when we heard a terrible noise in the same wood, on our left, only that it was farther onward the same way we were to go.

The night was coming on, and the light began to be dusky, which made it worse on our side; but the noise encreasing, we could easily perceive that it was the howling and yelling of those hellish creatures; and on a sudden, we perceiv'd 2 or 3 troops of wolves, one on our left, one behind us, and one on our front; so that we seem'd to be surrounded with 'em; however, as they did not fall upon us, we kept our way forward, as fast as we could make our horses go, which the way being very rough, was only a good large trot; and in this manner we came in view of the entrance of a wood, through which we were to pass, at the farther side of the plain; but we were greatly surpris'd, when coming nearer the lane, or pass, we saw a confus'd number of wolves standing just at the entrance.

On a sudden, at another opening of the wood, we heard the noise of a gun; and looking that way, out rush'd a horse, with a saddle, and a bridle on him, flying like the wind, and sixteen or seventeen wolves after him, full speed; indeed, the horse had the heels of them; but as we suppos'd that he could not hold it at that rate, we doubted not but they would get up with him at last, and no question but they did.

But here we had a most horrible sight; for riding up to the entrance where the horse came out, we found the carcass of another horse, and of two men, devour'd by the ravenous creatures, and one of the men was no doubt the same who we heard fir'd the gun; for there lay a gun just by him fir'd off; but as to the man, his head, and the upper part of his body, was eaten up.

This fill'd us with horror, and we knew not what course to take, but the creatures resolv'd us soon; for they gather'd about us presently, in hopes of prey; and I verily believe there were three hundred of them: It happen'd very much to our advantage, that at the entrance into the wood, but a little way from it, there lay some large timber trees, which had been cut down the summer before, and I suppose lay there for carriage; I drew my little troop in among those trees, and placing our selves in a line, behind one long tree, I advis'd them all to light, and keeping that tree before us, for a breast-work, to stand in a triangle, or three fronts, enclosing our horses in the center.

We did so, and it was well we did; for never was a more furious charge than the creatures made upon us in the place; they came on us with a growling kind of a noise (and mounted the piece of timber, which as I said, was our breast-work) as if they were only rushing upon their prey; and this fury of theirs, it seems, was principally occasion'd by their seeing our horses behind us, which was the prey they aim'd at: I order'd our men to fire as before, every other man; and they took their aim so sure, that indeed they kill'd several of the wolves at the first volley; but there was a necessity to keep a continual firing; for they came on like devils, those behind pushing on those before.

When we had fir'd our second volley of our fusees, we thought they stopp'd a little, and I hop'd they would have gone off; but it was but a moment; for others came forward again; so we fir'd two volleys of our pistols, and I believe in these four firings, we had kill'd seventeen or eighteen of them, and lam'd twice as many; yet they came on again.

I was loath to spend our last shot too hastily; so I call'd my servant, not my man *Friday*, for he was better employ'd; for with the greatest dexterity imaginable, he had charg'd my fusee, and his own, while we were engag'd; but as I said, I call'd my other man, and giving him a horn of powder, I bad him lay a train, all along the piece of timber, and let it be a large train; he did so, and had but just time to get away, when the wolves came up to it, and some were got up upon it; when I snapping an uncharg'd pistol, close to the powder, set it on fire; those that were upon the timber were scorcht with it, and six or seven of them fell, or rather jump'd in among us, with the force and fright of the fire, we dispatch'd these in an instant, and the rest were so frighted with the light, which the night, for it was now very near dark, made more terrible, that they drew back a little.

Upon which I order'd our last pistol to be fir'd off in one volley, and after that we gave a shout; upon this, the wolves turn'd tail, and we sally'd immediately upon near twenty lame ones, who we found struggling on the ground, and fell a cutting them with our swords, which answer'd our expectation; for the crying and howling they made, was better understood by their fellows, so that they all fled and left us.

We had, first and last, kill'd about three score of them; and had it been day-light, we had kill'd many more: The field of battle being thus clear'd, we made forward again; for we had still near a league to go. We heard the ravenous creatures howl and yell in the woods as we went, several times; and sometimes we fancy'd we saw some of them, but the snow dazling our eyes, we were not certain; so in about an hour more, we came to the town, where we were to lodge, which we found in a terrible fright, and all in arms; for it seems, that the night before, the wolves and some bears had broke into the village in the night, and put them in a terrible fright, and they were oblig'd to keep guard night and day, but especially in the night, to preserve their cattle, and indeed their people.

The next morning our guide was so ill, and his limbs swell'd with the rankling of his two wounds, that he could go no farther; so we were oblig'd to take a new guide there, and go to *Tholouse*, where we found a warm climate, a fruitful pleasant country, and no snow, no wolves, or any thing like them; but when we told our story at *Tholouse*, they told us it was nothing but what was ordinary in the great forest at the foot of the mountains, especially when the snow lay on the ground: But they enquir'd much what kind of a guide we had gotten, that would venture to bring us that way in such a severe season; and told us, it was very much we were not all devour'd. When we told them how we plac'd our selves, and the horses in the middle, they blam'd us exceedingly, and told us it was fifty to one but we had been all destroy'd; for it was the sight of the horses which made the wolves so furious, seeing their prey; and that at other times they are really afraid of a gun; but the being excessive hungry, and raging on that account, the eagerness to come at the horses had made them senseless of danger; and that if we had not by the continu'd fire, and at last by the stratagem of the train of powder, master'd them, it had been great odds but that we had been torn to pieces; whereas had we been content to have sat still on horseback, and fir'd as horsemen, they would not have taken the horses for so much their own, when men were on their backs, as otherwise; and withal they told us, that at last, if we had stood all together, and left our horses, they would have been so eager to have devour'd them, that we might have come off safe, especially having our fire arms in our hands, and being so many in number.

For my part, I was never so sensible of danger in my life; for seeing above three hundred devils come roaring and open-mouth'd to devour us, and having nothing to shelter us, or retreat to, I gave my self over for lost; and as it was, I believe, I shall never care to cross those mountains again; I think I would much rather go a thousand leagues by sea, though I were sure to meet with a storm once a week.

I have nothing uncommon to take notice of, in my passage through *France*; nothing but what other travellers have given an account of, with much more advantage than I can. I travell'd from *Bordeaux* to *Paris*, and without any considerable stay, came to *Calais*, and landed safe at *Dover*, the fourteenth of *January*, after having had a severely cold season to travel in.

I was now come to the center of my travels, and had in a little time all my new discover'd estate safe about me, the bills of exchange which I brought with me having been very currently paid.

My principal guide, and privy councellor, was my good ancient widow, who in gratitude for the money I had sent her, thought no pains too much, or care too great, to employ for me; and I trusted her so entirely with every thing, that I was perfectly easy as to the security of my effects; and indeed, I was very happy from my beginning, and now to the end, in the unspotted integrity of this good gentlewoman.

And now I began to think of leaving my effects with this woman, and setting out for *Lisbon*, and so to the *Brasils*; but now another scruple came in my way, and that was religion; for as I had entertain'd some doubts about the *Roman* religion, even while I was abroad, especially in my state of solitude; so I knew there was no going to the *Brasils* for me, much less going to settle there, unless I resolv'd to embrace the *Roman* Catholick religion, without any reserve; unless on the other hand, I resolv'd to be a sacrifice to my principles, be a martyr for religion, and die in the Inquisition; so I resolv'd to stay at home, and if I could find means for it, to dispose of my plantation.

To this purpose I wrote to my old friend at *Lisbon*, who in return gave me notice, that he could easily dispose of it there: But that if I thought fit to give him leave to offer it in my name to the two merchants, the survivors of my trustees, who liv'd in the *Brasils*, who must fully understand the value of it, who liv'd just upon the spot, and who I knew were very rich; so that he believ'd they would be fond of buying it; he did not doubt, but I should make 4 or 5000 Pieces of Eight, the more of it.

Accordingly I agreed, gave him order to offer it to them, and he did so; and in about 8 months more, the ship being then return'd, he sent me an account, that they had accepted the offer, and had remitted 33000 Pieces of Eight, to a correspondent of theirs at *Lisbon*, to pay for it.

In return, I sign'd the instrument of sale in the form which they sent from *Lisbon*, and sent it to my old man, who sent me bills of exchange for 32800 Pieces of Eight to me, for the estate; reserving the payment of 100 Moidores a year to him, the old man, during his life, and 50 Moidores afterwards to his son for his life, which I had promised them, which the plantation was to make good as a rent-charge. And thus I have given the first part of a life of fortune and adventure, a life of Providence's checquer-work, and of a variety which the world will seldom be able to shew the like of: Beginning foolishly, but closing much more happily than any part of it ever gave me leave so much as to hope for.

Any one would think, that in this state of complicated good fortune, I was past running any more hazards; and so indeed I had been, if other circumstances had concurr'd, but I was inur'd to a wandring life, had no family, not many relations, nor however rich had I contracted much acquaintance; and though I had sold my estate in the *Brasils*, yet I could not keep the country out of my head, and had a great mind to be upon the wing again, especially I could not resist the strong inclination I had to see my island, and to know if the poor *Spaniards* were in being there, and how the rogues I left there had used them.

My true friend, the widow, earnestly diswaded me from it, and so far prevail'd with me, that for almost seven years she prevented my running abroad; during which time, I took my two nephews, the children of one of my brothers, into my care: The eldest having something of his own, I bred up as a gentleman, and gave him a settlement of some addition to his estate, after my decease; the other I put out to a Captain of a ship; and after five years, finding him a sensible bold enterprising young fellow, I put him into a good ship, and sent him to sea: And this young fellow afterwards drew me in, as old as I was, to farther adventures my self.

In the mean time, I in part settled my self here; for first of all I marry'd, and that not either to my disadvantage or dissatisfaction, and had three children, two sons and one daughter: But my wife dying, and my nephew coming home with good success from a voyage to *Spain*, my inclination to go abroad, and his importunity prevailed and engag'd me to go in his ship, as a private trader to the *East Indies*: This was in the year 1694.

In this voyage I visited my new collony in the island, saw my successors the *Spaniards*, had the whole story of their lives, and of the villains I left there; how at first they insulted the poor *Spaniards*, how they afterwards agreed, disagreed, united, separated, and how at last the *Spaniards* were oblig'd to use violence with them, how they were subjected to the *Spaniards*, how honestly the *Spaniards* used them; a history, if it were entred into, as full of variety and wonderful accidents, as my own part, particularly also as to their battles with the *Carribeans*, who landed several times upon the island, and as to the improvement they made upon the island it self, and how five of them made an attempt upon the main land, and brought away eleven men and five women prisoners, by which, at my coming, I found about twenty young children on the island.

Here I stay'd about 20 days, left them supplies of all necessary things, and particularly of arms, powder, shot, clothes, tools, and two workmen, which I brought from *England* with me, *viz.* a carpenter and a smith.

Besides this, I shar'd the island into parts with 'em, reserv'd to my self the property of the whole, but gave them such parts respectively as they agreed on; and having settled all things with them, and engaged them not to leave the place, I left them there.

From thence I touch'd at the *Brasils*, from whence I sent a bark, which I bought there, with more people to the island, and in it, besides other supplies, I sent seven women, being such as I found proper for service, or for wives to such as would take them: As to the *English* men, I promis'd them to send them some women from *England*, with a good cargo of necessaries, if they would apply themselves to planting, which I afterwards perform'd. And the fellows prov'd very honest and diligent after they were master'd, and had their properties set apart for them. I sent them also from the *Brasils* five cows, three of them being big with calf, some sheep, and some hogs, which, when I came again, were considerably encreas'd.

But all these things, with an account how 300 *Caribbees* came and invaded them, and ruin'd their plantations, and how they fought with that whole number twice, and were at first defeated, and three of them kill'd;

but at last a storm destroying their enemies canoes, they famish'd or destroy'd almost all the rest, and renew'd and recover'd the possession of their plantation, and still liv'd upon the island.

All these things, with some very surprising incidents in some new adventures of my own, for ten years more, I may perhaps give a farther account of hererafter.

GLOSSARY

acted by: moved to action by
admiration (admire): astonishment (to wonder at)
affection: zeal, enthusiasm
affections: emotions, feelings
ague: fever, chills or fit of shivering (Crusoe probably has some sort of malaria)
alcamies: *see* curlieus
Algerines: pirates from North Africa, from Algeria
all adventures: great risk, all risk
alloes: aloes; a purgative or tonic drug derived from the dried juice of aloe leaves
amuse, amusement: to trick, befuddle; to be distracted, entertained
antick: grotesquely animated
antient and pendants: flags – ensign and pennants
attempted: attacked, tried to kill or capture

bays: baize cotton or woollen material napped to imitate felt
beachy rough: gravelly
better end: utmost length, bitter end
boltsprit: bowsprit, a spar or wooden pole extending from the stem of a ship
brand goose: species of wild goose, called in America, brant
breach of the sea: breaking waves
bruised: crushed into flour
bulg'd: bilged; with a hole or leak in the inner part of the ship's hull
burthen: cargo capacity
buskins: foot and leg covering or half-boot stretching half way to the knee

calenture: tropical fever, from Spanish, *calentura*
canes: sugar canes
carriage: ready to be hauled away
case-bottle: bottle designated for use in cases, fitting into divisions of the case

cassava root: tropical American plant with a large, starchy root, also called 'manioc'

casuist: one who determines what is right or wrong in matters of conscience

chickens meat: grain, chicken feed

chop'd: swerved or changed direction suddenly

colliers: ships carrying coal

come home: come loose

confus'd: assembled in a disorderly fashion, jumbled

conscience: consciousness

consequence: by-product

conversation: friendship, social interaction

converse of spirits: communication of spirits with human beings

cordial waters: liqueurs – sweet, syrupy alcoholic beverages, often with a brandy base

corn: in British usage, any cereal plant food such as oats, wheat, rye or barley

crowded to the utmost: spread all the sail possible in order to go as fast as possible

Cruisadoes (crusados): Portuguese silver coins, named after the cross inscribed on them

cur'd: cleared and ready for cultivation

curlieus: curlews – brownish, long-legged shore birds having long, slender, downward-curving bills

depending: impending, about to happen

design: plan, strategy

discover: explore; display, show

discover'd: showed, displayed

discoveries: revelations

doctor: teacher, scholar

Doubloons: Spanish gold coin, a double pistole

drills: rills or small streams

dubb: to strike, cut, or rub (wood or leather) to make them smooth

Ducats: any of various gold and silver coins formerly current in most European countries

eat: ate

embarrass'd: impeded by or encumbered with

entertain'd: preoccupied

Equinox: Equator, line dividing the northern and southern hemispheres; *see also* Line

fain: gladly, preferably, ready, willing

fancy: imagination, a fantasy, to imagine

fetch'd a compass: circled
fewel: fuel
flags: plants having long blade-like leaves
flea: to flay, that is, to skin
fleet: float
fluxes: dysentery
fore-castle: section of the upper deck of a ship located at the bow
fowling-piece: shotgun for hunting birds or small animals
frame: that is, frame of mind (p. 131)
freshning: increasing in velocity
frog: loop fastened to a belt to hold a weapon
fustic: tropical American tree that yields a yellow dye
fuzees: muskets

Generalissimo: commander-in-chief.
genius: inclination, talent, personal tendency
glaz'd powder: grains of the best gunpowder glazed with graphite to slow down combustion and thereby make it safer
graplin: grappling iron, an iron shaft with claws at one end used for drawing and holding an enemy ship alongside
ground-tackle: equipment (cable, anchor, etc.) used to anchor or moor a ship
gudgeons: metal pins joining the wheel, in this case, to the shaft of the wheelbarrow
Guinea grains: seeds of African plants
gyb'd: jibbed, swung around and shifted from one side of the boat to the other

hale, hal'd, hailing: to haul, hauled, hauling
hallow: *see* hollow
hanger: short sword
hawser: cable or rope used in mooring or towing a ship
head: fore part of the ship
hogshead: large barrel
hollow, hallow: to shout, to call

indifferently: neither good nor bad, mediocre
iron crows: crow bars

jealous: apprehensive, fearful
jealousy: suspicion
jerkin: vest or waistcoat

league: about 3 miles or 4.8 kilometers
lee: side of the land that provides shelter from the wind

Line: Equator
long-boat: longest boat carried by a sailing ship
luxuries: excessive, unnecessary or self-indulgent pleasures

magazine: storehouse or place where goods are stored
main: mainland
man of war: warship
Maresco: variant of *Moresco*, Spanish for Moor
meat: as used by Crusoe, often refers to food in general rather than specifically or exclusively to animal flesh
mechanical, mechanick: manual, of manual labour (also one who earns a living by manual labour)
medium: compromise
memento: reminder or example, an emblem or warning.
mere, meer: completely, perfectly, entirely, 'nothing more than'; see 'my meer fate', i.e. purely and fully my fate (p. 7)
misen-yard: the mizzen is the third mast aft on sailing ships carrying three or more sails, so the misen-yard is the pole supporting the mizzen mast
Moidore, Moydor: moidores, Portuguese and Brazilian gold coins
moiety: one half share
moletta: mulatto, since Crusoe is dark from exposure to the sun
molossus: molasses
moorish: like a moor, poorly drained and infertile land
move: urge
murthering humour: in the mood or disposition to commit murder

naked: defenceless
naturalists: those who study natural phenomena, scientists
Nicaragua Wood: South American redwood, also called Brazil wood
nice: particular, fastidious

oakum: hemp or jute fibre, sometimes treated with tar or creosote and used for caulking seams in wooden ships
obligation: contractual promise
observation: navigational reckoning
offing: position at a distance from the shore
opticks: eyes
original: originator or organizer
osiers: *see* sallows

pale: fence enclosing a field, or the area thus enclosed
pantaloons: men's tight trousers, normally reaching from the waist to the ankle

parch'd: cooked and dried

parly: to negotiate, negotiations

paste: flour moistened with water or milk and kneaded to make pastry

penthouse: shed or sloping roof attached to the main house

periagua: dug-out canoe made from a single tree trunk

perspective-glasses: prospective-glasses, telescopes

physical: medicinal, curative

physick: medicine, medical treatment

Pieces of Eight: Spanish silver dollars marked with a figure '8'

pinnace: small boat or tender attached to a ship

pipkins: small earthenware pots

presently: immediately

primitive: earlier or original

procuration: power of attorney

prospective-glass: telescope, 'perspective glass'

prudential: worldly wisdom, the prudent or practical thing to do

pumps: low-heeled shoes without laces

quarter: upper portion of the deck of a ship; mercy

rack: arrack, intoxicating liquor made of palm sap or coconuts

rankling: festering

regiment of foot: foot soldiers, infantry

rid forecastle in: with the bow of the ship underwater

round-house: cabin in the stern or rear of the ship, just below the poop or rear deck

Royals: Spanish silver coins, *reals* (from 'real' = royal)

rubb'd out: separated the kernel or grain of the barley from the chaff or straw

runlet: cask of varying sizes, usually holding about eighteen gallons

sallows: willows and osiers: trees in the willow family, all having long, rodlike twigs used in basketry

scuttle: hatchway

sheet anchor: large, extra anchor intended for use in emergencies

shoal: shallow

shoulder of mutton sail: triangular sail

simplicity: naive or foolish behaviour

skrew-jack: jack for lifting heavy objects, operated by a screw

softly: quietly or slowly

spatter-dashes: leather or cloth gaiters, leggings extending from the knee to the instep

sprit-sail: sail extended by a pole from the lower part of the mast to the peak of the main sail

step at the stern: platform to support the end of the mast

stern: rear of a ship

strike our top-masts: that is, lower the sails on those masts and secure them

stuff: woven material, especially woollens

stupid: in a stupor

sublunary: earthly

succades: candied fruit

supra cargo, super-cargo: officer on a merchant ship who has charge of the cargo, its purchase and sale

take a round: circle around

tell: count

thrash: thresh, to beat the stems and husks of cereal plants in order to separate the grain or seeds from the straw

toy: small article of little value but prized as a curiosity

traffick: business, trade

turn'd off: hanged, executed

twist: crotch

uncur'd: unprepared for planting

upon the ladder: upon the gallows, about to be hanged

vapours: anxiety or hysteria, depression

vesting: investing

virtue: said of plants, their efficacious medicinal properties

viz.: shortened form of *videlicit*: that is to say, namely (Latin); literally, 'it is easy or plain to see'

warmly: strongly, clearly

wave: to waive

whelming down: to place a hollow vessel upside down over something

willows: *see* sallows

yard: spar or pole used to support the sails on a ship

NOTES

1 *dispatch'd*: That is to say, stories such as this were meant to be read quickly (with dispatch) and inattentively, so that their truth or falsity did not matter.

2 *Robinson Crusoe*: Defoe's model for Crusoe seems to have been Alexander Selkirk: see Introduction. The 'Great River of OROONOQUE' (see title-page) is the Orinoco, in Venezuela, one of South America's longest rivers, extending about 2560 km (1590 miles).

3 *Bremen*: City in northwestern Germany, capital of the state of Bremen on the Weser River, near the North Sea.

4 *Dunkirk against the Spaniards*: Sir William Lockhart (1621–76), one of Oliver Cromwell's generals, captured Dunkirk from the Spanish in 1658.

5 *Wise man . . . poverty or riches*: Solomon, considered the wisest man in the Old Testament, as recorded in Proverbs 30:8 (though not directly attributed to him).

6 *1651*: The first edition has 1661, but this would make Crusoe twenty-nine years old. Subsequent editions correct the date to 1651.

7 *Humber*: Estuary in eastern England, flowing generally east from the junction of the Trent and Ouse rivers and then southeast into the North Sea.

8 *Prodigal*: Refers to Christ's parable of the Prodigal Son (Luke 15:11–24): this son goes on a journey to a 'far country' and wastes his money, but when he returns his father kills the 'fatted calf' for the celebration of his homecoming.

9 *Yarmouth*: Now Great Yarmouth, at the junction of the Yare and Waveney rivers with the North Sea. From medieval times, it was a port and centre of herring fishing.

10 *Winterton-Ness*: Promontory on the Norfolk coast.

11 *Jonah in the Ship of Tarshish*: Old Testament prophet on a ship bound for Tarshish was the cause of a fierce storm at sea because of his disobedience to God and was 'cast . . . forth into the sea' by the sailors to save the ship (Jonah 1:2–15); hence any person causing bad luck.

12 *Sallee*: Seaport in Morocco, which was a notorious base for pirates ('rovers'). From the seventeenth to the early nineteenth century, Morocco and the other Barbary Coast states were bases for piracy on the Mediterranean trade.

13 *athwart our quarter . . . stern*: The pirates draw their ship up alongside the 'quarterdeck' of the ship Crusoe is on instead of by the stern or rear part, and so are vulnerable to the mounted guns.

14 *Emperor's court*: Probably in Rabat, the capital. After a couple of centuries of struggle, the Moroccans expelled the Spaniards and the Portuguese, and by the end of the seventeenth century the country was ruled by the Alawite dynasty.

15 *Straits-mouth*: Straits of Gibraltar.

16 *Canaries . . . Cape de Verd Islands*: Canary Islands – seven islands in the Atlantic off the northwestern coast of Africa, which constitute two Spanish provinces; Cape Verde Islands – an archipelago, Portuguese territory, in the Atlantic about 400 miles west of Senegal. Crusoe is sailing southward away from the Canaries along the northwest coast of Africa, by the peninsula of Cape Verde (the westernmost point in Africa) and in the direction of the Cape Verde Islands.

17 *Gambia or Sennegall*: The Gambia river flows generally west through the nations of Senegal and The Gambia before emptying into the Atlantic Ocean by a wide estuary near Saint Mary's Island, the site of Banjul, the capital of The Gambia.

18 *All-Saints-Bay*: Harbour in northern Brazil where San Salvador, then the capital, is located.

19 *Assiento's*: Assiento (mod. *asiento*) was a monopoly on the African slave trade into their American colonies enforced by the Spanish and the Portuguese.

20 *the —th of —*: Spaces were left for the day, month and year in the first three editions. In the fourth and subsequent editions, these were replaced with 'the first of September, 1659'.

21 *120 tun burthen*: Having a cargo capacity of about 120 tons.

22 *Fernand de Noronha*: They are sailing toward the Fernando de Noronha Archipelago, which is a Brazilian possession in the Atlantic Ocean.

23 *Den wild Zee*: The wild sea.

24 *For sudden . . . confound at first*: Professor Geoffrey Sill has discovered the source of these lines: 'Wild's Humble Thanks for His Majesties Gracious Declaration for Liberty of Conscience, March 15, 1672', a broadside published in 1672 by Robert Wild (1609–79). The poem was written in response to Charles II's suspension that year of penal laws against Catholics and Nonconformists. Wild was a Nonconformist minister and a Royalist.

25 *Lord ha' mercy upon me*: Crusoe refers to the phrases used in Morning and Evening Prayers in the *Book of Common Prayer*: 'Lord have mercy upon us; Christ have mercy upon us.'

26 *Call on me . . . glorify me*: Psalm 50:15. Crusoe (or Defoe) misquotes slightly the Authorized Version: 'And call upon me in the day of trouble: I will deliver thee, and thou shalt glorify me.' See also p. 125.

27 *Can God spread . . . wilderness?*: Psalm 78:19: 'Yea, they spake against God; they said, Can God furnish a table in the wilderness?' Here and elsewhere Defoe is doubtless quoting Scripture from memory. See also p. 103.

28 *crossing and recrossing the Line*: One does not gain or lose a day by crossing the Equator, so Defoe may be confusing it with the International Date Line.

29 *He is exalted a prince . . . to give remission*: Acts 5:31: 'Him hath God exalted with his right hand to be a Prince and a Saviour, for to give repentance to Israel, and forgiveness of sins.'

30 *Jesus, thou son of David*: The Gospels of Matthew and Luke identify Jesus as belonging to the House of David. Matthew begins: 'The book of the generation of Jesus Christ, the son of David, the son of Abraham' (Matthew 1:1).

31 *Leaden-hall market*: One of the major London food markets in Defoe's time.

32 *I will never . . . forsake thee*: Joshua 1:5, cf. Hebrews 13:5.

33 *Solomon . . . the building of the Temple at Jerusalem*: In 1 Kings 5:3–6, Solomon resolves to build the temple in Jerusalem that his father, David, could not because of 'the wars which were about him on every side'. He recalls that the Lord 'spake unto David my father, saying, Thy son, whom I will set upon thy throne in thy room, he shall build a house unto my name.' Solomon asks King Hiram of Tyre to send him cedar trees from Lebanon for the building of the temple.

34 *hereafter*: Here 'after' death, from the next life.

35 *Father Abraham . . . gulph fix'd*: Refers to Jesus' parable of the rich man, Dives, and Lazarus the poor beggar, in which the Old Testament patriarch Abraham responds (Luke 16:25–6) to the rich man's plea from Hell that Lazarus in paradise dip the tip of his finger in water and cool his tongue, 'for I am tormented in this flame' (16:24).

36 *Lust of the flesh . . . pride of life*: 1 John 2:16.

37 *particular Providences*: That is to say, God's intervention in particular incidents of Crusoe's life. Theologians of the time debated whether God could be said to operate in such incidents as well as in the general disposition of events in the world.

38 *feeding Elijah by ravens*: As God commanded them; see 1 Kings 17:4–6.

39 *26 years after*: Crusoe's reckoning is slightly off: he was born in 1632 and shipwrecked in 1659, so he was twenty-seven.

40 *shoor*: Some editors have suggested that this is a misprint for 'shoot'; another possibility is 'sheer off', a nautical term, 'to turn aside'.

41 *great with young*: Pregnant.

42 *made a Stoick smile*: Stoic, a member of a Greek philosophical school founded by Zeno, *c.* 300 BC which maintained that wisdom is a matter of cultivating apathy, an indifference to passion and pain and other human feelings and emotions. Crusoe means that even an unfeeling Stoic would have been pleased by his good fortune on his island.

43 *checquer work*: 'Chequered' here means marked by great changes in fortune, unpredictable shifts and fluctuations; thus a pattern of changes.

44 *Wait on the Lord . . . strengthen thy heart*: Psalm 27:14. The Authorized Version says 'be of good courage'.

45 *Saul, who complain'd . . . that God had forsaken him*: 1 Samuel 28:15.

46 *As if the kingdom of Spain . . . generous temper in the mind*: Crusoe's evocation of the Spaniards as more cruel than other Europeans in their dealings with the native populations of America is to say the least one-sided and reflects the so-called 'Black Legend' that the English and their other imperialist rivals invoked to describe the conduct of the Spaniards in the New World. Conquistadors like Cortez and Pizzaro were ruthless as well as treacherous, and the Spaniards virtually exterminated some native groups, like the Arawaks in the West Indies. But other European colonists and explorers were equally cruel and exploitative in their dealings with the native people, and the English in North America were hardly morally superior to the Spanish in this regard. 'Bowels of pity': According to the traditional physiology, the bowels were considered the source of pity and the gentler emotions such as compassion.

47 *national*: Crusoe reasons that the cannibal community or nation as a whole is responsible for the crime of cannibalism and not any particular individual among them.

48 *that I shall not discuss*: The syntax here is confusing. Crusoe means that these 'secret intimations' may or may not come from God; he won't discuss that because he's not sure where they originate. But they prove, he then says, that spirits communicate with humans ('those embody'd').

49 *tinderbox . . . wild-fire in the pan*: Crusoe has made a container for starting a fire from part of one of his flintlock muskets (the pan is a small cavity near the lock of the musket) and put in a highly flammable substance.

50 *had just been to be kill'd*: Was just about to be killed.

51 *law to themselves*: 'For when the Gentiles, which have not the law, do by nature the things contained in the law, these, having not the law, are a law unto themselves (Romans 2:14).

52 *clay in the hand of the potter . . . form'd me thus*: Romans 9:20–21, and cf. Jeremiah 18:6 and Isaiah 45:9.

53 *Caribbees*: Caribs and the Arawaks were the native peoples inhabiting the Caribbean islands and the coast of Venezuela.

54 *St. Martha*: City in Colombia.

55 *worship'd instead of God, and as God*: Crusoe rehearses an old idea going back to the early Fathers of the Church that idolatrous and pagan worship was inspired by the devil and that the pagan gods were in fact devils.

56 *first cause*: Philosophical term for God the creator of the universe.

57 *a consuming fire*: Crusoe's discourse here and throughout his conversion discourse with Friday echoes the Bible, e.g. Deuteronomy 4:24.

58 *workers of iniquity*: A common biblical phrase for sinners. See, for example, Job 31:3, 34:8; Psalms 5:5, 6:8; Luke 13:27.

59 *tread him down . . . fiery darts*: More biblical echoes, from Romans 16:20 and Ephesians 6:16.

60 *reserv'd for the judgment . . . everlasting fire*: More biblical echoes, from 2 Peter 2:4, Matthew 25:41 and Revelation 20:1.

61 *new covenant*: More biblical echoes, this a phrase St Paul uses: 'Behold, the days come, saith the Lord, when I will make a new covenant with the house of Israel and with the house of Judah' (Hebrews 8:8). See also Hebrews 8:13, 12:24.

62 *foot stool of God's throne*: 'But I say unto you, Swear not at all; neither by heaven; for it is God's throne: Nor by the earth; for it is his footstool' (Matthew 5:34–5).

63 *seed of Abraham*: Common biblical phrase for the Jewish nation. Crusoe is quoting St Paul: 'For verily he took not on him the nature of angels; but he took on him the seed of Abraham' (Hebrews 2:16).

64 *lost sheep of the House of Israel*: Jesus instructs his disciples to preach to the Jews: 'But go rather to the lost sheep of the house of Israel' (Matthew 10:6).

65 *to know whom is life eternal*: Echoes several Gospel texts, especially John 17:3 ('And this is life eternal, that they might know thee the only true God, and Jesus Christ, whom thou hast sent').

66 *leading us into all truth*: 'Howbeit when he, the Spirit of truth, is come, he will guide you into all truth' (John 16:13).

67 *children of Israel . . . bread in the wilderness*: Exodus 16:2–3.

68 *Alicant*: Alicante, city in southeastern Spain; it is a seaport on the Mediterranean Sea.

69 *whipp'd and pickl'd*: Salt and vinegar were rubbed into the wounds on the back after a sailor's whipping, both to heighten the pain and to promote healing.

70 *River of Lisbon*: Tagus.

71 *to 38892 Cruisadoes*: All the 1719 editions leave this figure blank. In the early twentieth century, the Defoe scholar William P. Trent estimated the value of Crusoe's fortune in cruisados as 38,892, and most editions of the novel have used that number.

72 *the latter end of Job . . . the beginning*: Job 42:12. Tested by God, Job endures many afflictions, and at the end of his story is rewarded with even greater riches than he enjoyed before.

73 *master . . . estate of lands in England*: Crusoe's estate is substantial, the equivalent in cash and lands to what a member of the lower gentry in early-eighteenth-century England would have possessed.

74 *Start near Torbay*: Start Point in Devonshire, on the English Channel.

75 *Groyne*: Corruption of La Coruña, a port in northwestern Spain.

76 *Pampeluna*: Pamplona, capital of the Spanish province of Navarre.

77 *Old Castile*: Central province of Spain.

78 *Fontarabia*: Spanish port on the Bay of Biscay.

79 *Languedoc*: Province in southern France.

80 *Gascoign*: Gascony, a province in southwestern France.